I Am Behind You

D1425197

Also by John Ajvide Lindqvist

Let the Right One In
Handling the Undead
Harbour
Little Star
Let the Old Dreams Die

John Ajvide Lindqvist lives in Sweden and has worked as a conjurer and stand-up comedian. His first novel, the international bestseller *Let the Right One In*, was published in more than thirty countries and adapted into two feature films: one by Swedish director Tomas Alfredson, and an English-language version, *Let Me In. I Am Behind You* is the first book in a planned trilogy; John is currently working on the second.

Marlaine Delargy is based in the UK. She has translated novels by Swedish writers including Åsa Larsson, Ninni Holmqvist and Johan Theorin – with whom she won the CWA International Dagger 2010 for *The Darkest Room*.

I Am Behind You

JOHN AJVIDE LINDQVIST

Translated from Swedish by
Marlaine Delargy

riverrun

First published in Sweden in 2014 under the title *Himmelstrand* by Ordfronts Förlag.
This English translation first published in Australia in 2016 by The Text Publishing Company
First published in Great Britain in 2017 by

r

riverrun

An imprint of

Quercus Editions Limited
Carmelite House
50 Victoria Embankment
London EC4Y 0DZ

An Hachette UK company

Cover design based on original jacket design by Jeannine Schmelzer, © Bastei Lübbe
AG, Köln 2016
Cover image of caravan by Jill Battaglia / Arcangel
Page design by Text
Typeset by J & M Typesetting

A CIP catalogue record for this book is available
from the British Library

Hardback ISBN 978 1 78648 039 2
Trade paperback ISBN 978 1 78648 040 8
Ebook ISBN 978 1 78648 042 2

10 9 8 7 6 5 4 3 2

Printed and bound in Great Britain by Clays Ltd, St Ives plc

In memory of
Peter Himmelstrand
(1936–1999)

CONTENTS

1. Outside   3

2. Inside   109

3. Beyond   323

We know a person by their flaws.

We can form an impression of someone by noticing their talents and qualities, good or bad—everything that appears on the surface. But if we really want to understand who they are, we must step into the darkness and acquaint ourselves with their flaws.

The missing cog defines the machine. A picture is judged by a poor brushstroke, a dissonant chord makes a song fall apart. Or makes it interesting. That is the other side of the coin.

Without our flaws we would be like a well-oiled machine, and our actions and thoughts could be predicted through simulation, if we only had sufficient processing power. That will never happen. Our flaws are a variable outside the scope of such a calculation, and they drive us to great achievements or to utterly despicable deeds.

If you wanted to, you could say that this is what makes us human, imperfect and wonderfully interesting. You could also say that it makes us into reptiles, dragging ourselves along between heaven and earth, searching for something to fill the vacuum.

Whatever the truth of the matter, it is these flaws that drive us on, whether we know it or not. And just like everything else they can reach a critical mass, a point where they change character and become something else. Many events that we regard as inexplicable can be explained in this way. What follows is an example.

I switch on the light.

1. Outside

'Mum, I need a pee.'

'Well, go to the toilet then.'

'It's not there.'

'Of course it is. It's where you went yesterday. The service block.'

'It's not there.'

'For goodness sake, can't you let me sleep just for *once*?'

'But I need a pee. I'm going to wet myself.'

'So go to the service block. It's only fifty metres away. Surely you can manage that?'

'It's not there.'

'It is. Go outside, turn left and go around this revolting caravan, then carry straight on. That's where it is.'

'Which is left?'

'Oh, pee on the grass for heaven's sake, and let me sleep. Wake your dad if you insist on playing up.'

'Nearly everything has gone.'

'What are you talking about?'

'Come and look.'

'Look where?'

'Out of the window. Nearly everything has gone.'

Isabelle Sundberg props herself up on her elbow. Her six-year-old daughter Molly is kneeling by the window. Isabelle pushes her out of the way and pulls back the curtain. She is just about to point in the direction of the service block, but her hand drops.

Her first thought is: *scenery*. Like the backdrop behind Mickey Mouse's caravan on TV on Christmas Eve. Something artificial, unreal. But the details are too sharp, the three dimensions clearly distinguishable. This is no backdrop.

'I need a pee I need a pee I need a pee!'

Her daughter's voice grates on her eardrums. Isabelle rubs her eyes. Tries to erase the incomprehensible sight. But it is still there, just like her daughter's monotonous whine. She turns over and drives her knee into her husband's back. Pulls back the other curtain.

She blinks, shakes her head. It makes no difference. She clenches her jaw, slaps her own face. Her daughter falls silent. Isabelle's cheek is burning, and nothing has changed. Everything has changed. She grabs hold of her husband's shoulder and shakes it hard.

'Peter, wake up for God's sake. Something's happened.'

*

Thirty seconds later, Stefan Larsson is woken by a door slamming somewhere. His pyjamas are sticking to his body; it is hot in the caravan, very hot. He has had enough. Everybody else has air con. Later on today, when they go shopping, he is going to buy a couple of decent electric fans to sit on the table, at the very least.

'Bim, bim, bim. Bom.'

Stefan's son Emil is humming quietly up in the alcove, caught up in some fantasy as usual. Stefan frowns. Something is wrong. He reaches for his glasses with their thick black frames, puts them on and looks around.

The faithful old caravan looks the same. When he and Carina bought it fifteen years ago, it had been around for at least that long already, but after countless holidays and birdwatching expeditions, it feels like a friend, and you don't sell a friend online for a few thousand kronor. The worn surfaces have a dull sheen in the light penetrating the thin curtains. Nothing unusual about that.

Carina is asleep, facing away from him. She has kicked off the sheet and the generous curve of her hip is like something from an old painting. Stefan leans over her and picks up the salty aroma of her body; he can see tiny beads of sweat at her hairline. Decent fans, that's what they need. His gaze fastens on the tattoo on her shoulder. Two eternity symbols. The yearning for a lasting love. She had them done when they were both young. He worships her. It is a strange word to use, but it is the only one that fits.

His eyes widen. Now he knows what it is. *The silence.* Apart from Carina's breathing and Emil's humming, there is total silence. He glances at the clock: quarter to seven. A campsite is never silent. There

6

is always the hum of machinery on stand-by, air conditioning units. But not now. The site has stopped breathing.

Stefan gets out of bed and glances up at the alcove. 'Morning, kiddo.'

Emil is totally focused on his soft toys, moving them around as he whispers: 'But what about me? Can't I…? No, Bengtson, you're in charge of the guns.'

Stefan goes over to the sink and is filling the coffeepot with water when movements and voices on the grass outside catch his attention. The footballer and his wife are also up and about. So is their daughter. The child is pressed against her mother's bare legs as the woman gestures angrily at her husband.

Stefan tilts his head on one side. In a parallel universe he would be obliged to lust after that woman. She is in nothing more than her bra and panties, and she looks as if she has stepped straight out of an ad campaign. She is the woman men are supposed to desire. But Stefan has chosen something different, and he is not to be moved. It is a question of dignity, among other things.

The coffeepot is full. Stefan turns off the tap, pours the water into the machine, spoons coffee into the filter, then switches it on. Nothing happens. He flicks the switch up and down a couple of times, checks that it is plugged in properly, then thinks:

power cut.

Which also explains the absence of an electrical hum. He tips the water into a pan and places it on the hotplate. *Hello?* He scratches his head. If there's a power cut, the electric stove won't work either, obviously.

As he leans across to switch on the gas instead, he glances out of the window, past the quarrelling couple, to see what the weather is like. The sky is clear and blue, so it should be a lovely…

Stefan gasps and clutches the edge of the sink as he leans closer to the window. He doesn't understand what he is seeing. The stainless steel is warm to the touch; he feels dizzy and his stomach is churning. If he lets go of the sink he will plummet into emptiness.

*

Peter has found a sweet wrapper in the right-hand pocket of his shorts. There is a faint rustling noise as he scrunches the wrapper inside his clenched fist. Isabelle is yelling at him, and he stares at the exact spot on her cheek where the palm of his hand might land if it were not fully occupied with the sweet wrapper.

'How could you be so fucking stupid? Leaving the keys in the car when you were so fucking drunk that some idiot was able to drive off and dump us in this…this…'

He mustn't hit her. If he does, the balance of power will shift, temporary peace agreements will be torn up and everything will be sucked down into chaos. He did hit her once. The satisfaction was enormous, the aftermath unbearable. Both aspects scared him: the pleasure he took from inflicting physical damage on her, and her ability to inflict mental damage on him.

He thinks: *Ten thousand. No. Twenty thousand.* That's what he would be willing to pay for five minutes' silence. The chance to think, to come up with an explanation. But Isabelle's words hammer down on him and the taut strings of his self-control vibrate. He is capable of only one thing: smoothing out and screwing up the sweet wrapper.

Molly is clutching her mother's legs, playing the role of the frightened child. She does it well, exaggerating only slightly, but Peter sees through her. She is not afraid at all. In some way that Peter cannot understand, she is enjoying this.

He hears a discreet cough. The man with the thick glasses from the caravan next door, tedium personified, is coming towards them. Right now he is a welcome sight. Isabelle's torrent of words dries up, and Molly stares at the new arrival.

'Excuse me,' the man says. 'Do you have any idea what's happened?'

'No,' Isabelle replies. 'Do tell.'

'I don't know any more than you. Everything has disappeared.'

Isabelle jerks her head and snaps: 'You as well? You think

someone's come along and taken away the other caravans, the kiosk, the service block, the whole fucking lot? Does that sound reasonable? We've been *moved*, you idiot.'

The man with the glasses looks at the caravans, all that remains of Saludden campsite, and says: 'In that case it looks as if they've moved several of us.'

Molly tugs at Isabelle's panties. 'Who are they, Mummy? Who did this?'

*

Four caravans. Four cars.

The caravans are different ages, different sizes, different models, but they are all white. The cars have less in common, but two of them are Volvos. They all have a tow bar, of course. Two have roof racks.

Besides that: nothing apart from people. Three adults and a child, wandering among the caravans and the cars, the other occupants still sleeping, perhaps dreaming, unaware.

Beyond the little circle lies only grass. A vast expanse of grass, each blade just over three centimetres long, stretching as far as the eye can see in all directions.

It is an empty space.

It is impossible to know what lies beyond the horizon, under the ground, above the sky, but at the moment it is an empty space. Nothing. Apart from the people. And each person is a world within himself.

*

Molly insists that Isabelle accompany her when she goes behind their caravan for a pee. Peter crouches down and runs a hand through his hair, sighing heavily.

'Where the hell *are* we?' Stefan asks no one in particular. 'I've never seen anything like it.'

9

The corners of Peter's mouth twitch. 'I have. I've spent half my life on grass like this. First football, then golf. But how can it be so... neat?'

The grass has the appearance of a well-tended garden or a golf course. Stefan pulls up a small clump and rubs it between his fingers. It is real grass; there is soil attached to the thin roots. It would take an army of lawnmowers to keep it this short. Is there a variety of grass that only grows to a certain length?

Isabelle and Molly return. Isabelle is stunning, her daughter cute as a button. Long, wavy hair frames the girl's little round face and big blue eyes. She is wearing a pink nightdress with a picture of a fairy princess not unlike Molly herself. And then there is Peter: cropped blond hair and a strong jawline. Narrow hips, broad chest, biceps clearly defined beneath the skin.

Three people so close to perfection that they would be less than credible in an IKEA catalogue, let alone on a scruffy campsite. The change of environment has made their presence less unnatural; the endless field is a more appropriate setting for Isabelle than a run-down mini-golf course. And yet she is the one who is most agitated.

'This is absolutely fucking ridiculous,' she says. 'Where the hell are we?'

Stefan looks around at the grass, the caravans, the cars. He spots the black SUV parked next to the perfect family's caravan.

'Have you got GPS?' he asks.

Peter slaps his forehead and runs to the car. The others follow him, with Molly looking up at Stefan as they hurry along. He smiles at her. She doesn't smile back.

Peter opens the car door and slides in behind the gleaming dashboard. 'Hang on, I just need to check.'

He presses a button and the engine starts up with a low purr. Peter's posture changes. His shoulders were hunched; he straightens up, lifts his head. He is in the driving seat now.

The GPS screen turns purple, then a map appears.

Something is tugging at Stefan's trousers. When he glances down, his gaze meets Molly's. Her clear, unblinking blue eyes stare into his as she asks: 'Why don't you look at my mum?'

*

Benny has been awake for a while. He is lying in his basket in the awning, trying to understand.

The light is wrong. The smells are wrong.

His ears twitch as he hears human voices. His nose quivers, trying to pick up familiar scents from outside. They are not there.

Benny is seven years old, and he knows quite a lot. He is familiar with the concept of mechanised relocation. You get into Car or Caravan, there is a lot of rumbling and shaking, and rapid movement. Then you find yourself in a different place. New smells, new sounds, new light.

Benny knows that no such relocation has occurred. And yet he is not where he was when he went to sleep. This makes him feel insecure, and he decides to stay in his basket. For the time being.

*

'For God's sake, Peter, there must be something wrong with the bloody thing.'

'There's never been anything wrong with it before.'

'No, but now there is. I mean, does it look as if we're where it says we are? Does it?'

'All I'm saying is that...'

'Where are we, Mummy?'

'That's what Daddy's trying to find out with his little machine that doesn't work.'

'It does work! Look at the position indicator...'

'Peter, I couldn't give a damn about the position indicator. It's *broken*, just accept it! Oh yes, that's a good idea. Just give it a little tap, I'm sure it'll work. Know any magic spells while you're at it?'

'Okay, Isabelle. Give it a rest.'

'Mummy, why is Daddy cross?'

'Because his masculinity is threatened, and because he can't get it into his thick skull that we have been *moved*. He thinks we're exactly where we were yesterday.'

'But we're not.'

'No. You know that and I know that, but Daddy doesn't know that, which makes him feel stupid, and that's why he's cross.'

*

'Bom.'

A laser beam strikes one wing of the spaceship.

'Bim, bim, bim.'

Meteors, lots and lots of meteors crash into the windows.

'Bam!'

Magnetic shock! The meteors break up, but...

'Bom, bom.'

More lasers, warning, warning. There's nothing we can do. We've had it. The spaceship tumbles towards the sun.

'Heeeelp!'

It is warm in the alcove, very warm. Emil is so thirsty that his tongue is sticking to the top of his mouth, and yet he doesn't climb down to get a drink of water. Something isn't right. Mummy is snoring quietly below him and Daddy has gone outside. Emil can hear the faint sound of adult voices through the wall. He can't make out what they're saying, but he can tell they're worried.

He doesn't want to know why they're worried; he would rather wait until the problem has been solved. He arranges his cuddly toys around his head with Bengtson, his teddy bear, right at the top. Sköldis, Bunte, Hipphopp and Sabre Cat down the sides. Emil's eyes dart from side to side, meeting theirs.

We are here. We like you.

He licks the sweat off his upper lip and nods.

'I know. I like you too.'
Where shall we go?
'To Mercury—are you with me?'
We are with you.
'Good. Bengtson, you can be Chewbacca. Let's go.'

*

Peter has opted for a time-out.

The car doors are locked, and he sinks back in his seat. Isabelle is staring at him through the tinted side windows. He stares out through the windscreen.

An empty field is spread before him. It stretches as far as the eye can see, the horizon a curved incision between the shades of green and the shades of blue. That's right, curved. The world has not become flat. *Something* to hold on to.

He turns to the GPS screen once more. According to the data displayed there, everything is as it should be. The map shows the track leading to the campsite, the markers indicating that the car is exactly where it is supposed to be, fifty metres from the lake, which is also there. Peter looks out of the window. There is no track, no lake. Only the field, the field, and the field.

'Of course. Idiot,' he tells himself. It's so easy to check the GPS.

Peter releases the handbrake and applies gentle pressure to the accelerator. The car begins to move forward. He hears the sound of banging on the window; Isabelle is running alongside the car, yelling: 'You fucking lunatic! What the hell are you doing?'

Peter can't help smiling. She thinks he's going to drive off and leave her. And who knows, perhaps he'll do just that. He's fantasised about this moment often enough; maybe he should actually do it?

He glances at Isabelle, still dressed in nothing but her underwear, and feels his penis begin to harden. During the week they have been staying in the caravan he hasn't been allowed anywhere near her, and it was at least two weeks before that. His sexual sorrow is so obtrusive that it borders on hatred, and when Isabelle trips and falls, letting out a scream, he almost comes.

He blinks and concentrates on the screen.

The cursor is definitely moving, so the fault doesn't lie with the GPS. It moves smoothly towards the lake, closer and closer. Peter pulls up when he reaches the shore, in spite of the fact that there is no shore in sight. He sits there for a few moments, looking from his foot on the brake to the screen and back again. He just can't make himself drive out into the invisible lake.

More banging on the window, and this time he opens it. Isabelle leans in, demanding to know what the hell he's doing. He explains.

'And?'

'I just wanted to check.'

Isabelle catches sight of his erection and smiles scornfully. 'So what have you got there, then?'

'Nothing that would interest you.'

'Too right.'

Molly comes running, and in a voice much smaller than her six years says: 'Mummy? Is Daddy leaving us?'

'No, sweetheart, he isn't. He had a silly idea and he wanted to try it out right away, that's all.' Isabelle reaches into the car and takes the iPhone out of the glove compartment. 'I don't suppose it occurred to you to try this?'

Peter shakes his head and gets out of the car. He is fairly sure of how this is going to go, and he is right, as it turns out. He can hear Isabelle cursing behind him: 'What the fuck? No fucking...What kind of place *is* this?'

No connection. No signal. No contact. Peter's eyes sweep across the empty horizon, the clear blue summer sky. Then he brings his hands up to his mouth and whispers: 'The sun. Where the hell is the *sun*?'

*

The sun.

Stefan is standing outside his caravan, his arms hanging by his sides, his mouth wide open. He stares up at the sky once more, as if he had made a mistake the first time. Missed the thing that was right in front of his eyes. But there really is no sun, just the dazzling blue sky that seems to be illuminated by some internal light.

He takes a few steps in different directions to check the fragments of the horizon hidden by caravans and cars. No sun. He looks up again. The entire cupola of the heavens is equally bright, and exactly the same shade of blue everywhere. It doesn't even look like sky; it is more like something that has been put there to *resemble* sky. The absence of shifting nuances or clouds makes it impossible to decide whether it is ten or ten thousand metres above him.

He searches around on the ground and finds one of Emil's little toy cars; he picks it up and throws it in the air, as high as he can. It goes up perhaps twenty metres, then falls back down and lands on the grass, without having encountered any kind of obstacle on the way.

For as long as Stefan can remember he has lived with a feeling of fear in his chest. Sometimes it is stronger, sometimes weaker, but it is always there. If this fear had a voice, it would constantly repeat the same phrase: *Everything will be taken away from you.*

If the sun can disappear, then anything can disappear. Stefan's chest is aching, as if something is tugging at it from the inside. He looks over at the door of the caravan. As long as Carina and Emil exist, almost anything is bearable.

And what if they're not there? What if they've disappeared too?

Suddenly he cannot breathe. He takes a step towards the door, stops. He is seized by an insane urge to put his hands over his ears and simply run, run.

He makes a huge effort and takes a couple of deep breaths. The panic subsides, only to be replaced by a new torment. He doesn't want to wake Carina to this world, doesn't want to introduce Emil to a sky with no sun.

Stefan closes his eyes. Screws them shut as tightly as he can. He conjures up a sun in the sky, brings back the mini-golf course, the kiosk and the trampoline. He creates sounds: the morning breeze whispering through the trees, the shouts of children who have just woken up playing by the water's edge. Everything that is supposed to be there.

When he opens his eyes, it has all gone. He has no world to offer his family, and he cannot create one. He glances towards the door, and the fear returns. Is he looking at an empty caravan?

He can't stand it any longer. He dashes forward and yanks the door open, steps inside and stands there with his heart pounding, gazing at his sleeping wife and listening to his son's voice. As long as he stays there, not moving or speaking, it's as if nothing has happened. It's just an ordinary morning on their caravan holiday. In a little while they will have breakfast. Emil will come up with a tricky question about the world around him…

World? What world?

Stefan pulls himself together and climbs onto the bed so that he is lying face to face with Carina. He strokes her cheek and whispers: 'Darling?'

Carina blinks, then opens her eyes and says, 'Ooh.' She often does this when she wakes up, as if she is surprised that she has been asleep. 'Ooh. Morning. What time is it?'

Stefan glances at the alarm clock; it is ten to seven. Does that mean anything any more? He brushes a strand of hair from Carina's sweaty forehead and says: 'Listen. Something's happened.'

*

As there is no phone signal and no internet connection, Isabelle decides to look through her portfolio instead.

Synsam, 2002. A close-up that brings out her blue-green eyes in contrast to the black-rimmed glasses she is wearing. Her lips pout as if she is sucking on an olive.

Guldfynd, 2002. A luxurious full-length shot with chromatic lighting, a backless evening gown. A hunk in a dinner suit is approaching cautiously, as if he is unsure about speaking to such a beauty. Micro-spots glinting on a bracelet, a ring. The lighting alone took four hours.

Lindvalls kaffe, 2003. Her perfectly shaped nails around the bone-white coffee cup (false nails—she has always had a tendency to bite her own), the light that seems to come from the dark liquid creating shadows that emphasise her cheekbones.

Gaultier, 2003. The top of the tree in terms of professional credibility, but this was a men's fragrance campaign, so Isabelle is slightly out of focus behind the dark-haired man, his features as sharply delineated as if he were a cartoon character. Greek. The handsomest man she has ever worked with. Gay, unfortunately.

H&M, 2004. The most professional sessions ever. The summer campaign should have been her big break. At the last minute they decided to go down the ethnic route instead. Africans, Asians and an Eskimo. For the summer campaign. It was during this period that Isabelle started using Xanor.

Ellos, 2005. The only reason she has kept these pictures in her portfolio is because they show off her body to its best advantage. Swimwear and lingerie, fortunately. No frumpy blouses.

PerfectPartner, 2009. No one could fail to believe that she is madly in love with the man whose cheek she is caressing; her eyes say it all. Peter wasn't happy when the ad popped up as a banner on his email.

Gudrun Sjödén, 2011. When you're thirty you have to swallow your pride. But it was a pretty cool shoot in Morocco. Earthy colours, flowing fabrics, the afternoon light in the desert. Her eyes sparkling, hungry, as if she has just arrived in an oasis. As if she *is* the oasis.

Molly curls up beside her on the bed, moves her hand through the air in front of the screen.

'You're so pretty, Mummy!'

*

Benny has ventured as far as the opening of the awning. What he sees confirms what his nose and ears have already told him. There has been no transportation, but he is in a different place.

He sits down and scratches his ear with his hind leg, then tentatively pokes his nose through the opening. Certain scents are still there. The caravan that smells of Cow and contains Cat. Perfume.

He gazes out into the emptiness, blinks in the light. It is not at all like yesterday, and there are hardly any smells. Benny yawns, has a good shake. He turns around, then sits down again, peeps out and looks in the other direction this time.

Cat is lying in the window of the caravan that smells of Cow. Benny stretches and forgets his fear. He will give Cat a good telling off.

He has just stepped off the wooden floor of the awning and placed his front paws on the grass when he sees someone coming towards him. A big He. Benny stiffens, irresolute for a second. Then he withdraws, turns around and scuttles back to his basket.

*

For Peter, this holiday was a last attempt to save his marriage, a final shock with the defibrillator before declaring the patient dead.

They usually went to a five-star hotel in some exotic location, where Isabelle could indulge in a series of spa treatments while Molly was looked after in the children's club and Peter read crime novels by the pool. A luxury break made Isabelle more amenable, and they drifted along in a limbo that made them feel neither better nor worse. When they got home it was usually a few days before the quarrelling started again.

Needless to say, Isabelle had been less than enthusiastic about the idea of hiring a caravan, but Peter had insisted, on the grounds that he wanted to relive memories of childhood holidays with his mother. There was a certain amount of truth in that, but above all he wanted to give Isabelle one last chance. She hadn't taken it, and to be honest he had always known that was going to happen. He'd just wanted to be able to look back at this week and think: *That was when I'd had enough. That was when it all got too much.*

He has had enough, and it is all too much. He has to get away from here. Soon.

He walks over to Donald's caravan. A little beagle turns and scampers back into the awning as Peter stops and looks around.

The caravan is a Kabe Royal Hacienda, ten metres long and hooked up to a Cherokee SUV. Plus an awning at least twenty metres square. Teak furniture and a smallish garden made up of pots. On the supporting poles there are photographs of Elvis Presley, plus a couple of airbrushed pictures of wolves and native Americans. In the middle of the garden table there is a small flagpole flying the American flag. Half-hidden behind the beautiful plants is a gold brocade wall hanging: 'A kindly word at the right time helps the world go round.'

The beagle's basket is next to the door of the caravan, and the dog whimpers as Peter moves closer; its entire body is saying: *I know you're going to hit me, but please don't.*

The fear of a beating is provocative; one is tempted to become what one is presumed to be, and Peter has a sudden urge to give the dog a good kick in the head to make sure it keeps quiet. Instead he crouches down, holds out his hand and says: 'I won't hurt you.'

The dog's eyes dart from side to side, and it presses its chin against the bottom of the basket. *If we run out of food we can eat the dog.* Peter shakes his head and straightens up. He is not in his right mind. He has to get out of here. Soon.

He knocks on the door. After a few seconds the caravan rocks and he hears the sound of heavy footsteps. Peter thrusts his hands into his trouser pockets, screws up the sweet wrapper and clears his throat. The door is flung open.

The man standing there is in his seventies. He is completely bald, although his chest is covered in white curly hair. An impressive tanned belly conceals the upper half of a pair of red and white striped boxers. The slightly bulbous eyes give a kind of hunted intensity, as if he is

19

both prey and predator at the same time. His face lights up when he sees Peter.

'Wow! A visit from sporting royalty at this early hour!'

'Morning,' Peter says, lowering his eyes.

The previous evening Donald had come over uninvited and sat down to discuss the penalty against Bulgaria in 2005. In his opinion, Peter's career in the national team had been much too short, and he proceeded to go through a number of reasons for this, incidents that Peter himself had long forgotten.

Peter had supplied him with several drinks to keep him talking, in spite of meaningful sighs from Isabelle. He had served up a few anecdotes from his time in the Italian league, and Donald had taken it all in with admiring comments. Peter had basked in the glow of his fame, simultaneously ashamed of himself while revelling in the attention.

Donald had eventually weaved his way home, with an 'arrivederci, maestro' flung over his shoulder, and Isabelle had called Peter the most pathetic human being she had ever met. She had then proceeded to remind him that he had wasted the majority of his Italian millions on a failed restaurant project. And so on, and so on. A perfectly normal evening.

'What can I do for you?'

Donald steps down from the caravan, using the doorpost for support. Peter takes a step backwards to make room for the belly, and says: 'Something's happened. It's hard to explain, it's best if you take a look for yourself...' Peter follows the American custom and adds: '...Donald.'

Donald looks around. 'What do you mean, Peter? What's happened?'

Peter backs out of the awning and makes a sweeping gesture with his hand. 'You need to see for yourself. Otherwise you won't believe me.'

As Peter heads for the last caravan where the occupants are still sleeping, he hears Donald gasp and mutter something that sounds like: 'Holy shit.'

Emil has come down from his alcove and is kneeling between Stefan and Carina on the double bed, looking out of the window. He points at the horizon and turns to Stefan.

'How far is that?'

'The horizon, you mean?'

'Yes.'

'About five kilometres—that's what they say, anyway.'

Emil nods as if this is what he suspected all along, then says: 'Maybe there's nothing after that.'

'What do you mean?'

'Well, you can't see anything else.'

Stefan glances at Carina, who has hardly said a word since she first looked out of the window, then went outside for a minute before going back to bed. Her gaze is lost in the distance, and Stefan cups her shoulder with his hand. 'Are you okay, sweetheart?' he asks.

'This...' she says, waving her hand at the window. 'This is crazy. Have you tried the phone?'

'Yes. No reception.'

Carina's eyes flicker back and forth across the field, but find nothing on which they can settle. She hides her face in her hands.

'Don't be sad, Mummy,' Emil says, patting her back. 'Everything will work out. Won't it, Daddy?'

Stefan nods. The promise does not involve any kind of commitment; things always work out. Sometimes for the best, sometimes for the worst. But they will work out, one way or another.

Emil picks up a Donald Duck comic from the shelf above the bed and lies down on his stomach. He looks at the pictures, his lips moving as he spells out the words. He is old enough to realise that what has happened to them is very strange, incomprehensible in fact, but then a lot of things are like that in his world. Thunderstorms, elks, electricity and why eggs go hard when you boil them, while potatoes go soft. This is just something else to add to the list. He

has an enormous amount of trust. Mummy and Daddy will fix this, somehow.

Carina takes her hands away from her face, chewing on her lower lip as she asks: 'Is this for real?'

'What do you mean?'

'I mean...this just can't be happening. Is it for real?'

Stefan understands roughly what she means, but the thought hadn't occurred to him. Could this just be in their heads, like a hallucination or a mass psychosis?

'I think so,' he says. 'We're here now. Somehow.'

'Okay,' Carina says, turning away from the window. She takes a deep breath and straightens up. 'How are we for food? And water?'

*

There is a faint aroma of dung surrounding the dairy farmers' old Polar caravan, hooked up to a white Volvo 740. A ginger cat is lying in the window, glaring at him. Peter stands there contemplating the whole set-up. There is something homely about it, as if the caravan, the car and the cat have always been here, exuding *normality*.

The other evening Peter had passed by on his way to the laundry block. The two farmers had been sitting outside on deckchairs doing crosswords; from a CD player on the table came the sound of Abba's 'Dancing Queen'. They had got to their feet and introduced themselves: 'Lennart and Olof. Just like the former leaders of the Centre Party.'

Peter knocks on the door and hears movement from inside. Donald's caravan had rocked; this one creaks and squeaks, the metal complaining beneath the weight of the person who after a couple of attempts manages to push open the refractory door.

Peter has no idea whether the man in front of him is Lennart or Olof. They are so alike that he took them for brothers at first. The same round faces and deep-set, kindly brown eyes. The same age, just over fifty, and the same height. The same bodies marked by hard work, the same strong, callused hands.

The man is wearing a pair of blue dungarees with only one shoulder strap fastened. He blinks at the light, at Peter.

'Sorry,' he says. 'I'll just…'

He concentrates on the other strap and Peter peers into the caravan. Then he takes a step back so that the angle is different. So that he can't see.

With the strap in place, the man looks back at Peter, surprised to find him in a slightly different spot.

'Good morning?' he says.

Peter is still confused by what he saw inside the caravan. 'Er…The thing is…It's…'

The view from the caravan is not obscured by an awning, so Peter contents himself with waving his hand at the surroundings. The man looks around, leans out so that he can see to the right and the left, then stares up at the sky as he murmurs: 'Well I'll be…'

'I don't know any more than you,' Peter says. 'Perhaps we ought to have a meeting, all of us who are here. Talk about what we're going to do.'

The man looks back at Peter. There is something transparent about the deep-set eyes now, as if a fragment of the sky has settled there. He shakes his head and says: 'Do?'

'Yes. We have to…do something.'

'What can we do?'

Presumably the man is in shock, which is hardly surprising under the circumstances. Peter raises a clenched fist—the captain rallying the team before a match—and says: 'We'll have a meeting. Okay?'

Without waiting for a response he turns and sets off towards his own caravan. Behind him he hears the man's voice: 'Olof, wake up. You have to see this.'

So Peter must have been talking to Lennart. He rubs his scalp, hard. There is a lot to take in this morning, because through the open door he saw the farmers' bed. A double bed with a substantial body under the covers on one side. The other side was empty.

Peter isn't particularly bigoted, as far as he knows. But the thought of those two old men…it's hard to imagine. Really hard. Peter massages his scalp, trying to erase the picture. He has enough to think about without that.

What can we do?

That's the question. Personally, he has no idea. He doesn't know why he has taken it upon himself to go around and wake people, but he felt as if someone ought to do it. He can no longer remember why he felt that way. To avoid being alone, perhaps.

*

Five packets of instant noodles.
　　Just over a kilo of rice.
　　Half a box of macaroni.
　　Two tins of chopped tomatoes.
　　Two tins of sweetcorn.
　　Two onions.
　　A kilo of potatoes.
　　Four large carrots.
　　One pepper.
　　Half-full bags of oats, flour and sugar.
　　Lingonberry jam, apple sauce.
　　One litre of milk, one litre of yoghurt.
　　Four eggs.
　　Half a packet of crispbread, three slices of white bread.
　　Herbs and spices.
　　No meat, no fish. They were supposed to be going shopping today.
　　'At least the water tank is full,' Stefan says.

*

The area between the caravans is not large. A hundred square metres perhaps—half a tennis court. The occupants have gathered in this space. They are discussing what has happened as if it were some rare natural phenomenon—being transported to a different place, or the fact that their surroundings have disappeared.

Carina is not alone in doubting the authenticity of what they are experiencing. Majvor, Donald's wife, also thinks they are dealing with an altered reality rather than a geographical location. In the best-case scenario she thinks it is only temporary, like an optical illusion.

The men are more inclined to regard the situation as a problem to be solved, a nut to be cracked. If they have been moved, how has this happened? If everything around them has been dismantled, how is that possible? And why? *Why?*

Lennart and Olof follow the discussion, listening and nodding, but they say very little, offer no theories.

Mobile phone histories are examined with the aim of working out exactly when contact with the outside world was lost. Isabelle is the person who received the latest text, from a friend on her way home from a party. The message arrived at 2.26 am. Since then, nothing.

Molly woke up just before she roused Isabelle at about six-thirty.

It happened at some point during those four hours. Whatever 'it' might be.

*

The people are busy, and Benny seizes the opportunity. A quick thirty-metre dash and he is standing below the window where Cat is lying, puffing herself up to twice her size.

Cat is like Benny in some ways, and completely different in others. She is unpleasant and provocative, which is why Benny starts barking at her.

Cat cannot bark—it's just one of those things. Instead she gets to her feet and makes that noise that sounds like fast-flowing water. Cat makes her noise and Benny barks until he feels a hand seize him by the back of the neck, and hears his master's voice.

'Shut up, you stupid dog!'

Benny whimpers and scrabbles helplessly in the air with his paws as he is carried back Home by the scruff of his neck. The last thing he sees is Cat lying down and beginning to wash herself. As if she is pleased. This is so annoying that he lets out another bark, then he goes flying several metres through the air and lands on his back in his basket. He yelps in pain and curls up, hiding his head under his blanket.

*

'What do you think you're doing to that dog?'

Isabelle has never been interested in animal rights' issues, but there is something about the way Donald behaves that disgusts her. It is possible that the feeling is mutual, because Donald looks at her as if she were a slug in his garden. He smiles and says: 'No need for you to bother your pretty little head about that, my dear.'

Isabelle is not often lost for words. Donald is so lacking in self-awareness with his John Wayne–style machismo that it is almost frightening. She glances at Peter to see if there is any reaction to the way Donald has spoken to her, and indeed there is. He is staring down at the ground, unable to hide the smile tugging at the corners of his mouth.

'Right, listen up!' Donald says to the group. 'How about we give each other a little space to begin with—what do you think?' He pushes outwards with his hands as if he is knocking down invisible walls. 'I don't see the point in treading on each other's toes when we have all this room!'

Donald is wearing an old pair of tracksuit bottoms. Isabelle studies the area around the crotch, where a number of dried urine stains can be seen. Three steps forward and one good kick, right there. It's an option. For the time being she raises her voice and says: 'We can talk as much as we like about how and when we got here and how to arrange our caravans, but surely we have to start by finding out what's out there, for fuck's sake. There might be a supermarket just a few kilometres away! How about that? Freshly baked bread and some porn mags for good old Donald!'

She looks Donald straight in the eye as she says this. His cheeks flush, and Isabelle feels that the kick is no longer necessary. Peter steps between them and gives Isabelle a dirty look before he speaks: 'I'll go. My wife's choice of words may not always be…but I'm happy to go.'

Isabelle is about to say something suitably devastating to Peter, but Molly tugs at her hand.

'Mummy? I want something.'

*

Emil doesn't like it when there are lots of grown-ups around. Their voices and movements turn funny, as if they were on TV. Emil stays close to his mummy, Carina. Fortunately she doesn't say anything to the other grown-ups, just keeps her arm around his shoulders and lets him rest his head on her thigh.

The grown-ups are talking in loud voices, and Emil can tell they are frightened. He would like to drive away from here right now with Mummy and Daddy, but he realises this is impossible. There is nowhere to go. Not yet, anyway.

The lady that looks like a model is shouting horrible things, and Emil shakes his head. Somebody really ought to tell her off, but not Mummy or Daddy, because she might start yelling at them too. The model-lady's husband says he is happy to go.

Emil gazes out across the field. He has the distinct feeling that there is something horrible in the distance, beyond the point where they can see, and he thinks it is silly for the model-lady's husband to go. He seems nice, the kind of person who knows what to do.

Emil closes his eyes, screwing them up as he tries to push away the idea that there is something nasty out there. He pictures a great big broom, no, a vacuum cleaner that comes along and sucks up all his stupid ideas, down into the bag, then he removes the bag and throws it in the garbage. Then he takes the garbage bag out to the bin. And then a truck comes along and empties the bin and…he doesn't know what happens next.

Emil opens his eyes and is just about to ask his mother where the rubbish goes after it has been collected, but there is a girl standing in front of him. She is the same height as him, and she looks a little bit like the model-lady. There is at least one very similar girl at Emil's day care; she is nice but she shouts and screams quite a lot.

'What's your name?' the girl asks.

'Emil,' he says, pressing closer to his mother.

'I'm Molly,' the girl says. 'Let's go and play.'

Emil looks up at his mother. She doesn't look very pleased, but she removes her arm from his shoulders. Molly takes his hand and drags him away. Mummy is smiling and nodding now. Emil allows himself to be led to a strange caravan. He's not very keen, but he doesn't know how to say no.

*

Peter watches Molly and the boy disappear into the caravan as he heads for the car. His daughter always makes new friends. If that's the right expression. *She creates a court around herself.* Collects other children and tells them what to do. He knows that she had already noticed the boy, but had dismissed him as too pathetic to bother with. Instead she focused her attention on slightly older children, but not so much older that they were immune to her charm. Now they are gone, it seems that the boy will have to do.

Gone?

Peter leans against the car door and takes a deep breath. It is so quiet here. There is nothing but the sound of voices as the others continue to discuss the idea of rearranging the caravans. It is up to him now. He will find the way out and save them from emptiness.

A childhood memory pops into his mind. Peter is nine years old. It is November, and he is standing outside the door of the apartment where he and his mother are living temporarily. He fishes out his key, which is on a chain pinned to the inside of his pocket. As he is about to put the key in the lock, he hears a sound from the basement.

He jumps and drops the key, which dangles on the end of its chain, tapping against his knee. He gasps and reaches for it, then suddenly freezes. And straightens up.

For a few seconds he sees himself from the outside. The second-hand padded jacket that is far too thin, the frayed jeans. Standing outside the door of a sparsely furnished apartment that he hates. He sees how grey and boring his childhood has been, always on the run. And during those few seconds, as the fear subsides, he also sees what he really wants: to get away from here.

Peter clutches the car key in his pocket. Back then, when he was nine years old, he felt a vague desire to become an adult, to be able to make his own decisions about his life. Adulthood was the place where he longed to be, shimmering before him like a mirage. One day he would get there. But now? What if it is actually impossible to get away?

Peter shakes his head. People are relying on him. Obviously they are somewhere, and from somewhere it must be possible to get to somewhere else. Simple.

He slips in behind the wheel and closes the door with a soft click. The sound of a new car. When he starts the engine he glances in the rear-view mirror and sees that the group's attention is focused on him. He makes a slow U-turn and plasters on the smile he uses as an aerobics instructor, *that's terrific, you're all doing really well,* and raises his hand in a greeting as he drives past.

They wave back and he is struck by how *alone* they are. Cast out into emptiness by an unknown hand, for an unknown reason, with not even a tree for company. Paradoxically, Peter feels less alone in the car. The smell of the leather seats, the purr of the engine, the lights and diodes on the dashboard, the fact that he is moving forward creates a perception of self-sufficiency. A universe all of his own. *He* is leaving *them*, not vice versa.

Isabelle breaks away from the group and jogs over to the car. Peter opens the window; as usual he has no idea what to expect. It could be abuse, or an encouraging word.

'If you find a shop, buy something,' she says. Peter stares out across the field. 'Haven't we got anything?'

Isabelle shakes her head. 'Get some potato chips, or some chocolate. Anything.'

'We've got bananas.'

Isabelle sighs and raises a trembling hand. Her condition is called hyperthyroidism, apparently. A kind of excessive combustion. She can eat virtually anything without putting on weight. The price she pays is uncontrollable sweating and shaking when the engine no longer has anything to burn.

Peter looks at her hand and wonders what will happen if they can't get away, and run out of food. It's a terrible thought. And quite interesting.

'Did you hear what I said?'

'I heard,' Peter says, pressing the button to close the window. He puts his foot down, and a minute later he is surrounded by emptiness.

*

'Out of the question!'

When Donald suggested that the caravans should be spread over a wider area, it was with the proviso that his own mobile home should remain in place and be the starting point for this redistribution. People are now saying that he ought to move as well.

He looks at Majvor and shakes his head at the stupidity of others. From a purely practical point of view it is difficult for him to move, because his caravan is the only one with a proper awning, which would have to be dismantled and rebuilt. However, that argument should be surplus to requirements.

Donald and Majvor are long-term residents. They have rented a place on the campsite at Saludden for five weeks every year for twelve years so far. This year, however, they had to move across to the day campers' section, because a tree had fallen on their usual spot. They have had to endure three weeks among people who come and go as they please, just because the staff haven't pulled their finger out and chopped up that bloody tree. None of the others has been here for more than a week at the most. And now they're saying that Donald needs to move!

'Out of the question,' he repeats, pointing to his awning. 'It takes a whole day to put that up, besides which we've been here for three weeks already.'

The guy with the ugly glasses mumbles something. Donald stares at him and asks him to repeat whatever it was.

'But are any of us where we were?' the man says. 'From a purely technical point of view, I mean?'

Donald raises his voice and adopts the tone he uses when dealing with slippery suppliers. '*From a purely technical point of view* the issue is whether you can force me to move my caravan when I've explained how bloody difficult it is.'

The officious little prick backs down immediately; he holds up his hands and says: 'It was just an idea.'

Donald spreads his arms wide, embracing the entire group: 'You're all welcome to join me for a beer in our awning when you're done.' He indicates to Majvor that the conversation is over as far as he's concerned, and they head for home.

When they are out of earshot of the others, Majvor says: 'Why do you always have to be so unreasonable?'

'Unreasonable? You know how much bloody work it takes to get this thing set up!'

'Yes, and everyone else would have understood if you'd just explained yourself calmly and sensibly. And please don't swear at me.'

They step into the awning. Donald grabs a chair and slumps down on it, folding his arms. 'I'm not swearing at *you*, I just get so bloody... I'm telling you now, if anyone comes over here and starts messing with me, I'll...'

'You'll what, Donald?'

Donald bends down, supporting himself with one hand on the floor, and manages to extract a can of beer from the refrigerator, which runs on bottled gas. He cracks it open, takes a swig and wipes his forehead. 'I'll fetch my gun.'

Majvor stares at her husband, who is contemplating the entrance to the awning with practised indifference, as if he is just waiting for someone to come along and start messing with him. Majvor waits until his eyes flicker in her direction.

'You've brought the *gun* with you?'

Donald shrugs. 'Of course. You never know what might happen on a campsite these days.' He takes another swig of beer. Majvor's gaze is still burning into him, and he adds: 'Obviously I have no intention of *shooting* anyone. It's just a deterrent.'

'I assume the gun and the ammunition are in different places?'

'Yes. Yes of course.'

'Are they?'

'That's what I said.'

'*Are* they?'

'For pity's sake…'

Donald turns and rummages in the storage chest; he takes out the radio, which runs on batteries, and places it on the table. His only aim is to put an end to the uncomfortable conversation.

'I doubt if you'll be able to pick anything up,' Majvor says. 'Under the circumstances.'

But Donald has already switched on, and it transpires that Majvor is wrong. Music comes pouring out of the little red box. To be precise: 'Everyone Has Forgotten', by Towa Carson.

Donald and Majvor freeze and look at one another. Switching on the radio was an impulsive act. They had been told at the meeting that neither mobile phones nor computers were working, that there was no reception. They remain motionless, listening to the song as if it might contain some hidden message, something that could give them an answer. Neither of them liked Towa Carson back in the sixties, but now they sit there like lit candles, taking in every last syllable, as she sings of lonely nights spent with her memories.

The song fades away; the tension is unbearable. Will there be a voice, will someone say something? But no. After a brief silence they hear the opening chords of 'Your Own Melody' by Sylvia Vrethammar. And then Sylvia herself.

*

Molly and Emil are pretending to be dogs. For a long time they have been puppies, rolling around on the floor, yapping and scrabbling at each other with their paws. Molly has one of her sandals between her teeth. She jerks her head and tosses it into the darkness under the sofa.

Emil wriggles over and peers into the gloom, whimpering. He is a little dog who doesn't like dark corners.

'Fetch,' Molly says.

Emil whimpers again and shakes his head. Molly sits back on her hind legs and becomes slightly more human as she says: 'Fetch the shoe, or you're a stupid puppy!'

'Don't want to,' Emil says, still half-using his doggy voice.

'You *have* to!'

'Don't want to!'

'Why not?'

'Because...because...' Emil looks around for inspiration and catches sight of a roll of toilet paper. 'Because it's a horrible shoe and it stinks of *shit*!'

Molly stares at him for a moment, then she keels over backwards, giggling hysterically. It is a musical sound, nothing like the yelping of a puppy, and it makes Emil's little doggy heart swell slightly.

Molly carries on giggling and clutching her stomach as Emil sniffs the floor around her and pretends to pee up one of the kitchen cupboards. Molly stops laughing and gets on all fours. She straightens up as much as possible and says: 'Now we're a mummy dog and a daddy dog meeting one another.'

Emil abandons his loose puppy paws for stiffer legs and a more menacing expression. He lets out a low growl.

'No,' Molly says. 'You're a daddy dog who is in love with me.'

Emil blinks and widens his eyes the way the characters on *Bolibompa* do when they're in love, imagining a stream of pink hearts emerging from the top of his head.

'Good,' Molly says. 'And now you have to sniff my bottom.'

'Nooo!'

'Dogs *always* do that when they're in love!'

'Why?'

'Doesn't matter. That's what they do, so that's what you have to do.'

Emil crawls behind her and tentatively sniffs at Molly's bottom. He picks up the faint smell of pee before Molly whirls around, showing her teeth and letting out such a deep, aggressive growl that Emil is frightened. He shuffles backwards, waving his paws in front of him.

'What's the matter with you?' Molly says. 'Have you got cerebral palsy, or something?'

'No, I have not!'

'Well, you look like a dog with cerebral palsy.'

For a moment Emil feels as if he might burst into tears, but then he pictures a dog with cerebral palsy and starts giggling instead. Molly shakes her head. 'You try to sniff my bottom, I get cross, you try again, I get cross again, and *then* I let you sniff my bottom. That's what dogs do. Don't you know anything?'

'I don't want to,' Emil says. 'I'm a dog with cerebral palsy.'

Molly glares at him, but within a fraction of a second her face clears and she smiles at him. 'In that case you can lick my fur instead.'

Emil licks Molly's T-shirt until she nods and says: 'Time for a rest.'

They lie down on their stomachs side by side and pretend to sleep for a little while. Suddenly Molly gives a start; she raises her head, sniffs the air and whispers: 'Something dangerous is approaching. An enemy.'

Emil sniffs, but he picks up only dust from the carpet and a faint hint of perfume. 'There's no enemy,' he says.

'Yes, there is,' Molly insists, curling up. 'Something big and dangerous. The dogs don't know what it is, but it wants to eat them up.'

'No!'

'The dogs are scared. The enemy is like an elephant, but it's black, with a huge head and lots of sharp teeth. It's going to bite the dogs until it's got blood all around its mouth…'

'No!' There is a lump in Emil's throat, and his eyes are prickling.

'It's going to chew up the dogs, munching and crunching and breaking every bone in their body…'

Emil clamps his hands over his ears and shakes his head. He doesn't want to hear any more, because he can see it. The enemy. It is big and black and it has long, sharp teeth; it is surrounded by smoke as it moves along, and it is coming closer and closer because it wants to eat him up.

Molly pulls one hand away from his ear and whispers: 'But I know how we can protect ourselves. I'll protect you.'

Emil swallows the lump in his throat as best he can and looks at Molly, who is now wearing an expression of great determination. He knows that she is telling the truth about both the monster and her ability to save him, so he asks: 'How?'

'I'll tell you,' Molly says, glancing around. 'But first you have to do something.'

*

Carina lowers the caravan's supporting wheels so that the coupling fits over the tow bar. She doesn't bother with the electricity or the safety cable as they will be driving such a short distance. She wipes her hands on her shorts and gives Stefan the thumbs up. He starts the car, puts his foot down, and the caravan jerks forward. He drives ten metres out onto the field.

The two farmers have also moved their caravan. One of them is just getting out of the car, and raises his hand to Carina, who waves back.

Why are we doing this? Why are we moving? Surely we ought to stick together. For protection.

She glances over at the caravan into which Emil and Molly disappeared. There is something strange about that girl. It's as if she is only pretending, but what is she pretending?

'There we are,' Stefan says as he comes up to her. 'All done.'

Carina turns to face him. The thinning hair, the stocky body, the short arms ending in hands that are far too small. The man she chose. She loops her arms around his neck, rests her head on his chest. She knows every nuance of his smell, and she closes her eyes as he strokes her hair.

'Stefan,' she says. 'You have to promise me something.'

'Anything.'

'We don't know what's happened, or how long this is going to go on...'

'Carina, of course...'

'Wait. Listen to me.' She pulls back, looks up and takes his face between her hands. 'You have to promise me that we'll stick together. That whatever this is, we'll get through it together, not every man for himself. Do you understand?'

Stefan opens his mouth to answer too quickly, but closes it before saying a word. He gazes out across the field, frowning. Perhaps he does understand. He probably does.

'Yes,' he says eventually. 'I promise.'

*

Peter set off at fifty kilometres an hour, but now he is crawling forward. According to the GPS, the village of Västerljung lies a hundred metres ahead of him. Perhaps there would have been a small shop there, if only Västerljung itself had existed.

He has stopped trying to drive on what the GPS claims are roads; he has crossed streams without bridges and passed straight through dense forest without getting a single scratch on his paintwork. The only thing he can see is grass and more grass, the wheels of the car quietly passing over the unvarying field.

He looks in the rear-view mirror and is unsure whether the faint bumps on the horizon behind him really are the caravans, or merely an optical illusion. The sense of supremacy has left him, replaced by the loneliness of the penalty taker.

Bulgaria 2005. Everything disappears around him as he spins the ball between his fingers before placing it on the penalty spot.

He switches on the car radio to distract himself from the memories. As he presses the button he remembers that there is no reception. A second later it transpires that this is not in fact the case. He has been driving in silence, and the sudden onslaught of music is such a shock that he lets out a yell and slams on the brakes. The car shudders to a halt.

Peter sits there open-mouthed, staring at the cartoon-blue of the sky. His mother always used to listen to this kind of music when he was a little boy, and he knows who is singing. Kerstin Aulén and Peter Himmelstrand. This is obviously the last chorus; he hears a few bars of the wedding march on the organ, then the song is over. He is still so stunned by the fact that the radio works that he doesn't have time to wonder whether anyone is going to *speak* before Towa Carson kicks off with 'Everyone Has Forgotten'.

Peter switches off the radio and leans back in his seat, still gazing out across the field. Somewhere someone is sitting in a studio playing these records, broadcasting them into the ether. Who? Where? How? Why?

One thing is clear from the choice of music: they are still in Sweden. The radio and the GPS are in agreement there. But where is there a place like this in Sweden?

Peter opens the door, gets out of the car and gasps when he looks around. Only now is he able to appreciate the *depth* of the vacuum in which he finds himself. He holds up his hands in front of his face. They are there. He is real, even though he is so incredibly small. He pats the roof of the car, feeling the metal against his palm. The car is there too.

He screws up his eyes and peers in the direction from which he has come, but he can no longer make out any caravans. Peter and the car are in the middle of a vast green disc, suspended in a sea of blue. He spins around, and lets out an involuntary yell: 'Hello? Hello? Is anyone there? Hello?'

*

Lennart and Olof have moved their caravan a short distance, stripped and folded up their bed so that it has become two narrow sofas and a table. They are now sitting opposite one another at this table, contemplating a sparse breakfast: crispbread, fish paste and a tub of margarine that has gone runny in the refrigerator, which has stopped working. The gas cylinder is empty, and they have been running on electricity for the past few days. Electricity which is no longer available.

No coffee. This is a disaster. Neither Lennart nor Olof are particularly keen on breakfast; they are happy with a slice of bread cheered up with something out of a tube—soft cheese or fish paste. But they must have coffee. Always.

'Is there any way of mixing it with cold water?' Lennart wonders, waving at the pack of ground coffee.

'I doubt it. Maybe if we had instant.'

'Hang on, didn't we have a camping stove? One of those little ones?'

'Maybe, somewhere. Although I don't really feel up to looking for it at the moment. Do you?'

'No. Later, perhaps.'

'Okay.'

Lennart looks doubtfully at his rectangle of crispbread, with melted margarine dripping over the edge. 'How are we for food?'

'Not too bad,' Olof replies. 'We'll be all right for a few days. We've got plenty of potatoes.'

'Which means we have to dig out the camping stove.'

'Right. We can't live on raw potatoes.'

They carry on eating; the sound of crunching is animalistic in the silence. They look at one another and smile, with crumbs at the corners of their mouths. They are like two horses. Two horses chomping their way through their nosebags. The milk they are drinking to wash down the unappetising lumps of food is lukewarm.

'I'm not too keen on all this,' Olof says when they have finishing chewing and swallowing.

'No,' Lennart replies as he wipes crumbs off the table. 'Then again…I don't know.'

Olof waits. He can tell from Lennart's hesitant movements that he is trying to put something into words. When Lennart has tipped the crumbs into the bin and draped the dishcloth over the tap, he leans back against the cupboard, folds his arms and says: 'But this is just the way things are, somehow.'

'What do you mean?'

'You know what I mean. This is how things are. It's just been… clarified.'

'Right. I suppose that's one way of looking at it.'

'Is there another way?'

Olof frowns and concentrates on the situation in which they find themselves. It's difficult. His thoughts refuse to grow, because they have nowhere to take root. There is only emptiness. Eventually he shrugs and says: 'You're going to have to give me some thinking time, Lennart.'

'Take as much time as you want.'

Lennart picks up their current crossword magazines and places Olof's in front of him, along with his glasses and a pen. Similarly equipped, Lennart sits down opposite him and places his glasses on the end of his nose.

Olof manages to concentrate on the mega-crossword for only a minute before his thoughts run away with him. He looks up at Lennart, who is chewing on his pen, totally absorbed in the trickiest crossword of them all.

'What about the cows?' Olof says.

Without looking up, Lennart replies: 'I'm sure Ante and Gunilla will cope.'

Ante is Olof's son, and Gunilla is Lennart's daughter. An independent observer might easily conclude that the reverse is true. Lennart is always the first to praise Ante's all-round ability and skill with the animals, while Olof cannot say enough about Gunilla's financial wizardry and her willingness to pitch in when necessary.

Not that Lennart or Olof would wish for things to be different, but they find it easier to praise each other's child rather than their own. They have discussed the phenomenon and decided that it is probably only natural, and if it isn't, there is nothing they can do about it.

'Cynthia fifteen is due to calve in a couple of days,' Olof says.

'Ante will be fine.'

'Are you sure?'

'I'm sure.'

They sit in silence for a while, with Olof's pen doing the most scratching since Lennart is tackling the most difficult puzzle. After a few minutes Olof puts down his pen and says: 'Do you think something might happen? Between them? During our absence, so to speak?'

'Time will tell.'

'Yes. It would be a great help, though.'

'It would.'

Lennart smiles and strokes the back of Olof's hand. Then he taps his teeth with his pen as he stares at his crossword. His face clears as he suddenly sees the solution to one clue, which in turn unlocks a couple more, and he sets to work with renewed enthusiasm. Olof gazes out of the scratched plexiglas window, which distorts the view. Not that it matters, since all there is to see is the grass and the sky, the sky and the grass. He thinks about the other people who are seeing the same thing, and says: 'Things could get a bit tricky before long.'

'In what way?'

'I don't know, but most people aren't capable of dealing with a situation like this. And that could lead to…trouble.'

'You're probably right. The question is how much trouble.'

Olof's gaze is once again drawn to the window. The empty sky, the empty field that would make him feel utterly abandoned if Lennart wasn't here beside him. He says: 'Quite a lot, I should imagine. A hell of a lot, in fact. Trouble.'

Lennart also looks out of the window. He nods. 'You're probably right. Unfortunately.'

*

Stefan connects the stove and heats up a pan of water so that he can make himself and Carina a cup of instant coffee. Fortunately the refrigerator also works on gas, and the milk carton is cold against his fingers. He pours a generous splash into his coffee and a dash into Carina's, then carries the cups over to the table and sits down opposite his wife. He takes a sip, then says: 'We have a bit of a problem.'

'Oh?'

'I was going to ring the supplier today. They've been sending the same amount of herring since midsummer.'

'Why is that a problem?'

'Well, we're going to be stuck with half a pallet that nobody wants to buy.'

'If we get back.'

'Yes, but I'm sure we will. Sooner or later.'

'Really?'

'What's the alternative?'

Stefan knows what the alternative is, but has decided that it is pointless to acknowledge it until they know more, until Peter returns. It's no good assuming the worst, nor brooding unnecessarily about what has happened; that can only lead to unpleasantness.

If he avoids looking out of the window, there is nothing strange about the situation. Quite the reverse. He and Carina are sitting here with their hands around their coffee cups chatting about the minor problems of everyday life. Nothing could be more natural.

'We'll have to run some kind of campaign,' Carina says.

Stefan has been working so hard to imagine that everything is normal that he has lost the thread.

'Sorry? Campaign?'

'To get rid of the herring. A sales campaign.'

'Absolutely,' Stefan says. 'Good idea.'

*

Peter gets back in the car, starts the engine and gently depresses the accelerator. His perception of isolation is so complete that even his inner voice has fallen silent, and is no longer keeping him company. On the leather-upholstered seat is the shell of the man who was once Peter Sundberg, about to collapse in on himself and disintegrate into the empty field.

The GPS screen flickers and turns blue. Peter taps it a couple of times, even though he knows there is no point. He stops the car, turns off the GPS, turns it back on again. Nothing. Only blue, as if he were out at sea.

He randomly presses all the buttons, bringing up menus and settings, but no map or position indicators. Strangely enough this does not frighten him; it actually feels quite good, as if he has *escaped*.

On a whim he puts the car in reverse. After thirty metres the map reappears. He brakes and something shifts inside his head. The playfulness is gone. He rests his chin on the steering wheel and stares out of the windscreen. There is some kind of border a few metres ahead of him. He opens the door and gets out, walks towards the point where the map disappears.

Something happens, something striking. It reminds him of arriving in Thailand and walking out through the airport doors after spending many hours in an air-conditioned environment: the wave

42

of heat and humidity that strikes him, the instant change. It is just as powerful here, but completely different in character.

Peter sits down on the grass five metres from the car, his knees drawn up and his hands loosely linked over his shins. Total silence surrounds him. He is at rest. No Isabelle with her capricious demands and constant air of discontent. No Molly, hiding her nastiness beneath the guise of a princess. No one pulling him this way and that, wanting something from him.

Nothing. Just nothing. The perfect stillness when the free kick from thirty metres curves over the wall, half a second away from landing in the goal. When everyone knows. In half a second the opposing team's shoulders will slump as they accept the inevitable, his own team will raise their arms in celebration, but it hasn't happened yet. Right now the ball is hanging in the air, the whole stadium holds its breath, in awe. That moment.

Here he sits, Peter Sundberg. Over the years he has made hundreds of women feel better. And a few men, to be honest. But mostly women. They are sent to him if they are undecided. Is joining the gym, taking up aerobics really for them? After fifteen minutes with Peter, they usually sign up for annual membership. He does his best to meet their expectations. He remembers their names, always has a few encouraging words for them.

'How's it going, Sally? Looking good!' 'How's your foot, Ebba? I'm impressed to see you back so soon!' 'You can do it, Margareta, I know you can!'

They often fall for him. When he can't make their dreams come true in that respect, many want him to be their confidant instead, particularly those who have him as their personal trainer.

When they are relaxing after a training session, sitting together and assessing the client's progress, a sense of closeness can often arise, a bubble that forms around the two of them. Sometimes they want to tell him who they are, what their lives are like.

Peter is no psychologist; he rarely has any advice to offer beyond nutrition and stretching. But he knows how to listen. He can nod, he can shake his head, he can say 'mmm'. And that seems to be enough. He has received many bunches of flowers during the four years he has worked at the gym.

But that's not the most important thing. What gives him real satisfaction is to see a woman in her forties or fifties turn up at the gym looking like a sack of potatoes, an unhappy sack of potatoes, and then to watch the same woman walk in a year later looking like a different person. Not perfect, not necessarily happy, but with the strength to live, both physical and mental. A straighter back, a glint in the eye. That's what makes his job worthwhile.

Peter nods to himself and looks at his forearms, sinewy and muscular, covered in fine blond hairs. He feels a kind of vibration inside. And not only inside; as he gazes at his arms the hairs stand up, and he can feel his scalp crawling.

He gets to his feet, pictures the empty field before him filled with women. His women. The women he has steered out of incapability and apathy. He feels their gratitude pouring towards him, their love.

Eva, Aline, Beatrice, Katarina, Karin, Lena, Ida, Ingela, Helena, Margareta, Sofia, Sissela, Anna-Karin...

They are all wearing identical work-out clothes. Black tights, black tank tops. Their faces are radiant, and he feels a shudder of sensual pleasure. The vibration increases in strength; it has to find an outlet. He jumps up and down on the spot, shouting 'Yes! Yes!'

He rushes back to the car and switches on the radio. Mona Wessman's voice emerges from the speakers and he turns up the volume until the bass rattles. He doesn't lose heart, but shouts 'Okay!' and dashes back to his starting point.

Right leg lift, bam-bam-bam, other leg, bam-bam-bam, arms up, bam-bam, and again, bam-bam.

Everyone follows him, keeping to the beat, copying his movements; the group grows bigger and bigger until it fills the entire field. All the women in the world are obeying the smallest gesture, working with him. Their pulse is his pulse, the sweat running down his back is their sweat.

'Come on, ladies! Terrific!'

He increases the tempo, working twice as fast, and no one drops out, everyone is keeping up. This is the class he has dreamed of, but never achieved. The synchronised dance, the total unity. When the chorus comes along he just has to join in.

He has never been happier.

As the song fades away he releases his stiff cock from his shorts; it only takes a couple of tugs before he is overcome by an orgasm so powerful that his legs give way as his semen spurts across the grass.

Peace. He feels peace.

*

Benny raises his head, cocks one ear. He can hear a new sound, coming from far away. He glances at his master and mistress, who are sitting at the table, but they don't appear to have noticed anything. Benny edges along to the opening and looks out.

Several Hes and Shes are approaching. Benny turns his head and sees his master open the cold box next to his basket and take out a few cans. Benny has experienced this kind of thing before. There will be loud voices and lots of people trying to pat him, which he doesn't like. He screws up his courage and slips out, in the direction of the noise.

All the Hes and Shes go inside the awning, while Benny stares into the emptiness. It is impossible to see where the noise is coming from, but he recognises it. It is the same as the sound that comes from his master's box, the one on the table. Benny is satisfied, and decides to inspect the area while all the Hes and Shes are safely inside.

The absence of smells from other animals is distressing. There doesn't seem to be much point in marking his territory when there is nothing against which to defend it, but he goes through the motions anyway. You never know. A Fox or Dog *could* just turn up and get the idea that this is their place. Or Cat might start taking liberties.

Benny glances at Cat's caravan, wondering whether to go over and

45

show himself so that Cat won't forget about him, when a squeaking noise catches his attention. He heads towards it and spots the small He and She.

Benny is wary of small people. They sometimes pull his tail and behave unpleasantly in all kinds of ways. He stops at a safe distance and tilts his head on one side, trying to see what they are up to.

They have opened a flap and Benny senses that they are doing something that isn't right. She looks fine, but He doesn't. Benny is exactly the same when he has stolen a sausage. Benny knows all about Right and Wrong, and the small He is clearly doing something that is Wrong.

Benny cannot work out what this might be, but one thing he does know: the small He is going to get a good smack on the nose. Sooner or later. End up with no dinner. That kind of thing.

*

Majvor has been married to Donald for forty-six years. He proposed on his twenty-fifth birthday, and she said yes straight away. She saw no reason to give him a different answer. In those days Donald was just an ordinary employee at the sawmill, but Majvor knew that he would soon make progress. She was right.

She has given him four sons, and they are all decent men. She has run a large household, cooked, cleaned, shopped, done the laundry. She has had her hands full for almost thirty years, and has never felt the need to complain.

He has never hit her, and is not a big drinker. She is pretty sure he has been unfaithful, but this hasn't particularly bothered her. Men are men, and although she might have shed a few tears over a shirt carrying the scent of an unfamiliar perfume, she has quickly put the matter behind her and has never plagued him with questions.

He has accompanied her to church on high days and holidays even though he does not share her faith, which is kind of him. In return she has never tried to convert him or force him into a piety that is not in his nature.

They have been lucky, all in all. She'd grown up poor, with no special talents, and so had Donald, but together they have raised four fine sons, and can rest on their laurels in a large house by the sea, with two cars and a boat. The Lord has indeed smiled down upon them. To think anything else would be the height of arrogance.

Majvor doesn't know what to make of the situation in which they now find themselves. The Lord may or may not be involved, as is so often the case. When she has a moment to herself, she will ask Him for advice. He probably won't answer, and as usual she will be left to her own devices. That's how it should be.

But it looks as if it will be a while before that moment comes. The people from the other caravans are arriving, one by one or two by two, at Donald's invitation. Majvor gets up to welcome them. She is a good hostess, as she has been told so many times.

She intends to carry on being herself, a person who is basically kind. Whatever happens.

*

'Why are we doing this?'

'Because it's fun, of course.'

'How is it fun?'

'You'll see, you stupid dog.'

'I don't want to be a dog any more. Tell me.'

'Tell you what?'

'About the monster and so on.'

'Nope.'

'But you promised! You said that if I—'

'First of all I have to be sure you won't say anything.'

'I won't.'

'You swear?'

'I swear!'

'Do you swear on your mummy's life? If you say anything, she'll die?'

'...'

'There you go. You will say something.'

'I won't! I swear!'

'On your mummy's life?'

'…'

'On your mummy's life?'

'Yes.'

'Repeat after me: *If I say anything, my mummy will die.*'

'If I say anything, my…I don't want to.'

'In that case the monster can have you.'

*

Seven people are gathered around the teak table in Donald and Majvor's awning, three along each side, Donald at the head. Only Stefan and Donald have a can of beer in front of them; the others have soft drinks, or nothing. After all, it's only morning. Presumably.

Donald has told them that the radio is working, and together they have listened to Mona Wessman singing about the hambo, but there is no presenter.

If this was a meeting, it would have been abandoned by now. The atmosphere is oppressive, and no one is saying anything. From time to time someone turns to the opening in the canvas awning, looking for those who are not here. Everyone must be present. Perhaps that is why nothing is happening, nothing is being said.

Donald takes a swig of his beer and leans back, placing his hands on his belly. 'So…' One or two people nod as if to confirm he is correct. Stefan even goes so far as to say 'Right', mainly to thank Donald for the beer.

Majvor notices that Isabelle's hands are shaking. She reaches across the table and pats her arm. 'My dear, are you ill?'

Isabelle swallows audibly. 'Have you got any sweets? A Mars bar or a Dime, anything?'

Donald snorts. 'Are you a sugar addict? Oh well, sweets to the sweet, as they say.'

48

He looks around, but no one even smiles at his joke. He is about to try again, but catches Majvor's steady gaze and takes another swig from his can instead.

'We've got homemade buns,' Majvor says.

Isabelle rubs her arm and nods. 'That'll do, thanks.'

Majvor gets to her feet and waddles over to the door of the caravan, mounting the step with a groan. Donald watches her with displeasure and turns to Stefan. He looks as if he is about to say something, but changes his mind. Silence reigns once more.

Donald contemplates the assembled company, searching for an opening. He settles on Lennart and Olof, who are sitting opposite one another at the far end of the table. 'So what about you two?' he says. 'Tell me about yourselves.'

The two men shuffle uncomfortably.

'Lennart.'

'Olof. Think of the former Centre Party leaders.'

'I don't know any of their names. Apart from Fälldin. But I do know the name of every single American president.'

'Impressive,' Lennart says.

'Very,' Olof adds.

Donald narrows his eyes as he tries to work out whether they are making fun of him, but there is nothing to indicate that this is the case. Their expressions are open and interested, so he holds up his hands and begins to count on his fingers.

'Washington, Adams, Jefferson, Madison.'

Out of the corner of his eye he sees Majvor thud down the step with a plate of buns in her hand. He is well aware of her views on demonstrating his little party trick, but he doesn't care.

'Monroe, Adams, Jackson, Van Buren, Harrison.'

Majvor has barely put down the plate before Isabelle grabs two buns, one in each hand; it almost seems as if she can't chew fast enough to get them down. Majvor smiles and nods. It's nice when people eat what you're offering.

'Tyler, Polk, Taylor.'

Stefan glances towards the opening and sighs. He can't stop thinking about that bloody herring. Three hundred tins will be on their way to the warehouse. If only he could make a phone call. Why isn't that possible? There might be pockets in the depths of Norrland that have no reception these days, but this is not the depths of Norrland. Not by a long way.

'Fillmore, Pierce, Buchanan, Lincoln!'

Lennart and Olof are frozen, like two small animals caught in the headlights of Donald's gaze; his eyes are fixed on them as the names come pouring out. There is something vaguely frightening and possibly aggressive about the performance. They would like to hold hands, but of course they don't.

'Johnson, Grant, Hayes, Garfield, Arthur.'

Carina follows Stefan's eyes and assumes he is thinking the same as her. Emil. He has been with that girl for half an hour. She would like to go and fetch him, but knows she shouldn't. Emil doesn't find it easy to make friends; his shyness and reserve get in the way. So Carina ought to be pleased. She tries to feel pleased.

'Cleveland, Harrison, Cleveland again.'

Donald reels off his list of names triumphantly. Every one is a face, and every face is a period in American history. He is no expert, but taken altogether the names conjure up what America means to him. Opportunity. People who overcome the odds, who rise above their humble beginnings, breaking the chains of the past to be *free*. It is like a prayer, this litany, these names.

'McKinley, Roosevelt, Taft.'

Isabelle is on her fourth bun. She would really like to grab the whole plate and withdraw to a dark corner like some wild animal to devour the lot. She loves the slim figure her illness gives her, but hates the weakness. She doesn't want anyone to look at her while she is eating.

'Wilson, Harding…hang on a minute. Wilson, Harding…'

Carina is so busy trying to be pleased for Emil's sake that she doesn't notice he has come into the awning until he hurls himself at her and buries his face between her breasts. His body is heaving with sobs, and she gently strokes the back of his neck. 'Whatever's wrong, sweetheart?' Emil shakes his head and presses even closer.

'Wilson, Harding, then Hoover. But there's one in between. Who is it?'

Carina looks over towards the opening and sees Molly standing there, leaning against one of the supporting posts and staring at her. When their eyes meet Molly smiles, shrugs and shakes her head as if to say: '*I* don't know what's wrong with him either.'

'Help me out here,' Donald says. 'Wilson, Harding, and then…'

The sound of a car horn brings everyone to their feet. This is what they've been waiting for, although no one dared put it into words. Now they will know. There is anxiety on every face as they move towards the opening; Molly has already run away. Only Donald remains in his seat, staring blankly into space as he mutters: 'There's one missing. There's one missing.'

*

Isabelle's hunger has been appeased for the time being. She picks up the last bun on her way out. She is happy to leave the awning; the decor is possibly the most vulgar she has ever seen.

Bad taste can actually make her feel physically unwell. Both her parents are aesthetes, and she grew up in a home where every object was carefully chosen. Her bedroom was a monk's cell compared to those of her contemporaries. No posters, no photographs, no bits and pieces.

A week spent camping has been something of an ordeal. At every turn she has been confronted by barbecues and cheap tat, and by people who seem to enjoy that sort of thing. She hates the caravan and she hates Peter for persuading her to come along. Some of the best memories from his ghastly childhood, camping holidays with his mother, blah blah blah. Isabelle hates his rotten childhood too, and his constant references to it.

She has erased her own childhood, left it behind. She doesn't think about it, doesn't talk about it. Above all she doesn't use it as an argument to get her own way. She has other methods of achieving that.

Before she leaves the awning she glances back at Donald, who is sitting there with his mouth hanging open. *No need for you to bother your pretty little head about that, my dear.* No doubt he had a rotten childhood as well. She hopes so. She hopes he carries it with him, and that it really hurts.

Isabelle takes a few steps towards the car, then stops. There is something different about Peter, standing there by the open door with everyone gathered around him. She can't quite put her finger on it, but it is as if the light is striking him from another angle, rather than from above.

*

The first thing Peter says to the group is: 'Have you had a barbecue?'

They all look at one another. Everyone knows that no one has had a barbecue, and yet it is as if they have to check. *Have you had a barbecue? No. Me neither. How about you? No, when would I have done that? And why is he asking?*

It is Stefan who says it out loud: 'Why do you ask?'

'I thought I could smell smoke. As if someone was barbecuing. Meat.'

'Okay...' Stefan glances at the others. 'But what did you see? What's out there?'

'Nothing,' Peter replies. 'Same as here. Nothing.'

Stefan waits for him to go on. At a push he can accept what Peter says, that things are as bad as he feared. But what he can't get his head around is why Peter looks so *pleased*. It doesn't make sense.

Isabelle appears to feel the same. She walks up to Peter and says: 'What the hell is wrong with you? Don't stand there lying like a fucking idiot. This isn't the time or the place. What did you see?'

Peter looks down at the ground, blushing like a little boy whose mother has caught him dipping into the Saturday sweets in the middle of the week. No one understands him. His cheeks are burning as he raises his head and says: 'It's as if there's a border. When you cross it, things are…different.'

'What do you mean, different?' Stefan asks.

Peter scratches the back of his neck. 'I might have seen a person.'

Isabelle is on the point of slapping Peter. 'A person? You saw a person? And you're only telling us this now?'

'I'm not sure. They were a long way off.'

'So why the hell didn't you drive up to whoever it was?'

'The GPS stopped working. I was afraid of getting lost.'

Isabelle stares at Peter, then she turns to the group with a gesture that means something along the lines of: *You see what I have to put up with? I live with this pathetic waste of space.* She then grabs Molly's hand and heads towards their caravan as she says loudly: 'You poor kid. You were fathered by a man with no balls.'

*

Donald has a very specific fear that has grown stronger over the past few years. The name of this fear is dementia, senility, Alzheimer's.

He has started to forget things. Sometimes he opens a cupboard and can't remember why. He is about to say the name of a supplier with whom he has been dealing for over twenty years, and suddenly it has gone and he has to consult his diary. So far no one has noticed anything, not even Majvor, but he dreads the day when one of the children calls and he can't recall their name.

And now the list of US presidents.

If there was one thing he thought he would still be able to reel off when he was sitting in the care home, when the last ounce of sense had left him, it was the list of US presidents.

They're all there, every single one right up to Barack fucking Obama, apart from the guy who came between Harding and Hoover. Forty-three when there should be forty-four. Donald has gone all the way through the alphabet in the hope that the right letter would make the name jump out of its hiding place.

This is terrible. It's like owning a house and suddenly discovering that a door or a window is missing. It's not *complete*, it's not *whole*, and he can feel the mists of senility drifting in through the opening, forming a figure made of smoke that reaches into his mind with its long fingers, hollowing out his thoughts and memories.

He shakes his head and smiles apologetically. Only then does he realise that he is alone. He looks around in confusion, and hears voices outside. One of these voices belongs to Peter, which means he must have come back.

The teak chair creaks as Donald gets to his feet and arranges his face, turning himself into the man he is meant to be, the kind of man people turn to. He can't sit here philosophising over his minor lapses when more pressing problems are calling. He clears his throat, straightens his back, and steps outside.

The first thing he sees is Isabelle, marching past with her daughter. Donald sneaks a look at her bottom, and a vague rape fantasy passes through his mind before being replaced by a desire to spank that little rump until it is bright red and the redness

turns into blood, a fountain of blood gushing
Stop!

Donald stares gloomily at the group gathered around the car. Peter seems disorientated; he is waving his hands around, while the others have their eyes fixed on the ground. Someone needs to take charge of the situation, so Donald steps forward: 'How's it going?'

Peter looks at him as if he doesn't understand the question, and the boring little grocer answers on his behalf: 'Apparently he could smell smoke out there. And he saw someone.'

'Okay,' Donald says. 'What else?'

'Nothing else.'

'But where did the smoke come from? Who was this person? Peter? You did check, didn't you?'

Peter runs his hand over the roof of his car as if he is removing invisible dust; he doesn't look at Donald as he replies: 'No.'

'But why not, for God's sake?'

The dust seems to be pretty stubborn; Peter carries on rubbing away. 'I don't know.'

Donald shakes his head. He is disappointed. Among all the milksops surrounding him, he had thought Peter was an ally. Someone who could tackle things head-on. But now he is standing here gibbering like the rest of them. This can't go on.

Donald puts a friendly arm around Peter's shoulders. 'Come and have a beer and we can talk about this.'

*

The first thing Lennart and Olof do when they get back to their caravan is to switch on the radio, as if they need to check that the broadcast is not a localised phenomenon restricted to Donald's awning. But no. The music comes pouring out of their battered old Luxor too. And not just any music, but one of Olof's favourites: 'This Is How Love Begins' by Agnetha Fältskog and Björn Ulvaeus.

Lennart sits down on the sofa and watches with quiet amusement as Olof shuts the door, then begins to move in time to the music. Lennart likes the song too, but finds it a bit *too* romantic for his taste: a chance meeting in a crowd, dancing dance after dance.

Olof grabs Lennart's hand and pulls him to his feet, opening his arms as he sways on the spot. Lennart waves dismissively: 'I can't.'

'Of course you can,' Olof says, taking both of Lennart's hands. 'It's just a basic foxtrot.' The caravan rocks as Olof demonstrates the steps, pulling Lennart close. Lennart takes one step to the right, one to the left, and his cheeks grow hot. He pulls away and moves backwards until he bumps into the kitchen table.

'I *can't.*'

Olof frowns and turns down the volume. 'What do you mean?'

'I can't dance.'

'Yes, you can.'

'No, I can't. And it feels so...I don't know.'

Lennart sits back down on the sofa and looks out of the window. There is nothing to see, but he looks anyway. He hears a click as the radio is switched off, and in his peripheral vision he sees Olof sit down opposite him. He feels a gentle caress on his forearm.

'It's okay,' Olof says. 'It's okay.'

'I know,' Lennart says, glancing at Olof, who has tilted his head to one side, his expression full of concern.

'Was it too intimate?' Olof asks.

'No. Yes. Although it would be...I know. It's just that...'

Olof withdraws his hand and fixes his eyes on the table. 'We do sleep together, after all.'

'Yes, but that's different, somehow.'

'I know what you mean,' Olof says. 'I feel the same.' He scratches his head and pulls a face. 'Forgive me. I just felt...inspired.'

'You have nothing to apologise for. I wish...well, you know.'

They sit in silence for a while, then Olof says: 'Can you really not dance? Did you never learn?'

'No. I must have been off sick when we had dancing lessons.'

'My mother taught me, when I was fourteen or fifteen.'

'My mother wasn't much of a dancer, as you might recall.'

'No. Of course not.'

Lennart looks gloomy, and Olof wishes he had never brought up the subject. Lennart's mother was kicked by a horse, and Olof remembers her as old before her time, always leaning on a stick for support.

It was a silly idea anyway, trying to get Lennart to dance. It's all coming back to Olof now. Whenever he and Ingela went out with Lennart and Agnetha, Lennart would always have some problem with his back or his knees, and would stay at the bar while Agnetha danced with other partners. Olof had assumed he was just shy.

'Listen,' he says, tapping the table. 'Shall we go out and listen to our iPod?'

Lennart nods and gets to his feet, follows Olof. Before Olof has time to open the door, he feels Lennart's hand on his shoulder and turns around. Lennart's expression is serious as he slowly strokes Olof's cheek and says: 'Forgive me.'

'There's nothing to forgive.' Olof places his hand on Lennart's, presses it against his face. 'That's just the way things are. And it's fine.'

The gadgets are on the table between the two folding chairs. Olof knows the correct terminology—*iPod, dock, speakers*—but because he doesn't know how to operate the devices in question, he thinks of them as gadgets.

Lennart is astonishingly adept when it comes to modern technology. Mobile phones, computers, MP3 players. In his own defence, Olof can say that Lennart's daughter Gunilla is a much more patient tutor than Ante, whose pedagogical efforts rarely extend beyond: 'Read the instructions.'

Olof settles down in his chair and nods to Lennart, who looks much happier now he is dealing with something he is good at. Lennart slides his finger across the screen, and Olof says: 'It's a good job you know how to do that.'

'Shall I show you what to do?'

'If you like. As long as you let me show you how to dance. One day.'

Lennart can't help smiling. Then he nods. 'Sounds reasonable. *Super Trouper*?'

'Muy bien, gracias.'

'De nada, señor.'

Lennart places the iPod in its dock. Olof leans back and closes his eyes as he hears the first staccato notes of 'Lay All Your Love on Me'. Excellent.

*

Emil has calmed down, but he refuses to talk about why he was so upset. As soon as Stefan or Carina attempt to ask a question, he puts his hands over his ears and starts humming tunelessly.

Stefan is standing with his hands in his pockets, staring out across the field. *Nothing.* This can't be true. Vast expanses of emptiness like this do exist on the earth, but they are deserts or oceans. Where there is grass there are flowers, bushes, animals.

What if we're not on the earth?

The idea is ridiculous. Is he suggesting that a spaceship came along and beamed them up to this place, then started broadcasting Swedish pop music to keep them calm? It sounds like a bad film. Or a good film. But not like something that happens in real life.

He hears the sound of 'Lay All Your Love on Me' coming from the vicinity of one of the other caravans. Stefan has never been a fan of Abba; he has never really listened to their songs, but now he realises that the chorus almost sounds like church music, something sacred. A psalm or a prayer.

'Daddy,' Emil says. 'There aren't any birds here.'

'No, it seems that way.'

'That's stupid. That means we can't walk the line. And there aren't any trees either. So what is there?'

'There are people. And the caravans. And the cars.'

'But there must be more than that, mustn't there?'

'I guess so.'

Like many of the best games, Walk the Line came about by chance. Stefan had been measuring the distance between outbuildings in order to submit a planning application, and had run a length of twine through a small copse of trees.

Emil had been following this line in his gumboots when he spotted a bullfinch. After a couple more steps he saw a wagtail. When he reached Stefan they heard a knocking sound and looked up to see a woodpecker in the tree to which Stefan had secured the twine.

They decided to leave the line in place because it was obviously particularly easy to spot birds along its length. Every afternoon Emil solemnly walked along it with one foot on either side, gazing up at the trees. One day when Stefan and Carina were with him, Stefan had started to sing 'I Walk the Line', and that was how the game got its name.

'Stefan,' Carina says, getting up and looking out at the field. 'We have to find out what's out there.'

'Yes, but…we don't have GPS. I'm afraid of getting lost, if there are no landmarks. But you're right, of course. We can't just sit here.'

Carina pinches her nose and thinks for a moment. 'Couldn't we… or…'

'Hang on,' Stefan says. 'I know what to do.'

Emil tugs at his hand. 'What, Daddy?'

Stefan looks at him with a smile, and says: 'Walk the line.'

*

Majvor has been banished to the caravan so that Donald can have a private conversation with Peter. It is slightly humiliating, but she chooses her battles. For the most part she complies with Donald's wishes, but when she does object, he usually listens. This truce has not been achieved without cost, and harks back to an incident in the fourth year of their marriage.

At the time their one-year-old son Albert was still sleeping in a cot in Donald and Majvor's bedroom, while his brother Gustav, who was two years older, had his own room. Albert woke up crying several times each night, and Donald decided that he should go in with his brother so that he could get used to not being picked up and consoled all the time.

By the second night, Majvor had had enough. Albert screamed and screamed, and refused to go back to sleep. Gustav started yelling too, although he was slightly more articulate in his protests. Majvor got out of bed to go and fetch Albert, but Donald held her back, said that the boy had to get used to it, however long it took. Majvor lay awake for two hours listening to the child screaming, until he eventually subsided into exhausted sobbing, then silence. Her heart was in shreds by then, and she couldn't get to sleep.

The same thing happened on the third night, but with one difference. When she tried to get up and Donald held her back, she said:

'Let go of me, Donald. I mean it. Let go of me.' Donald gripped her arm even more tightly. Albert's despairing cries stabbed and tore at her breast. She said it again. 'Donald, let go of me. I'm falling apart. I mean it.'

But Donald didn't let go; instead he made a point of lying awake and watching her so that she couldn't creep off and console Albert, whose despair turned to pure fear. Every fibre of Majvor's body told her to go and get him, to take him in her arms, but Donald stopped her with sheer force.

The following day when Majvor was making chilli con carne for Donald's dinner, she finished it off with a spoonful of rat poison. She sat opposite her husband as he ate, grimacing at the strong chilli flavour; she had made the dish extra spicy to hide the taste of the poison.

Donald didn't even finish his meal before he was overcome by convulsions. He staggered into the bathroom and threw up, over and over again. When Majvor went in a few minutes later, he was lying on the floor, shaking. His lips were blue, his face bright red. Majvor held out a jug of cream.

'Drink this. You've eaten rat poison.'

Donald stared at her, unable to speak, but he managed to pour most of the cream down his throat, apart from a small amount that trickled down his chest and stomach. A little while later he threw up again. Majvor left him in peace.

When he emerged from the bathroom an hour or so later after a cavalcade of vomiting and diarrhoea, he held up a shaky hand and announced that he was going to report Majvor to the police for attempted murder.

'Fine,' she said. 'As you wish. Our marriage will be over, of course. Or you could try listening to me when I really mean what I say. If you do that, then this kind of thing won't happen again.'

Donald chose the latter option, and Majvor never again felt the need to resort to such extreme measures. Albert was allowed to sleep in their bedroom for another year, and when he moved into the other room, Donald didn't say a word if Majvor got up to comfort him.

Since then there had been only a few occasions when Majvor had got her own way by saying a very clear yes or no. Donald knew where the line was, and in return Majvor made sure that she didn't weaken her veto by overusing it. Peace reigned.

*

Without asking, Donald places two cans of beer on the table and waits until Peter has opened his and taken a swig. Then he says: 'If anything is going to get done around here, then you and I are going to have to do it. Would I be right in saying that you realise that too?'

The look Peter gives Donald suggests that he isn't quite so sure, so Donald feels the need to expand on his original statement.

'You're a *doer*, just like me. You don't sit around twiddling your thumbs and waiting for someone else to solve the problem.'

Peter shrugs, and Donald has to be satisfied with that for the moment. He leans forward and lowers his voice to indicate that this is just between the two of them. 'You can tell me what you saw out there, for a start. So we know what we're dealing with.'

Peter takes a deep breath, then he puts down the can of beer, straightens up and says: 'I saw my father.'

'Your father?'

'Yes. First of all I saw…something else. Something that was just my imagination. Then I saw my father. In the distance.'

'Okay. But what would he be doing here?'

'I've no idea. I didn't ask.'

Peter's voice and posture have regained most of their former confidence, but Donald can't make any sense of what he is saying. One thing in particular is bothering him.

'Pardon me for asking what might seem like an odd question, but…is your father still *alive*?'

'No,' Peter says. 'No, he isn't. Fortunately.'

Donald has a battery of follow-up questions, but is forced to put them on hold when he sees Stefan approaching.

'Here comes the shopkeeper. We'll talk more later.'

*

When Stefan reaches the entrance to the awning, he sees Peter and Donald sitting opposite one another at the teak table, each with a can of beer in front of them. Something about their posture makes Stefan hesitate for a second. They both have one arm resting on the table, the other on their thigh, as they turn to look at him.

This is men's talk.

Stefan cannot sit like that without looking ridiculous, and in spite of the fact that he is in charge of a fairly large store, he is always embarrassed when he has to drop off the car at the workshop and talk to the mechanics. There is a way of moving, a way of speaking that has never been accessible to him. That male thing.

'Hi,' Peter says, nodding towards an empty chair. 'How's it going?'

Stefan sits down. Peter seems to have recovered following his return, and that sense of disorientation is no longer in evidence. Perhaps Donald is a good psychologist, in spite of his bumptiousness.

'Well...' Stefan says.

Donald leans over to the refrigerator. 'Drink?'

The beer Stefan drank earlier is still swishing around inside his head like the prelude to intoxication, so he waves the offer away. Donald gets out a fresh can for himself, flips it open and says: 'So?'

'Well,' Stefan says again, trying to find a sensible sitting position that doesn't look as if he is trying to copy Peter and Donald, 'I suppose we ought to try and find out what's out there. More systematically, I mean.'

Donald gulps his beer and belches. He almost seems to be imitating Stefan as he repeats: 'Systematically.'

'Yes—I don't know about you, but I want to get away from here as soon as possible. I don't want to be here. And our only chance is if we find something beyond this.'

Peter seems interested. 'What do you mean by systematically?'

'We search the area bit by bit. We set out markers, or something. Then we drive off in four directions, setting out these markers at regular intervals. Then we'll know we've covered that particular direction. That will also work for those of us who don't have GPS, so we can find our way back.'

Donald and Peter look at one another. Donald pushes out his lower lip, nods and says: 'You know what? Stefan, wasn't that your name? That's not a bad idea. Are you sure you won't have a beer?'

*

Four cars. Four directions. Five people. Donald, Peter, Stefan. And Lennart and Olof, who have decided to go together. All the men.

Majvor has handed over her stock of garden canes, the supporting posts from the awning have been taken apart, and Carina has dug out the croquet set and straightened out the hoops. Isabelle is not participating as she is suffering from a headache.

Something must be done. Something must be found. The fear has started to grow.

They had thought the sun would reappear, that it was lurking below the horizon, but the minutes and the hours pass, and there is no sun. It is an absence so great it is impossible to comprehend. The things we take for granted are the things we miss the most when they disappear.

Hence the fear. Because the sun, like the moon, provides us with company. In our deepest loneliness, night or day, we can always turn to them. We have given them faces, ascribed them qualities, called them gods. This is unnecessary. Their silent, impersonal presence is enough. They shine with a power beyond us, confirming that something else exists. That we are not alone.

So however much the people on the campsite are hoping that those who set off will find a store, a village, a means of communication, they also have high hopes of the sun. That it is still there, in spite of everything. Beyond the horizon.

*

Benny looks over at the caravan where Cat is still lying in the window. He takes a couple of steps towards Cat, but stops, remembering the grip on the scruff of his neck, the flight through the air, the painful landing. He glances back at the awning; his master is sitting down, but that could change.

That feeling comes over Benny. The feeling that he has to catch something, chase something. There is nothing to chase, but that doesn't necessarily stop him trying. He sets off with a sudden jerk, speeding away from the camp in a straight line.

Running is good. The fear is washed away by the air flowing over his fur. Yes and No and Right and Wrong disappear in the drumming of his paws on the grass, the movement of his muscles.

There is nothing to obscure his view, no obstacles on the ground, so Benny can go at top speed. In less than a minute he has left the camp far behind him. He slows down a fraction, then he trots for a little while before sitting down with his tongue hanging out to help him cool down.

He sniffs the air. Now the smells of the camp are weaker, can he pick up anything else? Yes, he can. Fire. Benny spins around but can't locate the source of the smell. It is coming from several directions.

There is, however, something else that interests him. He puts his nose to the ground and sniffs, scampers a few metres. He recognises the smell, but can't understand how it has ended up here.

It smells of Grandchildren.

Sometimes different Hes come to visit his master and mistress. Two of them bring Grandchildren. There are big Grandchildren and there are small Grandchildren. The smell in the grass is the same as the small ones, the ones that aren't even as big as Benny. They lie on their backs waving their arms and legs in the air, making noises.

What are Grandchildren doing here?

Benny carries on sniffing, but cannot pick up the scent of a Him or Her. It is as if the Grandchildren are out and about on their own, even though they can't walk. It doesn't make any sense at all.

Benny is overcome by fear once more. He gives himself a shake and races back towards the camp, to his basket.

*

Peter is on his way out of the door when he hears Isabelle swearing behind him. She has opened the refrigerator and stuck her hand inside. She slams the door and demonstratively turns the knob on the stove.

'The fucking things are broken. Both the refrigerator and the stove. That's just fucking *perfect*.'

Peter leans over the sink and tries the controls on the stove. Nothing happens. He checks the connections, which look fine.

'There's something wrong with the bloody thing,' Isabelle goes on. 'This whole fucking caravan is one big...'

'I'll sort it out later,' Peter says. 'I have to go.'

'Oh yes? And what if you don't come back? Do you expect me and your daughter to sit here and rot with no stove, no refrigerator, no power? Do you?'

Molly is sitting at the table, drawing. She appears to be ignoring Isabelle's gloomy predictions, and calmly chooses a new felt-tip. Peter walks over to her.

'I'm off, sweetheart. Is that okay?'

'That's fine, Daddy. Look.'

Molly holds out her picture. It shows four caravans and four cars on the same level, with no perspective. Standing in a row in front of the caravans are eight adults and a child, a little girl. They are all smiling. Slightly to one side are figures that are presumably meant to be a dog and cat. They too are smiling broadly.

Peter points to the drawing. 'What about your friend? The little boy? Shouldn't he be there?'

Molly shakes her head. 'We don't need him.' She starts to draw a cheerful yellow sun in the sky, and Peter refrains from further comment. There is something about the picture that makes him feel uncomfortable, but he doesn't know what it is.

A few weeks earlier Molly had happened to see a news report from Iraq. A car bomb. Peter didn't manage to switch off the TV before the image changed to people weeping and screaming as injured friends and relatives were carried away on stretchers. The following day Molly had done a drawing. A jolly-looking man driving a burning car, surrounded by equally jolly men and women being blown to pieces. And up in the sky, that same beaming sun.

'Bye, Daddy,' Molly says as she begins to fill in the sun with a thick yellow felt-tip.

Peter turns away and is met by a searching look from Isabelle. He moves quickly towards the door, but she steps sideways and positions herself in front of him.

'Why are you so bloody keen to get away?'

'The others are about to leave.'

'You still haven't told me what happened.'

'Happened? Nothing happened.'

'You're lying. And I'm wondering why.'

Peter's cheeks flush red. He is neither willing nor able to explain to Isabelle. He just wants to get away, but she is blocking his escape, and the idea of moving her by force is unthinkable.

He is saved by Molly, who looks up and wags her finger at him. 'Lying is naughty, Daddy. Very naughty indeed.'

The tension is broken and Peter seizes the opportunity. 'See you later.' He slinks past Isabelle without meeting her eye.

*

GRAND CHEROKEE OVERLAND, 2012 MODEL. Donald can't imagine driving anything other than an American car. They produce decent vehicles with no frills. Admittedly this particular model has far too much unnecessary frippery on the instrument panel—Bluetooth and hands-free and MP3 and God knows what else—but the wheel is sturdy and the pedals a good size. You can tell you're driving a car. Four-wheel drive and the six-cylinder engine mean you can get just about anywhere. Donald likes to know that he can tackle rough terrain off-road, even if he never actually does. It's just the feeling that the car is built for it.

His gun is lying on the back seat, and the only thing missing is his hat. Donald revs the engine and grinds his teeth. Sitting here in his car, his chest expanding in time with the roar of the cylinders, he can't understand why he gave in to Majvor. He loved his stetson, his cowboy hat, but he had hung it up on the wall after Majvor said it made him look ridiculous.

That hat would have been perfect right now. Donald stares out across the endless field. He is going to explore the unknown, venture out into the unmarked areas on the map. *How the west was won.* He takes his foot off the gas a fraction, puts the car in gear and skids away.

VOLVO 740, 1990 MODEL. The good thing about a Volvo is that you can always get hold of spare parts. Olof has driven over four hundred thousand kilometres in his good and faithful servant, and has replaced this and that along the way. The external details, so to speak. There has never been a problem with the engine itself. The doors are warped, the seats lumpy, the gears are stiff and the boot is fastened with a hasp that Olof fitted himself, but she still goes.

Lennart is in the passenger seat, and as usual he has brought along a crossword. As a rule they take it in turns to drive on long journeys, and share the crosswords, but it seems unlikely that will be necessary on this occasion.

Olof puts the car in first gear and slowly releases the clutch. Lennart starts humming 'Seven Little Girls, Sitting in the Back Seat'.

TOYOTA RAV4, 2010 MODEL. Peter isn't particularly fond of SUVs, but Isabelle had pushed for this one 'for Molly's sake'. Safety and so on. Peter knows that Molly had nothing to do with it.

Isabelle isn't the kind of person who collects things, but the objects with which she surrounds herself have to be *right*. Evidently an SUV was right. Peter refused to buy any of the juggernauts Isabelle found on the internet, and they ended up with a compromise that pleases neither of them. Peter thinks the car is too big, Isabelle thinks it too small.

He sweeps the trash off the back seat so that he can put the garden canes there; he has brought them just to be on the safe side. Sweet wrappers, dried up bits of chocolate, a few films for Molly's portable DVD player. *The Little Mermaid, Princesses, Cinderella, Martyrs.* Peter picks up the last one and reads the back of the case.

Sexual violence…torture…intensely dark…a harder version of Hostel.

One of Isabelle's films. Maybe not such a good idea, leaving it among Molly's. He tosses the horror film into the glove compartment and switches on the GPS, which once again assures him that he is in the same place as yesterday evening. He sets off.

VOLVO V70, 2008 MODEL. Stefan is careful with his car. Not that he has any real interest in cars, nor does he believe that it is a part of his identity, but he does think it is important to be careful with expensive things. He cleans it once a month and has it serviced on a regular basis. Over the years he has had to change only the brake shoes.

Stefan places the thirty canes with scraps of torn sheet tied to them in the back seat. He has never bothered getting GPS, because he usually travels only short distances. He looks up at the field, and once again he feels dizzy. When he glances in the rear-view mirror, he sees Emil running towards him. Two of the other cars have already started to move, and Peter is just getting into his.

'Daddy, can I come?'

'I'm not sure…'

Stefan doesn't want to say that it might be dangerous, that they don't know what's out there, because Emil is an anxious child, prone to imagining terrifying scenarios. But with a resolve that is unusual for him, Emil marches around to the passenger door, and Stefan doesn't know what to do. Fortunately Carina appears.

'Let him go with you,' she says. 'He seems on edge for some reason. He says he *has* to come.'

Emil gets his cushion out of the back and places it on the passenger seat, then sits down and carefully fastens his seatbelt. It seems the decision has been made.

Carina bends down and kisses Stefan, whispers: 'Drive carefully.'

Stefan smiles and tilts his head in the direction of the field, as if to say: *Not much chance of hitting anything, is there?* He whispers back, 'I love you', then he starts the engine.

*

Carina is left alone, watching the cars drive off. As they grow smaller and smaller and the sound of the engines disappears, the usual horror starts crawling up her chest. *I'll never see you again.*

Perhaps it is because her mother died so suddenly and unexpectedly when Carina was only fourteen, but she finds parting difficult. When someone goes out of her sight, there is always a little voice murmuring inside her head: *That was the last time. You'll never see them again.*

As a teenager she numbed the constant feeling of loss with alcohol and drugs, a lifestyle that soon got out of hand, and could have killed her. When she went back to Stefan as a last resort, the need to drink had subsided, but the feeling itself never stopped gnawing at her. A sense of loss can hurl itself at you and sink its teeth in the back of your neck at any moment.

The cars turn into insects, then dots, until they are swallowed up by the endless field. She thinks about Stefan's last words to her: *I love you.* He has said it so many times before, but this was different. The tone of voice, the expression, what it meant in this particular context.

I. Love. You. It is easy to say those words—anyone can say them.

They are no more than a series of letters. A child to his teddy bear, a gangster to his pit bull; an actor can say them without wanting any more than to sound sincere.

So when Stefan says those words to her, does he mean the same thing she does when she says them to him? That he wants to share his life with her, that he thinks she is a wonderful person, that he just wants to get closer and closer? Is that what *she* means?

Carina looks towards the horizon, towards the point where she watched their car disappear, and whispers: 'I love you. I love you both.'

Her voice echoes in the emptiness. Something shifts in her mind, and for a moment she feels as if she no longer exists. As if she has been obliterated, along with the sound of her voice.

*

This time when Peter's GPS screen turns blue, he doesn't slow down, but simply presses the button and winds down the window, enjoying the smell of sweat mingled with perfume as he drives on.

If he stopped the car and got out, the women would be standing there waiting, ready to get going, to dance with him. But he resists the temptation.

The engine purrs, and after a slightly late night and a much too early morning, he allows himself to doze for a moment. After all, there is nothing in sight that he could possibly crash into. He drifts off into a waking dream, imagining himself among all those bodies moving in front of him and around him.

Like mermaids they undulate about him in the vast blue expanse, limbs floating…

Blue. Blue.

Peter gasps and opens his eyes, slams his foot on the brake. He doesn't know how long he has been gone. One minute? Two? Five? He shakes his head, looks in the rear-view mirror. Nothing.

How stupid is he? The map might have been incorrect, but at

least it enabled him to find his way back. The dot on the blue screen tells him nothing. He has no idea whether he might have turned the wheel while his eyes were closed, whether the car has deviated from the straight line.

The wonderful smells have disappeared, and it seems as if the air has grown cooler. Peter's throat tightens. There is no sun to help him work out which is backwards, forwards, right or left in relation to his starting point. He could well be lost.

He stares at the GPS screen, his broken contact with the rest of the world.

Hang on a minute.

He leans closer, screwing up his eyes. Something is appearing, so faint that it could be a figment of his imagination, an apparition lingering on his retina, but he thinks he can just make out a map amid the blue. A new map.

*

'Bit monotonous.'

'Yes.'

'Do you want me to drive for a bit?'

'No, you stick with the canes.'

Lennart and Olof have inserted seven garden canes in the ground since the campsite disappeared from view. When Olof pulls up to let Lennart get out with number eight, he hears a faint sound from the engine. A grating sound.

'That's just what we need,' he says. 'To break down out here.'

'Switch off. Let her rest for a while.'

Olof smiles at Lennart's habit of calling any kind of vehicle 'she'. The tractor is a she, the forklift truck is a she; he has even heard Lennart refer to the automatic milking system as female. *She's not programmed correctly.*

Olof kills the engine and jiggles the handle to get the door open. He steps out of the car. In the deep silence he hears a ticking sound from the engine; he places his hand on the bonnet, which is hotter than it should be.

'Does the radiator need topping up?' Lennart wonders as he pushes the cane into the ground on the other side of the car.

'I don't think so. I topped it up the other day.'

Leaning on the bumper for support, Olof kneels down and examines the undercarriage of the car. Nothing dripping. He gets up slowly to avoid a dizzy spell, and discovers that Lennart is now staring out across the field, arms folded.

'Can you see anything?' Olof asks.

'No. I'm just thinking. Fantastic arable land.'

'Or grazing land.'

Lennart crouches down and pulls up a few blades of grass, rubbing them between his fingers and sniffing. 'Seems a bit poor,' he says, holding out his hand to Olof. 'What do you think?'

Olof bends down and sniffs, then feels silly. He pulls up a few blades for himself and does the same thing. He has to agree with Lennart. There is something weak and diluted about the almost imperceptible smell of the grass, and the blades feel brittle between his fingers. As if the grass lacks both water and nutrients.

He carries on rubbing the blades between his fingers as he looks up at the sky. 'Do you think it rains here?'

'I suppose it must do. Otherwise how could the grass grow?'

'If it is growing.'

'You've got a point there,' Lennart says, gazing around at the grass, which is exactly the same length wherever you look. 'But it's definitely alive.'

Olof sniffs the blades in his hand once more, and says: 'I'm not so sure about that.'

*

Majvor's job is to monitor the radio. Keep it switched on and listen out for anything other than golden oldies. Make a note of what comes

72

on so that they can find out if the songs are on a loop, or if they keep playing new ones.

So far they have been new ones, although that's not strictly true. The songs are old. Wonderful old songs. Majvor has been a devoted listener to the Swedish pop chart for over forty years, and is ideally suited to this task. She doesn't need a presenter to tell her the name of the artist or the title of the song so that she can add them to her list.

Right now, for example, she needs to hear only the introductory bass notes before writing down: *Claes-Göran Hederström, 'It's Beginning to Seem Like Love'*. Not one of her favourites, but she still knows her Claes-Göran. Yes indeed.

She keeps time with her foot as she pours herself a drop of coffee from the thermos. She raises her cup in a toast to the empty chair on the other side of the table where James Stewart is sitting.

'So, Jimmy,' she says. 'How do you think this is all going to work out?'

James Stewart doesn't answer. He merely smiles his melancholy smile and looks at her with his soft, kind eyes. It is only in exceptional circumstances that Majvor imagines a conversation; his silent presence is usually enough.

Perhaps it is because this is such a crazy day that she has chosen to let Jimmy appear as Elwood P. Dowd, the man whose companion is an invisible six-foot-tall rabbit in the film *Harvey*. Jimmy's trademark expression of slightly confused niceness was never more appropriate, and Majvor knows the dialogue virtually off by heart.

They listen to Claes-Göran together, and Jimmy smiles at the words 'bang bang'. Perhaps he is thinking of one of his many cowboy films. No one can handle a revolver with such effortless elegance as Jimmy; the gun is simultaneously a necessary evil and an extension of his hand. Not like Donald and his shotguns.

James Stewart looks away, pretending to study Majvor's wall-hanging as her thoughts turn to Donald. She hopes he's okay. She always does. She knows his terrible story, and she has made it her life's work to look after him, make sure his life works.

What she can't say for sure is whether she has ever loved him. Probably not. She has nothing to compare her feelings to, but from books, films and what other people have said she has come to realise that there is a kind of love she has never experienced, and never will.

There is nothing she can do about it now. When she occasionally feels down about all those years wasted taking care of someone else, James Stewart is always there by her side. He is her secret, her Harvey.

*

Donald has been driving for fifteen minutes, sticking to around eighty kilometres an hour all the time, so he should have travelled about twenty kilometres. Still nothing. Still only the field and the field and the fucking field he can see through the windscreen.

This is a mistake. He doesn't quite know what he had been expecting, but possibly that he would drive up a hill, reach the top and be able to see all around. But it's just the same unbroken horizon out there in front of him, offering nothing beyond itself.

When the GPS screen turned blue, Donald didn't slow down at all, didn't even consider stopping to push sticks into the ground like those other fools. Okay, he can't carry on like this forever, sooner or later the deviation will be too great, but surely he can drive in a straight line for a few kilometres.

Strange images came into his mind as he drove into the blue. He thought he was driving through Las Vegas, where both John F Kennedy and Elvis were due to appear, and were just waiting for Donald so that they could get started.

With a wry smile Donald thought that dementia has its advantages after all. Fantasies become so real that you feel you could step right into them. On the other hand there are names for people who do that kind of thing: nutcases, fruit loops, loonies. So Donald had ignored the temptations of Vegas and put his foot down.

And there you go: after a little while his resolve begins to bear fruit. On the blank screen the map starts to appear once more. Donald nods with satisfaction, following a road that he will be able to follow again on the way back. The map becomes clearer and clearer, but he finds it difficult to see things close up, and he can only just make out the letters.

What the fuck?

He slows down and digs his reading glasses out of the glove compartment. When he sees what the GPS screen is telling him, he takes his foot off the accelerator and stops the car, sits there with the engine ticking over.

Åkerö, Gillberga, Lilltorp.

When he drove away, the GPS had claimed that they were in the same place as on the previous evening: the campsite ten kilometres south of Trosa. Then the arrow kept on moving west until the screen turned blue. Now it is saying that he is in the area where he grew up, *one hundred and fifty kilometres to the north.* It is physically impossible for him to have driven that distance. He puts the car into first gear and edges forward. He should now be crossing Norrtäljevägen and driving through the forest towards Åkerö and...Riddersholm.

A chill runs down Donald's spine. He pushes his glasses up onto the top of his head and gazes out across the field—towards Riddersholm, according to the GPS. There is nothing to see, but it feels as if the air has grown thinner, and it is difficult to get enough oxygen. Donald takes a few deep breaths to ease the pressure inside his skull. He studies the screen again. There is something wrong with Norrtäljevägen.

When the E18 was extended at the beginning of the 1970s, the route between Norrtälje and Kapellskär became five kilometres shorter, as a straighter motorway sliced through the landscape. But the road on the GPS map winds its way through the villages, and judging by the width, it isn't even a motorway.

Donald scrolls up and down, zooms out. There is no doubt whatsoever. The route on the screen is the *old* road, large sections of which have been forgotten and overgrown for almost forty years.

Donald rubs his eyes and breathes, breathes.

What the hell is wrong with the air?

Then he opens the car door and gets out.

It is colder now, and he gets gooseflesh on his arms when he leaves the interior of the car with its controlled temperature. There really *is* something strange about the air. Donald opens his eyes wide, relaxes, opens wide again, relaxes, but the phenomenon remains.

It's just like when you stand up too quickly after bending down, and tiny pinpricks of light seem to be floating in front of your eyes. Kind of like that, but the dots of light are smaller and there are more of them. The air is *shimmering*, as if it has a light of its own.

Donald rubs his arms as his eyes sweep the horizon. The movement of his pupils stops. He screws up his eyes. A shudder like a bolt of low-voltage electricity passes over his skin, and it is not the cooler air that is making the hairs on the back of his neck stand on end. He thinks he can see something. A figure.

He squints, trying to focus, but what he is seeing still doesn't make sense. Suddenly he knows what to do. The shudder runs down his back as he opens the car door and takes out his shotgun. He places the butt against his shoulder, looks through the sight and slowly traces his way along the line between earth and sky until he finds the figure.

Judging by its shape it must be human, but when Donald gets a closer look he almost fires, his index finger, resting on the trigger out of sheer habit, twitching in an involuntary spasm. The gun slips out of his hands and falls to the ground as Donald stands there with his lower lip trembling. It is one specific detail, a mutilation, that makes his stomach turn. He almost collapses, and leans on the car for support.

The car.

He has the car.

Donald lets out a sob, grabs the gun and throws it on the back seat. He catches his shin as he scrambles into the driver's seat and slams the door. His teeth are chattering as he turns the key, and for one dreadful moment he thinks the car isn't going to start, that he will be stranded here with

76

but the car starts with a roar because he has floored the accelerator. He tells himself to ease off and manages to put the car in first without wrecking the gearbox.

A second later he floors the pedal again and spins the wheel all the way round. He daren't even use the clutch to engage a higher gear. He just has to get away from here as quickly as possible. Away from the Bloodman.

*

Benny has been lying in wait for a long time. The door of Cat's caravan is open, and Cat's masters have gone. Benny's master has gone too. It is an interesting state of affairs. Cat is no longer visible in the window. Benny is waiting.

Behind him his mistress is singing, the same thing that is coming out of the box on the table. It doesn't sound good, and Benny turns his head towards the field to spare his ears.

He remembers the smell of Grandchildren and the strange feeling. The field is not good. In here among the caravans it is fine. This is his place. That is what he intends to make clear to Cat, if he gets the chance.

And what do you know—here comes Cat!

Cat is weird. Cat *runs* out of the door and starts washing herself without glancing in Benny's direction. Dog would have behaved in a completely different way. Been more alert. Benny fires off a short bark. Cat raises her head and gives him a look, then goes back to washing herself, as if Benny were of no interest whatsoever.

Benny takes a few steps towards Cat as a growl forms deep in his throat. Cat freezes. Benny moves closer and the growl feels good, makes him stronger. He will show Cat who is boss.

Cat turns to face him and grows. Benny stops. Cat is now almost as big as he is. He has seen the phenomenon before, but it doesn't make it any less alarming. How does Cat do that? But it is too late now.

Benny moves forward, the growl interspersed with little barks. He is angry.

At this point Cat does something unexpected, something Benny has not experienced before. She starts to come towards him, making her noise and showing her teeth. Benny isn't sure what to do. He stops. The growl fades away. Cat is not doing what she is supposed to do.

Before Benny has time to work out what is going on, Cat is standing in front of him. She hits him across the nose with her claws out. Cat has sharp claws, and it really hurts.

The capacity for thought leaves him completely and his body takes over. Benny lets out a howl, turns around and runs as fast as he can, back to the awning and into his basket.

When he raises his head he sees Cat stalking around the open space without giving him so much as a look. Benny buries his sore nose in his blanket and closes his eyes.

*

Stefan and Carina have lots of photograph albums. In this digital age they still take the trouble to order prints of their pictures, then they sit side by side at the kitchen table, cropping them manually with a craft knife and sticking them in. They find great satisfaction in the activity itself, reliving their memories, then sorting and cataloguing them. Creating an archive of their lives, concrete objects they can hold in their hands. Images stored on a computer can never be the same; there is no weight in a pdf file.

They have also produced a condensed version. They selected the best pictures over all the years, ordered copies, then stuck these in a special album that they always take with them on their travels. A little security measure, holding on to the very best moments.

Right now Carina is leafing through this best-of album.

Stefan and Carina in front of a waterfall in Norway, the year before Emil was born. Emil as a newborn, as a baby, his very first steps. Stefan in an impressive elf costume, Carina with the giant chanterelle she found behind the shed, the three of them together on that wonderful little beach on the island of Gotland. Stefan teaching Emil to use the binoculars. Stefan and Carina with the new sign for the store.

Carina glances over the pictures, her mind adding details, smells and feelings that cannot be seen in the photographs. Taken all together, these fragments form a composite of the last six years of her life.

A dog barks outside the caravan, and she looks up. The dog barks again, then suddenly whimpers and falls silent. As Carina returns to the album, she is struck by an unpleasant thought.

What if I had never existed?

What if she had actually managed to kill herself in her teenage years, or if she had never been born? Who would have been standing next to Stefan by the waterfall, who would have given birth to Emil and found that chanterelle? Someone else? No one at all?

She tries to place another woman beside Stefan, to give Emil a new mother, the store a new part-owner. It is impossible. The only thing she can do is to erase herself from the photographs and to add in a ghostly figure without a face, a non-Carina.

She carries on looking through the album, and the thought is actually not unpleasant at all, merely unaccustomed. When she was a teenager she often played with the idea: *I don't exist.* The last few years have been so hectic, so filled with practicalities that there has been no space, but it doesn't scare her. In fact it's a kind of consolation. A person who doesn't exist carries no guilt.

Carina closes the album and sneezes. Enough. She decides to make herself a cup of coffee.

She takes out the jar of instant, pours some water into a pan and switches on the gas stove. Or rather she doesn't. She presses the ignition button a couple of times and the little blue spark flashes, but nothing else happens. No sound of hissing gas. She tries the other ring, which is equally silent. She opens the door of the refrigerator, which also runs on gas, and sticks her hand inside. Only the faintest hint of a chill remains, so she quickly closes the door.

Stefan checked the cylinder before they set off, and it was half full. More than enough for a week, which means something else must be wrong. A blockage in the pipe, or God forbid, a leak.

Carina goes around the back of the caravan and sees that the door of the box housing the cylinder is partly open. If there's one thing Stefan is particularly careful about, it is making sure that door is kept shut. Carina opens it and gasps.

The hose that connects the cylinder to the pipe inside the caravan is broken. Only a short section remains attached to the cylinder itself. It doesn't make sense. Only last year they fitted a new hose in order to avoid this very situation, because rubber has a tendency to perish over time.

She checks the raw edge to see if the rubber is dry and crumbly to the touch. No. It is soft and pliable, just as it should be. When she pulls the two ends towards her, she realises that they are too short to meet, and therefore cannot be repaired. A fairly large section is missing, and the problem has not been caused by age or wear and tear. The ends are clean and smooth. As if the hose has been cut.

*

Peter has grabbed several garden canes and got out of the car. Now that he has deciphered the new map on the GPS screen, he feels it is absolutely essential to try to orientate himself, maintain some sense of direction, some kind of foothold.

He looks around. Nothing but grass, in all directions. Nothing to indicate that he is where the GPS claims he is: in Vällingby, to the west of Stockholm. Nothing except the feeling.

To what extent can we make our memories into a reality? If an event has been imprinted on us with the violence of the branding iron, or the joy of sheer bliss, if it is encapsulated within us like a moment that will live forever, does that also mean that we can really go back there, to some degree?

Maybe, maybe not. But we carry every defining moment of our

lives with us like an intangible perception, impossible to describe to anyone else. We think about that moment and there is something special there, a sensory label that applies only to that moment.

However much Peter pats the bonnet of his great big smart grown-up car that he was able to afford by playing grown-up football, the GPS does not lie. On some important level Peter is in Vällingby right now, on the evening when he was seven years old and started to believe in God.

When he was only five years old his mother had already taught him to say evening prayers, and she would sometimes tell him bedtime stories from the Bible. He liked it. She was a good storyteller, and he enjoyed the cosiness of sharing prayers, though he didn't believe in God. He would have liked to, but his father loathed everything to do with religion.

His father was often angry and unpleasant, especially when he was drunk, and sometimes he hit Peter's mother. Peter didn't want to be like him, and thought it would be nice to believe along with his mother, but he didn't have the courage. He could have believed in secret, but then again it did all sound a bit odd: God and Jesus and the mystery of the cross and the loaves and fishes, and it really, *really* is impossible to walk on water.

His father grew worse over the years. No job, friends who let him down, and more and more bottles in the pantry. Peter didn't understand why he and his mother had to stay; his mother said it was hard to explain, but they must trust in God and everything would be all right.

Until one evening when Peter was seven, and his father came home roaring drunk. Peter had gone to bed after half-heartedly saying his evening prayer when he heard the front door open. He could tell from the sound of the movements, the coughing, the way his father was breathing, the way he put down his feet: his father was extremely drunk and very angry. Peter pressed his hands over his ears before it started.

It took a couple of minutes, then came the usual noises. The thuds, the muffled cries, things falling on the floor. Peter shut his eyes tight to prevent any of it getting to him. Behind his eyelids he assembled an arsenal of weapons: machine guns, pistols, grenades and axes. He seized them in his dream hands and used them against his father.

It didn't stop. It usually stopped. It went on for a little while, then he could uncover his ears. If his mother was crying, he would cover them up again until that stopped too.

But not tonight. It just went on and on. And his mother was *screaming*. She didn't normally do that. An atom bomb fell through Peter's head, landed right on top of his father and obliterated him forever. His mother screamed again.

Peter usually just felt sick and embarrassed, but now he was really frightened, and started shaking. *What if he kills her?* His legs trembling, he got up and put on his Mickey Mouse dressing-gown, which was made of thick towelling and provided at least some protection. He opened his bedroom door.

His father was yelling something about 'putting stupid ideas in the fucking kid's head' and 'not even Jesus wants your fucking cunt', but the worst thing was what Peter could hear in the pauses. His mother's breathing. It was a kind of gurgle, as if she had something wet in her throat. His father let out a roar, then there was a clattering from the kitchen, heavy footsteps.

Peter reached the living room door as his father emerged from the kitchen, carrying a hammer. His mother was half-lying on the floor, with blood on her face and one eye swollen shut. She had one hand on her belly; the other was clutching a wooden crucifix.

Peter's father stepped forward, raised the hammer and bellowed: 'See how you like this, you fucking—' Peter opened his mouth to scream as loud as he could, and at the same time his mother looked up and held out the crucifix as a last defence against her husband.

That was when it happened. The scream that had been on its way out of Peter's mouth turned into a gasp as his father was hurled backwards, as if a shock wave of force had surged out of the crucifix and struck him in the chest. He staggered back two steps and dropped the hammer as he fell over the coffee table. He hit the edge of the table, then lay there shaking his head as if to deny what had just happened.

His mother crawled over and picked up the hammer. Peter's lips moved as he soundlessly whispered, 'Kill him. Kill him,' but his mother only managed to push the hammer under the sofa before she collapsed again, pressing the crucifix to her breast. Peter ran over and curled up beside her, putting his arms around her. Perhaps the faint warmth radiating from the crucifix onto his forearm was a figment of his imagination, perhaps not.

His father got to his feet and stood there swaying, looking down at Peter, his mother, the crucifix. Then he turned around and staggered out of the apartment, slamming the door behind him.

That same night Peter and his mother got a cab and went to a women's refuge, and a life in safe accommodation began. That night Peter started to believe in God.

Peter walks behind the car and pushes a garden cane into the ground. A new smell rises to meet him. Blood.

The smell of blood that surrounded his mother that night. The blood that wouldn't stop pouring from her nose, the blood that had dried on her hands, her face, the smell that filled Peter's nostrils as he sat close beside her in the cab.

Mum.

Tears fill his eyes. Angrily he dashes them away and turns to face the field and the car, expanding his chest muscles like a challenge.

Just you try it. Go on, just try.

He started to believe in God when he was seven, stopped when he was eleven. He has no illusions. In a couple of strides he reaches the car door, gets in and starts the engine. He drives until the cane has almost disappeared from view, then he stops, gets out, and pushes another one into the ground.

Then he drives on. Further and further.

Seven more canes, one kilometre further out. Lennart and Olof are leaning against the back of the car, letting the engine rest for a little while.

'I think it's got cooler, don't you?' Olof asks.

'Now you come to mention it, yes I do.'

They are contemplating the row of canes stretching back towards the campsite. They can see four. Lennart closes one eye and notes with satisfaction that they are in a perfectly straight line. Nothing slapdash about their work. He says: 'We create our own space, don't we?'

'I think you're going to have to explain that.'

Lennart nods at the canes. 'It's like putting up a fence. You have an area, and that's all there is to it. Then you put up the fence, and it becomes something else. Something you can call your own.'

'I suppose so, although the question is whether you are fencing something in, or keeping something out. And there are many different kinds of fence.'

'This one isn't much of a fence at all.'

'No.'

They stand there side by side, each lost in his own thoughts. Olof turns his face up to the empty blue sky, while Lennart gazes across the unchanging expanse of grass. Then Olof says: 'That time when Ingela shot through. I looked after the animals and so on, but I don't think I ate anything for three days.'

'I was the same when Agnetha disappeared,' Lennart said. 'I didn't bother eating. I just didn't feel like it.'

'I drank beer. You can get by on that.'

'Not in the long term.'

'No.'

'And it's a bad habit to get into.'

'Yes, but what can you do? I felt kind of disorientated, as if nothing was where it was supposed to be any more.'

'Everything seemed unfamiliar,' Lennart says.

'Exactly. Unfamiliar. I stroked the cat, and it wasn't the same cat, somehow.'

'Things were…mute. Dead.'

'Yes. Everything had moved away from me.'

They fall silent. Stare at the field. Olof blinks a few times, peers at the canes. Then he says: 'This is a strange conversation.'

'Is it?'

'No, not really. But it's unusual.'

'I thought it was good.'

'Me too.'

Lennart peers at the grass around his feet for a while. He crouches down and runs his hand over the surface, then digs with his fingers, moving them around until he has a handful of earth. He rubs it between his palms, then slowly shakes his head.

'Not much good?' Olof wonders.

'No. Although it is slightly damp in spite of everything.' Lennart cups his hands and pushes his nose between his thumbs, takes a deep breath. He frowns, draws back, then pushes his nose in once more. He seems confused. He holds out his hands to Olof. 'Smell this.'

Olof does as he asks, and he too is puzzled, has to check again. He can't be sure, but the earth seems to smell of something different.

'You used to slaughter calves,' Lennart says. 'So I thought you might be in a better position.'

Olof nods. 'I think you're right.'

'Blood?'

'Blood.'

Lennart lets the earth fall between his fingers, brushing his hands together to get rid of a few stubborn crumbs. 'Well, at least that solves the question of nutrients.'

*

Molly carries on drawing, while Isabelle sits opposite her leafing through an old copy of a TV magazine. There is a double-page spread of paparazzi shots of female celebs' bottoms in varying degrees of enlargement, showing their cellulite and lumps and bumps without the benefit of airbrushing. Admittedly Isabelle's skin has lost some of its elasticity over the years, but she has a long way to go before she is sporting a baboon's arse like the ones glowing out at her from the magazine.

But then again…Who's boarding a luxury yacht or sunning themselves on a Florida beach, and who's sitting in a run-down caravan without even so much as a plain fucking biscuit to eat? How did it come to this?

The answer is simple. It is sitting opposite Isabelle, wagging its curly blond head from side to side as it determinedly drags a black felt-tip across a piece of paper.

Suddenly Molly looks up. 'Mummy, is it possible to live without skin?'

'Sorry?'

'If you take away a person's skin, would they still be able to live?'

'Why are you asking me that?'

'I was just wondering. If you used like a potato peeler…'

'Stop it.'

Molly shrugs and returns to her drawing.

Sometimes it seems to Isabelle that her daughter is a complete stranger, while at other times they have a mutual understanding so powerful that it is almost like telepathy, which can be frightening. At some point while she was looking at the paparazzi shots an image from *Martyrs* had flickered through Isabelle's mind. The final scene. The flayed skin. Could it be a coincidence that Molly asked such a strange question just seconds later?

Occasionally Isabelle thinks it could have something to do with what happened in the Brunkeberg tunnel. But Molly was only two years old, and doesn't remember anything. Or so she says.

At the time the family was living on the fourth floor of an apartment block on Birger Jarlsgatan in Stockholm. Peter had been away for three days at a training camp, and was due to be away for three more. Isabelle spent her time meeting friends for coffee at Saturnus, lunching at Sturehof, and sucking up praise for her adorable daughter wherever she went.

She was perfectly capable of making Molly look pretty for outings in the three-wheel buggy, playing the role of the smart, proud, inner-city mummy, as long as she had a clear picture of what was expected of her. She did the same as everyone else, with her own added flair.

In the evenings, back in the apartment, the panic took over. Xanor helped, but only temporarily. Molly had a tendency to temper tantrums, kicking and lashing out at everything in sight, screaming for no reason, and Isabelle struggled to push away the images of herself hurling her daughter against the wall or stuffing her into the washing machine.

She was stuck in someone else's life, a life she was incapable of living, and everything around her was either false or meaningless. She hated the existence into which she had gradually slipped, bit by bit, and she hated herself because she had been so weak, believing that a child could alleviate her loneliness.

Because she had always been lonely. At fabulous parties where the champagne flowed and she was the centre of attention for every man in the room; in converted loft apartments and king-sized beds as she screwed her way around, searching for someone or something to free her from the feeling that her skin was a barrier against all living things.

A child had seemed like the obvious answer, and that was how she had felt during her pregnancy. But as soon as Molly was born, the separation had begun, and her daughter was just another person. On top of that, she constantly demanded Isabelle's attention without giving very much in return. A mistake.

Worst of all were the times when Molly was asleep and Isabelle simply wandered around the apartment. She could stand in the middle of the living room floor for half an hour staring at the print of *Guernica* while fear tore her guts to shreds.

At half past nine on one such evening, Molly woke up and was inconsolable. By that stage Isabelle felt so bad that the child's screams were a relief, a concrete manifestation of her own internal bellow of pain. She picked Molly up and carried her around, humming a lullaby between gritted teeth. Nothing helped.

As they passed the stove for the fifth time, and the pile of newspapers waiting to be recycled, Isabelle wondered whether to light all four rings, throw the newspapers on top, then hurl herself out of the window with Molly in her arms, just like Jonatan in *The Brothers Lionheart*. A beautiful death. The idea was so appealing that she had to bang her head against the refrigerator door a couple of times to get rid of it.

Only one thing helped in a situation like this. Isabelle dressed her screaming, struggling daughter, grabbed the buggy and took the lift down to the street as Molly's despairing cries echoed through the stairwell.

'Shut the fuck up,' Isabelle hissed. 'Can't you just shut your fucking mouth?'

Outside, Isabelle shoved Molly into the buggy and set off along Birger Jarlsgatan. It was early September, and darkness had fallen. The lights of Stureplan up ahead were tempting, but Isabelle would rather be French-kissed by a pig than turn up with her daughter in her present state.

She passed the Zita cinema, where people turned to stare at the screaming bundle. Isabelle bent her head and increased her speed. People, people everywhere, with their accusing, disparaging looks. In order to escape from them she turned into Tunnelgatan and carried on towards the Brunkeberg tunnel, which seemed to be deserted for once.

At first she felt a sense of liberation as she set off alone through the well-lit tunnel. The movement of her feet, the tapering perspective, the straight route ahead of her. But Molly was throwing herself back and forth in the buggy, her amplified screams bouncing off the walls, and soon it was worse than ever.

The tunnel closed in around Isabelle, and she was walking through a deafening nightmare. Everything went black before her eyes; something collapsed inside her chest. In a few seconds the madness would take her. She stopped in the middle of the tunnel and let go of the buggy. Then she turned on her heel and walked away.

She had gone only a short distance when the screaming behind her stopped. She carried on walking, faster now. With every step her body felt lighter, and by the time she left the tunnel she had regained her normal weight and was able to straighten her back. She drifted out onto Birger Jarlsgatan feeling as if she were drunk on laughing gas and turned right, heading for Stureplan.

Tomas, the doorman at Spy Bar, nodded to her and let her in. The two of them went way back. Isabelle floated into the club. Within a couple of minutes she was sitting at the bar with a treble Scotch. She knocked it back and ordered another.

Someone chatted to her and she chatted to this someone. Then she chatted to someone else. She gazed out across the room, looking for the guy who would have the privilege of taking her home with him tonight. There would probably be a better selection later, in the VIP room, but whether she would be allowed in there depended on who was in charge. Tomas would get her in if the worst came to the worst.

A final wave of euphoria swept over her; she wanted to spread her arms wide, to laugh, to dance. However, the way she was currently expected to behave was embedded in her very bones, so she merely glanced idly around, even though happiness was bubbling away inside her. It was a wonderful evening.

Reality began to catch up with her only when she had finished and paid for the second Scotch. It crept up behind her as she leaned on the bar, ran its cold, damp fingers down her spine, whispered in her ear. Almost an hour had passed since she left her daughter alone in the tunnel.

What have I done?

Isabelle got unsteadily to her feet. Dark shapes were circling in the dim light. She could hear terrible laughter, saw white teeth flashing in distorted smiles. The bodies around her exuded suppressed fear, greed, perversion.

She staggered out of the bar and was nearly hit by a cab; the driver sounded his horn angrily as she ran across the road, heading for the tunnel. Her brain trailed behind her, attached by only a thin thread. Molly would still be sitting where she had been left, Isabelle told herself, refusing to acknowledge how much time had passed. She had let go of the buggy's handle, but now she would seize it again and go home, forget that this had happened.

The thin thread almost snapped when she reached the tunnel and found it locked and in darkness. She pulled at the door, called out Molly's name, cupped her hands around her eyes so that she could peer into the impenetrable gloom. The light from the street reached the first ten metres or so, and then there was nothing but a black wall. She banged on the thick glass with her fists, then slid to the ground.

Isabelle? Isabelle? ISABELLE! Think!

They would never turn out the lights and lock up without checking whether there was anyone inside the tunnel. Someone must have spotted Molly, taken her to…the police. Yes, the police. She was with the police.

The police…

What was she going to say? Perhaps what she had done was an actual crime. She could end up in prison. Molly would be taken away from her. That couldn't happen. The story would leak out, spread everywhere. Her social circle's capacity for gossip was inexhaustible. Everyone would find out, and they would all turn their backs on her.

She's the one who left her little girl…as cold as ice…absolutely terrible…always knew there was something wrong…

Isabelle forced herself to stand up and looked at the notice next to the doors. The tunnel was open between seven o'clock in the morning and ten o'clock at night. Therefore it must have been locked just a few minutes after she walked away, and whoever had locked up must have found Molly.

'Someone has taken her.'

She said it out loud, and it sounded good. She said it again.

'Someone has taken her. I only…I saw someone I knew just inside the cinema. I left her by the door for no more than ten seconds. When I came out, she'd gone.'

Isabelle went back out onto Birger Jarlsgatan and paced back and forth for five minutes, polishing her story. When she was happy with the details, she called the emergency number. She was shuttled between different units and stations until she had bitten the nail on her left index finger down so far that bare flesh was exposed, and it was bleeding. She was finding it difficult to breathe, and just wanted to lie down in the street and go to sleep.

It was now almost eleven-thirty, and Molly was not at any police station.

'But she must be *somewhere*!' Isabelle yelled down the phone. She was now speaking to the duty officer at Norrmalm police HQ, and was asked to stay where she was. A patrol car was on its way, and she would be asked to provide a description and a more detailed account of what had happened. Perhaps she could…

Isabelle ended the call. The noose was tightening; she was sinking deeper and deeper. She felt sick and wanted to throw up. To get away from the crowds on Birger Jarlsgatan, she went back to Tunnelgatan and leaned against a railing as she stared at the bloody tunnel.

Molly was standing inside the doors with her hands pressed against the glass, looking out at her.

Isabelle managed to stop herself from retching and ran to the entrance, dropped to her knees and placed her hands against Molly's.

'Molly? Sweetheart? I'm so sorry. They'll be here soon. Very soon. Mummy will be there soon. I'm so sorry. I'll stay here until they come…'

Molly looked her in the eye without moving a muscle. There was nothing in her eyes, no joy, no sadness, no anger. Then she took her hands off the glass, turned around and toddled back into the tunnel.

'Molly! Molly!'

Isabelle banged the palms of her hands against the impenetrable barrier. Molly's pale jacket was swallowed up by the darkness and she was gone again. Isabelle carried on hammering on the glass and calling out her name until two police officers arrived and helped her to her feet.

Ten minutes later the tunnel was open and Molly, who had settled down in her buggy, was brought out into the light.

It was lucky that Isabelle had caught sight of Molly behind the doors, otherwise her story would have been less than credible. How could she have known that her daughter was in the tunnel?

Someone usually checked the tunnel before locking up, and the lights were normally left on. A series of unfortunate incidents involving a temporary employee and a fuse box had coincided with the even more unfortunate fact that Isabelle's child had been abducted and left in the tunnel on that particular evening. Taken altogether, this meant that Molly had spent almost two hours alone in the darkness of the tunnel.

How had she felt, what had she thought, what had happened?

Isabelle never found out, but after that night Molly changed. Her temper tantrums stopped, and she no longer cried without reason. When Peter came home he mentioned that Molly's behaviour had definitely taken a turn for the better.

Isabelle wasn't so sure. While it was nice to be able to sleep at night, it wasn't quite so nice to wake up and find Molly standing next to the bed, simply staring at her. It was liberating not to have the child whining around her legs all the time, but that was because Molly preferred to sit inside the wardrobe with the door closed, mumbling to herself.

After a year or so her demeanour and her games slowly came to resemble those of other children. And yet…There was an almost unnatural *calmness* about her, an air of authority that enabled her to take command of even four- and five-year-olds. Wherever Molly pointed, other children went. If Molly told them to eat dirt, they ate dirt.

*

Only five canes remain in the bundle that Emil is clutching. His father pulls up, but Emil doesn't want to get out and push another cane into the ground. He hands the bundle to his father without saying anything. His father leans down.

'What's the matter, chicken? You're so quiet.'

'Nothing.'

'Are you sure you don't want to do this one?'

'Sure.'

Emil has no intention of pushing in any more canes; in fact he has no intention of getting out of the car until they are back at the campsite. Perhaps he isn't safe in the car either, but it doesn't feel quite so bad.

And when they get back to the campsite? What is he going to do then?

By this stage Mummy is bound to have found out what he and Molly did to the gas feed. Emil isn't sure exactly *how* bad it is, or exactly what it means, but he thinks his mum is going to be cross. That was why he wanted to go with his dad, who is now getting out of the car with a cane in his hand.

Molly cut the hose from her caravan, then told Emil to do the same with his. He had to do as she said, even though he knew it was wrong. He doesn't understand it, and he doesn't like thinking about it.

Emil picks up the binoculars from the back seat and carefully loops the strap around his neck before bringing them up to his eyes. This is a very expensive pair of binoculars. Daddy has said that it's the only really expensive thing he owns, so Emil takes extra care. Breaking the binoculars on top of everything else would be a total disaster.

He looks through the windscreen, adjusting the focus the way Daddy has taught him. It's difficult, because there's nothing to focus on.

Or is there?

Emil turns the wheel one millimetre at a time until the figure far away in the distance becomes clear.

'Daddy! Daddy!'

His daddy looks in through the open side window. 'What?'

Emil points towards the field, pulling off the binoculars. 'Over there! Look!' He passes the binoculars out with both hands; Daddy looks rather sceptical. 'There's an old man!'

Daddy gives a thin smile and raises the binoculars to his eyes as Emil keeps on staring in the direction of what he saw. He can't make out anything with the naked eye, except perhaps a dot on the horizon. But he did see it. He's absolutely certain of that.

Daddy is standing perfectly still. He has not moved his head at all, which must mean that he can see it too. Emil grips the window frame, resting his chin on his hands and waiting for an explanation.

Daddy lowers the binoculars, then does completely the wrong thing. He opens the back door and *throws* them onto the back seat, slams the door, gets into the driver's seat and spins the wheel to turn the car around.

'Did you see it?' Emil asks. 'What was it?'

'I didn't see anything. We're going home.'

Emil's eyes prickle with tears and he can hardly get the words out: 'But there was someone there! You saw him too!'

Emil turns around to grab the binoculars, but Daddy grips his arm so tightly that Emil is paralysed. Daddy never usually hits him or hurts him in any way. Never.

'Leave that,' Daddy says. He is driving alongside the row of canes.

Emil slumps back in his seat, rubbing his arm. Daddy doesn't even look at him, and the lump in his throat is so big that he can't even cry. He knows that Daddy is lying. That Daddy saw the old man too.

An old man who was completely white.

Emil knows that there are dangerous things here. The white man didn't feel dangerous, yet Daddy is behaving like this.

It is a terrible day.

*

Isabelle watches as Molly frenetically moves the felt-tip across the paper. She thinks about the sensation in her body the day she let go of the buggy. All those coincidences.

There are nights when Isabelle lies awake and thinks that they were not coincidences at all. That it was somehow preordained. She doesn't really understand what she means by that, nor does she want to know.

Someone knocks on the door.

Isabelle is not normally keen on unexpected visitors, but this time she gets up from the table, grateful for the distraction so that she can stop thinking about things she just wants to forget.

The wife of the man with the ugly glasses is standing outside.

'Hi,' she says.

'Oh…hi,' Isabelle replies; her enthusiasm for the diversion has already ebbed away.

The woman peers into the caravan and nods in Molly's direction, then lowers her voice: 'Can you come outside for a minute?'

Isabelle steps down and closes the door behind her. The woman holds out her hand.

'We haven't been properly introduced. I'm Carina.'

Isabelle shakes her hand. Short nails and dry, callused skin. 'Isabelle.'

'I was just wondering, is your gas supply working?'

'No—why do you ask?'

'Ours isn't either. Have you checked to see why?'

'My husband takes care of all that stuff.'

Carina looks at her for a fraction too long before she speaks again. Of course. This is an independent woman who does things for herself.

'Do you mind if we check your cylinder?'

Isabelle shrugs. It's not that she despises Carina in the way that Carina clearly despises her, it's just that she finds the other woman beyond dull. If Carina were a film, Isabelle would already have fallen asleep.

95

Carina walks purposefully towards the back of the caravan, and Isabelle saunters after her, contemplating the other woman's substantial backside and thighs. Why the hell is she wearing *shorts*?

The door of the gas cylinder housing is already open when Isabelle rounds the corner, and Carina gestures inside. 'Look.' She points to the top of the cylinder. 'There's supposed to be a hose here, connecting the supply to the caravan.'

'Right. And?'

'It's not there.'

'I can see that.'

Carina purses her lips, and Isabelle waits. Is there going to be a sudden outburst? Is the woman going to snap at Isabelle in an attempt to rouse her from her lethargy? It looks that way. Or will she manage to control herself? Hard to say.

Isabelle knows perfectly well how the gas works; it was one of the first things she investigated when she was left alone in the caravan for the first time. She could see that the hose was missing before Carina pointed it out, and she is now wondering whether the valve is open or not.

It seems as if Carina has decided not to say anything. Instead she turns the knob until she hears a hissing sound, then turns it off again. 'You've got gas, but without the hose it's useless.'

'Oh,' Isabelle says.

A light dies in Carina's eyes. She takes a couple of steps and stands right in front of Isabelle, who is considerably taller, which means that Carina has to look up at her as she speaks. 'You know what? I can't cope with you right now, but I think your daughter has something to do with this. And I want my hose back.'

'She's been here all the time.'

'No, she hasn't. She was out a little while ago. With my son.'

'In that case perhaps he was responsible for this.'

The woman's hands are opening and closing. Is she going to slap Isabelle? That would be unexpected, and moderately interesting. Then again, perhaps not. If it does happen, should Isabelle fall to the ground, or grab the back of the woman's head and smash her face into the wall of the caravan? Probably the former. Almost certainly.

'My son...' the woman says through stiff lips '...is not that kind of child.'

'And you're saying my daughter is?'

Carina shakes her head wearily. 'Surely you could at least speak to her. Ask her.' She catches Isabelle's eye and her tone darkens: 'Otherwise I'll be back later.'

Isabelle holds her gaze calmly. Carina's nose is so short and flat that it wouldn't make much noise if she smashed it against the wall. On the other hand her front teeth do stick out, so they would probably provide a satisfying crunch. Isabelle tilts her head to one side and smiles.

Carina stomps off angrily towards her own caravan, but something in the line of her back and shoulders tells Isabelle that there is a hint of fear there too.

In her peripheral vision Isabelle sees a blond head disappear from the window. Molly has been listening. Of course.

*

Benny is on full alert in his basket, watching Cat's silhouette against the awning. Cat's long tail sways as she casually rubs against the canvas, moving closer to the opening.

Benny's muscles are trembling, shudders of displeasure chasing across his skin. Cat moves like water, like Snake. The shadow on the awning suggests that Cat has grown *even bigger* than before. Bigger than any Cat Benny has ever seen. A very dangerous Cat.

The shadow reaches the opening and Cat's head appears. It is no bigger than before, and some of the tension leaves Benny's body.

As if it were the most natural thing in the world, Cat slinks into the awning. Benny's mistress doesn't notice her; she is still listening to the sounds from her box. Cat's ears are pointing straight up and her tail swishes from side to side as she takes possession of the awning, a little bit at a time.

Suddenly that's it. Something snaps inside Benny and a reflex over which he has no control takes over. He leaps out of his basket and hurtles towards Cat as the corners of his mouth are drawn up, exposing his teeth, and a series of short, sharp barks comes from somewhere deep in his throat.

Cat jumps and almost falls over, but before Benny can get to her she has turned and shot out of the tent. She races across the campsite with Benny after her.

'Benny! Benny!' his mistress shouts, but Benny has eyes and ears only for Cat, who is running towards her own caravan. Benny's nose is still sore, and he is itching to get his teeth around Cat's neck.

Shortly before she reaches her own caravan, Cat stops dead, spins around, makes herself huge and growls, almost like Dog. Benny stops too, and barks. Cat moves towards him, and Benny backs away. Cat keeps on coming. Benny stops. Cat stops too.

They stand five metres away from one another, each equidistant from their own caravan. They threaten, Cat hisses, Benny barks. They both know the battle is over for the time being. The five metres between them constitutes a no-man's-land, a possible target for future skirmishes. But not right now.

They do what they have to do, then they go home. His mistress is standing outside when Benny returns.

'Bad dog!' she says, and Benny knows exactly what that means. 'Bad dog!'

Benny gets into his basket. He doesn't usually like it when Mistress says those words to him, but right now he couldn't care less. Regardless of what Mistress thinks, he is a good dog. *Good boy*, as they say.

*

'Look, Mummy.'

The drawing in Molly's hand represents nothing. It is merely a series of chaotic spirals, wavy lines in black ink.

'Lovely,' Isabelle says. 'Listen...'

'Do you like it?'

'Yes. I need to...'

'Do you really like it?'

'Be quiet, please. Did you take the hoses?'

'What hoses?'

'You know what hoses.'

'No.'

Molly's eyes are wide open. There is not the slightest twitch of an eyelid, not the hint of a blush on her cheeks: her whole face is the very picture of innocence and honesty. Isabelle doesn't know why she even bothered to ask.

Perhaps Molly has taken the hoses, perhaps not. Trying to find out by asking her is a complete waste of time. Isabelle might be a good liar, but she is a rank amateur compared with her daughter. Whatever proof of Molly's guilt might emerge, she will continue to insist that the opposite is true with that same utterly credible conviction.

Sometimes Isabelle almost allows herself to be fooled, just like most other people. She is almost ready to accept that perhaps Molly really has forgotten, perhaps she really doesn't know what she is supposed to have done. Almost.

In a case like this, where there is no proof, it is impossible to determine whether Molly is telling the truth or not, so Isabelle drops the subject and turns her attention back to Molly's drawing, or whatever you might call it. She has pressed so hard with the pen that the ink has gone through the paper, and there is a ghostly image of the drawing on the next page, a dark blob.

'What's it supposed to be?'

Molly opens her eyes even wider in a slightly exaggerated indication of surprise. 'Can't you *tell*?'

'No, Molly. No, I can't.'

'But it's us!' Molly smiles and nods. 'It's you and me, Mummy!'

*

Majvor has never seen Benny behave like that, chasing after a harmless little cat. She would never hit him as Donald sometimes does, but she has given him a real telling off, and she hopes he is ashamed of himself. Although he doesn't look as if he is, sitting there in his basket having a good wash.

Oh well. At least the incident got her on her feet, which is probably a good thing. She has been spellbound by the radio for the last quarter of an hour, song after song reminding her of the good old days. She wonders what station it is, whether it's possible to pick it up…at home?

There is no sign of anyone else. Majvor runs a hand over her stomach and frowns. It's not that she is hungry, or lonely, but there is an emptiness in her belly and her chest that she can't quite put into words. It's as if the field has moved inside her body.

Majvor is no fan of weird ideas. As a general rule she believes that people think too much, and that this is at the root of much of their unhappiness. The thought that the field has moved inside her is definitely a weird idea, and Majvor cuts it off before it can upset her, thinks about something real instead.

A party, with lots of cakes.

The empty space between the caravans, the lack of people, doesn't feel right. A party would bring everyone together. Majvor could bake a huge batch of cinnamon buns, then they could put a big table in the middle, covered with a gingham cloth, and everyone would sit around sharing the buns while they were still warm. With milk to accompany them.

Majvor walks around the outside of caravan, thinking it over. Is it possible? Yes, she has the ingredients, and the oven will do if she bakes two separate batches. They must have a table and enough chairs between them. The only problem is the gingham cloth, because it has to be gingham. Preferably red and white, but blue and white will do at a push. She doesn't have one herself, but perhaps someone else does?

She pauses at the back of the caravan, picturing the cloth as she stares at the cross painted on the wall. She is just about to go and ask

Carina if she has a suitable cloth when she stops dead.

A cross? Why is there a cross?

She can't recall ever having seen it before. The two intersecting lines are approximately six centimetres long. When she rubs her finger over them, a little of the paint comes off. If it is paint. The grainy pigment on her fingertip is more like…blood. Dried blood. But she's not sure.

Majvor goes round the back of Carina's caravan on her way to see her neighbour. Sure enough, she finds an identical cross. The gingham cloth is temporarily forgotten as she hurries over to the caravan belonging to the two farmers. The cat is lying in the window, and follows Majvor with her eyes as she passes by. Soon Majvor can add a third cross to her list.

Isabelle is leaning against the doorframe of her caravan. Majvor nods to her. Isabelle nods back, looking slightly puzzled as Majvor continues around the corner, where she is able to establish that there are in fact four crosses. One on each caravan. She stands there, trying to interpret this discovery, until she hears Isabelle's voice behind her.

'Excuse me, but what are you doing?'

Majvor turns around and points out the cross to Isabelle. 'This,' she says. 'There's one on each caravan.'

Isabelle shrugs. 'So?'

'Don't you understand?' Majvor says, pointing to the simple symbol. 'We are marked.'

*

With every kilometre Peter has driven, with every cane he has pushed into the ground, the map on the GPS has become clearer and clearer. But it is no longer showing Vällingby. He is now travelling through the area around Linköping. Soon he will be eleven years old, and his belief in God will come to an end.

Peter always had to use a false name when he started training with a new football team to minimise the risk of his father finding him and his mother, but they still had to move twice during that first year.

As far as the development of his skills was concerned, this was not a disadvantage. As the new boy he had to make an extra effort so that he would be accepted, and with the talent he already had, this quickly made him a star. However, even though he laughed and celebrated with his teammates, he rarely felt genuinely happy.

His other hobby was guns. He could spend hours daydreaming over the Hobbex catalogue's pictures of air rifles that were made to look like real guns. A copy of *Guns & Ammo*, found in a well-stocked newsagent's, provided even more food for his imagination.

By this stage he was nine years old. He and his mother had been living in Norrköping for just over six months with no sign of his father. Peter was playing for one of IFK Norrköping's youth teams, and seemed to have a very promising future; he was already playing alongside ten-year-olds.

After another year in Norrköping, Peter and his mother had begun to lower their guard and relax. Peter had stopped looking out for his father on his way to school every morning, and his mother no longer jumped when the telephone rang. Perhaps God had finally led them to safety.

Because God was with them.

After the night when He had saved Peter's mother from the hammer, Peter had started to say his evening prayer with sincerity and conviction. He thanked God, he asked God for advice, he placed his troubles in God's hands. God never gave a clear response, but Peter felt His presence, and every time they had to move and Peter was forced to leave new-found friends yet again, there was consolation in the knowledge that God was with them in the removal truck.

God didn't even object to Peter's interest in guns, although Peter was aware of His displeasure when it came to his gun-related fantasies. Then again, God wasn't the type to turn the other cheek if someone was mean to him.

Jesus was a different kettle of fish. Peter had no interest in Jesus, in spite of his mother's best efforts. And that business of God and Jesus somehow being the same just seemed like an unnecessary complication. God was the main man as far as Peter was concerned.

Until the summer when he was eleven years old, that is.

Peter stops the car and picks up a cane from the passenger seat; this is number fifteen. Before he gets out he glances at the GPS, which now claims that he is in the vicinity of Slite. As soon as he realised where he was heading, he tried to veer off, but to no avail. The GPS simply adapts itself to his driving, the map turns, and however hard he tries to get away, his destination always lies straight ahead of him. He has stopped fighting it.

Peter shudders as he puts his foot on the grass. He rubs his arms and blows, looking down towards his mouth. No, it isn't cold enough for his breath to form a mist, but it can't be far off.

The atmosphere around him has a strange, concentrated quality. As if the air were thicker, tougher than usual, as if it were in the process of turning into water. He waves his hand in front of him and can almost make out ripples in the air. It is difficult to breathe.

He gazes out across the field, screwing up his eyes to sharpen his focus. It could be his imagination, or something created by the saturated air, but he thinks he can see a change on the horizon. He would like a brighter light, a sign that the sun is somewhere below, but what he might be seeing is the exact opposite. A line of darkness. He hopes it is his imagination.

He looks behind him; he can still see the last cane he inserted. He walks in front of the car, takes a couple of steps, then pushes in the next one.

When he lets go he feels something tickling his palm. He looks down and sees that the cane is not a cane. The thing that tickled him is a fletch, and the cane is an arrow. He crouches down and runs his index finger across the smooth surface and up over the feathers.

It looks just like the arrow he had when he was eleven years old. No. It is the same arrow.

Just over two years had passed since the last time his father came hammering on the door, and during that summer's caravan holiday they decided to risk a few days on Uncle Joel's farm.

Uncle Joel had taken over his parents' place in Slite just outside Linköping, and it was okay for Peter and his mother to put their caravan on what had once been grazing land.

Peter got a pet rabbit that summer, and Uncle Joel helped him to make a wooden hutch and a run so that Diego could be outside without being watched all the time. At first he had called the rabbit Maradona, but that was difficult to say, so Peter had settled on Diego instead. Besides which, it seemed unreasonable to keep *Maradona* in a hutch and feed him on dandelion leaves, but with Diego it was fine.

One of the sad things about having to keep a low profile was that they hardly ever dared visit the friends and relatives Peter's father knew. Not that Peter thought it was all *that* much fun to visit Aunt Margaret or his mother's former work colleagues, but he had missed Uncle Joel.

There was plenty to do on the farm, and Uncle Joel was one of those grown-ups who was always interested, but didn't interfere. You could do stuff with him and wish it would never end.

The day before they were due to go home, while his mother was having a lie-in, Peter went out into the pasture with his bow. Uncle Joel had given it to him, and it was a 'top present'. His mother hadn't been very pleased, but Joel had placed his hands on Peter's shoulders and said that he was sure Peter would handle it responsibly—wasn't that right?

Absolutely, if only because Uncle Joel had said 'handle it responsibly' assuming that Peter knew what that involved.

The bow was made of fibreglass, and was almost as long as Peter was tall; he could only just manage to draw back the string. He had also been given five arrows; they too were top quality, with sharp, weighted points and rainbow-coloured fletching. Uncle Joel said the feathers had been plucked from a peacock's tail, but that was probably a lie.

There were a number of old pine trees on the edge of the pasture, and Peter had asked Uncle Joel if he could use them for target practice. Joel had inspected the thick bark and given his permission.

Halfway across the meadow, Peter stopped. It was a beautiful summer's day, pleasantly warm. The old pasture was strewn with dandelions, and the bumblebees were busy shuttling from flower to flower. One bee would take off, and another would land seconds later. Peter didn't understand how this could possibly be an efficient way of working, and made a mental note to ask Uncle Joel about it at dinner.

He turned his face to the sky and sent up a little message of thanks, a simple *here I am, thank you for letting me be here*, but without words. He sent the feeling instead.

Then he got an idea and immediately acted upon it. He placed an arrow in the rest, pulled the string back as far as he could, and fired the arrow straight up into the sky. In a fraction of second it was out of sight, and however hard Peter peered up into the blue, he couldn't see it.

Then he got scared.

He had sent the arrow straight up, which should mean that it would come hurtling back towards him once it had turned.

He ran a short distance towards the caravan, still looking upwards. His mind was racing. Presumably the shot hadn't been straight after all, and as the arrow flew higher and higher, it was impossible to say how great the deviation might be, and in which direction. Would he be able to see the arrow as it came down, and thus be able to avoid it, or would he—scary thought—see it only a nanosecond before it penetrated his eyeball? And what about God? What did God think about people shooting arrows at Him? Admittedly God was probably a lot further away than an arrow could reach, but...

A few more seconds had passed as Peter considered the problem; he spun around, but couldn't make up his mind. He didn't dare look directly up at the sky, but nor could he risk not looking up at all, because the arrow might land on his head, giving him no chance to get away.

He decided he had no alternative but to crouch down with both arms over his head and his eyes screwed tight shut. If the arrow landed on him it would hit an arm, which seemed like a better option.

He waited for five seconds, then another five, but nothing happened. He opened his eyes and looked around. He should have heard a thud when the arrow came down, but he had heard nothing, and there was no sign of an arrow anywhere nearby, so he concluded that his shot hadn't been straight after all.

He searched for a little while longer, then gave up and set off towards the pine trees once more. He spent ten minutes on target practice with the four remaining arrows, taking great care not to lose any more. Then he went back to the caravan to see if his mother had woken up.

She hadn't; the door was still closed, so Peter gathered a handful of dandelion leaves for Diego. When he reached the hutch, he dropped the leaves first of all, then the arrows. An ice-cold wind passed through the summer's day.

Diego was lying in the middle of the run with the missing arrow through the back of his neck. Blood spattered the grass all around him, the grass he had been nibbling, and his paws were splayed in all directions. The feathers on the shaft of the arrow protruded through the wire netting.

This just couldn't happen. Of all the millions of places the arrow could have come down, it had chosen to land in the rabbit run, in the exact spot where Diego happened to be at the time. Peter simply stood there staring for a long time, as rage and guilt overflowed in his breast, making his cheeks turn bright red and his eyes fill with tears.

He looked up at the sky and whispered: 'Why? Why? He was just a little rabbit!'

God was sitting up there watching, but as usual he didn't say a word. Peter carried on glaring furiously at the sky as tears blurred his vision. God refused to say anything in his defence. When Peter finally lowered his gaze, he saw a figure walking across the meadow, heading straight for the caravan. It was as if he was looking through a mist, but he rubbed the tears from his eyes and focused. A second later he was tearing open the caravan door, yelling at the top of his voice: 'Mum, Mum, wake up! Dad's coming!'

On that day Peter stopped believing in God. He was still aware of His existence, but he no longer believed. If God could do such evil things just because a person had fired an arrow in his direction, then he simply didn't deserve to have people believe in Him. He was worthless, or worse. Peter ended their relationship forever, broke off all contact.

Twenty-seven years later Peter is crouched down in an endless field with the wretched arrow in his hand. Now he knows what is wrong. He sensed it as soon as he realised that the sun had gone, but didn't dare follow the thought to its conclusion.

All his life he has felt God's silent presence, but since that day he has refused to respond to the wordless call.

Now it has disappeared. The presence has dissolved, the constant question is no longer being asked.

God is not here.

2. Inside

Everyone has returned to the campsite. Donald was the last to arrive, because he almost got lost. He tells the others about this, but nothing else. Stefan is not particularly communicative either. Like Donald, he seems uncomfortable with the meeting, and avoids the questions that are put to him.

When Lennart and Olof have come straight out and said that they saw nothing, but have started to take an interest in the soil itself, Majvor cannot keep quiet any longer.

'We're marked,' she says. 'Someone has marked us.'

The entire group follows her on a tour around the caravans as she points out the four crosses. As she suspected, no one can remember seeing these marks previously.

'So what do you think it means?' Olof asks.

'I've no idea,' Majvor replies. 'But there must be a connection, surely?'

'Then again, a cross can mean lots of things,' Lennart says.

'Lots and lots of things,' Olof agrees.

A discussion follows about the cross on a map showing the location of hidden treasure, the universal sign for *here it is*, the unknown factor in an equation, and the intersection between two lines. Majvor becomes increasingly frustrated during this debate, and for once she wishes that Donald would step in, but he is just standing there, staring at the ground.

'But don't you understand?' she says eventually. 'It doesn't matter what it means. The important thing is that it's there for a *reason*. Someone has marked us, done this to us.'

'But who?' Carina says. 'And how?'

'I haven't a clue,' Majvor snaps, gesturing towards the endless expanse of grass. 'But there's someone...something out there that wants to do something to us.'

*

Peter stands with his hands in his pockets, watching the others as they speculate on Majvor's discovery. He has nothing to add. His thoughts are not here, nor are they concerned with God's absence. Or perhaps they are, when they zoom in on the penalty against Bulgaria in the World Cup qualifier in 2005, as so often in the past. He can never work out what actually happened.

The match was absolutely critical to Sweden's participation in the World Cup. A win was vital. The score is 1–1 with a minute left to play. Sweden is awarded a penalty, and Peter is the one to take it.

He doesn't know how often he has gone over that moment in his mind, how many times people have reminded him of it.

He rotates the ball in his fingers several times before placing it on the penalty spot and taking four steps backwards. The whole Swedish team is behind him, thirty-two thousand spectators in the stadium, and many hundreds of thousands, even millions, watching on TV, all of them following his every movement.

Peter now has tunnel vision. The ball, the goal. The ball has to go over the line. His foot is going to kick the ball and put it in the net. Nothing else exists. This is what his life is about right now. Running forward and kicking the ball so that it…

Something happens. The blinkers fall away and the situation becomes crystal clear to him. He realises that right now he is as far from freedom as it is possible for a human being to be. The hopes of millions of people depend on his ability to carry out a fixed number of mechanical movements in a certain sequence. This is his job, his fate, his allotted task.

That is when he decides to protest. He knows which direction the Bulgarian goalie usually favours; Peter takes a couple of steps forward, and it is as if something within him breaks free from its chains, and eternity is his as he fires a loose ball exactly where the goalie wants it.

He knows that he is letting down an entire nation with this action, and that he will be the target of much venom and derision, probably for years to come. But at that precise moment it feels as if it is worth it, simply to experience that intoxicating sense of freedom. He lets the goalkeeper know just where he intends to shoot, and taps away a ball that even a rank amateur could stop.

And the stupid bastard hurls himself as far as possible in the opposite direction. The shot is so weak that the goalie has time to get back on his feet and dive the other way, but he misses by an inch, and Peter has scored the coolest penalty in the history of Swedish football.

He takes his hands out of his pockets and steps in front of the group, who are studying the cross on Majvor's caravan.

'Listen to me,' he says. 'There is nothing out there. Nothing. Nix. Nada. Something fucks with your head and makes you start imagining things. That's all. There might be a darker line on the horizon, and if you want to put a positive interpretation on that, then of course you can. But there's nothing here except us and what we have now. That's what we have to accept. If you want to speculate about other stuff, then carry on. But it's a waste of time. There is *nothing*.'

Peter flings his arms wide in a final, definitive gesture, then he walks away, heading back to his caravan. Something is bubbling inside him; it could be panic or happiness, it's hard to tell. But it's to do with freedom, and it is fizzing as if he has carbon dioxide in his blood.

He has to do something. Play something.

*

This business of the cross is a miscalculation on Majvor's part. She had thought that her discovery would have a particular effect on the group, and it hasn't turned out the way she imagined at all.

In her day-to-day life, Majvor regards it as her role to unite and to gather people together. It doesn't have to involve a big party, not at all; it could be something as simple as getting the whole family to settle down for an evening in front of the TV, or inviting friends along on a boat trip in the summer.

She hadn't thought that the revelation of the crosses would create any kind of festive atmosphere, or would cheer people up, but she had believed it would lead to a sense of *community*. We have all been marked in the same way, we are all subject to the same conditions, so let us unite on that basis.

But no. They're talking about hidden treasure and equations instead of seriously considering the idea that the crosses have a *meaning*. That's the way things are in society these days. A meaning isn't on the agenda. She stares morosely at the group. The little boy is tugging at his father's hand, 'Tell them, Daddy. Tell them what we saw,' but his father shushes him with a gesture.

Majvor notices that Isabelle has heard what the boy said; she crouches down and whispers something to her daughter, pointing at the boy.

Secrets. Secrets and nonsense, that's what people are really interested in. Despite Majvor's general goodwill, there is no denying it: sometimes she thinks everyone else is just a pile of shit.

Donald comes over to her. Majvor has hardly been able to get a word out of him since he came back. He grabs her hand and pulls her towards their caravan. Which is probably just as well, as Majvor is feeling increasingly bitter towards the group.

She's not the kind of person who solicits admiration or praise, but just once in a while it would be nice to have a little appreciation. Without her they would still be ignorant of the meaning they are now refusing to accept. Whatever. Majvor offers no resistance; she follows Donald into the caravan, and he closes and double locks the door.

'Sit down.'

Majvor does as Donald asks, or rather commands; she sits down on the sofa and watches as he walks around closing the blinds and making sure the windows are tightly shut.

'Donald? What are you doing?'

It is gloomy with the blinds drawn. Majvor can only just make out the shape of her husband as he stands there with his hands by his sides, looking around. He nods to himself, then sits down at the other end of the sofa.

'The thing is...' he says, holding up his index finger.

Majvor leans back and prepares herself for a lecture. The tone of voice and the finger suggest that this is what is about to happen. Donald has used the gesture for as long as she can remember, and whenever she saw Göran Persson do exactly the same thing during his time as prime minister, she always thought: *a damaged child who has acquired too much power.*

'The thing is,' Donald repeats, before going on to say something completely unexpected, 'I've realised that all this is just a dream. A nightmare inside my own head. I've had it before, but it's never been as clear or as real as this. But it's definitely a dream nevertheless, so all I have to do is wake up. So we're going to sit here and not let any more crap happen; we're just going to wait for it to end.'

Majvor has grown accustomed to the darkness, and she can see Donald's eyes shining in the dim light. They are wide open, to an unnatural degree, as if he is making a concerted effort to wake up. Tentatively she says: 'But what about me?'

'What about you?'

'Are you saying I'm having the same dream?'

Donald snorts. 'You're not here. I'm the only one who's dreaming. I'm sitting here talking to myself—fuck knows why. That's just the way it is in my dream.'

Donald folds his arms, rests his head on the back of the sofa and stares up at the ceiling. Majvor picks at one of the buttons on the seat; it is solid to the touch. She says: 'But...I've been listening to some music while you were away. I wouldn't be able to do that if...'

'Stop right there. What I don't understand is why I've made you exactly the way you are in my dream. I mean, I could be sitting here with Elizabeth Taylor, but oh no, it has to be Majvor. Same silly prattle, same stupid face.'

'Do you often dream about Elizabeth Taylor?'

'No, that was just an example. Be quiet. I've decided you have to shut up now. This is *my* dream, and in my dream you're not saying anything.'

Majvor can't understand where Donald has got this ridiculous idea from. It's not at all like him to come up with something so weird. But however crazy he is, she feels humiliated at the most basic level. He won't even acknowledge her *existence*. Her mind, her very own and completely real mind, is working feverishly to find a way to put an end to this delusion.

'Donald, listen to me…' Donald folds his arms even more tightly and makes a point of sinking deeper into the sofa, but Majvor takes no notice. 'While you were gone, Claes-Göran Hederström was on the radio—"It's Beginning to Seem Like Love". I wrote it down. How could I know that if…'

'It's part of my dream. You saying that, it's part of my dream.'

Majvor is getting frustrated. It's like talking to a wall. She slaps her hands on her thighs and gets to her feet. 'Okay, well in that case let's ask some of the others. Perhaps someone had the car radio on, and heard it too.'

As Majvor heads for the door she hears Donald behind her: 'You're just as stupid as you are in real life. The others are part of my dream too. It doesn't matter what they say. And come away from the door. I've locked it.'

Majvor pushes down the handle, but the deadlock requires a key. 'Give me the key, Donald.'

'No chance. No more running around outside. Sit down and shut the fuck up. I'm determined to wait this out.' Donald sneezes and shakes his head, mutters to himself: '"It's Beginning to Seem Like Love", for fuck's sake.'

Majvor goes and stands directly in front of her husband, who is now almost curled up on the sofa. 'Donald! Tell me what you really saw out there!'

For the first time since Donald got back, there is some contact. He looks away and says: 'Nothing. I saw nothing. Now shut up and sit down. I've never hit you, you know that. Not in real life. In my dream it could be different. So sit down.'

Majvor sits back down, her hands resting on her thighs. The air stands still inside the caravan. She looks at her husband, who is frowning, his lips moving as if he is silently trying to solve a difficult problem.

She isn't sure, but she thinks she might know what this is about. *The Bloodman*. If that is the case, there is a risk that they could be sitting here for a long time. A very long time.

*

There is a war going on inside Emil. He wants to be with Molly, and he definitely doesn't want to be with Molly. He is drawn to her, and he is afraid of her. The war makes him feel tired and apathetic. More than anything, he would just like to go to sleep.

As Molly walks towards him he doesn't know whether to go and meet her, or run away. His mother is kneeling in front of the cross on their caravan, running her fingers over its surface, so he can't hide behind her.

'Come on,' Molly says.

'I don't want to.'

'You have to. Otherwise I'll tell.'

Emil looks around to see if he can spot his father, but there is no sign of him. He shrugs with as much nonchalance as he can muster, and follows Molly. She leads him to her caravan, crawls underneath it and beckons him to join her.

They lie on their stomachs on the grass between the wheels, listening to Molly's father pacing back and forth above their heads. Emil whispers: 'I'll tell on you if you tell on me.'

'You don't get it, do you?'

'Get what?'

'The way things are.'

'What do you mean?'

'There you go: you don't get it. You're the one who's going to be in trouble. You and your mum and dad. If you tell. Now do you get it?'

'No.'

'Well, that's the way it is. What did you say?'

'When?'

Molly rolls over onto her back, sighing as she contemplates the underside of the caravan, crisscrossed by a tangle of dirty pipes and cables. She sticks her finger in her mouth, then runs it over a pipe that is black with soot. She draws four lines on her cheeks, runs her finger over the pipe again and holds it out to Emil.

'Come here.'

'What for?'

'You're going to be an Indian.'

Emil thinks for a moment. He can't see anything dangerous or forbidden about that, so he pushes his face closer to Molly, who draws on his forehead.

'There you go,' she says, wiping her finger on the grass. 'You're an Indian brave and I'm your chief.'

'Girls can't be Indian chiefs.'

'I'm not a girl.'

'Yes you are.'

'No I'm not.'

'So what are you then?'

Molly places her hand on his, looks into his eyes and says: 'If I told you, you'd die of fear. Shall I tell you?'

Emil shakes his head. He doesn't want the game to turn nasty again. When Molly says once again that she is his chief, he gratefully accepts.

'Good,' Molly says. 'You've been checking out the area. What did you see?'

Emil thinks as he picks at some bits of gravel stuck in the tyre next to him. 'I saw...I saw ten cowboys with guns.'

'No, no, no! You have to tell me what you really saw! When you were out there.'

'My dad said it was nothing.'

'So what was it?'

Emil peers towards the field as if he might catch a glimpse of what he saw, what he *knows* he saw. 'An old man. Or something.'

'What kind of old man?'

'He was white. And thin. And it was as if...he wasn't really *walking*. Although he was moving.'

'You mean he was flying?'

'No…I don't know. It was weird. And he looked like a person, but somehow he didn't.'

Molly's brow is furrowed as she digests this information. Emil glances at her and thinks that she looks more like a little girl than an Indian chief or something that might make him die of fear. He prods her shoulder.

'You were wrong,' he says. 'It wasn't a monster with big teeth.'

Molly smiles and wriggles over to him, whispers in his ear: 'How do you know?'

*

Carina runs her finger over the cross. A few flakes of the pigment loosen; she rubs them with her thumb and sees them disintegrate. It's blood—it can't be anything else. Someone has drawn a cross in blood on their caravan. It is difficult to put a positive interpretation on something like that.

She looks up and sees Emil and Molly crawling under Molly's caravan. She is concerned about the fact that they have started hanging out; she is all too well aware of what keeping the wrong company can do to a person. She touches her tattoo. She needs to talk to Stefan, but he has been avoiding her since he got back, even though they promised one another they would get through this together. It is up to her to bring him back home.

She doesn't normally hesitate to tackle things, but the emptiness all around is sapping her strength, and something within her just wants to run away, to take off in any direction.

Inside the caravan she is relieved to see that Stefan has boiled a pan of water on the camping stove and has made two cups of coffee, which he places on the table as a prelude to a conversation. Carina gestures towards the gas stove.

'I'm almost certain it was Molly who took the hose.'

119

Stefan nods, but the information doesn't seem to bother him at the moment. He asks Carina to sit down. They both take a sip of their coffee. Stefan stares out of the window for a long time, then says: 'When I was six years old I got a bike. With training wheels.'

He is sparing when it comes to stories from his childhood; he says he can hardly remember a thing. When Carina brings up some episode from the summers they shared as children, he rarely has anything to add. Carina is surprised by his opening remark, but merely says: 'Oh yes?'

Stefan's expression grows distant as he looks back. 'And then... something happened.'

His story is long and includes a certain amount of repetition, but it is the most cohesive account he has ever given from his early childhood, and Carina listens patiently.

Stefan had wanted a bike of his own for a very long time, and he finally got it on his sixth birthday. It had training wheels, because he hadn't quite mastered the technique yet. It was a great bike, and it had a shiny bell with a loud, clear ping, not like the grating noise the rusty bell on the bike he had borrowed used to make.

Stefan spent a considerable portion of his birthday riding around Mörtsjön on his new bike, around and around the lake. He pretended he was an astronaut, Lucky Luke, King of the Forest.

By the seventh or eighth circuit, the novelty had begun to wear off. New challenges were required. Stefan sat on his bike at the top of the hill leading down to the jetty. Now he was a secret agent. In the trees at the edge of the forest on the other side of the lake he could see a VW Beetle hooked up to a small, egg-shaped caravan. That was where the evil Doctor X had his headquarters! Soon Doctor X would escape in the motor launch that was moored at the jetty. He must be stopped! Stefan stamped on the pedals and zoomed down the hill.

For three more seconds he was a secret agent. Then he turned into a terrified six-year-old who was flying down a hill. He didn't dare brake because he was afraid of falling over, so he kept on going, out onto the jetty, where his pumped-up tyres clattered over the planks of wood.

He couldn't swim, so there was just one word flashing in his brain as a warning signal: *Armbands! Armbands! Armbands!* Then he shot over the edge.

'It's strange what you remember,' Stefan says. 'So much is gone, but I do remember that the surface of the water was black, and that the sun was so high in the sky that…for a fraction of a second I was dazzled by its reflection before I plunged into it.'

The cold forced the air out of Stefan's lungs, and a stream of bubbles rose from his mouth to the surface high above. Stefan would later learn that the lake was actually only three metres deep at the point where he went in.

He knew that he was in trouble, and yet it was the bike that preoccupied him the most. He mustn't let go of the bike, so he clung on to the handlebars. He felt the saddle thud against his bum, and the pressure in his ears stopped getting worse. A cloud of mud swirled up around him. He had reached the bottom of the lake.

A very simple thought came into his mind: *I'm going to die.* Stefan didn't want to die, but he didn't know what to do to avoid it. He looked at the bell, which had something of a dull shine now, and wondered what it would sound like if he rang it underwater. But he didn't dare to let go of the handlebars.

I'm going to die.

In a way the thought didn't frighten him; he just felt very, very sad. Mummy and Daddy, his sixth birthday. Drowned. It was so upsetting that he almost burst into tears, but it was impossible to cry underwater. His head throbbed as he screwed up his eyes and concentrated on *not breathing*.

After a while he couldn't do it any more. He raised his head, took a deep breath and opened his eyes. He hardly noticed the water rushing into his lungs, because something very strange had happened. He was no longer on the bottom of the lake; he was in a field. He was surrounded by light, by warm air. He was still clutching the handlebars, but something strange had happened to the bike. It was *shimmering*, as if it wasn't really there.

Stefan looked up and gasped. Coldness filled his chest once more. A figure was standing some twenty metres away, beckoning. A person, yet not a person. It wanted Stefan to join it, but Stefan had no intention of doing so. The non-person was horrible. It was completely white, and it lacked a number of things that would make it a person. If Stefan went over to it, he would end up like that. The icy cold in his chest banged and howled, and fear flooded his body as he tried to turn the bike that wasn't real; he opened his mouth and screamed.

Then he whirled around and the light changed and clouds flashed by and his stomach burned as he threw up onto the warm wood of the jetty and hands lifted him and it wasn't until he was lying in his bed with Mummy and Daddy sitting next to him and hugging and kissing him that he understood that it had actually happened. He had been rescued.

Stefan traces the rim of his coffee cup with his index finger and shakes his head. 'The first thing I asked about was the bike. What had happened to the bike. It was pulled out later.'

There is silence for a little while. Stefan is not only sparing with stories from his childhood; he rarely talks for long periods at a stretch. It's as if he needs to recover from the effort.

'I'm sorry,' Carina says. 'That was a good story, if I can put it that way, but why are you telling me this now?'

Stefan rests his chin on his hands, looking down and to the left. Carina has read something about the way the eyes move when we search our memory. Down and to the left. Was that an auditory memory? A visual memory?

'I was allowed to sleep in my parents' bed that night, although to be honest I hardly slept at all. As soon as I closed my eyes, that white figure appeared, and when I opened my eyes I was afraid it would be standing by the bed, beckoning to me. It was a long time before I could sleep in my own bed again. And I was always scared.'

Stefan blinks and returns to the caravan. He looks into Carina's eyes and says: 'I saw it. Out on the field. Here. Before.'

Stefan's story has explained a few things to Carina. She can just about remember the quiet but inventive boy she used to play with when they were little. How he changed, became a timid, hopeless child she just didn't want to hang out with.

'I don't understand,' she says. 'Do you mean you think....we're dead?'

'I don't mean anything. But that's what I saw. And I didn't want it anywhere near Emil.'

'Did he see it too?'

'Yes. That's what's so horrible.'

*

Freedom

Peter is looking at the rounders pitch he has laid out. The bats, the tennis ball, the cones to mark the corners. What the hell was he thinking? The usual, probably. The desire to make sure people were enjoying themselves. Peter Sundberg, humanity's tour guide.

Freedom

He goes back to the moment when he took the penalty against Bulgaria, allows his eyes to rest on the empty horizon. The feeling he'd had at that moment corresponds to this place. The same infinite expanse filled his breast before that idiot goalie went the wrong way and Peter became the hero of the match.

Freedom

There is no God here. The idea ought to be terrifying, but it isn't. Quite the reverse. The God who allowed Peter's father to smash up the caravan before Uncle Joel arrived with the police has not provided a protective embrace, merely a watchful eye guiding Peter's actions by the simple fact of His observation, whether Peter wanted it or not. Now that eye is gone. No one can see him.

Freedom

He can do whatever he wants, and the field is endless. So what does he do? Sets out plastic cones to mark the boundaries of a pitch so that he can run around and score points. He is creating an image of his life in miniature.

Peter picks up the bat and the ball. With a perfect strike he sends the ball rocketing towards the field. He watches it soar in a wide arc, then bounce a couple of times before coming to rest. He could have hit it in any direction; every direction is equally empty. To understand that, to really understand it.

*

It is while Carina is on her way to fetch Emil that she makes her decision. It is not like her to sit around, passively waiting for things to sort themselves out. She is going to find out for herself what is out there. Get in the car, drive.

She crouches down beside the caravan where the two children are lying close together, whispering. They look sweet. She is less impressed when she tentatively says, 'Emil?' and he turns his face towards her. He has tears in his eyes, and there is a cross drawn in soot on his forehead.

Carina almost recoils, because she has her own idea about those crosses on the caravans. People put a cross through something to indicate that it should be removed. Cancelled. However, she pulls herself together and remains calm: 'Come and have some breakfast, Emil. Or lunch.'

Emil glances at Molly as if he is asking permission, and Molly nods. That is the final straw as far as Carina is concerned. Emil will not be spending any more time with Molly.

When Emil has crawled out from under the caravan, Carina says: 'You too, Molly. Come out here, please.'

Emil tugs at her hand. 'Let's go, Mum.'

'Just a minute, sweetheart. Molly, could you come out here, please?'

'Why?'

'Because I want to talk to you.'

Molly lowers her face onto the grass, breathes in through her nose and says: 'I'd rather stay here where it's nice and peaceful, and I can smell the flowers.'

Carina forces a smile. 'Ferdinand the bull. Very amusing, Molly, but I'd like you to come out, please.'

Emil tugs at Carina's hand again. 'There's no point, Mum. Let's go.'

Carina shakes herself free. Emil gives up and walks off towards their caravan.

Molly watches him go. 'Is it urgent?'

'You could say that.'

'Why?'

'I'd like to be able to cook a meal, and I can't do that if the stove isn't working. So I'd like you to come out and give me back my gas hose.'

'What's a gas hose?'

'You know perfectly well what it is, because you took it.'

Molly frowns, thinking something over. Then she says: 'You'll get heavy if you eat.'

'What are you talking about?'

'You'll get heavy if you eat. And you won't be able to fly.'

'I don't want to fly.'

Molly yawns. She looks Carina in the eye and says: 'Yes, you do. Straight into the sun.'

Molly crawls out on the far side of the caravan and disappears from view, leaving Carina crouching there. There is a funny feeling in Carina's chest. As if a grubby little finger had been poking around inside.

*

Stefan slams his fist down on the kitchen table. Pain shoots up his forearm from his little finger. Would he be able to feel pain if he were dead? He straightens up. He's not dead, for fuck's sake, it's a ridiculous idea. And if he is dead, if they're all dead, then it's very similar to the state they are in when they're alive, and as long as you're alive, you *do* stuff.

He picks up the binoculars, goes outside and unfolds the roof ladder. Flakes of rust drift down onto his face as he climbs, but the ladder holds. When he gets up on the roof, he lets out a nervous laugh. The perspective is so weird. Now that he is able to take in all the caravans amid the vast expanse of grass, the little camp looks like an unnecessary anomaly, something that has dropped from the sky by mistake.

Carina is crouched down next to Peter's caravan; the two farmers are also crouched down next to their caravan, busy with something on the ground; Isabelle is pacing about with her arms wrapped around her body as if she is freezing; and Peter is standing motionless a short distance away.

Stefan puts the binoculars to his eyes and focuses on Carina, who is leaning in under the caravan with Emil standing beside her, tugging at her hand. Stefan moves on to Peter, who is now holding a bat.

Finally he does what he came up on the roof to do. He examines the horizon, methodically, bit by bit. He gasps when he sees something different, but realises that it is merely one of the canes that he and Emil set out. One hundred and eighty degrees further around, he spots a couple of the farmers' canes.

Nothing else. He lowers the binoculars and is overcome by dizziness once again. It is easier when this world is divided into sections, or when you have a task to perform. Naked and without purpose, the emptiness surrounding him is dreadful. He swallows down the feeling.

Below his feet, Carina is on her knees with her hands resting on Emil's shoulders, talking to him. Stefan is about to climb down and join them when he is struck by a thought. He is two and a half metres above ground. It's worth a try.

He digs out his mobile phone, a seven-year-old Nokia with a

screen the size of half a brick. He switches it on and hears the cheerful introductory notes; the image of hands reaching out suddenly appears. Stefan glances down and sees Emil frantically shaking his head.

When he looks back at the screen, he has *one* bar on his reception signal. It flashes and disappears, flashes again. Stefan holds the phone above his head, and the bar stabilises. He presses the button and hears the hum of the dialling tone.

'Listen!' he shouts to Emil and Carina.

*

'Can you do this, sweetheart?'

Carina mimes licking her fingers then rubbing her forehead. Emil looks at her with scepticism. 'Why?'

'Because…because you've got a dirty mark there. You don't want me to do it, do you?'

Emil shakes his head firmly, then sticks his fingers in his mouth and scrubs at his forehead. The cross is erased, leaving only grubby marks that can be washed off later. It looks a bit of a mess, but it's better. Much better.

'What would you like to eat?'

'Pancakes.'

Carina kneels down and places her hands on Emil's shoulders.

'Okay, sweetheart. If I'm going to make pancakes, then I need to use the stove. And if I'm going to use the stove, I need that hose.'

Emil's eyes dart from side to side, and he says: 'I'll just have a sandwich then.'

'But I need the hose. Where is it?'

Emil clamps his lips together and shakes his head. Carina feels sorry for him. He's a really bad liar, and she feels ashamed that she has forced him into it. Emil's body is tense beneath her hands as she goes on. 'You're not in trouble, chicken. Just tell me where it is. Do you…'

Two things happen at almost the same time. Stefan shouts 'Listen!' from the roof of the caravan, and a fraction of a second later Emil

127

clamps both hands over his ears and starts screaming. He stares at Carina as a single howl of despair comes out of his mouth and slices into her heart.

*

A child is screaming, and Isabelle realises that it must be Emil, since it can't be Molly. Her daughter neither screams nor cries, not ever. It is as if she used up her entire stock during the first two years of her life.

Isabelle was very obedient as a child. *A good girl*, her mother liked to say. An amenable soul who knew how to behave at a dinner party.

Right now she has wrapped her arms around herself so that she won't fall apart. Her body is screaming at her to find something sweet immediately, to stuff it in her mouth and swallow it, otherwise... She has broken out in a cold sweat, and doubles over as her stomach cramps. It will be over in a little while, then there will be a fresh attack in just over an hour, worse than this one. After that there will be a shorter interval, then she will be really ill.

Isabelle moves among the caravans, convinced that she is picking up the aroma of sweet things everywhere. It's as if the others are sitting inside their caravans, sneakily guarding mountains of sweets and chocolate.

She takes a couple of deep breaths through her mouth to avoid the sugary smells. She feels a little less anxious. By the time she passes the farmers' caravan, she is able to stand up straight and walk more or less normally.

The two men are on their knees, digging with a trowel. They are completely absorbed in what they are doing, and don't notice Isabelle until she coughs discreetly. They both look up at the same time, and it isn't difficult for Isabelle to produce her best smile, because they look really funny.

'Hi,' she says. 'What are you up to?'

Lennart and Olof glance at one another as if they were engaged in some secret activity, and have to reach a mutual agreement before they can reveal it.

Olof points to a potted plant on the ground beside them. 'We thought we'd try putting something in the ground. See what happens.'

Isabelle is still smiling. 'So we'll have more flowers.'

Olof laughs. 'We've got a few other things too.'

Isabelle is standing in that way. She is doing that thing with her eyes as she continues to smile. But she is getting nothing back. She *knows* when she has hit the mark, when a man would be ready to drop everything just to touch her. She scores that direct hit reasonably often, and she almost always lands *somewhere* on her target. But not this time. Which could mean one of two things.

There is no lack of gay men in Isabelle's industry: camp designers, photographers with a fetish for leather and the entire spectrum in between. She's seen most types, but picturing Olof and Lennart as a gay couple is beyond the reach of her imagination. Therefore she decides they must be asexual, that they have stopped having those feelings.

'Have you got any sweets?' she asks.

Once again the two men look at one another. Can't they say *anything* without a consultation?

'No,' Lennart says. 'Not exactly.'

It is clear that Olof is not entirely comfortable with this response. He looks down at the ground and busies himself with the plant. Isabelle holds Lennart's gaze for a few seconds. He doesn't even blink, but simply contemplates Isabelle as if she were a moderately interesting detail in his surroundings. This annoys her so much that she is on the verge of saying, 'Hand over the sweets, bum boy,' or something along those lines, but manages to resist. Instead she pulls a face and leaves the farmers to whatever it is they are doing. She can hear them murmuring to each other behind her back.

Only then does it strike her: the bastards are *planting* stuff. Which means they must think they're going to be here long enough for it to grow.

That can't happen. Rodebjer were supposed to be getting in touch with the agency today; Isabelle is in the running as a catalogue model for the new collection. The shoot has been delayed, and the decision must be made quickly. If Isabelle doesn't answer, the job could go to someone else. Rodebjer would be perfect; she can't lose it.

'Fuck,' she mutters. 'Fucking hell!'

She looks around and sees Peter, fifty metres away on the grass. He is standing absolutely still with a bat in his hand, like a statue proclaiming the glory of idiocy. Isabelle's hands begin to shake once more as she moves towards him.

*

'What the hell are you doing?'

Peter hears Isabelle's voice behind him and slowly turns around. Her lovely mouth is contorted in a sneer as she contemplates the rounders pitch. Peter weighs the bat in his hands. Isabelle has probably failed to grasp that the field is endless. What that means. 'Isabelle,' he says, 'I want a divorce.'

Isabelle screws up her eyes as if she is having difficulty seeing him. 'What did you say?'

'I said I want a divorce. I don't want to be married to you any more.'

'And you think this is the right time to mention that?'

'I do, actually. That's exactly what I think.'

Isabelle's eyes scan the horizon, back and forth, until they eventually come to a stop somewhere near where the ball landed. Then she sighs and says: 'I need something to eat.'

'Did you hear what I said?'

'Yes, I heard what you said. And? I need something to eat. You're friends with those weirdo farmers. They've got something.'

'We're never going to get away from here.'

Isabelle rolls her eyes. 'What is it you want? A blow job, maybe?'

'Some chance.'

'Can you sort it out? *Please.*'

Peter stares at Isabelle for a few seconds. She is so beautiful and so repulsive. He drops the bat and heads for the camp. He's said it. He thought he would feel better than he does, but he's said it. The words have been spoken.

He doesn't look up until he reaches the caravans. Stefan has put a folding chair on top of his caravan, and is in the process of clambering up onto it while holding his mobile phone above his head.

The field is endless.

The words keep going round and round in the back of Peter's mind like a mantra. It's as if there is some hidden meaning that he doesn't yet understand.

Lennart and Olof are sitting on the ground next to their caravan, and the mere sight of them makes something hard inside Peter soften slightly. He relaxes and walks over to them.

*

The folding chair is rickety even when someone sits on it. Stefan feels like an incompetent circus artist as he cautiously places one foot at a time on the frame while attempting to stabilise the structure of thin metal tubes with both hands. He daren't stand on the fabric.

Forty-nine kronor at Rusta. Serves you right.

At last he manages to straighten his legs. When he holds the phone at stomach height, the bar occasionally flickers into life; when he lifts it up to his face it becomes more stable, and when he raises it above his head, the bar is there almost all the time. He presses the button and hears a continuous dialling tone.

So? Now what?

There is one thing he definitely wants to do: call his parents and tell them that he and Carina and Emil are okay. That they might not be home tomorrow as planned. The opportunity to save his parents any anxiety would make this project worthwhile, even if nothing else comes of it.

But what next? Who else should he call?

The first thing that occurs to him is the distribution centre. That pallet of herring. He hears a grinding sound beneath his right foot, the chair moves slightly and Stefan almost loses his balance. He panics and jumps down, landing with a crash on the roof. He sinks down onto the warm metal, glaring at the telephone in his hand.

Who should he call?

Stefan moistens his lips with his tongue. There is one aspect of all this that he hasn't considered. *If* he manages to ring his parents and they answer…what exactly does that mean?

It means they are not lost. It means they are in a place that is in contact with the normal world, and that the normal world still *exists*. That makes a huge difference, if you think about it carefully.

Suddenly Stefan is afraid to make the call. It has become far too critical. He juggles the phone from one hand to the other as if it is a hot potato that needs to cool before he can deal with it. There isn't much battery left, and he ought to switch off the phone if he's going to sit here wavering.

Pull yourself together.

What is he so scared of? His parents will either answer, or they won't. If they don't answer he can ring the emergency number or something, just to check if he is able to contact another human being. Or even the speaking clock, for goodness sake.

There is, however, another possibility, and perhaps that is why he is still playing around with the phone. What if he calls…and *someone else* answers? Someone who is neither a person nor a machine? Someone who has been wanting to make contact with him ever since that day on the bottom of the lake.

Stefan stands up, picks up the binoculars and traces the horizon, looking particularly closely at the route he took with Emil. Nothing.

What was it he actually saw? A white figure, far away in the distance. How can he be so sure that this figure has anything to do with the one that beckoned him when he was six years old? What evidence is there? None. Nothing except that icy sensation in his chest; he felt as if he had swallowed several litres of cold water from the lake when he caught sight of that figure through his binoculars.

Stefan rests his forehead on his wrists, closes his eyes and goes back to the memory of his sixth birthday. The bike, the jetty, the dark water. The cold in his lungs, the field opening out before him, the beckoning figure. He fixes it with his internal gaze and examines it carefully.

It is not dangerous to make the call. As he remembers it, *the figure had no mouth*. It's not going to say anything to him. It had only eyes, as far as he recalls.

Without any further deliberation, he climbs up on the chair once more, trying to distribute his weight differently this time. Then he keys in his parents' number while holding the phone just above his head.

He hears it ringing at the other end of the line. Once. Twice. Three times.

Please pick up. Please.

He pictures the push-button phone on the kitchen window ledge, its old-fashioned ring echoing through the house with every electronic beep in Stefan's ear. He sees his mother put down her knitting and get up from the sofa in the living room. His father is too ill to be up and about.

On the fourth ring he hears a crackling sound, then a voice. His mother's voice.

'Hello? Ingegerd Larsson.'

Stefan wobbles and almost falls off the chair, but manages to steady himself without damaging it. He doesn't know what to say. He would like to press the phone to his ear instead of holding it above his upturned face, but he daren't risk it. The connection is fragile.

'Hi Mum,' he says. 'It's me, Stefan.'

'Stefan?' His mother's voice is so faint. 'Where are you?'

Stefan is looking up at the sky. He blinks a couple of times and realises that there are tears in his eyes. Where is he? If only he knew.

'I'm…I'm a long way away. But we're all fine.'

The bar flickers and Stefan picks up only disjointed words: '...worse...home...'

'What did you say, Mum?'

He raises the phone a little higher. The signal stabilises, but his mother's voice is now so distant that he can't hear a word.

'Sorry, Mum—say that again?' He brings the phone down a fraction, and just about manages to hear her this time: 'Your father is much worse. You need to come home.'

There is a loud crack as the crossbar of the chair snaps and the whole thing collapses. Stefan holds the phone close to his chest as he falls sideways and crashes down onto the roof, landing on his shoulder.

There is a certain amount of give in the metal and he doesn't break any bones, but when he looks at the screen, the contact has been lost.

You need to come home.

Stefan draws his knees up to his chest and whispers: 'Oh fuck.'

*

Lennart and Olof have dug three holes of differing sizes next to their caravan. When Peter comes over they are just removing a house plant from its pot in order to place it in the largest hole.

'Hi there,' Peter says. 'Are you making a garden?'

'Not really,' Olof says. 'We just wanted to see what's going on with the soil around here.'

'The thing is, we have our suspicions,' Lennart adds.

Peter sits down cross-legged beside them and looks at the items laid out on the ground. A trowel, an almost empty bag of compost, a bucket containing several litres of water, a wrinkled potato with two or three eyes protruding from the skin, a packet of dill seeds.

Olof follows his gaze: 'You use what you have, as Kajsa Warg said.'

Lennart pours a little water into the hole and Olof inserts the plant, a pelargonium, then both of them backfill with compost before watering it again. Peter watches the procedure and allows himself to forget that the field is endless. There is something restful in watching the two men work steadily, as if the world were normal, and all you had to do was carry on pottering as usual.

However, as Lennart and Olof place the wrinkled potato in the ground and begin to fill in the hole, Peter can't help asking: 'What kind of suspicions?'

Lennart looks up at Peter as if he doesn't understand what he's referring to, but then he remembers his last remark. 'We think that something isn't quite right about the soil here. It seems to be full of nutrients, yet nothing is growing. Apart from the grass.'

'So what do you think that means?'

Lennart shrugs. 'It could be toxic in some way.'

'Or it doesn't work like any soil we've ever come across,' Olof says.

Peter has the impression that there is something they're not telling him. They are very pleasant, yet there is a part of him that is frightened by them. They are so impenetrable; theoretically, they could be sitting on all kinds of secrets.

He pushes the thought aside and tentatively asks: 'Listen, guys, I don't suppose you have any sweets I could buy? My wife…' Peter stops, blinks and corrects himself. '*Isabelle* suffers from an illness which means she needs sugary things.'

Lennart and Olof look at one another, and after a silent conversation Olof raises his eyebrows meaningfully at Lennart, who sighs. 'Yes, we probably have.'

Olof leans on Lennart's shoulder for support as he gets to his feet and moves towards the caravan. Lennart glances shyly at Peter before calling after Olof: 'Just half, okay?'

Olof holds up a hand to reassure Lennart, who nods and turns back to Peter. 'I'm sorry to be so mean, but it's our Friday treat, so to speak.'

'What is?'

'The thing is, we have a packet of Twist and we always…' All at once Lennart seems embarrassed, and pokes at the soil around the pelargonium as he goes on. 'It's a bit of a special occasion.'

Tears spring to Peter's eyes: 'I'm sorry, of course you must keep your sweets. Isabelle will be fine.'

'No, no,' Lennart insists. 'We're happy to share. One sweet can make a special occasion, after all, if Isabelle needs our help.'

The tears are no longer pricking, but Peter has a lump in his throat, and that lump is made up of *loss*. When he was a little boy, a packet of Twist was a treasure worth waiting for, and he could make it last for days, but that has been replaced by pleasures that cost a thousand times more, yet give him only a fraction of the satisfaction. He has lost something that Lennart and Olof have managed to hold on to.

'I don't mean to pry,' Lennart says, 'but you look upset. What's wrong?'

Peter has a sudden urge to tell him everything. If Olof had asked, he might well have done so. Lennart somehow has a thicker skin and a less inviting embrace, so Peter merely shakes his head and thinks: *Nothing exists and the field is endless.*

Packets of Twist and the memory of packets of Twist and the feeling evoked by the memory of packets of Twist and the thoughts arising from the feeling evoked by the memory of packets of Twist— it's all essentially meaningless if nothing exists and the field is endless. Peter straightens his shoulders and when Olof returns he takes the plastic bag holding a dozen or so sweets that Olof offers him.

'I hope that will be enough,' Olof says, getting down on his knees once more.

'Thank you so much,' Peter says, reaching into his back pocket for his wallet, but Lennart pulls a face and waves his hand dismissively.

'Don't be ridiculous,' he says. 'It would be silly to accept payment for such a little thing. And anyway, what use is money out here?'

Peter aborts the unnecessary gesture; his wallet is in the caravan anyway. He sits there in silence as Lennart and Olof scatter the dill seeds in the smallest and shallowest hole. Their movements are so much in tune, their closeness so self-evident. When they have finished, Peter says: 'I'm sorry, I don't mean to pry, but...how come you're camping together like this?'

Lennart and Olof look at him with raised eyebrows, and Peter feels obliged to elucidate: 'I mean, it's a bit unusual, that's all.' Perhaps he has destroyed the warm atmosphere; he doesn't know how sensitive the issue might be.

To his relief, Lennart simply says: 'Our wives, Ingela and Agnetha, went on holiday together. To the Canaries. And when they came back...after a week or so...they just zoomed off. Both of them.'

The expression is so odd that Peter feels the need to repeat it: 'Zoomed off?'

'Yes. They must have talked it over while they were down there, and decided that was what they were going to do. And so they zoomed off. In different directions.'

'Seven years ago,' Olof chips in.

'But...You don't just...zoom off, surely?' Peter says.

'Well, no,' Lennart agrees. 'I don't suppose you do. But that's what they did.'

'That meant we were both on our own,' Olof says. 'And gradually we decided that...how shall I put it? That we didn't need to be alone. Not when we got on so well.'

Lennart doesn't seem to have any objections to this explanation; he nods thoughtfully, and Peter finds himself doing the same. He has more questions, but can't think of a way of asking them without over-stepping the mark, so they all sit there quietly for a while, nodding in unison, until they are interrupted by the crash as Stefan falls off his chair.

*

The bread bin is a sorry sight. It contains nothing but three dried-up slices of white bread, the kind that tastes good only if it is toasted. Carina considers making French toast instead. Then she remembers that they need to save the camping stove for essentials, in case they don't get the gas hose back.

She butters the bread and slices cheese, glancing over at Emil, who is sitting at the kitchen table playing with his Lego. Carina has realised that she must proceed with caution. The issue of the hose is sensitive in a way she doesn't yet understand.

As she places the sandwiches in front of Emil with a glass of luke-warm milk, there is a thud on the roof as if Stefan is jumping on it. Emil looks up.

'What's Daddy doing?'

'He's trying to get his phone to work.'

Emil takes a bite of his sandwich. 'So he can make calls.'

'That's right.'

'Is he going to call the police?'

Carina doesn't know what to say. Who should they ring? The person who marked their caravans with a cross. It's a pity whoever it was didn't leave a number.

'The fire brigade,' Emil says and Carina smiles, which makes him add: 'The bank. And the hairdresser.'

Carina knows that Stefan's main aim is to call his parents and reas-sure them. She has no one to call. No one at all. Both of her parents are dead, and she no longer has anything to do with her friends from the past. In any case, quite a lot of them are either dead or in jail. The people she has in her life are right here with her.

Emil manfully chews the dry sandwich. He can't help pulling a face when he takes a sip of the tepid milk, but he doesn't say a word. There is one slice of bread left, plus half a packet of crispbread.

We have to find a way out of here.

Carina's thoughts return to the impossible. To the fact that they are here at all, that they have been removed. Deleted. She picks up a piece of Lego, then three more. She stares at them in the palm of her hand, imagining a hand that lifted the caravans in just the same way, then dropped them on this incomprehensible field.

It is so counterintuitive that another possibility flashes through her mind: that she has got it wrong. That in fact it's all very simple; it's about a way of looking at things. An ant can grasp only two dimen-sions; if it is placed on a ball, it cannot understand that it will return to its starting point if it just keeps on walking. Something along those lines. Grasping the concept of a ball when a ball is an unknown entity. But how can you imagine something that you can't imagine?

'What's the matter, Mummy?'

Emil has finished his sandwich, and Carina realises that she must have been out of it for a few minutes. Her hand is tightly clamped around the Lego pieces, and when she tries to put them down, they stick to her skin for a couple of seconds before they drop, leaving red marks behind.

'Nothing, sweetheart. I'm just thinking, that's all.'

'Shall we build something?'

There isn't a sound from the roof, so Carina assumes that Stefan is still trying to get through. She doesn't want to go anywhere until he comes back and is there for Emil, so she nods. 'What shall we make?'

'A fortress. A strong fortress,' Emil says, placing the base in the middle of the table. He begins to construct a square frame. 'With thick walls so it can withstand the attack.'

Carina selects pieces of different colours and adds them to the base. She leaves a space on one side, but Emil pushes in a couple of pieces and closes the gap.

'Don't we need a door?' Carina asks.

Emil shakes his head. 'We're not having a door.' He picks up three knights, puts them inside the square and carries on building up the walls.

Carina points to the trio. 'So how did they get in, if there's no door?'

Emil looks at her, raises his eyebrows and shakes his head, as if he can't understand how he has ended up with such a silly mummy. 'Obviously there *was* a door,' he explains. 'But they've sealed it up.'

'Okay. And why have they done that?'

Emil sighs. 'I *told* you. Because of the attack.' His voice takes on a pedagogical tone beyond his years as he adds: 'The door is the weakest point.'

Carina slots in a few more pieces so that the frame is two bricks high before she asks another question: 'What kind of attack are we talking about here?'

Emil stops building and twists a Lego brick between his fingers. 'They don't know. That's what's so terrible.' His expression is grim as he resumes construction.

'What...?' Carina begins, but Emil interrupts her. 'No, Mummy. We have to finish the fortress. Keep building.'

They work in silence until the frame is four bricks high and the knights begin to disappear behind the walls. Carina points to them again: 'Won't they have problems in there? What about food and water? How will they manage?'

'It will be hard,' Emil confirms. 'But if they stick together, everything will be all right.' He leans forward and peers over the wall, then suddenly looks up at Carina. 'Mummy, what lives on blood?'

'Why do you ask?'

'I just wondered.'

'Well...you know about vampires.'

'Mmm. Like in *Twilight*. But in real life?'

'There are various insects, I suppose. And there's a species of bat that...'

'Bigger. Is there anything bigger that actually lives on blood?'

'Not as far as I know.'

'Are you sure?'

'Pretty sure.'

'But there *could* be?'

Carina runs her fingers over the knobbly top of the walls and asks: 'This...attack. Is the fortress going to be attacked by those who live on blood?'

'Yes,' Emil says, slotting in the piece in his hand. 'But not the dangerous ones.'

Even though Carina assumes that this is something Molly has told Emil, the quiet simplicity in his voice has created an idea that makes her scream out loud when she hears a crash from the roof.

At first Benny thinks it must be thunder, which makes him nervous. He doesn't like thunderstorms. He pricks up his ears, scampers to the opening and peeps out. The sky doesn't look the way it usually does when there is going to be a storm. Something else must have made the noise.

Cat is lying in the window of her caravan, and her owners are busy with something on the ground. The door is ajar. Benny stretches and yawns without taking his eyes off Cat. He sniffs and is confused. The smell of Grandchildren that he picked up from the field is here now. It's very, very faint. Grandchildren coming closer. It's strange, but not too alarming. Grandchildren are not dangerous, just hard on the ears.

Benny takes a few tentative steps outside. Cat is watching him now. A couple more steps. Cat gets to her feet. Benny is approaching the area that is no one's territory. When he is a nose-length away, Cat jumps down from the window. There is a clattering sound from inside her caravan, and a second later she is out on the grass, racing towards Benny, who stops exactly on the borderline of his territory.

Cat stops on her own borderline, sits down. Benny stays where he is. Cat starts washing herself. Benny scratches behind his ear. He can't decide. Should he go for it, or bide his time?

He settles on a compromise, and embarks on a circuitous manoeuvre, edging towards Cat in a semicircle. Cat watches him, then gets up and begins to move away from him in a semicircle of her own. After a while Benny is in the spot where Cat started off, and vice versa.

He scratches behind his ear again, debating whether to cut across the circle, step across the borderline. Instead he sets off again in Cat's footsteps, moving a little faster this time. Cat does the same, keeping her distance. When Benny gets back to his own starting point, he breaks into a run. Cat does the same.

It is no longer possible to tell who is chasing and who is being chased. Round and round they go; Benny lets out a couple of barks. Cat doesn't bark, but sometimes she fits in an extra little leap.

They carry on running until Benny starts to feel dizzy and can't go on any longer. He flops down outside his own caravan, panting heavily with his tongue hanging out. Cat lies down on the grass, her expression inscrutable as she stares uninterruptedly at Benny.

He fires off one last bark, then lumbers back to his basket. Before he goes and lies down he tries whimpering outside the door; something to eat would be nice. But no one comes.

*

Majvor is lying on the bed reading an old magazine by torchlight, since Donald will not allow her to open the blinds. Donald is sitting on the sofa, his hands constantly gripping, then releasing, the fabric of his sweatpants. His fists clench, then relax, clench, then relax. His mouth is filled with the taste of chocolate. The Bloodman is wandering through his mind. This is not a good dream.

Donald was the eldest child, born in 1943. Two sisters arrived shortly after him, and then his mother and father decided to stop, because they couldn't afford any more children. In spite of this, another sister saw the light of day in the spring of 1953. *A little accident*, his father said; Donald didn't understand what that meant.

The youngest member of the family was christened Margareta, and she was a real crybaby. There was no escape in a three-room cottage, so in the summer of 1953 Donald made sure he accompanied his father to his job at Räfsnäs Sawmill as often as possible. They even managed to find him an unofficial summer post as a kind of general dogsbody.

For twenty öre an hour, Donald sorted screws and nails, carried planks of wood to the storeroom and gathered up the waste timber which would eventually be shredded. He really enjoyed going on deliveries with his father, when they loaded timber for a building site onto the truck, then helped to unload it at the other end.

Donald and his father got on very well, and he would have happily worked for nothing just to spend time with his dad, exchanging banter about his mother and his little sisters. There was nothing wrong with them, nothing at all—they just weren't proper blokes.

It was no secret that Donald was his father's favourite, or at least the child he paid most attention to. It was only natural. Donald was the one who would learn the ropes, so that one day he could work in the timber industry. However, his father made sure that Donald worked hard in school, and liked to say: 'The boy has a good head on his shoulders.' If you were going to run your own business, it was important to be able to keep an eye on the figures.

One of their favourite games when they were driving the truck to some distant customer was to fantasise about the future, and what the sawmill or lumberyard Donald would own when he grew up might look like. Would he take care of the sawing himself, or contract it out? Would he perhaps have his own forest? What additional products should he sell?

June and the first half of July passed, and even if the work was sometimes physically taxing (a ton of battens to be distributed between five different storage areas) or boring (ten thousand nails to be sorted), Donald couldn't recall a better summer.

One very hot day in the middle of July, Donald and his father set off for the sawmill in Riddersholm. A small shipment of logs had arrived, and needed to be sawn into planks for a customer. Since the trunks were relatively slender, Donald's father decided they could do the job themselves.

When they had climbed up into the driver's cab, he nodded towards their lunch box and said he had a little surprise for Donald. The usual fare consisted of fried egg sandwiches which Donald's mother made in the morning, along with a small bottle of milk to share. There was rarely anything else. Donald couldn't guess what the surprise might be, so the lunchbreak hovered before him like a tempting mirage.

The circular saw used to split the logs was housed in a rectangular building with a corrugated iron roof. If it was hot outside, then it was boiling inside. Both Donald and his father worked with their shirts off, and the whirling sawdust combined with the sweat and the whining of the blade made for a less than pleasant experience. As Donald hauled away the cut planks and helped to load the logs onto the belt, he was really looking forward to that lunch.

After a while they just couldn't carry on. Only a few ugly logs remained, covered in gnarled, lumpy knots. Donald and his father stopped for a breather, wiping the sweat from their brows. Then they started again. Carrying the logs and dropping them onto the belt, sawing and lifting, carrying and dropping. Donald's head was spinning with heat and exhaustion, and even his father was blinking and shaking his head from time to time.

The penultimate log proved particularly difficult, and the blade of the saw got stuck twice in a root nodule near the end. Donald's father wrenched it free and told Donald to fetch the cant hook so that he could get a grip on the other end. If one of them pushed and the other one tugged at the same time, they ought to be able to force the bastard past the blade.

Donald used the metal hook to grab the narrow end of the log. His father was standing by the blade at the other end of the belt, ready to push. They nodded to one another and mimed: 'One...two...three!' Donald pulled, feeling triumphant as the log shifted a metre towards him with unexpected ease; it had gone through.

He glanced over at his father, ready to give him the thumbs up—only one more log to go—but before he could raise his hand he gasped and dropped the hook. The sudden jerk had made his father fall forward over the belt.

All his life Donald would keep going over what had happened, examining every second in minute detail. It had been so hot; the sweat had been trickling into their eyes, clouding his father's vision among the swirling sawdust; they had been tired; his father had misjudged the situation; or perhaps the log had an unusual structure which meant that the blade suddenly slipped through it like a hot knife through butter.

It couldn't be that Donald had tugged too hard, that his violent movement had caused his father to lose his balance, falling onto the blade which sliced off both his hands.

At first Donald couldn't process what he was seeing. His father slid down until he was on his knees. Blood was spurting from his wrists; it struck the spinning blade and was flung into the air. A few drops hit Donald's face; he looked down at the backs of his hands and saw the blood that had splashed onto them too, was still splashing onto them, and only then did his heart plummet in his chest like a lump of ice.

On legs that didn't want to obey him he ran over to his father, who managed to get to his feet, then fell back against the wall as the blood carried on pumping out of the stumps that were his arms, over his chest and stomach, over his face.

'Dad! Dad!'

'Donald,' his father wheezed above the whine of the saw. 'Pressure...tie...'

In a panic Donald looked around for their shirts, a piece of rope, anything that he could use to tie around his father's arms to try to stop the blood from gushing out of his body. He spun around and almost threw up when he saw one of his father's hands lying on the belt, the other on the floor in a clump of dark-coloured sawdust. No rope.

Our shirts, our shirts...

They had hung them on a tree. Donald raced outside and grabbed them, letting out a sob when his shirt got caught on a branch. He pulled at it until the sleeve tore off, then dashed back towards the building.

His father came staggering out into the light, and Donald stopped dead as the image that would haunt him as long as he lived was seared onto his retinas.

His father paused as if the blazing sunlight had taken him by surprise. His body was smeared with blood, shining like a fresh piece of meat in the harsh light. His hair was plastered to his head, and his eyes gleamed white through the blood that ran down his face when he raised his mutilated arms to the sky and dropped to his knees. There was no longer anything about him that resembled Dad; this was a horrific figure, a man covered in blood.

And yet Donald ran over to him, his hands shaking as he tried to knot the fabric around the Bloodman's forearms, where the blood was no longer spurting but merely trickling.

'Dad, please Dad, please!'

His father took no notice of his efforts. He was looking up at the sky, his body swaying from side to side. Donald had managed to apply a tourniquet of sorts around one arm; he tied the knot as tightly as he could and the flow of blood stopped.

Maybe, maybe, maybe...

Everything around him had disappeared. The birds were no longer singing, there was no sun in the sky, the trees had gone. There was only Donald and his father and the blood; he had to get the blood to stay in his father's body.

As he straightened out a shirtsleeve before winding it around the other arm, his father's chin fell onto his chest. He looked at Donald and whispered: 'My...boy,' then collapsed sideways.

Donald screamed and pleaded, he applied a tourniquet to the other arm, he shook his father and begged him to open his eyes, to say something, not to leave him alone. To no avail. His hands were red with blood by the time he got to his feet, his expression blank as he stared at the saw, which was still spinning, still emitting that monotonous whine.

He went inside and switched it off, stood and watched as it slowed down, stopped, fell silent. He considered picking up his father's hands and placing them next to his body, but he couldn't do it. Instead he went and sat in the truck.

He sat there for a long time. Now and again he glanced over at the driver's seat as if to check whether his father had come back, telling him that the whole thing was just a stupid joke, let's go home now. He felt nothing. He couldn't move.

The sun was no longer shining in his face when he noticed the lunch box on the floor. He picked it up and opened the lid. He saw the usual sandwiches, wrapped in greaseproof paper. And a bar of chocolate. A great big bar of chocolate. Hazelnut, his favourite, which they could hardly ever afford to buy.

He and Dad would have sat side by side sharing the chocolate, satisfied with a job well done. Sat side by side on a flat rock in the shade. Savoured every bite. Donald started to cry, and he was still crying as he walked to the main road, the chocolate bar in his hand. A car stopped and he explained what had happened.

Somewhere during the tears and screams of that afternoon and evening, with friends and neighbours coming and going and the realisation that his father wasn't coming back, Donald decided that he would keep the bar of chocolate, that he would never eat it.

All evening he sat on a chair with the chocolate bar on his knee beneath the oak tree where his father used to rock him when he was little, and gradually a dreadful realisation took root inside him.

He had somehow managed to accept that he would never see his father again. That his father as a living person could no longer mean anything to him. But what was even worse was that Donald no longer meant anything to his father. His father's eyes could no longer see him, because the light in them had died. On some essential level, Donald had ceased to exist. He sat on the chair beneath the oak tree and grew lighter and more transparent as his very being disintegrated and dissolved.

That night he lay in his bed staring up at the ceiling, listening to his mother sobbing in the room next door. He got up and fetched the bar of chocolate.

Carefully he removed the wrapper, then stood for a long time contemplating the rectangular block divided into squares as it began to melt in his hands. He broke off big pieces and stuffed them into his mouth, chewing and swallowing as fast as he could.

He remained standing in the middle of the room for a minute or so as the heavy lump grew in his belly, then he went to the outside toilet and threw up.

*

Carina, Emil, Peter, Lennart and Olof have gathered around the caravan as Stefan slowly gets to his feet on the roof. He seems shaken rather than hurt as he looks down at the assembled company; he raises his mobile phone like a trophy and says: 'I got through! I spoke to my mother.'

A grimace of pain passes across his face, and only Carina knows him well enough to suspect the reason. 'So what did she say? How's Bengt?'

The look Stefan gives her is answer enough. She is about to ask for more details, but Peter pre-empts her; he strides forward, and in a second he is on top of the roof standing next to Stefan. He fishes out his iPhone and looks at the screen, shakes his head. 'Nothing.'

'You have to be higher up,' Stefan explains. 'I stood on a chair. It gives you just enough of a signal.' He holds out his phone. 'And of course I've got this.'

Peter glances from his own brand-new iPhone to Stefan's Nokia. A Bugatti versus a Volvo 240. But old phones often have better reception, so Peter reaches out. 'May I...?'

Stefan shakes his head. 'The battery runs down in no time. If we're going to make calls, we have to be sure we can get through.'

'And how do we do that?'

Stefan looks at the sky. 'We need to be higher up.'

Both men stare at the sky as if they are waiting for a rope ladder to drop down. Lennart clears his throat and steps forward, raising a hand as if asking for permission to speak.

'Excuse me,' he says to Stefan. 'You said you spoke to your mother?'

'Yes.'

148

'And she could hear you?'

'Yes.'

'Thank you,' Lennart says. 'That's all.' Olof looks at him enquiringly, and Lennart shrugs. There is a brief pause as everyone considers the implications of this new state of affairs. Emil presses his body close to Carina and whispers: 'Can we go home soon, Mummy?'

*

One of the secrets to a good cinnamon bun is the *rolling*. How thin you can make the dough before you spread it with the mixture of butter and spices before rolling it up. Normally it is rolled four or five times, in a patisserie sometimes six. Majvor's cinnamon buns are rolled seven times.

The children never needed to feel embarrassed in school when they were asked to bring in homemade cakes to sell at some event. Majvor's buns always disappeared in no time. People with no skill in baking have no idea why these particular buns are so light and delicious, but those in the know raise their eyebrows and say: 'Seven, Majvor? How do you manage that?'

Skill with the rolling pin, that's all there is to it. The perfect balance between applying and releasing pressure. Plus of course lots of butter in the dough so that it doesn't stick to the worktop in spite of its thinness.

This is a concern at the moment. The kitchen worktops are a decent size for a caravan, but if Majvor is going to make a large batch of buns, she is going to have to divide the dough into seven or eight pieces and roll out each one separately, which to be honest would be a *hell* of a lot of trouble.

She has gone through the cupboards and laid out her ingredients. Flour, milk, sugar, yeast, butter, cinnamon and cardamom. Bowl, rolling pin, wooden spoon, dough scraper. The oven is also reasonably large, and she will probably be able to bake the buns in two batches. Only the work surface is lacking.

How many times have Majvor's good intentions been derailed by irritating deficiencies in her surroundings? If she had ten kronor for each one, she would be rich by now!

Come on, kids, let's build a snowman. The wrong kind of snow. *Donald, look at this lovely sweater I've bought you.* Too tight around the neck. *I've made muffins—I thought we could all have a lovely cosy evening together.* Everyone has other plans. *Wasn't that delicious?* No idea, I've got a cold.

And so on and so on.

Majvor stands in the middle of the caravan clenching her fists. Donald is still hunched on the sofa, his lips moving. Ridiculous man. Majvor remembers a letter he wrote her in the long-distant past. His final words were: 'You are my dream.' Who would have thought they would end up like this?

She wipes a tear from the corner of her eye. What Donald has said is pure *arrogance*, claiming that Majvor is not a real person, but merely a figment of his imagination. Who has brought up his children, run his household, washed his clothes and suffered through something like forty Åsa-Nisse films in the darkness of the cinema? A fantasy figure?

Majvor stares at Donald's bald head, allegedly the only place she exists. Then her eyes drift to the rolling pin. She could…

No, Majvor.

She draws a big cross through the picture, deletes it. The cross changes slightly, turns into the one on the outside of their caravan, on all four caravans.

Delete.

'Donald, can you move please?'

'Why?'

'I'm going to do some baking.'

'You're going to do some baking?'

'Yes, I'm going to do some baking.'

'Why?'

Sometimes Majvor feels so very tired. It seems as if she has spent *years* of her life having this kind of conversation. She sharpens her voice, finding the stern tone she so seldom uses: 'Donald. Move. Now.'

Donald may well regard her as non-existent at the moment, but he knows when she is serious. He mutters something, gets to his feet and goes and sits on the bed.

Right.

Majvor clears the table, which gives her a surface of approximately one square metre as she hums the Mona Wessman song she heard on the radio earlier. Now everything is as it should be. She is busy in her kitchen, making something nice for everyone to share. Not that anyone will thank her, but she's used to that. Her role is to nourish and nurture and care for others. People are just small children, when it comes down to it.

And no child refuses Majvor's cinnamon buns!

*

The group around Stefan's caravan has drifted away. Stefan and Peter have climbed down from the roof and are discussing the best way to construct something which will give them extra height. Lennart and Olof are heading back to their caravan.

'That question you asked,' Olof says. 'About his mother. Why did you do that?'

'Because it's strange. It means we are somewhere after all.'

'Didn't we think we were?'

'Well, no, I didn't,' Lennart says. 'Did you?'

Olof stops, his brow furrowed. After a while he says: 'No, I don't suppose I did, come to think of it.'

'No. But now…' Lennart gestures towards the open field. 'Now anything could happen. Perhaps it was a good idea to set out those canes after all.'

'But probably not.'

'Probably not, as you say. But we can't be sure.'

'Exactly.'

Lennart goes inside, while Olof checks on their experiment. This is completely pointless; it can't be more than ten minutes since they planted and sowed. In certain cases plants can react quickly to a change of soil, but not this quickly.

And yet...Isn't the colour of the pelargonium leaves a little darker? Under normal circumstances a plant will wilt slightly until it has recovered from the shock of moving, but that doesn't seem to apply here.

Olof is about to hunker down to examine the pelargonium more closely when Lennart pokes his head out and whispers: 'Psst. We've got a visitor.'

The visitor in question is Molly. She is curled up on the sofa and appears to be asleep. Lennart and Olof stand side by side, gazing down at her. In their scruffy caravan she seems like an elf who has strayed into the kingdom of the trolls and fallen asleep—indescribably cute.

The trolls themselves have no idea what to do. Lennart and Olof look at one another, whispering about the best course of action to take. Should they let the child sleep and tell her parents where she is, or wake her up? In the midst of their deliberations Molly sits up and makes a great show of rubbing her eyes. 'I fell asleep,' she says in a very small voice.

'That's all right,' Olof says. 'As long as your parents don't start worrying.'

Lennart glances around the caravan. 'What are you doing in here, by the way?'

'I'm just wandering around,' Molly says. 'Checking things out. I felt sleepy. I'll go home now.'

There is a faint rustling sound as she gets up. She is about to walk past the two farmers, but Lennart holds out his hand and stops her.

'Hang on,' he says. 'What have you got under your T-shirt?'

'Nothing.'

Lennart sighs and nods in the direction of the worktop so that Olof will understand what is going on. The half-full packet of sweets has gone. Molly tries to push past, but Lennart moves in front of her.

'Give us back our sweets, then you can go.'

Molly stares at him with big, frightened eyes and says: 'Help.'

'I won't say anything to your mum and dad,' Lennart goes on, 'but I want those sweets back.'

Molly opens her eyes even wider and says it again, louder this time: 'Help!'

Olof realises what Molly is playing at, and he doesn't know what scares him the most: what she is trying to do, or the fact that such a young child could think of such a thing. He is about to say that she can go, that they can manage without the sweets, but Lennart's grim expression stops him.

'Don't even think about it,' Lennart says. 'Your father saw us come in here a few seconds ago.' His tone sharpens and he repeats: 'Don't even think about it!'

Molly's expression changes as she faces up to Lennart, each taking the measure of the other. Then she shrugs and sits back down on the sofa, with more rustling. She rests her chin on her hands and contemplates the two men.

'Why do you live together?' she asks.

Lennart's mouth is set in a thin, angry line, and he doesn't answer. Olof also thinks that was a nasty trick on Molly's part, but perhaps she was frightened and turned to desperate measures. 'Because we get on well,' he says.

'Do you get on *really* well?' Molly asks, tilting her head to one side.

'Enough,' Lennart says. 'Put the sweets on the table, then go.'

Molly gazes at him for a couple of seconds, then says: 'I think you do. I think you get on *really* well.'

'Yes, we do,' Olof replies. 'What about it?'

Molly turns her attention to Olof. 'Shall we play a game?'

Lennart sighs. 'I think I'd better go and fetch your father.'

'No, don't do that. I might say something that would make him cross. Let's play a game instead.'

Lennart and Olof stay exactly where they are. Neither of them has ever encountered a child like Molly. It's like facing a completely different species, whose behaviour and instincts are totally unpredictable. Molly brings both palms down on the table, then waves to the chairs opposite her.

'Come along!' She lets out a theatrical sigh. 'We'll have a little competition. If I win I get to keep what I've got—if I have got something. Then I'll go home.'

Some of the tension in Lennart's body eases. The creature in front of him might be strange, but it probably isn't dangerous. 'That doesn't sound like much of a deal,' he says. 'What do we win?'

'You get what I've got, obviously. And I won't tell anyone that you two get on really really well.'

'You're welcome to tell people that we get on well,' Olof says. 'It's not a secret.'

Molly pulls a face and holds up one hand, fingers outspread. 'We're going to play scissors, paper, stone. And I have to win five times.'

'Best of five?' Lennart asks.

'No, five times in a row. Then I win. Otherwise you win.'

Olof can't help smiling. He wouldn't necessarily describe Lennart as competitive, but he does find it difficult to resist a challenge. He's also very good at scissors, paper, stone, insofar as it is possible to be good at it. He and Olof used to play the game when they had different views on how a problem should be addressed, but Olof refused to carry on when he realised that Lennart won three times out of four.

'Okay,' Lennart says, sitting down opposite Molly. 'Let's do it.'

Molly points to Olof. 'You're the referee.'

Olof moves over to the table. Lennart and Molly raise and lower their clenched fists in time, chanting: 'One, two, *three*!'

Lennart has paper. Molly has scissors.

'One, two, *three*!'

Lennart has paper. Molly has scissors.

'One, two, *three*!'

Lennart has stone. Molly has paper. Lennart licks his lips and

154

clears his throat, straightens his back.

'One, two, *three*!'

Lennart has paper. Molly has scissors. Four–nil. 'Come on, Lennart!' Olof says, but Lennart's eyes are locked on Molly's, and he doesn't seem to hear.

'One, two, *three*!'

Lennart has stone. Molly has paper. She says it out loud—'I've got paper'—upon which she removes the bag of Twist sweets from underneath her T-shirt and places it on the table. She takes one out, unwraps it and pops it in her mouth. Lennart scratches the back of his neck and says: 'Well, I'll be…'

'Mmm,' Molly says with her mouth full of caramel. She chews for a little while, then points at Olof and mumbles indistinctly: 'You too.'

'What?'

'You play too.'

Irrespective of whether or not there is anything to win, Olof can't help being fascinated by Molly's self-confidence in what is basically a game of chance. He wouldn't mind having a go; it would wind Lennart up, if nothing else.

Lennart is about to get up and make room for Olof, but Molly waves her hand, indicating that he should move along the sofa. Olof slips into his usual seat. It feels odd to have Lennart next to him instead of opposite. Molly nods; she finishes off her caramel and swallows.

'Both,' she says.

'What do you mean?' Olof asks.

Molly holds up both hands, fingers outspread. 'You use one hand each. I use both.'

Lennart and Olof extend their right hands, fists clenched, and Molly keeps her hands wide apart, one in front of each of the farmers. Four hands bang on the table three times, and they're off. Molly's right hand is scissors to Lennart's paper. Her left hand is paper to Olof's stone.

They do it again. And again. After the fifth time it is like a ritual incantation, as if they are in a trance: 'One, two, *three*!', 'One, two, *three*!'

They play ten times. Molly wins every hand, twenty matches. There isn't even a single draw. Molly takes another caramel and pops it in her mouth, then picks up the bag and gets to her feet. Before she leaves the caravan she says: 'You have to be nice to me. Now do you get it?'

*

Stefan and Peter have drawn a sketch on the back of an old receipt. The structure they want to build resembles the kind of tower used in the forest when hunting elk, and should serve its purpose—to bear the weight of a person high enough in the air to get a stable mobile phone signal.

As far as they know, no one has a hammer or nails, so Stefan has come up with a system of knots that will tighten when pressure is applied; he used the same idea when he built a little cabin for Emil, and didn't want any nails around.

There is, however, a weakness in their plan: the material itself. The only planks of wood in the camp are the ones that make up the floor of Donald's awning. There has been no sign of Donald since Majvor pointed out the crosses, and they have no idea what mood he is in. That's the key question.

Stefan and Peter have spent ages on their plan, and have had a lovely time. What they haven't talked about, however, is the purpose of the tower: who they are going to call. Stefan has an idea, quite a strange idea, and he is about to share it with Peter when Carina comes over to them.

'Can you look after Emil?' she says to Stefan.

'Of course, but why?'

As if she is talking about popping out for a newspaper, she replies: 'I'm just taking the car for a little while.'

Stefan is going to ask, 'Where are you going?', but realises that the question is meaningless. There is nowhere to go out here except everywhere, so instead he asks: 'Why?'

'There's nothing out there,' Peter chips in.

'Sorry,' Carina says, looking searchingly at Peter, 'but I'm afraid I don't believe that.'

*

'What are you doing, Mummy?'

Isabelle is sitting at the kitchen table with a bottle of whisky and a glass. When Molly comes into the caravan, Isabelle picks up the glass and knocks back the last few drops.

'I haven't got anything sweet, so I'm drinking this crap instead to get some sugar.'

Molly sits down opposite her mother with exaggerated care. She is pretending to be scared, but in fact she is trying to make sure the bag of sweets doesn't rustle.

'So,' Isabelle says, slurring slightly. She's not exactly drunk, but the whisky has had a rapid effect on her hungry body. 'Did you find anything out? About what your friend saw?'

'He's not my friend. Can I play on the computer?'

Isabelle's eyes narrow, her lips tighten. 'Are you trying to do a deal?'

Molly shrugs and Isabelle takes down her laptop from the shelf, runs her hand over the surface and says: 'Ten minutes.'

'Twenty.'

'We can't charge the battery. When it runs out, that's it. Do you understand? Ten minutes.'

'Fifteen.'

Isabelle sighs. 'Okay, fifteen. If you have something to tell me, that is. About whether he saw anything.'

'He did.'

'And what was it?'

'A man.'

Molly reaches for the computer, but Isabelle moves it away. 'What kind of a *man*, Molly? Tell me, for heaven's sake!'

Molly rolls her eyes. 'He saw a man out on the field—he was completely white and he was thin and he moved in a funny way and he looked like a person but somehow he didn't.'

Isabelle doesn't protest as Molly grabs the laptop and opens it up. Isabelle's jaw has dropped and her eyes are wide open.

White and thin and looked like a person. Out on the field.

Isabelle can see the image, she can see it very clearly, because she has seen it before. The music from 'Plants vs. Zombies' starts to play on her computer. Molly's index finger moves over the touchpad and her thumb clicks on the command button as she captures suns and arranges flowers as protection against the zombies who are trying to invade her garden.

Suddenly Isabelle gets up and goes outside. When Molly is sure that she has gone, she retrieves the bag of sweets and pauses the game as she unwraps a slightly gooey chocolate and pops it into her mouth before playing on.

*

Carina is surprised by her own ruthlessness as she slips behind the wheel and closes the car door. It's as if she is on her way to a vitally important meeting, and mustn't be late.

To fly. Into the sun.

There is something she doesn't understand. A movement inside her, like troops relocating under cover of darkness. She *knows* that something is going on, but can't decide if it involves enemies or reinforcements, destruction or redemption. It could also be a group of civilians without any particular significance, but something is on the move.

She is about to turn the key when she hears someone tapping on the window. She sighs when she sees Isabelle standing there. *What does the stupid cow want now?* She considers ignoring her, starting the car and driving off. Then again, perhaps it's about the gas hose. She really would like it back, so she winds down the window. 'Yes?'

Isabelle's eyes rake over the car. 'Are you going somewhere?'

Her expression is slightly glazed, and when Carina picks up the smell of alcohol on her breath, she realises why.

'Yes. Why?'

Isabelle nods in the direction of the instrument panel. 'You don't have GPS.'

'No,' Carina says, imitating Isabelle's earlier response as she adds: '*And?*'

Isabelle doesn't appear to notice the sarcasm; instead she simply states: 'You won't be able to find your way back.'

'I'm sorry, but what's it got to do with you?'

Carina doesn't think she could sound any more off-putting, but for some reason Isabelle doesn't move a muscle; her expression doesn't change at all. All becomes clear when she points to the black SUV.

'We could take our car,' she says. 'That one.'

'*We?*'

'Yes. You and me.'

'You can go on your own. Unless you're afraid of getting picked up by the cops, of course.'

Isabelle shakes her head. 'I don't have a driving licence.'

'What does that matter out here?'

Isabelle makes a vague, limp-wristed gesture, tucks a strand of hair behind her ear. Carina suspects she knows the truth, and milks the situation for a moment longer before she says, in a voice oozing with fake sympathy: 'You can't drive, can you?'

Something nasty flickers in Isabelle's eyes, but she shrugs and says: 'No.'

Carina gazes out across the field. Her plan was to drive in the same direction as one line of canes, but with GPS it would be possible to check out a different route. On the other hand—Isabelle. She considers the pros and cons, and eventually gets out of the car.

Isabelle holds out one of those keys that you don't actually have to insert in the ignition. Carina takes it and says: 'Maybe we won't need to talk much.'

'Maybe we should,' Isabelle responds as they walk over to the car. 'We could have a real girls' outing.'

Her tone of voice has regained most of its earlier sarcasm, and Carina is already wishing she could change her mind.

*

As Carina and Isabelle get into the Toyota and start the engine, Peter remembers the sweets that are still in his pocket. The car moves off and he starts to run after it, then stops and watches as it grows smaller.

She's not your wife any more.

The actual divorce will be messy, with papers and lawyers and a whole load of crap, but as far as Peter is concerned it is already a reality, because he has made the decision. He is no longer Isabelle's servant. He doesn't have to do anything she asks him to do, he doesn't need to care about her wellbeing, and he doesn't have to give her any sweets if he doesn't want to.

He can hear how childish his thoughts sound, but they excite him, and he laughs to himself as he takes out a sweet, removes it from the wrapping with his teeth and begins to chew.

Yumyumyum.

This is the sword slicing through the Gordian knot, the apple falling before Newton's eyes, the long putt dropping into the hole. One small event that changes everything. *Not being with Isabelle.* Being free. Peter feels like clapping his hands at his own cleverness. Life stretches ahead of him, wide open like the field, and he realises that he is starting to get a hard-on. The thought of going to bed with someone who *wants* to go to bed with him, to lie in someone's arms, to thrust into…

'Peter?'

He hears Stefan's voice behind him and forces himself to think of roadkill. Squashed badgers, foxes with their guts hanging out. It works, and after a few seconds he is able to turn around without covering his crotch as if he is about to face a free kick. He waves the sketch in the air: 'Okay, shall we go and speak to Donald?'

Stefan glances towards the field; his wife is no longer in sight. 'I've got an idea,' he says gloomily. 'About who we can call.'

They walk towards Donald's caravan, and Peter waits for him to go on. He is clearly in need of some encouragement, so Peter says: 'Great—who?'

'It's a bit weird.'

Peter waves his arm towards the vast expanse of grass. 'Can't be any weirder than this. Tell me.'

Stefan stops a couple of metres from Donald's caravan, takes a deep breath, then says: 'I think we should call the campsite. Where we were.'

'Because…'

'Because then we can check if we're still there.'

Stefan looks at Peter as if he is expecting a dismissive laugh, but Peter is not laughing. He has been thinking along the same lines himself, but without formulating the concrete idea of calling the campsite. The possibility makes his head spin.

'And if we are there? As well as here? What do we do then?'

'Haven't a clue,' Stefan says. 'But it might be helpful to…have access to that information. If that's the case.'

For a long time they stand and look at one another, at the field, at the caravans. What if Molly is bouncing up and down on the trampoline right now while Isabelle texts her agent, and Peter, the other Peter, the real Peter…

'I can't think about that right now,' says the Peter who is here at the moment.

'Nor me, actually,' Stefan agrees.

Together they step inside Donald's awning, where the radio is still switched on. Peter picks up the piece of paper on which Majvor has made a list of all the songs that have been played.

'It's Beginning to Seem Like Love', 'Keep to the Right, Svensson', 'You Know Where I Am'. And so on.

The artists are many and varied. Towa Carson, Rock-Boris, Jan Sparring, Mona Wessman and Hasse Burman, among others. But thanks to his mother's taste in music, Peter can see a common denominator.

Stefan is about to knock on the door when Peter says: 'Have you heard of Peter Himmelstrand?'

Stefan frowns at this apparently irrelevant question. 'Wasn't he the one…who smoked himself to death? And wrote about it?'

'Yes, although he was a songwriter too.' Peter points to the sheet of paper. 'It looks as if these are the songs that have been on the radio. He wrote every single one.' Peter nods at the radio, from which Hasse Burman's spiky Norrland tones can be heard. 'Including this one.'

It is a song about Stockholmers, how they should all be shot with specially poisoned gunpowder, or sprayed with DDT to get rid of them all.

'Not exactly overflowing with the milk of human kindness,' Stefan says.

'Not really. But don't you think it's strange?'

Stefan looks at the little box, from which Hasse Burman continues to hurl abuse at the residents of the capital city. Then he shrugs: 'The strange thing is that the radio is broadcasting. At all.' Then he knocks on the door.

*

Donald is sitting on the bed and suffering. There has to be an end to this soon, otherwise he fears for his sanity. The temperature inside the caravan has begun to rise since Majvor switched on the oven, and the mere sound of her humming as she messes about with her cinnamon buns is enough to drive a person crazy.

He longs to be back in the lumberyard, moving among his seven employees and making sure that everything is running smoothly, chatting to a regular customer who doesn't like to deal with anyone except Donald, helping out a new arrival who wants to replace his guttering.

He usually values his holidays—he has no problem with sitting around and doing nothing for a few weeks, drinking beer and catching up with old friends, letting the days slip by. Recharging his batteries while the yard runs itself and the money comes rolling in during the high season for DIY enthusiasts, hallelujah.

But this. What's all this?

Donald interlaces his sweaty fingers, his head slumping between his shoulders. He closes his eyes and silently begins to count. When he gets to one hundred he will open his eyes and everything will be back to normal. Otherwise he doesn't know what he's going to do.

Ninety-eight, ninety-nine. One hundred.

Donald opens his eyes. The oven is humming away, blowing yet more heat into the caravan. The satin coverlet on the bed is sweaty and slippery beneath his thighs. Majvor is creaming butter and spices on a plate. A whining sound passes Donald's ear, and for a second he thinks it is the dentist's drill of insanity boring into his skull.

But it's a mosquito. A real live mosquito. It hovers above his linked hands before landing on the back of his right hand; it pierces the skin with its proboscis and begins to suck. Slowly Donald brings his hand up to eye level and studies the insect.

There is something unsettling about this detail of his dream, because it is so ordinary compared to everything else that has happened; a visitor from the real world, its rear end bobbing up and down as it pumps blood from Donald's system into its own.

Something flickers before Donald's eyes like the brief darkness between two slides, and it seems to him that the mosquito is the protagonist here, the subject. That he, Majvor, the caravans and the field are just part of the mosquito's dream. He dare not pursue that thought; instead he forces his mind back to the original image.

A mosquito. Here.

It must have been hidden away in some corner, and now it's woken up, gone hunting. With great success! The rear half of its body is now swollen like a balloon, and through the thin skin Donald can see the drop of his own blood which is now the property of the mosquito.

If he raised his left hand and slapped it down, the whole enterprise would be for nothing. Instead of a happy, successful mosquito there would be nothing but a sticky smear. He has the power.

There is an empty schnapps glass on the window ledge next to Donald. As the sated mosquito slowly begins to withdraw its proboscis, Donald captures it beneath the glass. He holds the glass in place with two fingers as the mosquito makes a couple of vain attempts to escape, then it resigns itself to the situation and once again settles down to rest on Donald's skin, the back of its body heavy with blood. He glances over towards the kitchen area and sees that Majvor is now greasing baking trays, and is taking no notice of him. He is free to have a little fun.

On the back of Donald's hand is a little bloodsucking terrorist, an invader into his kingdom. Or perhaps…Perhaps! The omnipotent God whose dream we are all a part of. Or simply another creature in Donald's power. Whatever.

Think of the decisions one must make as president. Sending troops to kill and be killed. Giving the go-ahead for this or that air strike, where this or that number of civilians could be killed. Should we secretly liquidate this spy? Yes or no? Thumb up or thumb down?

When there is emptiness all around us, and everything else has fallen away, it boils down to this and this alone: I have a life and you have a life, however different they may be. The question is: who has the power?

Donald brings the glass as close to his eyes as possible without losing focus, and studies the miracle of nature that a single mosquito actually is. The precision in the fragile limbs, the almost invisible membrane of the wings, the tiny head turning from side to side as if questioning, wondering.

You and me, Donald thinks. *You and me.*

For a moment Donald sees himself and the mosquito as two equals on the earth. He picks up a playing card and carefully slides it under the glass, then turns the glass over and places it back on the window ledge with the card as a lid. The mosquito's legs scrabble at the smooth walls; it makes an attempt to fly, then settles on the bottom of the glass once more.

Donald scratches the back of his hand, where a faint redness is beginning to appear. He stands up and his perspective shifts. On the window ledge is a glass containing a drop of his blood, enclosed within an alien.

My blood.

He rubs his eyes; he can't really remember what he's been thinking about over the last few minutes. What it's like to be the president, perhaps. To be the one who decides. That's what he usually thinks about, so it's a reasonable assumption.

The president's blood.

There is something radically wrong about this whole situation. As soon as he manages to gather his thoughts, he's going to do something about it, but first of all...

With another glance at Majvor, who is still busy with her baking, Donald takes a lighter out of a drawer full of bits and pieces. He sits back down on the bed, then presses the button and brings the flame close to the glass. After a couple of seconds the mosquito starts to move.

In a desperate frenzy it rushes around the enclosed space, and Donald smiles as the drop of his blood catapults between the glass walls, until it lands on the bottom as the mosquito lies there with its wings burnt off. One of its legs waves helplessly as smoke rises from its body, then it is still. Donald extinguishes the lighter and nods.

That's the way it goes. Be under no illusions.

There is a knock on the door. Majvor looks enquiringly at Donald and he shakes his head. He doesn't want to engage with any more figments of his imagination; he just wants to be left in peace.

When the knock comes again, Majvor says: 'Enough of this nonsense, Donald. Open the door.'

Donald runs a hand over his breast pocket and feels the key. At that point a very simple idea comes into his mind. Strange that he didn't think of it before; habit, no doubt.

When Majvor comes over to him and says, 'Give me the key,' he grabs hold of her arm, gets to his feet and drags her along behind him. With his free hand he unlocks the door and flings it open. He catches sight of Stefan and Peter outside, opening their mouths to talk, talk, talk, then he pushes Majvor outside, slams the door and locks it.

There you go. Peace at last. He places his ear to the door to listen to what they are saying out there, *what they are saying in his dream, in his imagination.*

*

However close Stefan thinks he and Carina are, however intertwined their lives might be, there is something of the stranger about her, something he cannot reach. She never wants to talk about her childhood or youth; she is like a film where he has missed the beginning, and therefore cannot understand certain parts of the action.

He knows that this is to do with darker elements than the eternity symbols on her arm and the longing for a love that will last. There was a hunger in her eyes when she said she was taking the car, a hunger that is alien to him.

And his father is dying. As the key turns in the door in front of him, Stefan thinks that everything is being taken away from him, and he doesn't know what he can do about it. Then he has other things to think about.

The door is flung open, and before Stefan or Peter have the chance to speak, Majvor comes tumbling out. They catch a glimpse of Donald's florid face before he slams the door. Peter reacts quickly and catches Majvor before she falls headfirst to the ground.

The lock turns. Peter helps Majvor to her feet and asks: 'What happened?'

Majvor pushes a few strands of sweaty grey hair out of her face and says: 'My buns.' She staggers forward and hammers on the door, shouting: 'Donald! The buns need to go in the oven in ten minutes—I don't want them to over-prove!'

There is no response from inside the caravan, and Majvor turns to Peter and Stefan. 'I was making cinnamon buns.'

'Right,' the two men say simultaneously. There is a brief silence. Majvor moves to pat the dog, who is lying in his basket and watching them, but changes her mind.

'I'm sorry—was there something you wanted?'

'The thing is…' Peter says, his eyes taking in the wooden flooring before he explains about the poor mobile phone reception, the need to get higher up. Majvor listens and nods. When Peter has finished describing the tower they hope to build, she says: 'That's all very interesting, but what can I do?'

'We need wood,' Stefan says, nodding towards the floor. 'And the only planks of wood around are…these.'

Majvor seems taken aback as she stares at the teak floorboards. No doubt she has never thought of them as anything other than the floor of their awning; the fact that they are also planks of wood that could be used to build something else has probably never occurred to her. 'You mean you want to…?'

'Take it up, that's right,' Stefan says.

Peter places a hand on Majvor's shoulder, and in a tone that implies he is revealing a great secret, he says: 'But we can put it back together. Afterwards.'

Majvor glances towards the caravan. When no guidance is forthcoming from that direction, she looks at the dog, who tilts his head on one side and pricks up one ear, as if he too is waiting for her decision.

'Well,' she says. 'That…that's fine.'

'Excellent,' Peter says, whipping out his pocketknife. He finds the Phillips screwdriver and hunkers down. The screws securing the boards are short, and he needs only a few turns to remove the first one. He passes it to Stefan, who puts it in his breast pocket before changing his mind and slipping it into his trouser pocket instead. There will be a lot of screws.

Or not. As Peter begins to undo the second screw, the caravan door flies open with a crash that makes the dog leap out of his basket in terror. Donald is standing there holding a shotgun, which is pointing at them.

'Leave my fucking floor alone!' he yells, waving the barrel of the gun. 'Fuck off!'

Peter slowly gets to his feet, hands in the air. He clasps the knife between his thumb and forefinger so that he can show Donald an empty palm. 'Donald,' he says with exaggerated calm, 'we need the planks to build a...'

'I heard what you said.' Donald raises the gun to his shoulder so that he can take aim properly. 'It's not happening. Now fuck off!'

The dog is the first to obey Donald's order. With his tail between his legs he slinks out of the awning as Peter and Stefan back away. Only Majvor remains where she is; in fact she takes a step towards her husband. 'Donald. Pull yourself together. Put down the gun.'

This is the first time Stefan has been threatened with a firearm, and he doesn't take his eyes off the barrel of the gun. There is something hypnotic about that dark hole, the black eye of the snake determined to paralyse him before the fatal strike. The cramp in his legs eases slightly as the barrel shifts towards Majvor, and Stefan turns his head a fraction just to check that he really is on his way to the exit.

He is. The dog is standing a couple of metres outside, gazing up at him. Their eyes meet. Then a shot rings out.

*

Molly's fifteen minutes on the computer are almost up when she hears the bang. The only reaction this provokes is a raised eyebrow before she places the final flower and brings down the last of the zombies on that level.

She wrinkles her nose and looks bored as the next level begins. She exits the game and clicks on the computer's battery saver. It is set so that the laptop goes into sleep mode when it hasn't been used for ten minutes. Molly alters the setting so that it never goes into sleep mode, then leaves the laptop open on the table.

She wanders over to the sink, turns on the tap and spends a little while staring at the running water. Then she goes to the bathroom and turns on the shower, flushes the toilet a couple of times.

The flow of water has already begun to slow down by the time she clambers up onto the kitchen worktop and rests her hands and forehead against the plexiglas, staring out across the field in the direction Carina and Isabelle took.

'Come on then,' she whispers. 'Come now.'

*

Emil hears the bang and assumes that someone has a puncture. He had one once, and it sounded very similar. He doesn't bother to investigate; he is far too busy with the story in front of him, the tale of the Lego fortress.

Molly has a way of saying stuff so that it sounds real, and Emil has to make up his own narrative to counter hers. For example, she said that creatures wanting blood would soon come, and that Emil would bleed and bleed.

Emil knows that this isn't really true, but it *feels* true, and therefore he has put himself inside a story where there are high, strong walls and a good defence. There are three people inside the fortress: Emil and Mummy and Daddy.

Outside there is a skeleton Lego man, and Emil makes him bang his head against the wall as he says: 'Let me in. Give me blood.'

'Ha ha,' say the occupants of the fortress. 'You will never get in here, you stupid bloodsucker, you stupid...' Emil searches for the right phrase: '...bag of bones!'

The skeleton gets angry and starts picking up pieces of Lego, which he hurls at the fortress, growling. But the walls hold. The skeleton jumps up and down, gnashing his teeth.

Emil frowns. This isn't what Molly said was going to happen. He can't quite remember what she said, but he thinks they were going to *give away* their blood to whoever came. Voluntarily.

That doesn't fit in with the game, so instead the skeleton carries on throwing himself at the wall until his head falls off. Emil bursts out laughing. That's what's going to happen. That's the way it will be.

*

Lennart and Olof have dug out their old primus stove and are in the process of filling it up so that they can make a decent cup of coffee when they hear the gunshot. They immediately stop what they are doing, because they know exactly what it is.

Maud slides out through the door ahead of them as though she too wants to see what is going on, but in fact it is something else that has caught her attention. The beagle is on guard just a few metres away from his caravan, and Maud keeps going until she is about ten metres away from the dog. Then she sits down and hisses at him.

Lennart and Olof are hurrying over when Peter, Stefan and Majvor emerge from the awning. Majvor's eyes are wide open, and one hand is resting on her heart.

'What's happened?' Lennart calls out. 'Is anyone hurt?'

Majvor moves her hand to cover her mouth. There is no sign of blood on her blouse, so presumably she is simply in shock. When Lennart and Olof reach her, they can see that this is the case. She stares at them, takes her hand away from her mouth and whispers: 'He…he shot at me.'

Olof can see that the caravan door is closed. Cautiously he edges forward and peers into the awning. Everything looks just as it did the last time he was there. No. There's one difference. The photograph of Elvis Presley is lying on the floor. The glass is broken, and there is a hole in Elvis's cheek. When Olof examines the awning itself, he finds another hole there.

What an idiot. Firing a gun when there are people around.

He goes back to the others; Stefan and Peter have moved Majvor a safe distance away, and sat her down on the ground. In his peripheral vision Olof can see Maud and the dog running around in circles.

170

'We wanted to borrow a few planks of wood to build a tower so that we could pick up a mobile phone signal,' Peter explains. 'And then Donald appeared with a shotgun. He…' Peter checks that Majvor isn't looking at him, then points to his temple, rotating his forefinger.

His discretion is unnecessary, because Majvor says exactly what he is thinking: 'He's gone mad. Completely mad. He's convinced all this is a dream.'

*

His master is very cross, and when that is the case, Benny never knows quite what to do to make sure he doesn't take it out on him. Cat is better. Cat is weird, but manageable. Cat makes her noise and Benny barks. Cat runs around in circles and Benny runs after her. Or in front of her.

No. Benny is absolutely not being chased by Cat! He puts on a burst of speed to reduce the distance between them and to show who is the hunter. Cat races across the grass and shakes her head, her tail swishing to and fro.

Benny has temporarily forgotten the claws and the swipe across his nose. He is gaining on Cat, and it's a wonderful sensation. He is a good dog, a fast dog, and he feels neither dizzy nor tired as he gradually gets closer and closer to that long, waving tail. This time he's going to catch Cat!

Suddenly something unexpected happens. Cat stumbles and falls, rolling over on the grass. Before she can get to her feet, Benny is standing over her, growling and showing his teeth as a drop of saliva trickles from his jaws.

Cat flattens her body, folds back her ears, curls up. Benny is ready to sink his teeth into the back of her neck, put an end to this. He draws back his lips, showing his teeth even more, still growling. Cat turns her head to one side, exposing her throat.

Benny is confused. This doesn't feel right. He licks his lips and lets out a short bark. Then he lifts one paw and brings it down on Cat's belly. But not hard.

Cat raises her head and hits him across the nose, but without claws. Benny whimpers, but he's kind of joking. It didn't hurt. He doesn't really know what to do next, so he turns around a couple of times then plonks his bottom down. Cat sits up. They look at one another.

Cat starts to wash herself, and Benny sniffs the air. It is very clear now—the Grandchildren are getting closer. Benny wonders whether Cat is aware of this too. He can't tell by looking at her, and he doesn't know how to ask.

*

When Molly told Isabelle about the thin, white figure Emil had seen out on the field, Isabelle understood why she had ended up here. She was twenty-three when she saw the figure for the first and so far only time, and since then she has been waiting to see it again. On that occasion, she wasn't ready.

Is she ready now? Yes, she's ready now.

Isabelle had just met a football player called Peter, and they had spent a few nights together before he had to go back to Italy and Lazio. They had said they would keep in touch, but Isabelle didn't really care. Her main focus was on her career, and at the age of twenty-three she had reached her peak. She didn't know that at the time; she just thought she had taken a huge step up.

H&M's summer collection. First the show itself, to be followed no doubt by the advertising campaign.

Isabelle had served her time on the catwalks of Milan and Paris; she had been on the cover of *Femina* and could be regarded as well-established, but without that final push that made her a *name*. The summer collections could change all that.

The salons at Berns Hotel in Stockholm had been booked for the event, and in the hours leading up to the show Isabelle was in a contradictory state of intoxication and sharp focus. She felt one hundred per cent present in the moment, while at the same time the edges of her existence were dissolving. As if it were someone *else* who was in the moment.

She was sharing a dressing area with her sidekicks, three younger girls. She gossiped and sparkled while the final adjustments were made to the one-off pieces she would be modelling. When no one was looking at her, she glanced furtively around the room. There was something there, something she couldn't quite catch sight of. Or at least it felt that way. The hum of a machine, a pressure inside her skull. She dismissed it as nerves.

She was ready. The final unnecessary stitch at her waistline, the final unnecessary dab with the powder puff, ritualistic movements. Then she headed for the ramp.

'Survivor' by Destiny's Child was blasting out of the speakers and the thump of the bass sucked through Isabelle's skull as the stage manager counted down on his fingers. She stood in the darkness, dressed up and ready, tortured by the conviction that she had *missed* something. Something vital. Then came the signal: *Go!*

She mounted the few steps to the catwalk. She went out there, took the steps she was supposed to take, adopted the posture she was supposed to adopt, all the way to the end, where she nonchalantly placed her hands on her hips. An explosion of camera flashes. Then she realised.

This is what I've dreamt of.

Her eyes grew accustomed to the light. Right at the back of the room there was a screen with the image of a green meadow projected onto it to help create a summery atmosphere. Next to the screen was a small, silver-coloured, egg-shaped caravan, giving a three-dimensional illusion. The audience was a dark mass of human shapes, crowding around the sushi buffet, the Riesling and the chillers full of Absolut vodka, their faces occasionally looking at her with vague interest.

Is this what I've dreamt of?

The gaps between beats grew longer and longer, as if someone had slowed down the track. The thump of the bass turned into a long-drawn-out rumble of thunder that grated inside Isabelle's sinuses, and a thought that was both banal and crystal clear in equal measure took over her mind.

I am an object.

A disposable commodity. A commodity whose function was to sell other commodities. A lone commodity that could be used.

A camera flash exploded, and time was now passing so slowly that Isabelle was able to follow as it burst into life then died away. White light filled her field of vision and there was a tickling sensation in her nostrils. She blinked. Her eyelids were also moving in slow motion, and for a long time she hovered in darkness as the taste of blood filled her mouth.

When she opened her eyes again, her gaze fell on the screen. There was a figure standing in the meadow. A thin, white figure. It was coming towards her, even though it didn't appear to be walking. Then it beckoned to her. It was the only thing in the room moving at normal speed; everything else had more or less stopped.

Come. This is where you belong.

The figure wanted *Isabelle* to come. Not her hip or waist measurement, not her sultry eyes or well-shaped lips. Not the object, but Isabelle herself. She hesitated, because this invitation from the depths of existence brought with it the obvious follow-up question: *Who am I?*

A blinding flash, right next to her. The music resumed its usual tempo; she could hear the hum of conversation, and the image in front of her was now nothing more than a photoshopped summer meadow with unnaturally bright flowers. She spun around in a half-turn and sashayed back along the catwalk, to the sound of polite applause.

When she stepped out of the light the stage manager pointed to his mouth, then to her. She ran a finger over her lips and it came away covered in blood. She had a nosebleed, and had to do the rest of the show with a couple of hastily trimmed, flesh-coloured earplugs blocking her nostrils.

When it was all over and the audience had gone, Isabelle stood in front of the screen for a long time, but she saw nothing but the green meadow. Then the projector was switched off and the screen rolled up. The silver-coloured caravan had already been removed. She had missed her chance.

That was how she thought of what had happened during the days and weeks that followed. Something had been offered to her, something

Come. This is where you belong

that was fundamentally *different* from the life she was living, the life of an object. When she found out that they had gone for an ethnic look complete with Eskimos, it was merely confirmation that she had done the wrong thing when she ignored the call. Fear and anxiety sank their claws into her, and she was prescribed Xanor. After a while she called Peter and offered to come down to Italy.

Yes, she is ready now. For ten years she has waited to see the figure again, to be given another chance. During those years she has tried the conventional methods available to create meaning in her life. She got married, had a child. It didn't really help at all.

So now Isabelle is sitting next to Carina, her gaze sweeping across the field.

This is where you belong.

Whatever is demanded of her, she will do it. Anything at all to be freed from life, but to go on living.

*

Lennart and Olof's neighbour, Holger Backlund, once went mad. He picked up both of his hunting rifles, went to Olof's cow pasture and started methodically shooting dead every single animal within range. He had managed to kill five excellent dairy cows before Lennart and Olof put a stop to the massacre by reasoning with Holger, gently and calmly, until he put down the gun.

This means they have experience, so Lennart and Olof approach Donald's caravan slowly, looking relaxed, as if they are just paying him an ordinary social call and are not in any particular hurry. In some ways it is similar to the occasion when they talked Holger down; in other ways it is very different.

One similarity is that as on so many other occasions they would really like to hold hands to find strength in each other, but who knows what reaction this would provoke in someone like Donald? Therefore they approach the awning as two separate and, to tell the truth, pretty scared individuals.

When they are five metres away, they can see that one of the caravan's side windows is open, and that Donald is sitting inside watching them.

'Hello, Donald,' Lennart says, pointing to the small fridge outside. 'We were just wondering if you had any of that beer left.'

'We haven't really had a proper chat,' Olof adds.

They stop outside the entrance to the awning. Lennart pushes his hands into his back pockets and manages to sound completely relaxed: 'How about it? Shall we sit down and have a drink together?'

Olof admires Lennart's courage; he doesn't move a muscle when Donald sticks the barrel of the shotgun out of the window, while Olof himself can't help pointlessly stooping over slightly to reduce the target area.

'You're having none of my fucking beer!' Donald bellows. 'And you're not touching my fucking floor! You can both fuck off!'

Lennart only has time to say, 'But...' before a shot is fired. A tuft of grass just centimetres away from Lennart's foot flies up in the air and crumbles, scattering soil all over his legs. Lennart pulls Olof to the right so that they are hidden by the awning as they back away from the caravan.

'Stay away!' Donald roars, and they hear a series of clicks. 'Fuck off! All of you, fuck off!'

Lennart and Olof turn and run back to their own caravan, where Peter and Stefan are waiting. Majvor has gone over to Stefan's caravan to recover. The four men sit down at the kitchen table, slightly hunched because one of the windows faces Donald. Lennart is out of breath, and speaks in short bursts.

'So. That didn't. Go too. Well.'

'We'd better leave him alone,' Stefan says. 'If we leave him in peace, maybe he'll...'

'Daddy?' Molly's voice comes from the open door. 'Daddy, I'm frightened.'

Peter leaps to his feet, rushes over and picks her up. Just as he takes her in his arms, they hear another shot. Fragments of plexiglas fly everywhere as the window shatters, and there is a dull thud as the bullet penetrates the fridge.

Everyone crouches down even further, and Peter sinks to the floor with Molly in his arms, with a kitchen cupboard behind him for protection. They wait for ten seconds, thirty seconds, a minute without any further shooting. Molly extricates herself from Peter's grasp and crawls under the table, where she attempts to tie Lennart and Olof's shoelaces together.

'There's only one thing to do,' Peter says. 'We can't have someone sitting there shooting at us. He has to go.'

*

To Carina's relief, Isabelle hasn't said much since they left the camp. She has spent most of the time sitting in silence, staring out at the expanse of green. The emptiness around them is counterintuitive and ought to be frightening, but Carina doesn't feel that way.

For the first kilometre she sat up straight, looking out for signs of people or habitation. From time to time she checked the GPS to make sure that they were following a route that could be retraced, in spite of the fact that the roads shown on the GPS didn't exist in the world they could see.

Then something happened. She stopped searching, and was perfectly happy to gaze out at the field before her. By now her brain is completely empty, and it would be extremely difficult to recall what was so important about finding buildings or people. Moving through the emptiness is all she requires.

When she happens to glance at the GPS screen, it seems perfectly logical that it has now turned blue, and is no longer showing a map. *Blue, blue, my love is blue*, she thinks listlessly, staring out through the windscreen once more. She feels so contented that the hairs on her arms stand on end. She is *resting* in the empty space, resting in a way that she so rarely does. Suddenly she hears Isabelle's voice: 'Heil Hitler.'

It's like having a bucket of cold water poured over her head. Carina gives a start and looks at Isabelle, who is staring at Carina's shoulder.

'Are you crazy? What did you say?'

Isabelle nods at Carina's tattoos. 'Heil Hitler.'

'Those are two eternity symb—'

'Like hell they are. They're two figure eights. H H. Heil Hitler.' Isabelle's eyes widen as a thought occurs to her, and she laughs out loud. 'Does *your husband* think they're eternity symbols? Perhaps I ought to put him straight.'

Carina rests her hands on the wheel and stares at the horizon. Isabelle is right. They are two eights, and they represent the eighth letter of the alphabet. H H. Heil Hitler. She has kept the tattoos as a reminder of a life she never wants to go back to. She lets go of the wheel and opens the door, gets out of the car and begins to walk away.

Behind her she hears frantic movement as Isabelle shifts across to the driving seat. Apparently she can drive when things get tricky. Carina hears her push the ignition button, then swear. The key is in Carina's pocket, and the sensor can't pick it up. She hears fabric sliding over leather, footsteps on the grass, then a hand touches her shoulder.

'Carina,' Isabelle says. 'Give me the…'

Oddly enough, what happens next is probably a consequence of the peaceful place in which Carina finds herself, on one level. An emotional MRI scan of her brain would show various levels lying parallel to one another, linked together but without any direct internal relationship. On one level peace, on another rage, on another fear. But they are *clear*. Everything is so clear.

With this same clarity she spins around, feeling her right hand clench into a fist. Defined muscle groups radiate strength as she swings her hand upwards from the hip so that it meets Isabelle's chin with a dry crack.

Isabelle staggers backwards until she bumps into the car door; she slumps to the ground, mouth gaping, eyes wide open. Her long blond hair swirls around her face as she shakes her head as if to clear it. Or as if she can't believe what's happened.

Carina walks up to her and grabs the neck of Isabelle's T-shirt with her left hand as if to drag her to her feet and punch her again. She's done it before, although it was a long time ago. The key thing is not to hesitate, not to stop until the job is done and the victory beyond doubt.

There is a tearing sound as the seams of the T-shirt rip, and Isabelle sinks back down before Carina has time to let her have it. Isabelle's right foot shoots out and kicks Carina on the shin. She screams and instinctively bends forward, which exposes her cheek to a kick from Isabelle's left foot. Carina goes down and lands on her side.

'You fat cow!' Isabelle screams, hurling herself at her opponent. 'What the fuck do you think you're doing, you stupid bitch!'

Isabelle sits on Carina's stomach and smashes her fist into Carina's left cheek, which makes a lump of bloodstained phlegm fly out of her mouth. A red curtain descends over Carina's eyes. She braces the muscles of her back against the ground and smacks her fist straight up into Isabelle's chin. There is no cracking sound this time, just a muted, fleshy crump, suggesting that Isabelle's tongue was between her teeth at the moment of impact.

Spot on. Isabelle falls sideways, blood pouring from her mouth. Carina stands up and looks down at Isabelle, who is now on all fours, blood still dripping onto the grass. Perhaps she has actually bitten right through her tongue? That would be good. Carina takes a step forward and kicks Isabelle in the stomach so that she rolls right over, away from the car. When Isabelle makes an attempt to get up, Carina kicks her again.

Isabelle has an amazing body. Those slim legs, those rounded hips, that peachy bum. And that beautiful long hair. The adrenaline courses through Carina's veins and she smiles. She knows what she is going to do. She is going to smash that pretty little face until it is no longer recognisable, then Isabelle can walk around in her pants wiggling her backside as much as she likes.

She just needs to get on with it. Carina walks over to Isabelle and uses one foot to push her over onto her back. Her chin and throat are covered in blood, which is still trickling from one corner of her mouth.

There is something familiar about this scene, something buzzing away in the back of Carina's mind, trying to get her attention, something that is making her flesh creep

It's here

but she shuts it out, pushes it away as she sits down on top of Isabelle, locking the other woman's arms with her knees. With an expert eye she assesses Isabelle's jawline—still visible in spite of the blood—and her straight nose. Right. Shatter the jawbone and smash the nose, but in which order? Best to go for the nose first, because tackling the jaw could damage the hand that Carina is now raising

It's here

as Isabelle whispers in a voice thick with blood: 'Stop. Please. Stop.'

So she hasn't bitten through her tongue after all. Oh well, you can't have everything. Carina is about to bring her fist down on Isabelle's nose when she sees something out of the corner of her eye, something that is between her and the car. Carina's hand hovers in the air as she looks up.

A black tiger is lying on the grass, staring at her. It is not a beautiful tiger. Its body is emaciated, its coat matted. One side of its mouth is drooping, exposing yellowish-brown, decayed teeth. The tiger blinks; it has lumps of dried pus in the corners of its eyes. Those bloodshot eyes continue to stare at Carina, and the expression in those elliptical pupils is ancient, a gateway to eternity. It is *that* tiger.

Carina's arms drop and she begins to scream.

*

'Stop. Please. Stop.'

The words are repeated mechanically by Isabelle's swollen tongue, because that is what she ought to say. A plea for the violence to stop. At the same time, there is something deep inside Isabelle that doesn't want it to stop at all. Something that just wants it to go on and on.

As far as she knows, she has never had any masochistic tendencies; she has never been attracted to men who would mistreat her, as some others within the modelling industry have done. Quite the reverse: weaklings who were easily kept under the thumb have been her choice.

But now…Carina's first, totally unexpected blow had sent Isabelle into a fury, and as long as the fight was evenly balanced, she wanted nothing more than to kick the shit out of Carina. But with the blow to her chin, when she bit her tongue and blood started pouring out of her mouth, something changed.

Any desire to beat Carina poured out of Isabelle's body along with the blood. When the first kick in the belly took her breath away, she experienced a moment of clarity, a eureka-moment more powerful than the kick when cocaine grabs hold of the synapses. Isabelle saw herself in the world, she saw her path and her end in a way that couldn't be put into words.

The sensation was beginning to fade when the next kick came, and it burst into life once more. Isabelle was *present*, she was *participating*, and when Carina sat on her and locked her arms by her sides, there was a part of Isabelle that was looking forward to what was to come with a certain level of excitement, while at the same time another, instinctive part of her made her swollen tongue shape the words: 'Stop. Please. Stop.'

Through half-closed eyelids Isabelle sees Carina raise her fist, and an involuntary sigh escapes her. But the blow does not come. Instead Carina freezes, then lets out a piercing shriek. She shuffles backwards, holding her hands up in front of her.

Isabelle's chest aches as she pulls herself up into a sitting position. Carina's eyes are fixed on something behind Isabelle, who slowly turns around and

oh there you are

The white figure is lying on its stomach on the grass, just a few metres away from her. Its big, dark eyes look into hers. As if she was wearing the wrong glasses, Isabelle has difficulty focusing on the face. As soon as she tries, the image blurs.

It has no hair. Its skin is chalk-white, and is completely lacking in any indication of age. No wrinkles or variations in pigmentation. The ears and nose are no more than suggestions, slight protuberances with holes in the skull. Isabelle screws up her eyes and tries to make out the mouth, but there is no mouth. Taken as a whole, the face is no more than a setting for the eyes

the eyes

which are looking straight into Isabelle.

It is said that eyes are expressive. That they can be sad or happy or indifferent. In fact they are simply two spheres, incapable of expressing anything without the help of the muscles surrounding them. The angle of the eyebrows, a wrinkling of the nose, the shape of the mouth: altogether these elements formulate what a person wishes to communicate, while the eyes remain a pair of lifeless globes of vitreous jelly.

The figure in front of Isabelle lacks anything that could help with an interpretation. There are only those eyes, two dark wells, the iris and pupil barely distinguishable. It is a gaze totally without intention, without evaluation, without calculation. It is a *pure* gaze that washes over Isabelle, sweeping away her aching body, the taste of blood in her mouth, the pounding in her head.

She crawls towards the figure, whispering: 'Here I am. I'm here now.'

The white figure gives no sign of having heard her. It remains lying flat on its stomach on the grass, its head raised a fraction so that it can look at Isabelle. She keeps on crawling until their faces are no more than a few centimetres apart. Isabelle's eyes are dry, because she has not blinked since their eyes met. She doesn't want to blink and break the contact, but she has to. She blinks.

Just like that day on the catwalk, it is as if time slows down. Isabelle sees her eyelids slowly slide down over her eyes like a curtain being lowered. Then she is in darkness; she has to make a real effort to force her eyes open again, but it is a slow, difficult process. First there is a tiny gap that lets in a hint of light, then they open in slow motion, gradually widening and letting in the world.

By the time her eyes are fully open, the figure is standing up. It has no sex organs or nipples. It has no fingernails. There is nothing but white skin, like the first draft of a human being, or the final phase of a human being, when everything that is unnecessary has been removed. It turns and moves away from her.

'Please,' Isabelle whispers. 'Please…'

Only when the white figure is several metres away does Isabelle realise that Carina is still screaming.

*

There are many things Carina regrets from her youth, but if there is one thing she would sacrifice a great deal to erase from her past, it is the night she saw the tiger.

Summer 1991. She was eighteen years old. The gang she hung out with consisted mainly of older boys and girls. Some were minor criminals, or worse; some were on drugs of various kinds, and some just thought that everything was crap.

They would meet up at someone's place and drink, shoot up or sniff whatever happened to be around while listening to music that often belonged to the White Power genre, since several members of the gang had sympathies in that direction.

Carina had no sympathies in any direction whatsoever. From time to time the boys—they were mainly boys—would sit and talk to her about the Swedish tribe, the dangers of contaminating the race, pride in their heritage, the battle that must be fought. Carina thought it all sounded okay. Most things sounded okay as long as she was drunk enough. Communism and world revolution and unrestricted immigration would have been fine too, as long as she could drink with people who had no plans for life, or even the next day.

The week before she saw the tiger, something had happened that was not okay. She had got completely pissed at a party and collapsed on a sofa to the sound of 'Hurrah for the Nordic Lands' by Ultima Thule. When she woke up in the morning with the hangover from hell, she was naked from the waist down and there was dried semen on her thighs. By that stage she had sunk so low that she didn't really care. Shit happens. She staggered to the bathroom to have a shower.

When she had pulled off her T-shirt, she glanced at herself in the cracked mirror. She looked fucking terrible. Her hair was sticking out in all directions, her mascara had run and her eyes were red. She wondered who on earth had managed to rape such a monster.

Her right shoulder was swollen and inflamed, and at first she thought the bastard must have bitten her. Then she saw the black symbols, clearly visible against the red skin. Two eights. She knew all too well what they stood for; a couple of the guys had the same thing.

The hangover had turned her brain into a ball of spikes bouncing around inside her skull as she sat down on the toilet and put her head in her hands.

No. Fuck. No.

For the first time in months Carina took a step back and looked at herself. She was sitting in a bathroom that stank of piss and vomit in a disgusting apartment, with people lying around sleeping off whatever they had taken. During the night someone (or more than one person?) had taken the opportunity to rape her while she was unconscious, and had finished off, or possibly started, by tattooing *Heil Hitler* on her shoulder.

This was her life. This was what it had come to.

As she stood in the shower letting the hot water flow over her skin, she felt as if she was washing something away, as if she was being cleansed. She thought there might be a chance to start again. Perhaps this could be the turning point, the wake-up call.

She found a relatively clean towel and wrapped it around herself, then went searching for her underwear and jeans. When she found them she would leave the apartment and…register with Komvux, the adult education service, see if she could get some qualifications. Sort out a job at McDonald's, anything. Go to the right places, fill in the right forms, make the right calls.

Before she found her jeans she came across a bottle of vodka with a reasonable amount left in the bottom. She sat down in an armchair and took a couple of swigs, just to get her thoughts in order. Then a couple more. And that was the end of that.

When she was out on the town with the gang a week later after a major session of front-loading, it was all forgotten and forgiven, or at least it was as unimportant as everything else. She had been fucked and pricked, as someone put it, and it was just one of those things, of no significance. She didn't know who had done it, and she didn't care. No yesterday, no tomorrow, no problems. As the gang moved along Sveavägen heading for Monte Carlo, they were invincible, pulsating with an energy that came from the knowledge that they owned the city, they owned the night.

A plastic bottle of bootleg vodka and Coke laced with quarter of a gram of speed was passed around the group, which consisted of Carina, three guys who were all into White Power, plus a girl she hadn't met before who belonged to one of the guys. Her name was Jannika; she had empty eyes and wore a bomber jacket and a short, neon yellow skirt. She laughed much too loudly at everything that was said.

As they were passing the offices of Bonniers publishing house, Micke gave the Sieg Heil salute to the Jewish mafia, which made Jannika fall about laughing. She carried on laughing as they walked on, and after about a hundred metres she announced that as a result she needed a pee. By then they had reached the junction of

Tunnelgatan and Sveavägen, and weren't far from Monte Carlo.

'Cross your legs, for fuck's sake,' Johan said. 'We're nearly there.'

'Can't,' Jannika whimpered. 'I need to go now.'

Micke looked around and saw the plaque on the ground that marked the spot where Olof Palme had been assassinated. 'Piss there,' he said, pointing.

'*There?*'

'Why the fuck not? Piss on Palme. I mean, he was always cuddling up to the blacks. Piss on him.'

Jannika giggled and grabbed her crotch, then she went over, pulled down her pants and squatted over the plaque. Urine splashed down onto the metal and trickled away between the paving stones.

'Piss on Palme,' Johan mumbled, taking a swig from the bottle. 'Too fucking right.'

Carina had followed the conversation with a listless lack of interest, leaning against the wall by the entrance to the subway. Then something happened. She suddenly had goose bumps on her arms, and a shudder ran down her spine as if an icy blast had come rushing up from the underworld. She didn't have time to reflect on this, because two men emerged from the subway. They were both wearing suits, and they both had coal-black hair.

'What are you doing?' one of them said, with a noticeable accent. His companion gestured to him to be quiet as all three boys turned to face them.

'What's this I hear?' said Hasse, the heaviest and strongest of the three. 'Doesn't sound much like Swedish to me.'

'Nothing,' the other man said. 'We go here now.' His Swedish was worse than the first man's.

'So you like Palme, do you?' Micke said, taking a couple of steps towards the men with the other boys following in his wake.

What happened next could hardly be described as a fight. The submissive man was quickly knocked to the ground, where he stayed. When his rebellious companion rushed at Micke, Carina stuck out her foot and tripped him up, so that he went down headfirst.

It was instinctive. Her foot shot out before she had time to think. As soon as she made contact with his leg she regretted her action, and backed away towards the Brunkeberg tunnel. Cold darkness licked at her spine, making her shiver and shake.

A spasm in the leg, an outstretched foot, a small movement that would never let go of Carina because of the subsequent course of events. The boys dragged the man over to the memorial plaque, where Micke grabbed him by the hair and held his face just above the metal.

'So you like Palme, do you? Okay, well give him a kiss then!'

He slammed the man's face against the plaque. Pulled it up, slammed it down. The third time something shattered. Teeth, nose, possibly both.

'Kiss the piss!' Micke yelled. 'Kiss Palme!'

He slammed down the man's face yet again, blood pouring over the metal and mingling with Jannika's urine. The others had moved back a little way, and Johan said: 'For fuck's sake, Micke, that's enough.'

Carina was still edging backwards towards the tunnel; she covered her mouth with her hands as Micke repeated his mantra—'Kiss the piss! Kiss Palme!'—and continued to mash the man's face.

It's here.

She had no idea what the thought meant; it was a message from the same deep recess of the human psyche as the fear of fire, heights, sharks, everything that can kill us. Like the cold darkness a moment ago, it licked at her back, just as diffuse as smoke or mist. And just as concrete. Slowly she turned around.

The summer evening was still light, and she had no difficulty in making out the lump of darkness lying outside the entrance to the tunnel. As she looked at it, it stopped being a lump; it stood up on four legs and took the shape of a tiger. A black tiger.

It padded softly towards her, and she was so paralysed with fear that she couldn't move a muscle. The tiger had no stripes; it was entirely black apart from the eyes, which caught something of the light from the sky. They shone as they stared past Carina towards the violent attack, which judging by the noise was still going on. The tiger drew back its lips and bared its teeth, emitting a low-pitched sound that was more of a purr than a growl.

The tiger stopped five metres away from her, pricked up its ears and looked up towards the hill on Luntmakargatan. With a supreme effort of will, as if she were freeing herself from a collar of ice, Carina turned her head to see what the tiger was looking at. Two seconds later a police car rounded the corner and drove down the hill. It turned left when it reached Carina, heading towards Sveavägen.

Only then did she make the connection. Violent attack—police. When she looked back at the tunnel she saw the tiger running up the steps towards Malmskillnadsgatan. She didn't see whether it carried on up the steps or disappeared on the way, because she had regained her ability to think, to a certain extent at least, and she spun around just as the police car screeched to a halt and three cops jumped out.

She didn't stop to see what happened to the rest of the gang, or to give the police time to wonder about the girl they had driven past. She took to her heels as if the tiger was after her and ran along Luntmakargatan in the direction of Tegnérgatan.

She had gone no more than twenty metres when she was struck by that very fear: what if the tiger was after her? She glanced back, but the street was empty. And yet it felt as if the tiger was there. As if it would always be there. She ran…

*

…and she had carried on running, until she crashed into Stefan's arms a few years later. Or rather crawled into them. That's another story. But even when her life had stabilised and her focus had shifted from the abyss to an ICA store in the country, she had never stopped looking over her shoulder.

As time went by, the memory of the tiger had grown diffuse, and she would happily have dismissed it as a hallucination if the feeling hadn't stayed with her. It was no longer panting at her heels, but it was lurking somewhere behind her, waiting for the right moment to pounce.

And now it is here. Carina stops moving backwards, stops screaming as the tiger turns around and begins to walk away from her, but she doesn't take her eyes off it until it is so far away that it could be something else. Something normal.

Her body has been so tense for such a long time that it hurts when she relaxes. The left side of her head is aching, and she has to make an effort to remember why.

Isabelle. The blood.

Every scrap of aggression has left her when she looks around and sees Isabelle sitting not far away. She too is staring at the spot where the tiger is shrinking on the horizon. Carina gets up on shaky legs, staggers over to Isabelle and slumps down on the grass beside her.

'Can you see it?' Carina asks.

The thick sound that emerges from Isabelle's mouth seems to be a 'Yes'.

Images of their fight come back to Carina. The blow to the chin, the blood pouring out of Isabelle's mouth, her own compulsion to smash, to crush. Isabelle's chin is covered in coagulating blood: Carina wants to apologise, but cannot find the right words. Perhaps it is because no apology is necessary. They were caught in the eye of the tiger.

What Carina cannot understand is the expression on Isabelle's face. Not fear or disbelief, but sorrow, longing. As if the tiger is a dear friend who has left her.

The tiger is no more than a black dot against the blue sky when Carina gets to her feet, walks towards the car and stops halfway. She stares down at the grass around her feet, and two things strike her simultaneously. The tiger is moving in the direction of the camp. And there is no blood on the grass.

She can still make out the indentations left by their bodies. This was where they fought, and blood was pouring out of Isabelle's mouth, but the blood has gone. As if it has been washed away.

Lapped up.

*

There is not a sound from inside Donald's caravan as Peter creeps over and begins to raise the tow bar, a millimetre at a time. It takes him almost five minutes to get it to the right height, and as he locks it in place his hands are slippery with sweat and his mouth is dry.

Cautiously he opens the back door of Donald's car and roots around in the side pocket until he finds the spare key that Majvor told him was there. As he slides behind the wheel and starts the engine, he doesn't take his eyes off the rear-view mirror for a second. He is watching the curtains, making sure they stay closed, that the front window doesn't open. He stops when he hears the tow ball scrape against the bar, leaving the engine running as he gets out.

Peter has positioned the car perfectly, and the hitch is directly above the tow ball. He lowers the bar as slowly as he raised it. Stefan is standing outside his caravan, and gives Peter the thumbs up. His job is to watch Donald's door, because the awning is blocking Peter's view.

Peter licks the sweat from his top lip as the hitch drops into place. All he has to do now is raise the stabiliser, but the locking mechanism is sticking. Peter pushes and pulls, but is unable to release it. He glances over at the window, then takes a step back and gives it a good kick.

Idiot!

The mechanism releases, but the entire caravan rocks as all its weight falls on the tow ball. Peter quickly lifts the wheel, but it is too late. The curtain is jerked to one side and Donald is staring into his eyes.

'What the hell—' Donald yells, lifting the window latch, but Peter doesn't wait to hear what else he has to say. He leaps into the car and puts it into first gear. In the rear-view mirror he can see the window opening. He puts his foot down. The car doesn't move at all.

The barrel of the gun is already poking through the window by

190

the time Peter realises that old habits die hard; he put the handbrake on before he got out of the car. The stress is making it difficult for him to coordinate his movements, and he still has his foot on the accelerator when he releases the brake, fortunately for him. Both car and caravan jerk forward, and Donald disappears from the window as he falls backwards.

The tyres skid on the grass as Peter hunches over the wheel, driving out into the field without bothering about the direction. He switches on the GPS, intending to follow the first road that appears. The plan is to leave Donald close enough to the camp so that they will be able to find him again, but far enough away so that he will have difficulty getting back without the help of satellites.

Satellites?

The timing isn't ideal, but as he crouches low over the wheel Peter catches himself looking up at the sky, as if he might catch sight of some small probe up there. After all, the GPS is working, so there must…

His train of thought is interrupted as the car lurches to one side. There is no sign of Donald, but a glance in the wing mirror tells him what the problem is. The awning is dragging along the side of the caravan. It is still being kept upright to a certain extent by the pegs that remain in place, but a long strip has become caught in one of the caravan's wheel arches, which means that wheel is no longer turning, but is simply sliding across the grass, leaving a long skid mark behind it.

The car is powerful and can still manage to tow the caravan, so Peter changes up to second gear and floors the accelerator. After a hundred metres he realises that the plan isn't going to work. Why the hell would Donald need satellites when he can follow the mark left by the wheel all the way back to camp whenever he feels like blowing all their heads off?

The engine is racing and the smell of burnt rubber is being pumped into the car via the air con system when Donald reappears at the window, his eyes burning with hatred. He pokes the barrel of the gun out, and Peter ducks so far down that he can't actually see through the windscreen. His body is curled into the shape of a question mark as he rests his cheek on the passenger seat, while keeping one hand on the wheel and his right foot on the accelerator.

This was a bad idea, a seriously bad idea.

The key point in their plan had been the belief that Donald probably wasn't crazy enough to actually try and shoot someone, but given the look in his eyes, it seems they might have been wrong.

The burnt rubber smell is blowing right in Peter's face. He feels sick, and risks reaching up to turn off the fan. Instead he manages to switch on the radio, halfway through 'It Always Gets Worse When the Night Comes' by Björn Skifs.

Himmelstrand, of course—that melancholy line about being far away from all the lights and the laughter.

The engine roars, the car lurches sideways, and Peter is driving without looking, to the accompaniment of yet another Swedish Eurovision entry. There is only one possible reaction. Peter starts laughing. His foot bobs up and down on the accelerator, making the car jerk forward as the spasms pass through his stomach.

'You fucking bastard!' Donald bellows behind him, which sounds like the punchline to a really funny sketch. Peter is laughing so hard that he can hardly breathe.

Then comes the explosion, and he stops laughing abruptly as fragments of glass shower down on his face. Tiny, tiny fragments, that's all. Not like when a windscreen shatters in an action film. He glances up and sees that the windscreen is still intact, unlike the GPS screen, which has exploded in a cascade of plastic, glass and electronic components.

Peter isn't sure, but through the music and the roar of the engine he thinks he hears a three-step metallic click. The sound of a gun being reloaded. Seconds later the next shot is fired.

This is impossible.

Peter screws up his eyes and takes a deep breath. In a single movement he sits up and slams his foot on the brake. The car has ABS, and he feels the impact all the way up his leg. A glance in the mirror confirms that the desired result has been achieved: Donald has lost his balance. When he straightens up to take aim once more, Peter floors the accelerator.

The car responds beautifully, and Donald is hurled away from the window. When Peter checks the wing mirror, he sees that the manoeuvre has also caused the awning to free itself, and the wheel is now running smoothly. Peter nods to himself, phrases as meaningless as football chants echoing in his brain.

All I have to do is drive. Foot down. Keep on keeping on.

He changes up to third, maintaining a lower speed so that he can shoot forward if Donald reappears. Peter stares out across the empty field as if he were looking for someone to cross the ball to. When he can't find anyone, he automatically looks back at the GPS which is no longer a GPS, but merely a jagged plastic box.

Focus. Drive like a pro...

Think!

Apart from sheer technical skill, there are two things that distinguish a good footballer: the ability to have an overview, and to improvise. To be able to read the game on a wider scale, and to make creative decisions in an instant. Zidane was a master of the former, Maradona the latter. Without making any further comparisons Peter is more of a Maradona, because although he has improvised pretty well so far, at the moment he is experiencing a distinct lack of any kind of overview. He can deal with each individual situation as it arises, but what is he going to *do*?

When Donald's face pops up yet again, his forehead is bleeding; this doesn't seem to have improved his mood. Before Peter has time to react, Donald pokes the gun out of the window and fires without even bothering to take aim. The bullet passes through the back window and the passenger seat before slamming into the glove compartment. This is followed by the sound of breaking glass, whereupon a yellow liquid the colour of urine starts trickling out of the hole.

Peter speeds up, and yet again Donald falls backwards. The trick isn't going to work forever, and there is a problem. A big problem.

How the hell is he going to uncouple the caravan without getting shot?

Of course one option is to stop the car, jump out and run as fast as he can, hoping that Donald won't shoot him in the back. This course of action seems less than appealing, partly because he saw the look in Donald's eyes in the rear-view mirror, and partly because he now knows that the gun is equipped with a rangefinder.

He's got the gun. I've got the car. Exploit the situation.

Perhaps the idea that comes into Peter's head is just as bad as the idea of driving off with Donald, but at the moment he can't think of anything else. He increases his speed to eighty kilometres an hour while twisting the wheel from side to side so that the caravan swings and sways behind him, hopefully making it nigh on impossible for Donald to keep his balance.

Only when 'It Always Gets Worse When the Night Comes' finishes does Peter realise that it has been playing all that time. When it is replaced by 'Helledudane, What a Guy', he switches off the radio. He fastens his seatbelt, grits his teeth, and makes a sharp turn to the right.

He wishes he knew more about mechanical engineering, physics or whatever the fuck would help him to predict the precise effect of his action. The plan is to shake Donald up so much that it will give Peter a few precious seconds in which to uncouple the caravan, but there is the impetus of the turn and the speed to which a caravan weighing at least two tons is about to be subjected, and that caravan is attached to a comparatively small car.

The taste of gall rises in Peter's throat as he watches the caravan swing around; the wheels on the left-hand side leave the ground. Peter turns the wheel to the left to compensate, but the weight of the caravan makes it impossible to stop its progress. It forces the car forward in a skid as the tow bar creaks and grates.

Peter puts his foot on the brake, but the caravan pushes him forward. The acrid stench of burning rubber once again fills the car, the wheels smoking as the brake pads struggle to cope. The caravan slides sideways, accompanied by a cacophony of breaking glass and china as the cupboards fly open. It is about to tip right over, and Peter feels the car's wheels on the left-hand side leave the ground. For one quivering second everything is in the balance, then the caravan crashes back down on all four wheels.

Okay. Okay.

Peter allows himself to sit still for two seconds, expelling the air from his lungs. When he tries to get out of the car his fingers are locked onto the steering wheel, and he has to prise them free like a bandage from a festering wound.

Sometimes you find your own space. It doesn't happen often, but it does happen. You've passed the back line, you're in control of the ball, and the goal is straight ahead. Then it's important not to think, but to let your instincts take over. The body knows what to do, if you leave it in peace. The goalie's position in relation to the goal, the position and speed of the ball and the body. It is all so complicated that you could fill a whiteboard with calculations. If you thought about it. So you don't think.

Something similar happens to Peter as he gets out and rushes around the back of the car on surprisingly steady legs. He doesn't waste time checking on Donald's whereabouts, he doesn't even bother winding up the tow bar, he simply stands with one leg firmly planted on either side of it, pushes down the handle of the locking mechanism and *lifts*. He knows it is the only possible course of action.

Under normal circumstances he might not have managed it. But he isn't thinking, he is just assuming he can do it. And he does. The muscles in his arms and legs are screaming as he lifts the caravan off the tow bar with one single movement and drops it onto the stabilising wheel to the sound of more breaking glass and china from inside. And Donald's voice.

'Fucking bastard! I'm going to shoot you dead, you fucking...'

Peter is in the car with the door shut, cutting off the stream of invective. He reaches for the start button and his brain suddenly shuts down when his fingers find a key instead.

Key. Lock. Why is there a key?

Then he remembers that this is not his car; he turns the key, depresses the clutch and puts the car in first gear. As it begins to move, the caravan door flies open and Donald staggers out clutching the shotgun.

Peter changes up to second and puts his foot down. He glances in the mirror and sees Donald drop to his knees and put the gun to his shoulder. Peter hunches over the wheel, grateful for every nanosecond, every metre between him and Donald before the shot is fired.

He hears a sharp, dry crack followed by a bang, much closer this time, like a reverse echo, and for one terrible moment he thinks maybe that's what it sounds like when the spinal cord is shattered by a bullet; he closes his eyes to deal with the pain. But there is no pain. Instead the car begins to shudder, and Peter realises that Donald has burst one of the rear tyres.

The car is pulling slightly to one side, but the four-wheel drive keeps it moving steadily away from Donald. The next crack is much more distant, but Donald must be a good shot, because judging from the sound he has managed to shatter one of the rear lights.

When Peter looks in the mirror again, the caravan is over a hundred metres behind him, and he should be out of range. He keeps on driving.

The relief at having escaped from mortal danger and achieved his objective lasts for about thirty seconds. Then Peter realises that he is driving out of the frying pan into the fire, so to speak.

During the manoeuvres with the caravan he has lost all sense of direction. The GPS has been destroyed, and there are no markings to show him the way. The field stretches out in front of him, vast and unchanging, and he has no idea whether he is heading towards home or away from home or somewhere in between.

He is driving. That's all.

*

It's time for revenge, and it's not going to be pretty...

Carina sets aside *Martyrs*, the DVD she has found, and carries on rooting through the Toyota's glove compartment, her hands shaking. Make-up bag, instruction manual, advertising leaflets. Right at the back she finds a duster; that will have to do.

Isabelle, who is still sitting on the ground, pulls a face as Carina holds out the dirty rag, but she scrunches it up and pushes it into her mouth to stem the flow of blood from her tongue. Carina looks over towards the field where the tiger is no longer visible, then she tugs at Isabelle's arm.

'It's on its way to the camp. We have to go.'

Isabelle offers no resistance as Carina pulls her to her feet, but Carina stops in mid-movement. There is something strange about the expression on Isabelle's face. Carina is still frightened following her encounter with the tiger, but Isabelle's eyes are saying something completely different. Carina lets her fall back down.

'You saw it too, didn't you?'

Isabelle nods and makes a noise that could mean absolutely anything as the corners of her mouth turn up. A thought strikes Carina, and she crouches down in front of Isabelle, who is still gazing out at the field. Eventually she catches her eye and asks: '*What* did you see?'

In spite of her battered body Isabelle manages an elegant gesture which cannot possibly relate to the terrifying figure that Carina saw. Isabelle tries to remove the duster from her mouth, but winces and decides to leave it where it is.

'I'm sorry about that,' Carina says. 'It was...it became...'

She doesn't know how to explain the madness that came over her, but nor does she need to, because Isabelle gives her the finger, thus erasing Carina's desire to apologise. Isabelle is now staring at the ground next to Carina, her eyes flicking from side to side.

'Yes, I noticed it too,' Carina says. 'The blood has gone. It's taken it.'

Isabelle closely examines the grass. She nods to herself, then looks up at Carina, stares at her for a long time. Carina gets the impression that she is being *assessed*, like some antique objet d'art. Or a piece of meat. It is not a pleasant feeling.

Isabelle drags herself to her feet and walks over to the car. Carina follows her. She gets behind the wheel and reaches for the start button with a sense of dread. Part of her just wants to turn the car around and drive in the opposite direction, away from the tiger.

But not Isabelle. As soon as she is settled in her seat she waves towards the horizon in front of them. Eagerly. Longing to get there.

*

Majvor sits in Stefan and Carina's caravan and watches Peter drive off with Donald. She stretches her neck so that she can follow them for another thirty metres before they are out of sight, and the only thought in her head is: *My cinnamon buns.*

Given the current situation, what are the chances of Donald putting the buns in the oven before they are over-proved? About the same as the chances of her winning the Olympic long jump. Today has been one miscalculation after another.

However, she does realise that it was necessary to remove Donald. He is much too volatile; he can blow up over nothing, and this time he really did go too far. Firing the shotgun at her! She could have had a heart attack. On these occasions there is only one thing that helps: time. When Donald gets worked up there is no point in arguing with him, no point in doing anything except staying out of his way and letting him cool down.

Majvor hopes that a few hours' calm and contemplation will have the desired effect on her husband, and might even bring him to his senses with regard to this insane idea that she and the others are a figment of his imagination.

Where does all this come from?

Like the time he decided they should start selling soft-whipped ice cream at the yard. The customers could buy a cone while they were waiting to be served. There would be three sorts of sprinkles. Nobody thought it was a good idea, but it was only Majvor who dared to speak up.

Not that it helped. Donald was adamant, and installed the most expensive machine on the market. It was meant to be a gimmick, he explained. Something that would make his yard stand out. And indeed it was a gimmick. The customers laughed and wondered what the hell that monstrosity was doing there, but hardly anyone wanted sticky ice-cream fingers when they were about to handle their goods. Donald was the one who made the most use of the machine, and by the following summer it had been consigned to the loft insulation store room. He refused to sell it, because that would have meant admitting that he had made a mistake, so he insisted that it had just been put away temporarily 'until the time was right'.

Majvor continues to run through the catalogue of stubborn decisions and ridiculous ideas that Donald has come up with over the years, until she is interrupted by a child's voice.

'Hello?'

A little boy is looking down at her from the sleeping alcove above her head.

'Hello yourself,' Majvor says.

'What are you doing here?'

She smiles at the directness of the question, and responds in the same way: 'My caravan has gone, so I'm sitting here for a little while. Is that okay?'

'Of course. Why has your caravan gone?'

'It needed…a little outing.'

The boy frowns, but seems to decide that her answer is acceptable. He clambers down and stands beside Majvor. He looks her up and down, then asks: 'Have you got children?'

'I have. Four of them. All boys.'

'They must be really old.'

'They're quite old, yes. And some of them have children of their own.'

199

The boy nods, pleased that he has drawn the right conclusion. He sits down opposite Majvor, lowers his voice and asks: 'When your children were little…did you ever lie to them?'

'I might have done, now and again. Why do you ask? Has someone lied to you?'

'Mmm. Grown-ups shouldn't tell lies.'

'No. You're right, of course, but sometimes….was it about something important?'

'Quite important.'

'Would you like to tell me?'

The boy straightens up and looks out of the window, chewing his lower lip. The muscles around his eyes are twitching in the way they do when we dream; he is probably studying some internal image. Majvor places her hands on top of one another on the table and waits. She enjoys the company of children; she always has done. Their needs and wishes are not so tangled up in dark urges and unhealed traumas as is often the case with adults.

On the table next to Majvor is a Lego construction that looks like the beginning of a chimney, with four high walls. When she leans forward, she can see three figures down at the bottom.

'Did you build this?' she asks.

'Mmm. Me and Mummy.' Still staring out at the field, the boy says: 'What are we doing here? Why are we here?'

'Goodness, that's not an easy question!'

'Do you know the answer?'

'No, but I can tell you what I *think*.'

'Okay.'

'I think…' Majvor's gaze rests on the Lego as she remembers how she felt when she first saw the crosses on the caravans. 'I think everything has a purpose. That there's a reason why we're here. And that it will all become clear.'

The boy looks disappointed. 'Is that all?'

No, that's not all, but Majvor doesn't know how to explain the rest, so instead she asks: 'Do you believe in God?'

The boy shrugs. 'I suppose so.'

'Would you like to say a prayer with me?'

Once again the boy frowns as if he is concentrating hard, weighing up the pros and cons of her suggestion. After a moment he says: 'Okay. If you promise to play with me afterwards.'

Majvor holds out her hand to seal the deal. The boy looks a little lost, then does the same. As Majvor's fingers close around his fragile little hand, for the first time today she feels a real *confidence*. A conviction that everything will sort itself out, one way or another.

Then she lets go and interlaces her fingers in prayer. The boy copies her, a determined look on his face. Majvor begins to recite the Lord's Prayer, and the boy repeats it after her, one phrase at a time. When she reaches 'For ever and ever', she adds: 'Show us the way we should go and lead us back home. Amen.'

'Amen,' the boy says. They sit for a few seconds looking into each other's eyes, struck by the seriousness of the moment. Then the boy asks: 'Do you know Star Wars?'

'The film?'

'*Films*. Yes.'

'Not very well.'

'Do you know Chewbacca?'

Majvor and Donald's son Henrik had the first three Star Wars films on video, and Majvor watched the first one. She can't remember anyone called Chewbacca, but she thinks they might have made more films later on.

'No. Who's he? Is he the one in the black mask?'

Her comment provokes an unexpected reaction. The boy throws himself backwards on the sofa and bursts out laughing. Majvor picks at the Lego building. It can't have been *that* funny, but the boy is laughing so hard that he is clutching his stomach, legs waving in the air.

'Darth Vader,' he shouts. 'That's Darth Vader!'

'I see,' Majvor says, and in spite of the fact that there is no reason to do so, she feels herself blushing slightly. 'So who's Chewbacca?'

The boy's face is flushed as he sits up, gasping for breath. 'He's... Han Solo's co-pilot. He's all furry and...he talks like this...' The boy makes a noise that could be a cross between a tiger and a goat, and something stirs in the back of Majvor's mind.

'The one who looks like an ape?'

She is afraid that this might cause another fit of hysteria, but the boy nods thoughtfully. 'Yes. I suppose he does look a bit like an ape.'

'So what about him?' Majvor says.

'You can be him.'

'Do I have to sound like you just did?'

'Of course. See if you can do it.'

Majvor tries to imitate the sound the boy made, and he laughs again, but appreciatively this time. Then he explains the game. They are going to blow up something called the Death Star, there will be lots of enemy spaceships, and Chewbacca must be ready to man the guns. Majvor makes the noise to show that she has understood, and they're off.

Majvor used to play games with her boys when they were little, and it's amazing how quickly it all comes back to her. After a few minutes Majvor steps back and watches herself. She is sitting there grunting and waving her paws and pretending to fire laser guns, while at the same time her mind feels clearer than it has done for a long time. She doesn't give a thought to Donald or her cinnamon buns, or anything else outside the situation.

Since the children moved out she often feels incapable of grasping what it's all *about*, what is important, what she should be doing with her life. That kind of egotistical brooding doesn't exist right now. She knows what she should be doing, and she knows what is important. She must defeat Darth Vader!

*

Stefan has never had unrealistic expectations of himself or his life. When he left school with acceptable grades, he immediately started working full-time in his father's grocery store. His little cabin in the grounds was extended, and he lived there until he was twenty-three, when he was able to buy a house of his own just three hundred metres away, with a loan secured by his parents.

For two years he lived with Jenny, a girl he had met at school. Then Carina came back to Ålviken, and a few difficult months followed before everything settled down. They married when they were twenty-eight, and two years later Stefan took over the store.

It was a couple of years before they decided to try for a baby, and another three before they succeeded. By the time Emil was born in 2006, the store was flourishing as well as a store in a small community could be expected to flourish, and they had renovated the house from top to bottom.

Stefan remembers that moment a year or so later very well indeed. It was a Sunday morning at the beginning of June. He was looking forward to opening up the store; this was the best time of the year. Enough customers to make him feel secure, but the frantic rush of high summer was still to come.

He was humming 'Hey Hey Monica' as he walked downstairs and stopped three steps from the bottom. Carina had got up with Emil an hour ago and the two of them were in the kitchen; Stefan had a perfect view from where he was standing.

The morning sun was shining in through the window, casting its soft light over the oiled wooden floor and rag rugs. The aroma of coffee and freshly baked bread filled the air. Carina was moving around the floor with Emil's feet balanced on her own as she held his hands. Emil was laughing, his downy blond hair almost transparent as Carina kissed the top of his head and nuzzled him with her nose.

Stefan stood motionless, watching. And that was when the thought came to him: *This moment. Take it in. Save it.*

This was perfection. He had everything he had ever wanted. Everything. If Nirvana means freedom from demands and desires, he had achieved it in that instant. And yet he hadn't. Because he still had one wish: that it would never end, that things would stay like this forever.

With one hand resting on the banister he absorbed the light, the aromas, the sound of Emil's laughter and Carina's murmurs of encouragement, the image of a strand of hair falling forward as she bent over her son, turning to gold as it was caught by a sunbeam. The lawn outside the window, the wagtail on the veranda rail. He wanted to save it all.

He had been standing there for perhaps ten seconds when Carina caught sight of him, smiled and said: 'Good morning. Coffee's ready.' Emil toddled a few steps under his own steam and shouted : 'Offee!' Then down he went.

Perhaps it isn't unusual for people to think this way at moments of particular happiness: *Let me hold on to this forever.* What was special about Stefan's situation was that he had succeeded.

It took some work, that was undeniable, but Stefan was a stubborn individual. If he had set himself a task, then he carried it through. This was about preserving ten seconds of his life, and methodically he set to work.

Over the next few days he made sure he went over the scene time and time again, rerunning it in his mind and making use of his other senses until it was imprinted within his consciousness as securely as a photograph on the desk that you glance at every day.

He didn't stop living for the present, or enjoying the happiness that continued to come his way, but from time to time—when he was unpacking a delivery of mineral water, for example—he would go through every detail of the image. The fringes on the rug, Emil's toes, the gleam of the toaster, the dust motes swirling in the sunlight.

Weeks, months, years later, he continued to keep it alive by taking it out and examining it every so often, playing with it by looking at it from different angles from the one he actually saw.

No, Stefan has no unrealistic expectations of life. He has been given everything he could have wished for. And if he doesn't have it right now, at least he had it once. He finds great consolation in that thought.

When Stefan hears Emil, now five years older, laughing in the caravan, the picture opens up inside him once more, settling like a comforting blanket over the anxiety that is tearing at him from all directions. Carina's absence, his father's illness or possibly imminent death, the lack of food, the fact that the situation they are in makes no sense at all. He will deal with all that in a little while. First he needs some peace.

Stefan places the remaining folding chair at one end of the caravan so that he can keep an eye on the direction in which Carina drove off. He settles down, plugs himself into his MP3 player with one hand and flicks through the track list to 'MZ' with the other.

At difficult times Monica Zetterlund's voice can reconnect him with life; she has a tone that sounds to him like the *truth*. He has felt that way ever since he found *Ohh! Monica!* among his father's record collection when he was fourteen years old.

He selects 'Little Green Apples', presses Play and leans back with his eyes closed. As soon as he hears the first few notes of the flute, he begins to relax. When the orchestra softly joins in, accompanied by a single note on the xylophone, Stefan lets out a long, shuddering sigh. Then Monica begins to sing about waking up in the morning with her hair down in her eyes, her lover greeting her with a 'hi'. A smile plays around Stefan's lips as he listens to the description of an ordinary, loving morning routine. He doesn't know how many hundreds of times he has listened to this song, but he tries not to play it too often these days. He doesn't want it to lose its ability to bring the world to life for him.

It is about him and Carina, and about how love does not manifest itself through grand gestures, but through tenderness, through consideration for each other on Mondays, Tuesdays, Wednesdays and every other day of the week. How this is the most beautiful thing in the world. The anxiety that has been gnawing at his body ebbs away a little more, and Stefan takes a deep, relaxed breath as the chorus kicks in.

Then he frowns as Monica tells him there are no seas, no islands, if God didn't make those little green apples. It's as if he is hearing the words for the first time, as if he has no idea of how the chorus goes. His grip on the MP3 player tightens and he holds his breath, waiting for what comes next. Monica sings about the lack of laughter and children playing, the fact that the sun is cold. He switches off the player and opens his eyes, looks up at the empty sky. He glances to the right, to the left. Nothing. No seas, no islands. No mountains, no lakes.

If nothing exists, can love exist?

The love in Monica's song is so great that it is as impossible to deny as the existence of the mountains and the seas. But what happens when there are no mountains, no seas?

The little details. The things that make up everyday life. Working together, sharing leisure time. If all that has been eradicated, what is left?

Stefan removes his earbuds and gets to his feet, still clutching the MP3 player. An object made of plastic and metal. And perhaps God didn't make the little green apples after all. They just exist, like everything else. Until everything ceases to exist.

Tears fill his eyes and he stares out across the field. Then, unsure if he is really seeing what he thinks he is seeing, he scrubs the tears away with his sleeve and takes a closer look.

Ten seconds later he is on the roof of the caravan with the binoculars to his eyes. There is no doubt whatsoever. From exactly the direction in which Carina disappeared in the car, the white figure from the bottom of Mörtsjö lake is now approaching, moving slowly as if it has all the time in the world.

Stefan knows what it wants; he has known ever since their first encounter, which is why he refused to acknowledge its presence when he saw it with Emil. It wants to take everything away from him. Back then he had only his pathetic little life to offer, but now he has more. He has love, he has those happy moments that he has saved, he has a family.

All this is now going to be taken away from him. He knows this with the same clarity as the condemned man knows that this is the end as he faces the firing squad. Thus far but no further.

*

'I want to do a puzzle.'

Molly is sitting on the sofa, her penetrating gaze fixed on Lennart and Olof.

'I'm not sure we've got anything like that,' Olof says. 'We're not used to...'

Molly interrupts him, pointing at the pile of crossword magazines. 'In there. The children's pages.'

'Help yourself, in that case,' Lennart says, peering out of the doorway to see if there's any sign of Peter or Donald.

'But I'm sitting over here,' Molly says, turning to Olof. 'Please can you pass me one?'

'Of course,' Olof says, ignoring the cross look Lennart gives him. He takes a ballpoint pen out of the kitchen drawer and puts it down in front of Molly with a magazine.

Molly gives him a winning smile and flicks through the pages until she finds a join-the-dots puzzle. Olof joins Lennart, looking over his shoulder. Lennart says quietly: 'You shouldn't just do what she says.'

'What harm can it do?'

Lennart gives Olof a look: *Wait and see, wait and see.*

The caravan is small, and neither Lennart nor Olof wants to sit at the kitchen table with Molly, so they both start busying themselves with things that don't need doing. Lennart decides to check out the fridge. He rummages around, then holds up a flattened bullet.

'Hit the side,' he says. 'What kind of ammunition do you think it is?'

Both of them know that they are just talking for the sake of it. They know next to nothing about guns, but Olof takes the irregular piece of metal, turning it over and over. The only result is an unwelcome reminder of the bullets filed down to sharp points that he found outside the grazing pasture on the day that Holger Backlund shot their cows—bullets that were never fired, fortunately.

'No idea,' he says, handing back the bullet as if it was burning his fingers. Both Lennart and Olof pick up a cloth and start wiping down worktops and cupboard doors.

Molly is bent over her puzzle, the rose-pink tip of her tongue sticking out as she concentrates on joining up the dots. Without looking up, she says: 'Why did the cows die?'

Lennart and Olof stop cleaning.

'What cows?' Lennart asks.

'Your cows, of course,' Molly says, drawing several short, jagged lines.

'Our cows aren't dead.'

'Some of them are,' Molly says, leaning back to study her work. 'Why did it happen?'

Lennart goes over and leans on the table, lowering his head to try and catch Molly's eye. 'How do you know about that?'

Molly looks dissatisfied, and adds a couple more lines. 'You told me.'

'No, we didn't.'

'I must have dreamt about it then.'

Using the table for support, Lennart crouches down so that his face is level with Molly's. She draws two more lines, and seems happy with the result.

'Molly,' Lennart says. 'What are you up to?'

Molly looks at him with such a big smile that her entire face seems to be made up of a smile. 'I don't know what you're talking about. What are *you* up to?'

'I'm not up to anything,' Lennart says, his tone less pleasant this time. 'But we haven't mentioned those cows, so...'

Olof places a hand on his shoulder. 'Lennart. Leave it.'

'Yes,' Molly says. 'Leave it. If you know what's good for you.'

Lennart raises his eyebrows and turns to Olof with an expression that says *did you hear that?*, but Olof shakes his head and says: 'Let's go and see how our plants are getting on.'

'Oh, you've got plants!' Molly says, getting up from the table so quickly that she bumps into Lennart, who loses his balance and has to support himself with one hand on the floor to stop himself from falling over. Olof glances at Lennart to check that he's okay; Lennart waves a dismissive hand, and Molly and Olof go outside.

If you know what's good for you.

Lennart was nine years old when his mother was kicked in the head by a horse. After that she was bedridden for long periods, although no one could say what the problem actually was. After years of fruitless visits to doctors she started to pin her hopes on 'wise women' as she called them. Lennart's father had another name for them: 'charlatans'.

Most of them were probably harmless, with their salves and concoctions and amulets, but Lennart remembers the woman who came on the scene when he was thirteen: Lillemor. She was a different kettle of fish.

Unlike many of the others, she made no attempt to convert Lennart and his father to her approach; in fact she didn't even bother to explain it. She did, however, demand full access to the patient with no interruptions. For two hours three times a week the door to his mother's room would remain closed; Lillemor also asked Lennart and his father to leave the house, if possible.

The only reason his father didn't throw Lillemor out, bushy red hair first, was that her treatment was the first that seemed to have any effect. Lennart's mother was able to stay up for longer periods, and there was a clarity in her eyes that had been absent for many years. His father was so pleased that she appeared to be on the road to recovery that Lennart didn't want to rock the boat by saying there was something in that clarity that scared him.

During the fifth or sixth week something changed. His mother started mentioning long-dead relatives as if she had spoken to them recently, and in spite of her isolation she had an astonishing grasp of what was going on in the village. She also began referring to herself in the third person: 'Kerstin needs to rest for a while', 'Kerstin thought that was delicious'.

One day Lennart came home on a Lillemor-free day and went into his mother's bedroom to find Lillemor sitting there anyway. The curtains were closed, and a large candle was burning on the bedside table. As soon as Lennart opened the door he recoiled, because there was something...*distorted* about the image that confronted him.

Lennart had just been learning about perspective in his art lessons in school, but that wouldn't have helped him if he had tried to draw his mother's room at that moment. The angles were strange, and things that should have been far away seemed close, and vice versa. He could count the legs on a fly sitting on the bedstead, while the door handle seemed far out of reach.

Lennart closed his eyes and rubbed his eyelids. When he opened them again the room looked just as it always did. Lillemor had got up and opened the curtains.

'Mum?' Lennart said.

His mother turned her head towards the sound of his voice, but her eyes were unseeing, fixed on a point far beyond him.

'We are not to be disturbed,' Lillemor said, taking a step towards him.

Lennart swallowed and moved forward. 'I didn't think this was one of your days.'

Lillemor tilted her head on one side and gave him a smile that revealed unusually white teeth. 'I had a space in my diary.'

'Right. But I need some help with my homework.'

Lillemor studied him for a moment as Lennart's eyes darted around the room. That was a straight lie; he had no homework, and when he had, he was perfectly capable of doing it on his own.

'No,' Lillemor said. 'You need help explaining where the key to the school storage shed has gone.'

Lennart stood there, feeling as if it had just started snowing in his belly, cold and fluttery. A week ago he had come across a key that the caretaker had dropped, and with this key he and his friends had been able to unlock the shed outside school hours and help themselves to hockey sticks and footballs which they replaced when they had finished playing. It wasn't exactly the crime of the century, but the possession of the key was far more serious.

Lillemor nodded at his confusion and said calmly: 'So off you go, and close the door behind you. If you know what's good for you.'

If you know what's good for you.

That same evening Lennart plucked up more courage than ever before and told his father everything, except the bit about the distorted appearance of the room. The business of the key had been on his conscience anyway, and the blow his father delivered felt like a kind of penance. When he got up from the floor with his ears ringing and the imprint of his father's hand on his cheek, his father asked as if nothing had happened: 'Did she really say that? *If you know what's good for you*? She threatened you?'

'Yes,' Lennart said, trying to stand up straight. 'And there's no... Dad, she couldn't *possibly* have known about the key. It's just like when Mum said that Östlund's Karin had...'

His father interrupted him. 'Be quiet.' He sat there for a while with his head in his hands, then he looked up. 'Well. That's a shame.'

The next time Lillemor turned up, Lennart's father sent her away and told her not to come back. As she left she gave Lennart a long look, a look that said, *you'd better hope that our paths never cross again, if you know what's good for you*, then she got into her silver Volkswagen Beetle and disappeared out of their lives.

Lennart has had a feeling about Molly, a feeling he couldn't put his finger on until she spoke those words. She reminds him of Lillemor. The look in her eyes, the smile, the air of calm, and something else, something hard to define, a kind of *distortion*. Everything around her is slightly skewed, as if the eye has been unable to focus for a moment.

Lennart gets up and hurries out of the caravan; he is suddenly afraid to leave Olof alone with Molly. He shakes his head at his own stupidity. Those things happened over forty years ago, but

If you know what's good for you

he still feels as if it has started snowing in his belly. He shivers as he steps outside and to his relief finds Molly and Olof standing side by side.

'Look at this, Lennart,' Olof says. 'You won't believe your eyes.'

Molly kneels down, hands resting on her thighs, beaming at their little garden.

'What a pretty flower!' she exclaims, stroking the pelargonium's dark green leaves with her fingertips.

No, Lennart doesn't believe his eyes. It looks as if the pelargonium has grown, which is ridiculous; it's only a little while since they planted it. Anyway, the flower is glowing with rude health, so they must have been wrong about the soil being toxic. Then Lennart glances at the rest of their plantation. If there had been a chair nearby, he would have slumped down on it, but instead he links his hands behind his head and simply stares.

The first pale green buds of the potato leaves have begun to peep out of the ground, and right next to them he can see a couple of slender dill shoots. A process that would normally take something in the region of ten days has taken just over an hour.

'What the hell…' he whispers.

Molly wags her finger at him. 'No swearing. It's naughty.'

The whole thing is so bizarre that Lennart can't help clutching at the only straw he can find. Narrowing his eyes, he looks at Olof: 'Have you done this? Is it some kind of joke?'

'When would I have had time? It's crazy, isn't it?'

Lennart shakes his head, utterly bewildered. The only time he has seen something grow like this is when they use those time lapse films on TV; he finds them slightly unpleasant, but this is a hundred times worse, because this is *for real*.

Lennart looks out at the empty field, spreads his arms wide and says, with an anger directed at everything and nothing: 'But this doesn't make any sense! There ought to be a *jungle* here if...' he waves at their rapidly growing plants, '... if this is what's happening!'

'It's very strange,' Olof agrees.

'It's more than strange,' Lennart says, so loudly that Molly tenses and jumps to her feet. 'It's completely... *unnatural*!'

Olof goes over and places his hand on Lennart's shoulder. 'Calm down, Lennart. Calm down. You're frightening the girl.'

It is obvious that Lennart and Olof have widely different perceptions of Molly's character, but Lennart takes a deep breath, allows his arms to drop and nods to Olof to indicate that he is calm, in spite of the cold front in his belly now spreading and covering large parts of his body.

He looks at Molly, convinced that it wasn't the fact that he raised his voice that made her leap up. Quite right. The girl's eyes are screwed up in concentration as she peers out at the field behind Lennart, and her nostrils are twitching as if she is sniffing the air.

'Molly,' Olof says, but the child merely shakes her head and quickly walks away from them, out into the field. Olof hurries after her, telling her to stop, but Lennart stays where he is long enough to see Stefan hurry down from the roof of his caravan, rush inside and come straight out again clutching his son's hand. He drags the boy to their car, pushes him into the passenger seat, then runs around to the driver's side.

'Stefan?' Lennart shouts. 'What's going on?'

Either Stefan doesn't hear or he decides to ignore him, because five seconds later he has started the car and set off in the opposite direction from Molly and Olof.

The girl has broken into a run now; Olof is lumbering after her as best he can, but he is falling further and further behind, still shouting to her to stop. Lennart looks down at the glorious pelargonium, swears to himself, then sets off after them.

Isabelle's tongue is a lump of meat in her mouth, so swollen that it seems to fill the entire cavity. She would like to stuff her face with snow, ice, ice cream to cool down the burning, throbbing pain that is bringing tears to her eyes. Now that Carina is no longer the avenger, destroying all before her, Isabelle feels nothing but hatred towards her.

Isabelle's lips are numb, and as they approach the white figure she feels something trickling from the corner of her mouth. She wipes it away and discovers that it is not blood, but saliva. Her mouth is watering.

She is intimately acquainted with the meaninglessness of life, more so than most. Just as some people have genes that make them good at maths, while others have a high pain threshold or can draw a perfect circle freehand, Isabelle is gifted with two defining qualities: her beauty and her constant terror over the emptiness of her existence.

Just as someone who is capable of multiplying two-digit numbers in their head cannot be called a mathematical genius, so someone who says that 'life seems a bit empty sometimes' cannot be compared with Isabelle when it comes to her capacity for experiencing the futility of life, every second and with every fibre of her being.

She doesn't know when the realisation struck her; it has been there for as long as she can remember. Everything is an illusion, a pretence, an *as if*, and its only purpose is for life to continue until it is over. When the bookmark angels she had made were passed around her father's guests to cries of delight, when some boy told her she was the most beautiful girl in the world, she knew exactly what to say and how to behave, but nothing touched her, because these people were just as empty and unreal as her.

Only extreme horror films evoke a response and create an illusion of being in the moment, with the lower bar set around the level of *Hostel*. The sight of people being hunted down, tortured and slashed to pieces with close-ups of plenty of gore can give her peace of mind, temporarily at least. The French wave is her favourite—*Frontiers*,

Inside, Martyrs. She has spent many sleepless nights watching those films over and over again. As dawn approaches, the madness is lurking.

Paradoxically, it is her illness that has kept her comparatively healthy. The hyperthyroidism has given a direction, a partial goal to her days. She has to eat to avoid intense physical discomfort. Without this discomfort she might just have sat down in an armchair and faded away. There is nothing for her in the world anyway.

Hence the saliva. The white figure does not belong to the same conceptual world as everything that Isabelle perhaps renounced even before she could talk; it is the first indication that her feeling is justified. There is another world, a world that is purer and more real. Isabelle has understood what the white figure wants, and she intends to oblige.

They have now caught up with the figure, which keeps on moving, its dark eyes fixed on the horizon. Isabelle's eyes caress its perfect white skin, its body unmarked by human degeneration.

'What shall we do?' Carina asks; for some incomprehensible reason her voice is trembling.

Isabelle makes a two-part gesture which means: *Drive a bit further. Then stop.*

Carina turns to her and nods, fear shining in her eyes. 'Yes. We have to stop it. Before it reaches the camp. And the children.'

'Mm-hm,' Isabelle says.

Carina speeds up and drives a couple of hundred metres beyond the figure, then stops, leaving the engine ticking over. Isabelle indicates that she should turn it off, which she does. She seems to have lost any capacity for taking the initiative, which suits Isabelle perfectly.

They get out of the car and go round to the boot. Isabelle takes out the heaviest rounders bat. When Carina reaches out for it, Isabelle points to the other one. The flat one. The girl's bat.

Carina leans over and Isabelle considers whacking her right away, but decides the angle isn't right. She needs a clean blow to the back of the head to avoid any difficulties. Then there's the bleeding. Even if Isabelle manages to crack Carina's skull, there is no guarantee that there will be much blood. She will need to open a vein, and she lacks the tools for such an operation.

Hang on a minute.

Her emergency make-up bag in the glove compartment also contains a pair of nail scissors. For her *toenails*. She takes care of, or fails to take care of, her fingernails with her teeth. The scissors should do the job of opening up the jugular vein.

'Should we wait here, or what?' Carina says, glancing nervously towards the figure, which is approaching across the grass.

'Mm-hm,' Isabelle says, studying her head. It's probably best to hit her really hard if she's going to bring her down with a single blow. But…She mustn't kill her, because then her heart will stop beating and the blood won't be pumped out. Then again, surely there will be some blood? When she strikes the blow? Isabelle blinks a couple of times.

Jugular vein. Nail scissors.

Absolutely. That's the way. But it is as if she has forgotten one detail: that *she* is the one who is going to do it. Isabelle Sundberg, who was so well placed for the Rodebjer contract. She was going to *call* them, that's what she was going to do.

She no longer wants to call them, the contract is no longer important, it never was. So is the alternative to smash Carina's skull, to open the vein, get the blood out?

Yes? That's right, isn't it?

They are standing next to the car clutching their bats, waiting for the white figure, which is getting closer and closer. Isabelle is slightly behind Carina, at exactly the right angle and the right distance for a direct hit that would send the ball flying into the forest, if there was a ball and if there was a forest.

'Shit,' Carina says when the figure is perhaps twenty metres away from them. 'I'm so fucking scared.'

Isabelle lowers the tip of the bat to the ground so that she can get a decent swing. She fixes her gaze on the back of Carina's head and waits for a sign, a word of exhortation.

'Mummy!'

Molly is racing across the field, with the two farmers lumbering along behind her, and when Isabelle narrows her eyes she can see the outline of the camp. She didn't know they were so close. She lifts up the bat and holds it in her arms, squeezing it tightly.

*

Majvor isn't quite sure how it happened, but she seems to be alone in the camp. Stefan came in and dragged his son away before they had even started the attack on the Death Star, and when Majvor stepped out of the caravan she saw Lennart and Olof shambling across the field after Molly, just as Stefan drove off.

So.

Majvor looks at the spot where her own caravan stood, and it is a sorry sight. What used to be the floor of the awning is now a lonely expanse of wooden decking, with upturned chairs, tables and plant pots. It needs tidying up, and guess whose job that will be?

The sound of Stefan's car fades away, and all is quiet. Majvor hears a noise she can't identify, a quiet smacking and slurping coming from somewhere nearby. She bends down to look under Stefan's caravan, but her back is so stiff that she has to get on her knees to see properly.

Benny. It's a while since she thought about the dog, but he is lying here with that cat he was barking at before. The cat yawns, apparently not in the least bothered by the proximity of her former arch-enemy, while Benny carries on chewing.

What's he chewing?

For a moment Majvor imagines that Benny is chomping away at the cat's tail. She crawls forward and takes a closer look. There are a few scraps of black rubber between Benny's front paws, and Benny is determinedly destroying the larger piece in his mouth. A hose, or what was once a hose.

'Benny,' Majvor says, and he looks up at her. 'Have you made a new friend?' Benny snorts and shakes his head, then resumes his chewing, as if the question is too stupid to warrant an answer. With some difficulty, Majvor gets to her feet.

So.

Funny how things can change. Yesterday evening she and Donald had sat there peacefully watching the music festival from Skansen, then Donald went off to talk to Peter while Majvor read the latest instalment of the serial in her magazine. Now Peter, Donald and the magazine have gone, and she is standing here all alone in the middle of a field. How did that Gunnar Wiklund song go?

Something about walking alone on a deserted shore, as the waves... hm, hm...What was it the waves were doing?

Majvor wanders aimlessly towards the decking, because at least it is a place that is somehow hers. The fridge is lying on its side with the door open and the cans have rolled out. She looks around and thinks she sees something glinting in the grass where their caravan used to be. What can it be?

Ouf!

Down on her knees again, that's all she seems to be doing these days. She scrabbles in the grass until her fingers close around an object made of metal. It is a ring. A gold ring, one half blackened and pitted as if something has been eating away at it, while the other half is more or less intact.

Majvor peers at the inscription on the inside. Part of it has been destroyed, but she can just make out what remains: '& Erik 25/5/1904'.

A wedding ring. Belonging to someone called Erik, or the person he married one hundred and ten years ago. Judging by the size, it was probably Erik's ring; women don't usually have such large fingers. Then again...Majvor tries it on her own ring finger, pushing it down until it meets her own wedding ring, and it's not a bad fit. Only slightly too big.

She crawls around, searching in the grass, and she is rewarded with another discovery: a small, irregularly shaped lump of gold. When she bites it to check if there is any softness in it, she immediately realises what it is: a gold filling from someone's tooth. It probably isn't all that far-fetched to assume it was Erik's.

A few metres away she finds a blackened gold chain and two more fillings. Then another ring, but this one is so badly damaged that it is impossible to read the inscription.

Majvor jingles her collection in her hand. Very interesting. First the crosses, and now this. It's astonishing what discoveries you can make if you don't spend all your time rushing around and coming up with stupid ideas. If you just take things a little more slowly.

*

When Lennart and Olof reach the Toyota, Molly has already been there for quite some time. They are puffing and blowing, and the sweat is making their eyes sting, which is why they don't see anything strange about the group. Two adults and a child, just as they expected.

They catch their breath and look over at the car; only then do they realise that Carina is sitting inside, clutching a rounders bat and staring out of the side window at a *complete stranger* who is talking to Molly. A man in a suit who is crouching down, his head so close to Molly's that the brim of his hat is touching her forehead as they whisper together.

Lennart gives a start when he sees Isabelle, who is leaning against the back of the car looking very unhappy. There is blood around her mouth, and her face is swollen and discoloured.

'What's happened?' he asks, pointing at the man. 'Did he…?'

Isabelle shakes her head. What has happened to her is a question for later, but at least the man wasn't responsible, so Lennart walks over to him, holding out his hand. 'Hello. We didn't think there was anyone else around. I'm Lennart.'

With a nod to Molly, the man stands up. 'Bengt,' he says, shaking Lennart's hand. 'Bengt Andersson. Travelling salesman.'

Lennart can't help suppressing a laugh. *Travelling salesman.* When did that profession cease to exist? People schlepping around the countryside selling underwear, with their entire stock in the back of the car. Lennart is clearly dealing with a joker here, so he answers in the same vein: 'Lennart Österberg. Vagabond and tenant farmer.'

Bengt raises his eyebrows. 'Excuse me, sir, but are you jesting with me?'

He seems to be genuinely annoyed. Lennart looks him up and down: his suit is old-fashioned, the pomaded hair is reminiscent of men's hairstyles when Lennart was a child, and there is no denying the overall impression: from his appearance and manner, Bengt Andersson could be any boring, ordinary man from the 1950s.

Lennart's doubts turn to confusion when Olof says: 'Are you just going to stand there, Lennart?'

'What do you mean?' Lennart says. 'We're having a conversation.'

Olof bursts out laughing and looks to Isabelle for support, but she refuses to meet his eye. 'No you're not,' he says. 'You're just standing there.'

Lennart has only Molly to turn to for confirmation, but the girl is simply staring at him with a supercilious smile.

Bengt tips his hat and says: 'You must excuse me—I'm late for a meeting.'

Aren't we having a conversation?

Lennart expands his examination to take in Bengt's face, and his confusion turns to discomfort when he realises that he somehow can't *see* it. Bengt has a face, of course, but it is kind of unclear, like the memory of a person you haven't met for a long time. If Lennart were giving a witness statement to the police he might possibly be able to help with a rudimentary ID sketch, but nothing more. The mouth in particular would create major problems. Lennart has no impression of it at all; it's as if the man has no mouth.

Lennart takes a step to the side and places himself directly in front of Bengt, who is about to leave.

'Hang on a minute, mate,' he says. 'Who exactly are you, and what...'

Bengt interrupts him. 'I'm sorry, sir, but I really don't think it's appropriate for you to address me as *mate*.'

Olof comes over to Lennart and says: 'That's enough.' He holds out his hand and Bengt shakes it. After a brief silence, the two men let go of each other's hands. Lennart looks at Olof; it is clear from his expression that he is reacting to something that is being said, and is saying something in reply. But his mouth doesn't move. Bengt turns to Lennart: 'If you will excuse me, I'm afraid I really do have to leave now.' He tips his hat once more and sets off towards the camp.

'Hang on a minute,' Lennart says again; now that he is aware of the phenomenon, he realises that talking requires no effort whatsoever from the muscles in his tongue and lips. It is as if an imaginary mouth inside his head is producing the words. 'Wait. What kind of meeting are you going to, *sir*?'

Without slowing down, Bengt says over his shoulder: 'I'm meeting a colleague. Good day to you.'

*

Emil is sitting in his car seat staring sulkily at the floor. It was really stupid of Daddy to drag him away like that. He was having fun with the lady. People who talk about God and Jesus are usually a bit of a pain, but the lady was cool. She knew how to play, and old ladies are often rubbish when it comes to playing.

Emil also thinks Daddy's behaviour is strange, not to mention alarming. He isn't saying anything, and he seems scared. That's the worst thing in the world as far as Emil is concerned: grown-ups who are scared. It's okay for children to be scared for a little while, of Alfie Atkins and the ghost for example—although that doesn't frighten Emil any more—but it soon passes. When grown-ups get scared, they stay that way.

They have been driving for a little while now, and Emil doesn't like the fact that they have gone away from Mummy. Daddy never does that. Perhaps this is what it's like when children are kidnapped? That's it. Emil will pretend he's been kidnapped, and everything will feel much better.

How much will the kidnapper demand as a ransom? Would Mummy and Daddy pay a million to get Emil back? How much is a million anyway? Perhaps it's the same as the cost of a house. Would Mummy and Daddy sell the house?

Emil thinks it over. Yes, they probably would, because they've told him over and over again that he's the best thing in their lives, that they think the world of him. In which case he must be worth more than the house. It's a strange thought. The house is huge, and the cooker is brand-new, with those hotplates you can't burn yourself on.

Emil feels quite pleased. A million. He is worth a million. Probably. He comes out of the game for a moment to ask a question.

'Daddy? If someone came and kidnapped…'

Daddy holds up his hand to shut him up. Emil really doesn't like it when Daddy does that, treating him as if he was a little kid. Emil is about to push the hand away and ask the question anyway when he realises from Daddy's expression that this is serious, that Daddy can see something. Emil turns his head to look through the windscreen, and what he sees makes him gasp and let out a sob.

About two hundred metres away there is an elephant, coming towards them. It is heading straight for them on its four tree-trunk legs, and it looks exactly like Molly said it would look.

Emil has seen ordinary elephants at the zoo in Kolmården, and although they're a bit scary because they're so big, there is something really nice and gentle about their slow, heavy movements. It's as if they are always thinking carefully about everything they do.

This elephant is not nice or gentle. For a start it isn't pale grey, the colour that dolphins are too; no, this elephant is covered with so much dirt and mud that it is almost black, and Emil knows that it isn't thinking about anything except moving forward with its thick, dark trunk swinging from side to side.

Ordinary elephants don't have any teeth, at least not that you can see, but this one has. Jagged yellow teeth that are so long they don't fit in its mouth, so the elephant's jaws are open as it lurches along on a collision course with their car.

And it is smoking. Just like when Daddy burns piles of leaves in the spring, a pillar of smoke is rising from the elephant and dispersing against the blue sky. With his hands pressed to his tummy Emil stares at the elephant, struck dumb with terror, because he knows what it is: *the most dangerous thing in the whole wide world.*

That is when Daddy does something terrible. So far they have been driving at forty kilometres per hour; Emil has glanced at the speedometer from time to time. Instead of turning the car around, Daddy puts his foot down, and their speed climbs to fifty, sixty.

'No, Daddy! No!' Emil screams.

'We have to,' Daddy says through gritted teeth. 'Close your eyes, there's a good boy. Keep your head down and close your eyes.'

Emil realises what Daddy is intending to do. He is going to drive straight at the elephant, which is crazy. If it was an ordinary elephant the impact might have broken its legs so that it wouldn't be able to walk, but that's not what is going to happen in this case. This elephant is going to pick them up in its trunk, lift them to its mouth and chew them up.

Emil tears his eyes away from the speedometer and looks up. He blinks a couple of times and looks again. The elephant is gone, but walking towards them now, so close that Emil can see the details of his mask, is Darth Vader. His black cloak is billowing around him, and through the roar of the engine Emil thinks he can hear the deep, wheezing sound of Darth Vader breathing. He is carrying his light-saber in his right hand, and his left hand is pointing straight at Emil. In a few seconds the car will hit him.

At that moment Emil has a sudden flash of insight. He can't put it into words that would convince Daddy, and time is short, so he simply yells: 'It's just pretend!' He twists towards his father, grabs the steering wheel and pulls it towards him.

Daddy is much stronger, of course, but Emil's unexpected intervention makes the car swerve to the side, and they miss Darth Vader by a metre. They carry on for another twenty metres or so before Daddy manages to brake. His face is red, his mouth is opening and closing, but no words are coming out.

Emil has never felt so strongly that Daddy might be about to hit him; he remembers the iron grip on his arm, and shrinks as far away as his seatbelt will allow before he says: 'It's not real, Daddy. It's just pretend.'

He glances out of the rear window and sees that Darth Vader is still walking along as if nothing has happened, moving away from them so that only the back of his shiny black helmet and his cloak can be seen.

The Groke, Emil thinks. *He looks like the Groke.*

Daddy read a couple of the Moomintroll books to Emil when he was five, but they had to stop because Emil found the Groke so upsetting; everything she touches will freeze, and as a result she is rejected by everyone, and is terribly lonely. Suddenly Emil understands. If he was still five years old, and if he hadn't seen Star Wars, it might have been the Groke out there.

Daddy has stopped opening and closing his mouth, and Emil thinks he might be able to find the right words to explain now. 'It's just stuff we've made up,' he says. 'It's not really there. It's just... nothing.'

Daddy's eyes are starting to look more normal, and as if Emil were the grown-up he places a hand on Daddy's arm and says reassuringly: 'Daddy? I'm right, you know.'

*

Donald is sitting on the bed with the gun on his knee, gazing at the devastation. Everything that was loose inside the caravan has ended up on the floor or the worktops, at least half of the plates and glasses were smashed to smithereens when they fell out of the cupboards, and Majvor's ingredients are all over the place. Her unbaked cinnamon buns are plastered across the sofa, where they continue to rise.

Donald is so fucking furious that he has stopped reflecting on whether this whole thing is a dream or not. If it *is* a dream then it would be pointless to retaliate, which would be unfortunate, so from now on he intends to act as if it were real, whether it is or not.

One of the speakers from the surround sound system has fallen off its shelf and cracked against the bed frame. Donald pokes at it with the barrel of the gun. Twenty-two thousand kronor; that's how much it cost to have a home entertainment package installed in the caravan, but now both the DVD player and the TV have been torn loose and are lying on the floor, so presumably they're fucked.

There are people who go around being grateful and humble, whatever life throws at them, thanking God or Fate or Winnie-the-Pooh for the gifts they have received. Donald is not one of those people. He has earned every penny through hard work and good decisions. He's been given nothing, not one fucking thing.

His stomach ties itself in knots as he thinks about how he sucked up to Peter, a mediocre footballer who made millions running around after a lump of leather in Italy, and who now has the gall to sit there moaning because he's been booted out of the national team too soon, in spite of the fact that he can easily live on the money that has simply fallen into his lap. The little shit!

And then the little shit comes along and wrecks Donald's caravan, for which Donald has toiled in the sweat of his brow, before taking off like a frightened rabbit in *Donald's* car!

Donald kicks the speaker so that it flies across the room and lands on top of the dough smeared across the sofa. He is so angry that his hands are shaking when he gets up, slips the gun over his shoulder and goes outside.

All around him there is nothing but emptiness as far as the eye can see. He checks out the caravan and discovers that the fixings for the awning have been torn away, which will mean an expensive repair job. This makes him even more livid, if that were possible. He wants to shoot something, any fucking thing, but there is nothing in sight.

He goes to the back of the caravan and lowers the ladder, then stands hesitating with one hand on the bottom rung. He's not in the best shape, and if he fell and hurt himself out here it could prove fatal.

They didn't think about that, the bastards. What if Donald had been seriously injured when Peter drove off with him? Would they just have left him out here in the middle of nowhere to bleed to death like an injured animal? Would they?

Tears of rage spring to Donald's eyes as he hauls himself up the ladder. Anger gives him strength, and he doesn't stop until he is on the roof. He unhooks the gun and peers through the sight in the direction in which Peter took off in his car. Nothing. The little bunny has scampered home to mummy.

Or...

Donald lowers the gun. Only now, standing on the roof with nothing to obscure his view, does he realise that there is nothing to say that the camp lies that way. Donald has no idea where the camp is.

He positions the shotgun against his shoulder and slowly sweeps the barrel across the horizon, moving no more than a centimetre at a time so that he can search the entire area for a deviation, a hint of unevenness. When he is looking in precisely the opposite direction from the route Peter took, he spots something. He gasps and lowers the gun, as if to make sure that the sight isn't playing a trick on him.

Yes. Even without magnification he can see the tiny figure in the distance. He looks through the sight again, and the figure moving across the field becomes clearer. Its body is blotchy red, and it has no hands.

The Bloodman

The gun begins to shake and Donald is no longer able to fix the figure in the sight. When he lowers the weapon his body is tense, hunched as if to defend itself against an attack, while the old fear slashes and tears at his belly and the guilt presses him down, down. Then something happens. A simple thought takes root in Donald's head and flowers in a second.

Enough.

Enough. Everyone and everything is trying to break him, to bring him to his knees. Peter and those other milksops sitting there shaking in their little camp, noses trembling; even this fucking place is trying to scare him into submission. Enough. This is not How the West Was

Won—no, we set off into the wilds with our guns in our hands and we took the land that had been given to us, if we just had the courage to be men.

A man or a mouse, Donald? A man or a mouse?

Donald nods to himself, slips the gun over his shoulder once more and climbs down from the roof without even considering that he might fall. He doesn't fall.

When he reaches the ground he inserts a cartridge in the magazine, then sets off resolutely towards the Bloodman. After a short while he starts to whistle 'John Brown's Body'.

Enough.

*

Peter has been driving around aimlessly for fifteen minutes, sometimes heading to the left or the right without seeing anything but the horizon all around him. This is just what he was afraid of. He is hopelessly lost. Nothing about the field changes: there is only that endless expanse of green everywhere he looks.

He has sniffed at the liquid that ran out of the glove compartment and established that it is whisky; he caught a few drops in his cupped hand and lapped it up. This made him feel better for a little while, but the monotony of the field is taking its toll. It is as if he is being hollowed out, becoming as empty as the landscape in which he is driving around, with no goal and with the same view constantly before his eyes.

At the same time, something is growing within his body. An irritation, an itch, as if the soft tissue of his intestines is slowly hardening, chafing from the inside. He is *itchy* in places where it is impossible to scratch without the help of a knife.

To distract himself he switches on the radio and smiles in spite of himself when he recognises that cracked, croaky voice. It's Peter Himmelstrand himself, singing one of the last songs he wrote, and possibly the most bitter. 'Thanks for All Those Slaps'. It's about things going wrong just when everything seems okay. Peter stops thinking about driving and focuses on the song, which seems to him to be truer and more real than the place in which he has ended up. When it gets to the part where Himmelstrand says his old man always hit him, he starts to sing along.

Yes, there are so many occasions in life when it might be appropriate to give up, to stop trying. There have been so many times when he could have done just that.

He could have given up when a knee injury ended his career in professional football. Or when the Italian restaurant chain he and Hasse had started up went bust. When all possible routes were closed off, one by one. When it became clear that he had married a woman with whom it was impossible to be happy, and had a daughter who turned out to be a stranger.

To allow his legs to give way, to fall over. Inside. Shoot down the energetic little devil that always drives him on. Kill him. How liberating would that be?

The refrain dies away: 'At last I know my place…' Peter stops the car and turns off the radio. The air has thickened once more; it is pressing on his head. He leans back in his seat and examines how he is feeling.

The itching sensation has become even more noticeable. It is as if a huge spider is squatting somewhere inside his chest and stretching out its long legs right to the tips of his fingers, tickling and tugging at him. No, not a spider. A tree. A tree has taken root in his heart and is reaching out with its branches.

Peter closes his eyes. And sees the tree. How stupid is he? Coming up with such complicated images when the answer is much simpler. It is *the circulation of his blood* that he can feel. He has become aware of the blood that usually passes quietly around his body. And it is pulling at him.

He gets out of the car and takes a few steps in the direction in which his blood wants him to go. When he sees what lies in the distance up ahead, he stops. There is a thin band of darkness on the horizon.

Over there. Come on. Let's go over there.

He doesn't know how high the wall of darkness is or how far away, but he has to physically resist the compulsion to go towards it.

Why resist? That's where you have to go. You know that.

Peter holds out his hand with the fingers spread wide, and relaxes his muscles. The hand really is being drawn towards whatever is beyond the horizon. He walks around to the passenger door, opens the glove compartment and takes out a shard of glass from the broken whisky bottle. It has a sharp point, so there is no need to slice; he can simply stab.

It takes a couple of attempts before he manages to pierce the skin of his left middle finger. He squeezes out a fat bead of blood with his thumb, then turns his hand palm down. The blood slowly becomes a drop, then falls.

There is no doubt whatsoever. It's not just in his head. The drop of blood does not fall straight down, but turns off towards the darkness. Peter wipes his finger on his shorts, then clamps his arms to his sides as if he were standing to attention, his gaze fixed on the horizon, swaying slightly because of the power that is pulling at him, at his blood.

Life is no picnic, for heaven's sake.

What does it matter, after all? He could go back to the camp, to Isabelle and Molly, maybe manage to get away so that he can carry on ploughing through the mud for another year, and another year after that. He has been offered an alternative.

I'm coming, Peter. Peter is coming.

He gets back in the car and drives towards the band of darkness.

*

So.

After replacing the cans in the small fridge, Majvor has settled down in her chair with a can of Coke by one foot and a Budweiser by the other. She rarely allows herself a treat, but sitting here alone with her treasure trove she has decided to take a little holiday.

She has the occasional glass of low-alcohol beer with herring or a prawn sandwich, but how long is it since she simply sat down and opened a can of strong beer? Twenty years? Longer? She feels free and slightly naughty as she tips back her head and allows the cool liquid to run down her throat.

It doesn't taste very nice, but she takes another swig simply because she *can*. Under normal circumstances she prefers not to sanction Donald's alcohol consumption by following his example. When he really gets into the swing of things he can sit there knocking back can after can, which he then crumples and throws on the floor, building a pile of growing evidence of his achievement. He can be so…Majvor wrinkles her nose at the bitter taste and puts down the can as she searches for the right word. *Unsavoury.* That's it. *Repulsive*, in fact.

It is many years since anything of a sexual nature happened between them. It was different when they were young, oh yes. But after Majvor gave birth to Henrik, their youngest, it was as if a light went out, and stayed that way.

Majvor was usually too tired, and if she was in the mood occasionally, it seemed that more and more frequently Donald wasn't up to it. They never talked about it because *you don't talk about that kind of thing*, but each of them slowly withdrew and stopped trying.

Majvor sighs and reaches for the can of Coke. Admittedly she's no Liz Taylor; she's overweight and her legs aren't up to much, but could things have been different between her and Donald? Could they still have had a sex life?

She opens the can and swills the cola around her mouth to wash away the taste of the beer. No. With the way Donald looks and behaves these days, it's out of the question. Nononono. Just thinking about Donald in that way almost makes her feel sick.

So it's come to this. To tell the truth, at the moment she feels as if it would be best if Donald never came back. She would be able to lead a quiet life instead of running around trying to please him all the time.

She has dedicated her life to being a mother, and now that job is done, perhaps she could have a rest?

Majvor puts down the can, leans back and folds her hands on her stomach so that she can really, really relax. She manages five seconds. Then she looks around and everything changes. She sits up straight, narrowing her eyes as she stares out at the field. It's impossible.

Jimmy?

She is not a crazy person. When she imagines her conversations with James Stewart, she knows exactly what she is doing: using her imagination. Sitting him down opposite her in the role that suits her at the time, making him speak Swedish.

The slightly knock-kneed figure approaching across the field, dressed as Will Lockhart in *The Man from Laramie*, is no figment of her imagination. Majvor hasn't thought about James Stewart for over an hour, and she has done nothing to conjure him up.

And yet it's definitely him. She can hear the jingle of the spurs on his boots, visible below the turned-up jeans; she can see the gun belt hanging low on his hips, and his brown suede jacket is dusty, as if he has just come back from riding across the plains. His face is weather-beaten and sunburnt, his blue eyes shine beneath the brim of the characteristic white hat that Jimmy wore in so many of his cowboy films. Those eyes are looking at Majvor as he moves closer.

Majvor's hands flutter nervously over her body as if to brush something away: dirt, several kilos of fat, quite a lot of years. It's not fair of him to turn up *now*, when she's old and such a sight. However, she still gets up and goes to meet him.

She knows that James Stewart has been dead for seventeen years, and that what she is seeing must be a particularly detailed vision, or perhaps she is well on the way to being as crazy as Donald, but right now none of that matters at all. He's *here*. That wonderful, incomparable man whom she has seen on the screen in so many roles, the best of them all: James Stewart.

Majvor accepts what she sees so completely that the only thing she finds strange is that he doesn't have his horse with him. Pie, who accompanied him throughout his career in Westerns—how did he get here without Pie?

That's the first question she asks when they meet in the open space in the middle of the camp: 'Where's Pie?' she says in Swedish.

James Stewart pushes back his hat with one finger, and Majvor, who is already weak at the knees, is quite overcome. She curses herself, feeling like a silly little girl.

He doesn't speak Swedish, you idiot.

She blushes, partly because of her stupidity and partly because she is now going to have to speak English, which is not her strongest suit. Whenever she and Donald visit the USA, he always teases her about her limited vocabulary and terrible accent.

But her fears are unfounded. James Stewart smiles in that gentle, sad way as only he can and says in Swedish: 'He couldn't come along this time. Unfortunately.'

In the last word Majvor picks up a hint of Roslagen, as if he comes from her home area. Her overwhelming feeling is one of relief, because she will be able to talk freely. She decides to start again.

'Please forgive me,' she says with a little curtsey. 'Good afternoon. I'm Majvor.'

She holds out her hand and James Stewart takes it. His handshake is firm but not painfully so, his hand warm and dry. It is a hand that makes her want to shrink, to shrink and become tiny so that she can curl up inside it like a baby bird.

'James,' he says. 'Call me Jimmy—most people do.'

Majvor swallows and nods. She is *not* going to start babbling about how much she loves his films, how she has dreamt of meeting him all her adult life, because no doubt every woman he comes across says exactly the same thing, so instead she asks: 'What are you doing here?'

It is a reasonable question, and she hopes he won't think she is being too brusque. Jimmy doesn't seem to be offended; he simply nods as if the question is justified.

'I'm meeting someone,' he says.

Majvor nods too. This is going well. A reasonable answer to a reasonable question. Suddenly a jolt of fear shoots through her belly. What on earth is she doing? She's still holding on to his hand, even though he has loosened his grip! What a faux pas!

Majvor quickly lets go of the beloved hand and strokes her stomach. Another source of embarrassment is that she is wearing her scruffy sweatpants, her house clothes. She really would have liked to be a little better dressed on such an occasion, but Jimmy doesn't seem to mind; he smiles at her and asks: 'So how are you, Majvor?'

There is no denying it any longer. Ever since Jimmy turned up and Majvor realised that it really was him, she also realised something else. That Donald might just be right, and this is all a dream. What other explanation can there be for the fact that Jimmy Stewart appears to be standing here talking to her, saying her name and wondering how she is?

But in that case…in that case it is Donald who is a product of her imagination, not vice versa. *Donald* would never dream up Jimmy Stewart, oh no; he's more likely to come up with Åsa-Nisse, the cunning farmer/inventor loved by Swedish film audiences and hated by the critics in equal measure.

'What are you smiling at?'

Majvor has been impolite enough to lose herself in her thoughts while Jimmy was standing there waiting for a response.

'Oh…Nothing. It's just so nice to meet you. At long last. So I'm fine, thanks.'

Jimmy nods thoughtfully, as if she has said something profound. She really would like to come out with something wise or witty, anything to show that she's not just some flibbertigibbet, but the only thing she can think of to ask is how he could possibly have had a romance with Olivia de Havilland. That's not really acceptable, so instead she says: 'Who are you meeting?'

Jimmy nods towards the field, in the opposite direction. Majvor turns around and wobbles slightly; she would have fallen if Jimmy hadn't taken her arm and helped her to keep her balance. Unfortunately she cannot enjoy his touch, because her mind is fully occupied with trying to process what she is seeing.

Walking across the field, or rather *strolling*, his face glowing with amiability and the joy of life, is Elwood P. Dowd, Majvor's favourite incarnation of Jimmy. But that's not what made her wobble. Fifty metres behind him is Harvey, a six-foot-tall rabbit, kind of waddling along behind Elwood on his hind legs.

It's Harvey who tips the balance. Majvor has often conjured up Elwood P. Dowd for a chat; she has frequently dreamt of being hugged by Will Lockhart, the Man from Laramie. But Harvey? Harvey doesn't even exist in the film, or rather he does, but Harvey isn't... *real*. There are no six-foot-tall rabbits, and on top of everything else this one is wearing a bow tie, just like...what's his name...Little Hop in the *Bamse* cartoons!

Majvor no longer thinks this is fantastic, or even pleasant. As she watches the oversized rabbit waddling towards the camp, a shiver runs down her spine and she is scared. This is crazy stuff, and crazy stuff is dangerous.

'Majvor,' Jimmy Stewart says, but Majvor doesn't want to listen to him any longer. She has noticed a detail which only a dedicated Jimmy-fantasist would pick up. The colour of the handkerchief knotted around Will Lockhart's neck is *exactly* the same shade of pink as Harvey's bow tie, and that's not right. Lockhart's neckerchief should be medium-red.

There is something dubious going on here, and even if she can't work out what it is or why, it makes her feel uncomfortable, and in spite of everything she wishes Donald was here. He knew there was something in the air, even though he drew the wrong conclusions.

She ignores the attractions of Jimmy Stewart; she goes over to Stefan's caravan and crouches down. Benny has stopped chewing the hose, and is now staring out at the field, tension in every line of his body. The cat also seems on edge; she has pricked up her ears, and is looking in the same direction as Benny.

'Benny,' Majvor says, and the dog looks up at her as if he is waiting for instructions, which is exactly what Majvor intends to give him.

234

'Benny,' she says again, clapping her hands. 'Go and find your master, Benny. Find your master.'

*

It's nice to be given an order. Benny has been feeling confused for quite some time; he hasn't known what to do with himself. Nothing is as it should be. The strangest thing of all is this business with Cat. They are getting on really well. Benny no longer has the slightest desire to chase or bite Cat. Cat makes sense, unlike almost everything else.

The Grandchildren, for example. At a distance the Grandchildren smell was exactly as it should be—brand-new, sweet and gentle. But now they have arrived in the camp, Benny can smell something else, an old smell like stuff that has been lying around in the forest for too long. It's faint, but it's there, and it's not right. No Grandchild smells like that.

Besides which, it's almost impossible to look at them. The Sun has disappeared, but instead it is the Grandchildren that are hurting his eyes, so Benny doesn't look at them, he just sniffs, and he can't make any sense of the way they smell.

'Find your master,' the Mistress says, and Benny is only too happy to oblige. He wants to get away from here, away from the old Grandchildren. He crawls out from under the caravan and runs over to his basket, which is lying upside down on the grass, and sniffs all around it. He sneezes and looks out across the field. The sniffing isn't really necessary; he knows what his caravan smells like, and there is a clear scent trail to follow.

He gives himself a shake, then sets off at a reasonable speed. Since Benny finds it difficult to keep several things in his head at once, he hasn't given Cat a thought since he was told to find his Master, but as he runs he becomes aware of a soft, rhythmic sound beside him.

He turns his head and sees that Cat has come with him, taking long leaps as she runs in that peculiar way of hers. Benny doesn't

235

know whether Cat understands what they are supposed to be doing, but it feels good to have her there. He gives a little bark, and Cat makes a humming sound.

Benny has no idea what that means, but he thinks it means that Cat is happy, that Cat thinks this is good too.

They run.

*

Isabelle's hands begin to shake as the voracious hole in her body opens up and grows bigger and bigger. The hunger tears at her like a physical sensation, and her skin crawls as sweat drips from her armpits. Her tongue is numb; she might not even be capable of eating anything anyway. Torment has taken over her body, and disappointment is clouding her judgement.

Everything is ruined.

The white figure is not interested in her, and her yearning was misdirected. There is no other life, no other existence; she is trapped inside her screaming body. Nobody wants her, nobody is going to come and save her. Isabelle smacks herself in the face as she walks towards her caravan, welcoming the pain that floods her body as something bursts in her mouth.

Falling apart. I am falling apart.

She goes inside, and her hands are so sweaty and shaky that she has difficulty opening the drawer under the bed. There are only three Xanor tablets left, and it takes her a minute to push them out of the blister pack and cram them into her mouth, where they are pushed to one side by her tongue and end up tucked in her cheek. She staggers over to the sink and turns the tap, but the tap is already fully open, and no water comes out. The taste of blood mingles with the bitter taste of poison as the binding agent within the anti-anxiety medication dissolves. She bangs the taps, she bangs the draining board as tears of rage fill her eyes.

Molly. Molly. Molly.

When she turns around she sees that her laptop is open and the screen is black. She presses the Start button, and nothing happens. A low growl comes from deep in her throat as she grabs the whisky bottle and swills down the tablets, making her mouth explode with pain as if she had sucked on the flame from a welding torch. She screams, and beyond the scream she hears: 'What are you doing, Mummy?'

Molly's tone is the same as if she was asking Isabelle to show her how to paint her toenails, and a blue flame flickers before Isabelle's eyes as she looks up and sees her daughter standing in the doorway, smiling at her with her head tilted on one side.

It just happens. Before Isabelle has time to think she flies across the room and slaps her daughter so hard that the child goes flying, crashing headfirst into the kitchen cupboard. And yet Isabelle does not come to her senses; the rage is too black and all-encompassing. As Molly slides to the floor clutching her head in her hands, Isabelle kicks her in the stomach. Molly doubles over and collapses on the carpet, whimpering faintly.

Isabelle is about to stamp on her head when a door opens in her mind and a glimmer of light pushes its way in; instead she brings down her foot on Molly's hair, spread around her skull like a blond puddle.

Skull. Her little. Skull.

The door is flung wide, and Isabelle shakes her head in disbelief. Molly is lying at her feet, coughing as she curls into a ball and clutches her stomach.

I hit her. I kicked her. I was going to…kill her.

Every scrap of strength leaves Isabelle's body and she falls to the floor next to Molly. She tries to say something, but all that emerges is a soggy gurgle. She closes her eyes, she flies away, she isn't here. This is not happening. A space opens up beneath her eyelids, stars in lots of different colours. She steps out into that space, and time disappears.

Somewhere far away, in another part of the universe, she hears a drawer opening, the clink of metal. She doesn't know how much time has passed when Molly's voice reaches her.

'Mummy.'

She opens her eyes and sees Molly kneeling beside her. The child's right cheek is bright red, and she is offering something to Isabelle. A knife. The small fruit knife, the sharpest knife they have.

'There you go, Mummy.'

*

Carina dare not enter the camp. She has walked around the perimeter for twenty minutes, noticing that their car has gone and that the black tiger has been joined by two identical beasts. Lennart and Olof have told her that *they* see only a harmless travelling salesman with two colleagues, but that doesn't help Carina at all. She already knew that the tiger isn't the kind you see in a zoo. This tiger belongs only to her.

Delete. Delete.

That word is circling inside her mind like a vulture above a cadaver.

Delete.

The situation in which they find themselves defies all reason, but they have been given *one* concrete detail. The crosses on the caravans, the crosses drawn in blood, the crosses that mean *delete*. But who put them there? And why? If she could only solve the puzzle, then perhaps it would be possible to find a way out of here, to escape from the tiger.

On top of everything else, she has an urgent practical problem. The sheer terror has loosened her bowels, and she needs to go to the toilet. She daren't go into the camp, and even if she did pluck up the courage, they can't afford to waste valuable water flushing the toilet.

She can't hold out much longer. If she can't find somewhere to go, it's going to come spurting out into her pants. Why haven't they discussed what to do with human waste?

She knows the answer, of course: because no one wants to talk about the situation as if it is a long-term problem. A wave of pain rolls through Carina's belly, strongest towards the rectum, and she clamps her buttocks together, forcing herself to stand upright and push back. When the pain recedes her teeth start to chatter and she lets out something between a laugh and a snort.

The fear is here, the creature from her darkest nightmares is waiting for her, but what does any of that matter when you really need a shit?

On stiff legs and with her arms wrapped around her belly, Carina moves towards the camp. She has been so preoccupied with her internal affairs that she hasn't taken in her surroundings for a couple of minutes. When she looks up she sees

thank God

that their car is approaching from the field. She could hardly bring herself to think about what the fact that it was gone might have meant, but now it's on its way back. They will be together again, talk their way out of this madness, they will...

But first she has to go. Has to.

A new wave is building in her belly, and Carina uses her hands to press her buttocks together so that she can keep moving. As she approaches Isabelle's caravan she hears noises that sound like a fight, but by the time she gets there it has gone quiet.

With her back against the wall, Carina slides down into a squatting position, pulling down her shorts and pants at the same time. The diarrhoea explodes out of her, splashing onto the grass, and the stench sears her nostrils. She lets out a long breath and thinks: *From me to you, Isabelle.*

As she pulls off her socks to wipe her bottom, she hears movement inside the caravan, then Molly's voice saying something. As she cleans herself up she also hears their car drive into the camp. Then she hears Stefan screaming.

*

'Why are you so scared, Daddy?'

The white figure has vanished from view through the rear window

239

when another appears on the field in front of them. It looks exactly like the first one, except that it is moving faster, as if it is in a hurry. Without realising it, Stefan has locked his hands together and tensed his whole body.

'Look, Daddy, it's just…it's just *another one.*'

Stefan and Emil have spent the last fifteen minutes talking. Emil has told Stefan about Darth Vader and the elephant; he has explained that the white figures can change, that none of it is real. Stefan has told Emil about what happened when he was six years old, about his new bike and the incident in the lake. He was worried that the story might frighten Emil, but just like Stefan back then, Emil was mainly interested in what happened to the bike.

They have talked and talked, comparing their experiences. However, Stefan is far from convinced, because when the second figure appears, the childish terror returns immediately. But with Emil's last comment, something happens.

It's just another one.

The significance of that remark hits home. The white figure is not the only one of its kind; it is not an ever-present signpost to the kingdom of the dead, or some evil divinity able to manifest itself to people when life is about to leave them. It is just one of two, of three, of many. Stefan looks at Emil, spreads his hands wide and puts it as simply as possible: 'It's just…a white figure!'

'Mmm,' Emil says. 'Or a stormtrooper.'

'Is that what you can see?'

'Mmm. It's not right, though. It hasn't got a lightsaber. Stormtroopers always carry a lightsaber.'

'But you're not scared of stormtroopers, are you?'

'No. I'm scared of Darth Vader, but he wasn't right either. It's strange, isn't it, Daddy?'

'Very strange indeed.'

They sit together, watching as the white figure veers to one side to avoid bumping into the car.

Like reindeer in Norrland. Like rabbits on the island of Gotland.

They're just here.

'Emil,' Stefan says. 'You're the cleverest little boy in the world, did you know that?'

Emil gives a modest shrug and Stefan is overwhelmed by a love so strong that it hurts his chest. He wants to pull Emil close and kiss his head, but he knows that the gesture would be more pleasurable for him than for his son, so instead he decides that it's time.

'I've got something for you,' he says, opening the glove compartment and taking out a small padded envelope, which he gives to Emil.

Emil's favourite Star Wars character is Darth Maul, the demonic figure who wields his dual-blade lightsaber like a taekwondo staff. It hasn't been easy to get hold of the Lego version, but by searching on an online auction site Stefan has managed to track down two different models, and has paid approximately five times as much as they cost to begin with. Darth Maul is very popular.

Stefan had intended to wait until Emil's birthday, or at least his name day, but he has to do something for his son right now, he just has to.

Emil's delight when he sees what is in the envelope is out of all proportion to the two tiny figures. He holds them up, his eyes sparkling.

'Wow!' he says. 'Wow! Two *different* ones!'

'That's right. Those are the only two that exist.'

'I know that. Wow! Thank you, Daddy!'

Emil clicks the lightsabers into place and makes the two figures have a little fight. 'The battle of the century! Darth Maul versus his twin brother!'

'Darth Miaow?' Stefan suggests, which makes Emil flop back in his seat, helpless with laughter.

'Darth Miaow! His mother was a cat!'

A stone has fallen from Stefan's chest, a great weight has been lifted from his back. For the first time since he woke up this morning he feels as if he can breathe properly. *We got here somehow. Somehow we can get away from here.* He reaches for the key, ready to turn the car around, but before he can start the engine Emil asks: 'Daddy, do you think other worlds exist?'

'You mean on other planets, that kind of thing?'

'No.'

'So what do you mean?'

Emil pulls a face and blows through his nose as he waves the two Lego figures. 'I mean, like, sort of...'

'Do you mean other worlds *inside* our own world?'

'Yes. Or outside it. No, that's not what I mean. It's...oooooh!' Emil bangs his head with his wrists, frustrated at his inability to explain.

Stefan grips his slender arms. 'Calm down, Emil.'

Emil pulls away, stares at both Darth Mauls for a few seconds, then says: 'It's *the same* as ours. But different.'

'What do you mean by *the same*?'

Emil shakes his head. 'I can't explain.'

Stefan waits as Emil walks the figures to and fro across his thighs. It's obvious that he is still thinking, that in spite of his last remark he is trying to find the right words. After a couple of minutes Stefan looks out through the windscreen and sees yet another white figure approaching in the distance. He checks the side windows: nothing.

Why do they all come from the same direction?

No, that's not true. The first time he and Emil went out in the car, they went in precisely the opposite direction, and that was also where the white figure he saw when he was on the caravan roof came from. So they don't all come from the same direction, but they are all following the same *line*.

Emil removes the lightsabers and puts everything in his breast pocket before buttoning it carefully. Then he says: 'We can kind of decide what's real.'

'I don't understand.'

'No,' Emil says, stroking his pocket. 'Neither do I. Can we go home now?'

*

Home...'

It's amazing how quickly we adapt. As soon as he spots the caravans, Stefan experiences a little of the relief that is always part of coming home, of knowing that we can switch off from the tension involved in transactions in the outside world. The relief is even greater when he sees the Toyota. Carina is back, and without her the concept of 'home' has no real meaning.

The two white figures he has already seen are standing in the middle of the camp along with two others who must have come from the opposite direction, if his theory is correct. They are all facing one another, apparently deep in conversation.

Stefan drives slowly, heading for his caravan. There is no sign of anyone apart from the white figures, who slowly turn their heads to look at him.

Even if 'the white figure' is no longer a single entity, and has therefore lost something of its dramatic impact, it can't be denied: there is still something ghostly about that silent contemplation, those expressionless faces.

Stefan is ten metres away from the group when Isabelle comes flying out of her caravan with a knife in one hand. Stefan automatically brakes and covers Emil's eyes, because Isabelle is obviously heading for the figures, intent on harming them. *Why* is a question for later, but he doesn't want Emil to see.

'Stop it, Daddy!' Emil says, trying to twist free.

'Sweetheart, I don't want you to see...'

When Isabelle reaches the white figures, she falls to her knees in front of them.

'...this.'

What is she doing?

Isabelle is slightly obscured by the figures, and it is only when she holds up one arm that Stefan understands. Blood is pouring from two long, diagonal gashes running from wrist to elbow. As Stefan looks on, Isabelle begins to slash at the other arm.

He lets go of Emil, and as he opens the door he says: 'Close your eyes, Emil! Don't look!' He gets out of the car and sees that Lennart and Olof have also realised what is going on. But they are too far away, and as Stefan runs towards Isabelle, she brings the knife up to her throat.

'Isabelle!' he shouts. 'No!'

His cry makes her stop in mid-movement and look at him. Her face is swollen, and there is not a trace of sanity in her wide, staring eyes. Her face contorts in a horrible smile as she tips her head to one side to give her better access to the jugular vein. Stefan hurls himself at her with his arms outstretched, knocking her over before she has time to carry out her plan.

Blood spurts over his shirt, his face, as Isabelle's arms flail wildly; the deep gashes in her arms have opened up several arteries, which continue to pump out their contents in a steady stream. Stefan screams when Isabelle manages to stab him in the right shoulder; a second later the knife is wrenched from her hand.

'What the hell are you doing?' Lennart says, tossing the knife aside. 'Have you gone completely mad?'

Stefan's shoulder is throbbing, a red stain is spreading on his shirt, and yet another thing can be added to the list of things he could never have imagined.

Stabbed. I've been stabbed.

All at once Isabelle goes limp. Her bleeding arms flop to the ground, and she lies there staring up at the sky with empty eyes. Pain radiates outwards from Stefan's shoulder, and he can no longer feel the fingers of his right hand. From somewhere he hears Majvor's voice: 'Does anyone have any bandages?'

Together Olof and Lennart lift Isabelle and carry her towards their caravan, her arms leaving a trail of blood on the grass. Majvor follows them.

Stefan touches the wound with his left hand and his fingers come away sticky with blood. He swallows and closes his eyes, opens them again. Blood, blood, there is blood everywhere.

Emil didn't close his eyes. He saw the four stormtroopers, who no longer look like stormtroopers because their armour and weapons are slowly fading away, he saw Daddy jump on Molly's mum to stop her from cutting herself. When Daddy got stabbed Emil wanted to get out of the car, but he was too scared. He might get stabbed too, so he tucked his hands between his legs and carried on watching.

Things got a bit better when one of the farmers took away the knife, but Molly's mum is covered in blood, and Daddy is bleeding too. It's really horrible, all this blood. The worst thing Emil has seen in a film was when Darth Vader chopped off Luke Skywalker's hand, but there wasn't any blood. Emil has never thought about it before, but there should have been lots of blood! The grass where Molly's mum was lying is covered in the stuff, litres of it, and she's still bleeding as they carry her away.

But here comes Mummy! She runs over to Daddy, and is horrified when she sees the blood. She gives him a big hug and Emil feels a little calmer, but still he doesn't move. He wants them to come and get him, pick him up and give him a cuddle, because he's terrified.

Then the stormtroopers do something Emil has never seen real stormtroopers do. All four of them get down on their knees at the same time, then they lie down. Emil leans closer to the windscreen so that he can see more clearly. They are lying exactly where Molly's mum was, in all that blood—they must be crazy.

Then something happens to their armour. Emil can't see properly, and he daren't get out of the car, so instead he reaches into the back seat for the binoculars. He adjusts the focus until he achieves perfect clarity.

The whiteness which is a mixture of armour and skin now looks as if someone has drawn faint, uneven lines all over it with a pencil. All four of them are covered in a network of red lines.

Emil lowers the binoculars and sees Molly, who is standing outside her caravan staring at the four figures lying on the grass. She doesn't appear to be the least bit frightened. Her expression suggests that she is trying hard to work something out. As if she suddenly becomes aware of Emil, she raises her head and looks him in the eye. She ought to be really upset about her mum, but she doesn't look upset at all. Just focused. She waves to Emil.

Although it feels weird, he waves back. Then Molly smiles. But Emil can't do that. No way.

*

When Donald set off to meet the Bloodman, he felt invincible. The lone cowboy heading off across the prairie to confront his enemy. The endless expanse, the shotgun in his hand, and *John Brown's body lies a-mouldering in the grave, but his soul goes marching on.*

Donald isn't much of a one for hunting; he lacks the necessary patience. Give him a few hours lying in wait for elk, and he begins to understand why there are so many hunting accidents. You just want to shoot something, any fucking thing. The third time he went out he eventually shot a squirrel. All that was left of the little creature was a few shreds of flesh, and Donald got a real telling off from the leader of the hunting association. In fact he had only applied for a licence so that he could own a gun, because the concept of guns appeals to Donald.

Donald and Majvor had visited Graceland a few years earlier, and one of the highlights was Elvis's extensive collection of weapons. The revolvers and pistols were rather too ornate, embellished in a style more suited to Liberace than the King, but there was also a display case filled with impressive rifles and shotguns and an assault rifle. Donald spent a long time in front of that particular case.

There is something about the idea of being *armed*. The potentially lethal object in your hands, under your control. The finger on the trigger, yes or no, and the revolutionary changes that decision can bring about. To have that power. A gun is more than a composite of wood and metal; it is a way of becoming master of your own destiny.

These were Donald's thoughts as he moved across the field, whistling 'John Brown's Body'. He was finally on the way to making himself the master of his own destiny. Whether this was a dream or not, the gun felt pretty real in his grasp.

After a while the feeling began to fade. The Bloodman was further away than he could have imagined, and on top of everything else he was moving away from Donald in a diagonal line. Donald was definitely gaining on him, but it was a slow process, and his bad knees and general lack of fitness were beginning to make themselves felt.

His knees are creaking and his back is aching by the time Donald gets close enough to make out the details of the Bloodman's appearance. He has no hands, and his body is blotchy red with dried blood. He has no hair on his head.

Donald is clear about *one* thing, otherwise he would not have embarked on this mission. The figure in front of him is not his father. It is the image of his father that he created after the accident, the image that supplanted every other image. The Bloodman. Donald's greatest fear, yet at the same time something that is not real.

So what is it then?

Donald's favourite Åsa-Nisse quip comes from the film *Åsa-Nisse Goes a-Hunting.*

Åsa-Nisse and his sidekick Klabbarparn are lying in wait in the forest. It is dark, and visibility is poor. They don't know it, but their wives have come looking for them. Klabbarparn spots them and thinks it might be an elk. Because he's not sure, he wonders out loud whether he ought to shoot.

At which point Åsa-Nisse says: 'Go on, shoot it so we can see what it is.'

On many occasions when Donald has been unsure about a decision, those words have popped into his mind, and never have they been more apposite than right now.

Shoot it so we can see what it is.

Donald keeps on walking with this mantra going round and round in his head, but with only twenty metres to go, he comes to a halt. The

Bloodman is still moving away from him, but Donald just can't do it any more. His lungs are hurting, his back is aching, and his knees feel like a mechanism that has seized up in the locked position.

There is an alternative, of course. He could shoot the Bloodman in the back. But that would be wrong. We must meet our fears face to face, cowboy ethics or whatever. Anyway, it would be wrong.

'Hello!' Donald shouts, leaning forward with his hands on his thighs. 'Hello, you bastard!'

The Bloodman stops. And turns around.

If you've worked in a sawmill all your life, you've seen plenty of blood, both your own and other people's. The upper body and face of the figure in front of Donald are covered in blood, but the blood isn't right. It is far too pale. A child might imagine blood looking that way, but that's not what it's really like. It's a con.

Donald staggers closer. Beneath the blood that isn't blood he can see that the figure has a face which resembles Father's face, but it is blurred and unclear, like an old photograph.

'Are you trying to frighten me, you bastard?' Donald shouts, raising the gun. Then he meets the Bloodman's gaze.

There's one missing. There's one missing.

Why does that fucking list of presidents have to pop up *now*? Against Donald's will the presidents start chanting inside his head, searching for the missing name.

Roosevelt, Wilson, Harding...

Roosevelt, Wilson, Harding...

A hole as black as the creature's eyes opens up in Donald's mind when he tries to fill in the missing name; he is afraid the hole will widen, sucking in more and more things until he ends up a babbling dementia case.

Blood.

Yes, the blood will carry on pumping around his body while he sits there pointlessly dribbling. What kind of future is that, what kind of life is that? Think of Hemingway. When his strength began to fail and his thoughts were no longer of any value, he picked up his gun, went out into the forest and shot himself. That's how a man dies.

Blood.

The figure has taken a couple of steps towards Donald, who is seeing things more and more clearly. How much better and more dignified it would be to put an end to everything here and now. To fall like a warrior, like a Lone Ranger on the prairie, letting his

Blood

spread across the ground.

Father comes closer, Father is by his side now.

'I know,' Donald says. 'I know.'

Blood. Blood.

He should have done it on that day when he was ten years old. After Father had bled to death, Donald went inside and shut down the saw. Instead he should have put his neck on the bench beside it. One sideways jerk and

Blood

the black hole that looks into his eyes as he turns the gun around and pushes the barrel into his mouth. The metal is cold against his lips, and as he fumbles for the trigger he thinks *cold* and he thinks *cool* and he thinks *Coolidge.*

Donald gasps and pulls the gun out of his mouth.

'Coolidge!' he yells to the figure, who is standing there looking at him.

Blo—

'Don't start with me, you bastard! It's Coolidge! Wilson, Harding, Coolidge!'

Donald takes two steps backwards, raises the gun to his shoulder and screws up one eye. The sight's eyepiece is set for a greater distance, and the Bloodman's head is no more than a blurred, pale mass, with the eyes visible as dark pools. Donald aims for a point between and directly above those pools. Then he pulls the trigger.

This is the first time he has fired a gun in an open space where there is nothing for the sound to bounce off. The report when it goes off spreads in all directions, like dropping a stone in a pond, but in three dimensions. The noise fills the field and soars up into the sky as the recoil smashes into Donald's shoulder, making his weakened body wobble.

The Bloodman is still on his feet, but he has acquired a third eye between the other two, a bright blue eye. It takes Donald a couple of seconds to work out what he is seeing. The bullet has drilled a tunnel straight through the Bloodman's skull, and Donald can see a patch of sky about the size of a ten-öre piece.

The astonishing thing is that the Bloodman hasn't fallen over. He is simply standing there with his arms dangling at his sides, gazing at Donald with a look that expresses nothing. No surprise, no accusation, not even pain. But he isn't dead. Donald reloads the shotgun.

As he puts the gun to his shoulder again, something happens that makes him stop with his finger on the trigger. The Bloodman begins to *run*. Skin, trousers, blood start to dissolve, as if someone has poured a jug of water over a watercolour painting.

Donald lowers the gun, and it falls from his grasp without him even noticing. The Bloodman is no longer the Bloodman. Wet, sticky noises like the sound of bursting membranes can be heard as his face and clothing lose their solidity and turn to liquid, which defies gravity and flows towards the hole in his head.

The figure in front of Donald grows paler and paler as layer after layer of colour and form are sucked into the diminishing hole, and as the Bloodman disappears, something starts to grow inside Donald.

'Dead...' he whispers.

The metamorphosis is complete. Donald is now facing a white creature with no distinguishing features. No mouth, no nose, no ears. Just those two eyes, still gazing at him. The hole in the forehead has disappeared. The figure turns and walks away from Donald, who stands there watching it go as the process of growth within him reaches its conclusion. When the creature is ten metres away from him, he yells: 'Dead! You're dead, you bastard! Completely! Fucking! Dead!'

He sinks down on the grass next to his gun, strokes the barrel.

He takes it in his arms, crooning to it like a baby as he continues to caress it.

You killed him. You're such a good gun. You killed the Bloodman.

What happened at Riddersholm sawmill on that summer's day was just a terrible accident, nothing more. Donald tries to think about Father, and discovers that it is possible. He sees a bright, kind person with callused hands and hair that has begun to turn grey at the temples, eyes that look at Donald with love and appreciation. No taste of chocolate mixed with blood in his mouth, no accusing figure with stumps where his hands should be.

All his life Donald has been oppressed by that figure, and now it's over. He's dead. Donald has killed him. He puts down the gun, places his hands on his heart, and what he feels inside is a powerful machine, pumping the blood around his body. He leans back slowly until he is lying down, looking up at the sky. That vast blue surface belongs to him, and he embraces it with his entire being. If this is his dream, then he is

God. I am God.

the sovereign of this place. Nothing can limit him any longer; whatever his eyes can see is his and his alone. It is wonderful. Donald lies there for quite some time, revelling in the feeling that he owns the world.

Only when he sits up and looks around does he remember what happened. Peter, the caravan, the car. He has been dumped here. Driven out, cast out like a scapegoat in the desert.

Fucking bastard.

Donald grabs the gun and uses it as a support to help him get to his feet. He waves the barrel at the sky and shouts: 'What the fuck?' He has so much energy, but no outlet for it. He looks all around, and is rewarded with the sight of something approaching from the direction in which the white figure disappeared. Fine. He's quite happy to deal with whatever it might be. The pleasure of the report, the thud against his shoulder, the fleeting sensation of reaching beyond himself with lethal power. Wonderful.

He looks through the gun sight, sees what is approaching, lowers the gun and smiles. He sticks two fingers in his mouth and whistles.

'Come on, little man! Come on!'

In a couple of minutes Benny is standing there panting, his tongue hanging out. In Donald's current state of mind he doesn't find it strange that Benny is accompanied by a cat. The animals have come to fetch him, bless them.

'Good boy,' Donald says, scratching Benny behind the ears. 'Good dog.' The cat looks at him, but when Donald reaches out to stroke it, it moves away. 'All right. Good cat.'

Donald peers beyond the animals, but can see nothing but the horizon. Benny is lying at Donald's feet with his head resting on his paws as he looks up at his master. Donald lets him catch his breath, then says: 'Can you find your way home?'

Benny pricks up his ears and cocks his head on one side. Then he glances at the cat, which has started washing itself. If the cat could shrug, it would; it seems to have no interest whatsoever in the question.

'Find your mistress?' Donald says. 'Find your mistress!'

Benny gets up and goes over to the cat. They look into each other's eyes, and Donald feels as if they are conferring on some level that is inaccessible to him. The cat abandons her ablutions and the two animals set off, heading back the way they came.

Donald hooks his gun over his shoulder and follows them.

*

'Bandages,' Majvor says. 'Do you have any bandages?'

Isabelle is lying on the ground outside the farmers' caravan. Majvor and Lennart are kneeling on either side of her, squeezing above Isabelle's elbows as hard as they can to stop the flow of blood. The stab wounds are long and deep, and Isabelle's face has a yellowish tinge.

Olof hurries inside and Majvor catches a glimpse of Isabelle's eyes, somehow transparent, before her eyelids slowly close. She dare not loosen her grip on Isabelle's arm to pat her on the cheek, so instead she leans forward and blows on her face.

'Isabelle,' she says. 'Wake up, Isabelle. You have to stay with us.'

Isabelle's eyelids flicker, and she looks towards the middle of the camp. Majvor follows her gaze and sees that all the incarnations of James Stewart are lying flat on their faces on the grass. Harvey is there too, and with his chalk-white fur and round body he resembles a pile of snow that has been shovelled to one side in the summer.

Olof emerges with a roll of gauze and a roll of duct tape. He and Majvor work together; it feels as if they are trying to zip up an over-full suitcase. Olof clamps together one section at a time, then Majvor places a piece of gauze on the wound and winds the tape around the arm. She is worried about cutting off the blood supply to the hand, but then again there can't be much blood left.

Isabelle's eyes are closed as Majvor and Olof turn their attention to the other arm. Lennart grabs hold of Isabelle's ankles and lifts her legs; it is more important for the blood to reach the brain than the legs.

When they have finished, Lennart gently pulls Isabelle across the grass and places her feet on one of the folding chairs. Majvor and Olof remain where they are, just looking at one another, until Olof breaks the contact by waving to Lennart and saying: 'Can you give me a hand here—I just need to...'

Lennart helps Olof to his feet. He nods to Majvor—'Sorry, I...'—at which point he staggers over to the corner of the caravan and throws up.

Majvor doesn't think any less of him for that. There is no denying that it was a very unpleasant task. Clumps of coagulated blood are stuck to her hands, her nose is filled with the smell of blood, and she is astonished at how calm she feels.

'Good job,' Lennart says. 'I guess you're the kind of person who always comes through in a crisis.'

That's actually true, but not many people have seen that side of Majvor, and even fewer have praised her for it. It may be inappropriate under the circumstances, but Majvor can feel herself blushing.

Olof returns, wiping his mouth and apologising. All three of them stand there contemplating Isabelle as if she were a work of art they had created together, or rather restored and preserved for posterity. Hopefully.

Lennart goes into the caravan to fetch a blanket, which he lays over Isabelle. The movement of her chest shows that her breathing is shallow, and from time to time she whimpers quietly. Olof shakes his head. 'Why did she do it? Can you make any sense of it?'

Lennart has pushed his hands deep in the pockets of his dungarees, and is now looking towards the middle of the camp. His eyes narrow.

'Majvor,' he says in a tone of voice that Majvor seldom hears. It is respectful, as if she is someone to reckon with. Lennart nods towards the four prostrate bodies. 'When you look at those...figures, what do you see?'

Majvor turns to face Will Lockhart, Elwood P. Dowd, Mr Smith who went to Washington, and the impossible Harvey, who, like the others, is lying motionless, face down on the grass. While she was working to save Isabelle, Majvor's mind was crystal clear, and she doesn't like the mist that threatens to drift in when she looks at her dreams come true. 'I'd rather not say,' she replies.

'Okay. But let me ask you this. Do you see four identical men in suits and hats, lying on the ground?'

Majvor doesn't need to check to know that Elwood P. Dowd is indeed wearing a suit and a hat, while Mr Smith looks as if he is delivering his filibuster to Congress. A suit, but no hat. But then there's Will Lockhart. And Harvey.

'No,' she says. 'Why do you ask?'

'Because that's what I see. And Olof.' Lennart points to Isabelle. 'I wonder what *she* saw.'

He turns to Olof, who seems lost in thought as he stares at Isabelle's caravan. 'That's right, isn't it? You see the same thing as me, don't you? Four travelling salesmen?'

'Mmm,' Olof replies without taking his eyes off the caravan. Majvor is suddenly struck by a pang of guilt. Molly! They can probably be excused for not thinking of her during the critical phase with Isabelle, but to stand here chatting when there is a child whose mother is seriously injured is an oversight bordering on cruelty.

Majvor is about to go and speak to Molly, but stops in mid-movement. Molly is there, outside the caravan, her eyes wide open, staring at the four figures on the ground. Her hands are folded over her stomach, a smile is playing around her lips, her cheeks are flushed and her whole appearance conveys an impression of rapture.

'I wonder...' Olof says. 'I wonder what *she* sees.'

*

The wound in Stefan's shoulder is not deep, and a compress and a few strips of surgical tape from the First Aid box in the boot of the car soon stem the flow of blood. While Carina is fixing him up they talk about the field, agreeing that there is some kind of pull, something drawing them outwards, but that they will not allow it to separate them again. From now on, they will stick together.

Emil crawls onto Stefan's knee, fishes out his Darth Maul figures and shows them to Carina. When she leans forward to take a closer look, Stefan notices the swelling on her cheek for the first time. 'What happened to you?'

'I had a fight. With Isabelle.'

'Why?'

Carina sighs, and she glances over to the four figures, still lying face down on the grass. 'It's a long story.'

'We've got plenty of time.'

'I'll tell you later. If I'm feeling brave enough.' Carina admires the Lego characters and hands them back to Emil. 'Listen, I don't want you to play with Molly any more.'

'Why not?'

Stefan looks at Molly, whose eyes are fixed on the middle of the camp, a blissful expression on her face. She is taking no notice what-soever of her injured mother; her attention is totally focused on the figures on the ground. She is *glowing*.

'Do as your mother says. And I agree. You're not to hang out with Molly.'

'I don't *want* to hang out with Molly. But *why*?'

Carina gently puts her hands on Emil's cheeks and looks into his eyes. 'Because she's evil, Emil. She's evil.'

'Hang on,' Stefan says. 'That's a bit...'

Carina lets go of Emil's face so that her hands can move. With uncharacteristically jerky movements she underlines her words.

'No! It's not going too far! There's something about her and this place. And those...things. I don't understand it, and I don't need to understand it, but you are not to hang out with her, Emil. She's dangerous!'

Carina is getting louder and louder, and Stefan realises that Emil is frightened. Carina rarely raises her voice, and the element of panic in her tone is making him nervous too. He rubs Emil's back and asks Carina as calmly as he can: 'What do you see? When you look at... them?'

Carina's body is tense, alert as she looks across. She shakes her head, and there is an uncomfortable silence. Stefan tries to change the subject. 'They follow a line. I'm just wondering...'

Before he can finish the sentence—*what's at the end of the line*—Carina has clamped one hand to her mouth and is waving towards the field with the other.

'What is it?' Stefan asks.

'I saw...When I was walking around the camp before, I thought...'

She starts the car and slams it into reverse. When she has shot back twenty metres, she puts it into first and swings to the right so that they drive past the three caravans in an arc. Carina edges forward, her eyes fixed on the field.

'There!' she says, braking and pointing in one of the directions the figures came from. 'Can you see it? You can see it too, can't you?'

Stefan peers through the windscreen, searching for something that is sticking out, sticking up, but he can't find anything. He is about to say so when Emil shouts: 'I can see it! It's in the grass, isn't it?'

Carina nods, and Stefan lowers his gaze. He starts by the car, then gradually moves outwards. And there it is. The grass has been trodden down along a faint track leading from the horizon and into the camp. Presumably it comes out the other side and continues, because it follows exactly the same line as the white figures he saw. Even though the outline of the track is unclear, it has obviously been used by several pairs of feet over a fairly long period.

'It's a track,' Stefan says as the thought strikes him. 'And it was here before. They *always* follow this route.'

'Yes,' Carina says, putting the car into gear once more and continuing to circumnavigate the camp. 'But that's not what I saw.'

When she has completed ninety degrees of the circle that began at the track, she pulls up again and points. 'There.'

Now that Stefan's eyes have acclimatised and he knows what he is looking for, he sees another track leading either to or from the camp, at right angles to the one they have just discovered. It is not unreasonable to assume that this track also runs through the camp and out the other side. He peers towards the horizon; nothing has come this way, and there is no sign of anything now.

But something walks here. Something…tramples down the grass.

'Do you understand?' Carina asks.

'Yes,' Stefan says. He feels as if a door has opened behind his back, letting in a blast of ice-cold air. He holds on tightly to Emil.

'We are exactly where the tracks meet,' he says. 'At the crossroads.'

*

Carina is pointing almost directly at Peter. She doesn't know it, because he is beyond her field of vision, but if you drew a straight line from Carina's index finger, it would miss Peter by only twenty metres or so.

He has stopped the car, but dare not get out. In front of him is a wall of darkness so high that he has to lean forward and twist his neck to see the top. In the rear-view and wing mirrors he can still see blue sky, but the windscreen is covered by a darkness so compact it is as if the glass has been painted black.

Ahead of the car there is still green grass, but it covers only a couple of hundred metres. Then the darkness takes over, and it is not a dark wall, but *a wall of darkness*; in spite of its dense appearance, it has a living quality, a depth. If he put his foot down, he wouldn't collide with something; he would travel *into* it.

His body is urging him to do just that. The pull of the darkness is so strong that he decides to stay in the car; he is afraid that if he gets out, he will be physically dragged forward. It is as if thousands of invisible threads are attached to his skin, trying to haul him in with inexorable force.

Peter sits there clutching the wheel, feet braced on the floor as he stares into the gloom. The darkness stares back, and gradually Peter is able to make out textures and nuances. It is warm, it is moist, it is soft. And it smells of shower gel. Shower gel and disinfectant.

Anette.

Yes. It smells of Anette.

When Peter was seventeen, he was given a trial by the national youth team. By that stage his father had found a new woman, but he had abused her so badly that he had been jailed for four years, which meant that for the first time in ten years, Peter and his mother could walk down the street without feeling as if he was watching them.

Peter had found it remarkably simple. Only a couple of days after his father was sentenced, Peter was able to shake off the potential threat, and he felt free. This was partly because he already knew that he was capable of outrunning his father; he was no longer so vulnerable.

It wasn't so easy for his mother. When she was informed, having

258

not heard from her ex-husband for five years, it was less of a reassurance and more of a reminder that he still existed and was just as violent, if not more so. He became a *reality* once again, an evil colossus sitting in his cell and thinking about her, sending his hatred out into the ether and touching her. This made her so weak that she had to take time off work. She was signed off due to ill health for a long period, and eventually took early retirement. His father's violence was so effective that it transcended time and space.

When Peter went away on his first training camp with the national youth team to Stockholm, he couldn't help feeling guilty because he was leaving his mother alone with her demons. She persuaded him to go, although her words didn't hold much conviction. There was so little strength left in her that she was incapable of saying or doing anything with conviction, but he went anyway.

Because football was his life. Things weren't going too well in school because he trained three evenings a week, and he usually had a match at the weekend. It would have been easier if he could have attended a football academy, but that would have meant moving away from Norrköping, and given his mother's condition that wasn't an option.

He turned up at school, but he wasn't really *there*. He was well-built and good-looking, and to his embarrassment had been named one of the five 'hottest guys in school'. Fortunately he was narrowly beaten into second place by Patrik Schmidt, who later became a model. But of course Peter received plenty of female attention too.

Lots of the girls would have liked to get it together with Peter, but there wasn't really anywhere to go. He hardly ever went to parties because he didn't drink, and on the rare occasions when he did go, he felt as if the conversations were entirely concerned with a world he hadn't had time to be a part of. A couple of times some drunken girl had thrown herself at him and tried to snog him, but the smell of her breath put him off from the start.

He didn't think he was gay. He would jerk off over his mother's Ellos catalogues while fantasising about a world of slim, clean women with perfect figures, and so the ground was already prepared by the time he met Isabelle.

But football was the real focus of his existence. It was a language he understood, and a social environment with clear goals: to win the next match, to progress in the competition. As long as he belonged there, he didn't need any other company.

He was a reserve with the A-team by the time he was sixteen, and had a permanent place at seventeen. Of course it wasn't long before he was spotted by the national youth team, so one weekend in September he went off to Stockholm to show what he could do.

The training camp was held at Zinkensdamm sports ground, which Peter quickly learned to refer to as Zinken. They trained, ate and stayed in the area, and all Peter saw of Stockholm was Tantolunden and Hornsgatan. On the other hand, he had no desire to see any more. Because of Anette.

She had played for the national women's team, but had been forced to give up three years earlier due to a cartilage injury. She now worked as an assistant coach with the various youth teams, among other things. Anette had medium-length blond hair, a square face, and she had put on a few kilos since she stopped playing. She was thirty years old, and looked just like anyone else, in the widest sense of the concept. She could have been on the checkout in a supermarket, a support teacher in a school sports department, or a local government politician. She was the kind of person you pass on the street without paying any attention.

'Hello...Peter,' was the first thing she said to him on the Friday afternoon after consulting her list. 'It's going to be hard work for the next couple of days—are you up for it?'

When she shook Peter's hand, something happened. Her hand was slender, her grip was firm, and in a way that Peter didn't understand he had a sense of *here, now* as they touched. It was as if he was holding something he had missed, but without knowing it. Perhaps she felt the same right from the start, perhaps not. She didn't show it, anyway.

Saturday's training went well, and Peter had no problems fitting in with the team, from both a technical and a social point of view. By the afternoon he had already acquired the nickname Hammerhead after crashing into a goalpost and getting up as if nothing had happened. Hiding his pain was something of a speciality for Peter.

That evening they all had dinner together, and Hammerhead ended up sitting next to Anette. They chatted about this and that, mainly her time with the national team and the goings-on at IFK Norrköping, but even though it was a perfectly ordinary conversation, there was also that undertone of *here, now*, just like when they first touched.

Peter assumed that the feeling was entirely one-sided, that he had developed some kind of fixation that he could neither control nor define. Surely he couldn't *fancy* Anette; she was so much older than him, and bore more than a passing resemblance to his Swedish teacher, and he'd never given her a thought.

During dessert, which was ice cream with chocolate sauce, they were both chatting with their neighbours when Peter became aware of a sensation on the skin of his forearm; it was like a faint charge of static electricity. When he glanced down he saw that Anette's arm was right next to his on the table, and that the hairs on his arm were standing up. But that wasn't all. The fine, downy hairs on Anette's arm were doing exactly the same.

He said something to his neighbour. Anette said something to hers. They looked at one another. Peter's expression was completely open, searching, a question mark based on the electricity that she too must be feeling. In Anette's eyes, however, there was a tinge of sorrow as she looked down at her arm, then back at Peter.

It would be a few years before Peter understood that sorrow. Understood that it was about age, about the fact that things can happen at the wrong time, when it's already too late, but that you still have to pretend that it's not too late. They looked at one another and a decision was made, even though they had no idea how to carry it through.

The group started to break up, and Peter got to his feet, his mouth dry. Some people were going into town, but not for long; they had training in the morning. Others were going to play cards or watch TV. Peter turned down a couple of invitations, said he was going to do a few laps of the pitch, which of course led to comments such as 'Looks as if Hammerhead can't get enough', 'Going back for a rematch with the post?' and so on.

However, when he got out onto the pitch, faintly illuminated by the odd floodlight, it felt right. Because he had just eaten he could only jog, but it was nice to exercise in the semi-darkness, concentrating only on the movement of his body. Round and round, the fabric of his tracksuit bottoms flapping against his legs.

He was halfway through the fifth circuit when he noticed Anette, leaning against the wall by the players' entrance. A tingle ran up through his belly from his crotch, then dissolved in his chest. He cut across the pitch and jogged up to her.

Her hair was wet; presumably she had just showered. A few damp patches were visible on her tracksuit, which was identical to his, as if she had got dressed in a hurry without drying herself properly. Peter took all this in, interpreting the signs as the tingle started up again and grew.

He was starting to get a hard-on, and pushed his hands deep in his pockets. Under cover of darkness he grabbed hold of his cock with one hand and held it against his body so that the situation wouldn't get any more embarrassing than it already was.

'Hi,' he said.

'Hi. How's it going?'

'Good. It's a bit chilly, but...' He couldn't think of anything else to say.

'Yes, it does get quite cool in the evenings.' Anette's voice sounded strained, as if her throat had closed up. She blinked and shook her head. When she spoke again, she sounded regretful. 'Peter, I...'

Perhaps it was the fact that she used his name, confirming that this was really happening to him; it gave him the courage to act. He moved forward, took his hands out of his pockets and kissed her.

For one terrible moment he thought he had got it wrong; her lips were tense and didn't respond to him. He was standing here trying to force himself on the assistant coach with his erection poking her in the stomach, and apart from the fact that it was so embarrassing that he wanted to die, it would mean that his career in the national team was over before it had even started.

A second later, everything changed. He had kissed a few girls, those half-hearted snogs at parties. But this was something different. When Anette relaxed, softened and kissed him back, she did so with her whole body, and all the warmth that was within her came pouring out through her lips.

'Come with me,' she said.

They walked along the corridor to the changing rooms, side by side and so close that the fabric of their tracksuits rustled as they touched. Everything was in darkness as they moved away from the faint light on the pitch. When they were halfway along the corridor they could see nothing but the gleam of each other's eyes, the faint shimmer of the reflective band on their clothing. And yet it wasn't enough. Anette opened the door of one of the changing rooms and they went inside. When she locked it behind them, they were in pitch darkness.

The room was warm, and the moisture from the showers hovered in the air. The lack of light intensified the sensory impressions, and Peter was aware of the strong scent of shower gel, which he thought was Axe, plus the smell of disinfectant from the toilets. A tap was dripping, he and Anette were breathing, and he knew that *now, now,* but he didn't know how. He groped for Anette and found her hip, squeezed it, but she moved away and said: 'No. Get undressed.'

As he took off his tracksuit he could hear her doing the same. There was a faint crackle as she pulled her top over her head and the polyester reacted with her hair, sending a shower of tiny sparks into the darkness. The smell of Axe mingled with her shower gel, a girl's gel, a *woman's* gel that he couldn't identify.

He heard her voice: 'Lie down.'

This wasn't how he had pictured his first time, this wasn't how he had pictured *any* time, but when Peter lay down on the damp floor in the total darkness it felt better than he could ever have imagined, it felt *right*.

His penis was throbbing and burning so much that he thought he ought to be able to see it, that it ought to be glowing, but when he looked down there was only blackness, and he felt a breath of Anette's scent as she straddled him, guided him inside her and began to rock.

It was so glorious that he stopped breathing. The concrete floor beneath him disappeared, the walls of the room dissolved, and it was only when flashes of yellow began to dance before his eyes that he realised he was feeling dizzy due to lack of oxygen. He gasped and thrust into her as deeply as he could; it was as if he was screwing the darkness itself. The warm, engulfing, all-forgiving darkness. His hands fluttered over her far from perfect body, with flabby skin here and there, but to him it was the perfect body, the body of the darkness.

He didn't even bother trying to perform or to hold out. He had no idea how much time had elapsed when everything that he was flowed inwards from his limbs, from the very tips of his fingers, was concentrated in his crotch and then exploded into the darkness. His arms fell away from his body, his head went back, his eyes flew open, and as if his pleasure really had created *light*, he found himself staring at an upside-down sign that said, 'Will the last person to leave please turn out the lights!' before he floated away on a cloud of sweat and shower gel and became one with the darkness and the moisture.

Twenty-two years ago. Twenty-two years and ten months. They had got dressed in the darkness, parted in the darkness, and the following day they had barely looked at one another. It was a few years and quite a few girls before Peter realised that the first time had been the best, and would always be the best.

On the Sunday he had gone back to the changing room to check. On the wall by the door, just above the light switch, was a hand-written sign: 'Will the last person to leave please turn out the lights!'

264

He had torn it down and taken it, but at some point during all the subsequent moves it had disappeared.

Sitting in Donald's car right now, his fingers clutching the wheel, his feet braced against the floor, he can smell spilt whisky mingled with shower gel, disinfectant, and the thick odour of aroused bodies. Out there in the darkness is what he wants. The place where he wants to be.

He nods to himself and starts the engine. As he is about to put the car in gear, something changes. The light dims, and he hears a noise. When he leans forward and looks up at the sky, he sees that the top of the wall of darkness is shifting. Thick black plumes rise up, as if the darkness has turned into clouds, hiding the light of the sky. The clouds grow and come away from the wall, turning into heavy rain showers, moving towards him as the noise gets louder, and he realises that it is the sound of screaming. Screams of pain, many voices.

'What the fuck....?'

Just as the darkness in the sky has metamorphosed into clouds, it has also taken on a physical form on the ground. A hundred metres or so ahead he can see a number of distorted figures running towards him. They are moving rapidly but jerkily, as if they are suffering from painful cramps, and the agonised screams now make sense, because the flesh has been virtually burnt away from their bones, with only scraps of blackish-brown leathery skin remaining to shield their skeletal bodies. They are screaming with pain and running towards the car.

*

When Stefan, Carina and Emil return from their tour around the camp, the others have gathered outside Isabelle's caravan. They have laid Isabelle on her bed, after establishing that her condition does not seem to have deteriorated.

'Mind you, it would be good if Peter came back before too long,' Lennart says. 'That would help...'

What he would really like to say is that he's not very keen on the idea of leaving Isabelle alone with Molly. Since the four figures got up, she has finally taken an interest in her mother, announcing that she wants to sit beside her and hold her hand. Of course it is impossible to say no, but it doesn't feel quite right.

Another thing that doesn't feel right is those four travelling salesmen. Their old-fashioned suits ought to be covered in blood from lying on the grass, but this is not the case. On the contrary; the jackets that looked slightly shabby before are now glowing with a new freshness, and the limp trousers are now sporting a razor-sharp crease. Four diffuse, faceless figures have become four separate individuals with their own characteristics. One has prominent ears, another a long, straight nose. And so on.

The blood that was spattered all over the grass has disappeared, and it is not difficult to draw the obvious conclusion. Lennart looks over at the group of travelling salesmen, who are now waiting quietly once again. He rubs his eyes.

Yes, it is possible to draw conclusions, but what is the point of those conclusions when you don't understand what they mean? It's just like the old days, when Gunilla used to come home with her maths homework, asking for help with her equations: x and y and z. Lennart never even went to high school, and he wasn't exactly a star pupil in maths in junior school. He said as much to Gunilla, and she explained: 'Yes, but if $2x$ plus y equals z...' But by then he was already lost.

What does it matter how these letters relate to other letters, when you have no idea what those letters *mean*? You could just as easily say that one Gupp plus two Hupps make eight Plupps. Where exactly does it get you?

That's how he feels now. There are a number of variables, and when you put them together, they make this or that. But he doesn't understand the system.

Whatever they put in the ground grows unnaturally quickly, in spite of the fact that the sun is gone. Okay. And yet there is only grass here. The four figures he can see look different to different people, and these figures clearly benefit from absorbing blood. Okay. Lennart felt considerably more optimistic a few hours ago, when he and Olof sat gazing out across the empty field. Emptiness is only *one* concept, and in some ways it is quite normal. But now there are all these other aspects that need to be interpreted.

Carina's account of what she has noticed hasn't improved the situation. Apparently they are at a crossroads, where two tracks intersect. In the middle of a cross, just like the ones painted on their caravans. What does that mean?

The whole thing is insane; he has experienced nothing like it since the moment when he opened the door of his mother's room and found that the perspective had shifted. It makes him uncomfortable, and he has some sympathy with Donald. The best and most sensible explanation is that the whole thing is a dream. Unfortunately he doesn't believe that, but it would be nice.

'How are you?' Olof asks. 'You don't look too good.'

'I don't feel too good either,' Lennart replies. 'Isn't all this making *your* head spin?'

Olof glances around. 'Yes, but I'm sure it will sort itself out, one way or another. We've been in tricky situations before, haven't we?' Olof laughs and shakes his head. 'Do you remember that summer when a thunderstorm knocked out the power? All the stock got out because the fence was no longer electrified, and we had to round them up in the dark and the pouring rain? But we got them in. Every single one.'

Lennart looks at Olof with a measure of scepticism, but his friend's expression is open and honest. He really does think that the two situations are comparable.

Lennart remembers that night very well. He and Olof were out in the rain until daybreak, searching for their cows, driving them back to the barn in small groups or one by one. After only a couple of hours normal life had been washed away in the wind and rain, and they both ended up wandering around like restless spirits, with just enough strength to persuade the cows to go home. Then they were off again, hunting for the next one.

It was a very difficult situation, which made everyday concepts disintegrate. But still. However tricky it was, they had a job to do. A job that might have seemed impossible at times, but it was clearly defined. Find the cows, get them inside the barn. But here? What is their job here? What is it they're supposed to *do*?

No, however much Lennart would like to share Olof's confidence, the innate unnaturalness of this place has begun to chafe at him like the sight of a fly trapped between two panes of glass that cannot be opened. There is nothing you can do except wait for the buzzing to stop. Or smash the glass, which of course you don't do.

Under normal circumstances Lennart is not much of a one for brooding, but now he finds that he has been so lost in his own thoughts that he has no idea why Majvor is standing in front of the group holding out her hand, palm upwards. She has said something, but he missed it. He moves closer and sees that she is showing them several objects made of gold: a chain, rings, and some irregularly shaped lumps.

'Sorry,' he says. 'What have you got there?'

'I found them,' Majvor says, pointing. 'Spread out over there. The wedding ring is from 1904.'

They all look over at the spot where Majvor's caravan used to be, as if that might somehow help them.

'Could I have a look?' Stefan says, and Majvor hands over the items with a certain amount of reluctance. As Stefan examines the rings, Majvor says: 'I think the small lumps are fillings.'

'Why are they here?' Emil wonders, standing on tiptoe so that he can see what is in his father's hand.

Everyone else looks enquiringly at Stefan and Carina to check what they think about discussing such matters in front of Emil.

'Well,' Lennart begins, 'the obvious explanation is that they used to belong to people who are no longer with us. But...' He turns to Majvor. 'You didn't find any bones?' When she shakes her head, he frowns. 'Not even *teeth*?'

'No,' Majvor replies. 'I did look, but I couldn't find anything else.'

Lennart thinks about the deer skull nailed to the wall at the back of the old brewery. It was hung up by his great-grandfather, and because it has been there for so long, it has just been left. Exposed to wind and weather, it is still intact, and if there is one thing that the passage of time has barely touched, it is the teeth.

Then again, it doesn't take a genius or any knowledge of his ancestor's macabre idea of what constitutes a decorative object to be aware that skeletons and teeth have a tendency to stay around when everything else has gone. At least after a relatively short period such as a hundred and ten years. And of course there is nothing to say that it happened then, whatever it might have been. It could have been considerably later.

'Erik,' Stefan says, reading the inscription. 'His name was Erik.'

The group falls silent. At some point long ago there was a person called Erik who also ended up in this place, together with some other people. Something befell Erik and his companions, and as a result all that was left of them was their jewellery and the fillings from their teeth. That is the first thing that occurs to everyone; it creates a moment of reverence, hence the silence.

But it doesn't stop there. The reverence metamorphoses into something far less pleasant as they all draw the obvious conclusion: whatever happened to those other people could also happen to us. Or even worse: whatever happened to those other people is *going* to happen to us.

They all look at one another, then out towards the field.

The crossroads, Lennart thinks. *Just like us, they were at the crossroads. And that's where they stayed.*

*

Isabelle is lying on her back on the double bed, her arms by her sides. Her face is swollen, her tongue is throbbing, and the pain in her forearms feels like an army of vicious, biting ants. She is a piece of meat wrapped in plastic, but fortunately she is not here in the moment and she is not in her body.

She is in the past. She is ten minutes ago, running towards the white figures with the knife in her hand. She knows they want blood, and she intends to give them blood. Her guts are so full of black, surging shame

I kicked my daughter, I wanted to kill my daughter

that she feels nothing but relief when the blade slices into her skin and lets out some of the

bloodshame

the pressure that grows and grows, threatening to make her explode from the inside. She falls to her knees, holding out her arm to the white figures, offering them the blood gushing out of her body. She wants them to take her, embrace her, carry her away and suck her dry. But they simply look down at the ground where her blood is staining the grass dark red.

She changes hands and cuts open the other arm. The relief is diminished this time. It is merely a task, a series of movements which must be carried out to get this out of the way. The white figures do not deign to look at her. Their dark eyes are focused on the grass, where the blood...

Isabelle sways, down on her knees with her arms outstretched. She doesn't understand. The blood is vanishing. As it spurts out of her arms, it is absorbed by the ground the second it lands. There is blood on the grass, but only a fraction of the amount she has already sacrificed and

More. More.

continues to sacrifice.

More.

Clearly it is not enough. The arteries in her arms are too thin, she must give them more

All of it.

and she raises the knife to slice open her jugular vein. As she tilts her head to one side to get a better angle, two things happen in rapid succession.

She looks up at the white figures hoping for confirmation before she makes the ultimate sacrifice, but suddenly her attention is caught by a movement in her peripheral vision.

Up and down. Up and down.

Someone is bouncing. A child. Bouncing on a trampoline. And right alongside is an overweight guy in a Hawaiian shirt, raising his arms in triumph as his long putt rolls into the hole on one of the mini-golf courses. The smell of fried food from the kiosk wafts past Isabelle's nostrils, and she hears someone say something in Finnish from a nearby mobile home.

For a second she is able to grasp that she is back on the campsite, the place she hated so much, then something enormous comes flying towards her and crashes into her. She falls backwards, drops the knife, and she sees nothing but blue sky. Then everything goes dark as her consciousness gives up.

Little mummy, little mummy,
the sweetest little mummy.

Isabelle opens her eyes a fraction, lets in a glimmer of light. Molly is sitting cross-legged beside her on the double bed, singing as she strokes Isabelle's fingers, her bitten nails.

She grew claws, long sharp claws,
because she was a whore.

Isabelle feels dizzy, and she is falling back into the memory that is playing on a loop inside her head. The fat man on the mini-golf course appears. The bottom buttons on his brightly coloured shirt are undone, and when he raises his arms a pale, hairy belly is revealed, spilling over the waistband of his trousers.

Ugly people. All these ugly people. Where do all these ugly people come from? From Finland. Fat ugly Finns. Fat ugly Finns from Finland.

A shudder runs through her body. She is shaking and her teeth are chattering as she picks up the smell of that hairy belly; she can taste the salty tang of sweat mixed with beer fumes just as strongly as if she had licked that belly and felt the curly hairs against the papillae.

Are you awake, Mummy dear, are you awake?
Your teeth are chattering, chattering.

Molly's voice brings her back to the caravan. Isabelle opens her eyes a little wider and sees that Molly is smiling at her, wagging her head from side to side. Isabelle is finding it difficult to focus. Molly's face is blurred, like a pencil drawing that someone has gone over half-heartedly with an eraser. The memory of a face.

Isabelle assumes she is having a problem with her vision because of her dazed state, but in that case how come the princess on Molly's T-shirt is crystal clear?

Molly leans closer, but her face remains blurred. More so, in fact. What Isabelle had thought was her mouth looks more like a dirty mark that disintegrates when Isabelle looks at it.

'Mummy,' Molly says. 'Do you remember the tunnel? It was dark in there. Really, really dark.'

*

Peter was once responsible for Lazio losing a vital league match against Milan. In the final minute of play he raced towards the left post just as a perfectly executed lob curved over the goalie's head. A gentle tap and the matter would have been resolved. Instead Peter caught the ball with his shin, and it landed just outside the goal. Thirty seconds later the game was over. He had to put up with a lot of ribbing from his teammates, but it didn't really affect his position within the squad. These things happen; it was just unfortunate that it came at such a critical moment.

The newspapers had a different view. It was all Peter's fault, and they borrowed the Spanish expression *hacerse el sueco*, which means to act like an idiot.

A few of Lazio's more fanatical supporters read the articles and took the criticism very seriously. One evening when Peter was on the way home to his apartment, he heard a drunken yell from a bar: 'Lo svedese! Guardate lo svedese!' Seconds later four guys were running towards him. Nobody had told them that 'these things happen', and they intended to teach lo svedese a lesson.

The memory flickers through Peter's mind as he sits in the car watching the distorted figures approach. For a moment he had stopped dead in the middle of the piazza. There was something hypnotic about the sight of the four men coming at him with the intention of beating him up. To be the quarry, alone and exposed to the hunters' thirst for blood.

The paralysis soon passed, and Peter turned and fled. He had no difficulty in getting away from four drunken louts, and he suffered no lasting damage, apart from the unpleasant feelings that the incident aroused: the sense of being the focal point to which violence is drawn with the aim of smashing him to pieces, crushing him.

Something of that same fascination has gripped Peter now, and all he can do is stare open-mouthed. The figures are running, but not particularly fast, since every step seems to cause them pain. The screams Peter can hear are coming out of mouths that have been robbed of their lips, white teeth gleaming in charred faces. When they are close enough for him to see that the reason why their eyes are wide open is because they have no eyelids, he comes to his senses and lurches towards the passenger door to lock it, but there doesn't seem to be a button.

The blackened figures are now only a couple of metres from the car, and their screams slice through Peter's chest like ice-cold knives.

Central locking! Central locking!

Donald's car is fairly new, as is Peter's, and somewhere there must be a button that locks all the doors from the inside. In case of carjacking. In case of a zombie attack. Peter's fingers flutter over the instrument panel, desperately seeking the right symbol. He glances outside; this isn't the time to consult the manual. The expression on the face of the figure whose hand is already on the car bonnet lacks any vestige of human sanity. Those eyes convey only one thing: hunger.

The thin, claw-like hand scrapes across the metal; the creature's hip catches the wing mirror and bends it inwards as it reaches for the door handle.

Two buttons. One with an open padlock, one with a closed padlock. Peter presses the closed padlock and hears a reassuring clunk from all four doors in unison. The creature tugs at the door, but to no avail.

Peter has been so preoccupied with what has been going on in front of him and inside his head that he has forgotten a pretty vital fact: he is sitting in a car. A car that can be started up. A car that can be driven. Away from the creatures who are now surrounding him, trying to find a way in.

And yet he doesn't move. Now that the immediate danger has passed and the wave of panic in his belly has receded, he can see that even though the creatures look terrifying, they are not strong. Their dried-up, burnt fingers scrabble at the car or clench into fists, banging feebly at the windows as they scream and scream.

Are they…people?

One of them clambers up onto the bonnet and leans towards Peter, who instinctively recoils. They look at one another.

The creature has no more individuality than a skull. Everything that would confer personality has been burnt away. The ears and nose are no more than charred remains, and the parchment-like skin is stretched over the cheekbones. It looks at Peter. And screams.

When it opens its mouth Peter can see that one single muscle is more or less intact: the tongue, obscenely pink among the black and brown as the creature leans closer and screams. Most people go through life without ever hearing such a scream, fortunately, but in its expression of bottomless pain it is nonetheless human.

'What do you want?' Peter shouts. 'What do you want?'

It is obvious what they want. They want to get into the car. Peter has no intention of allowing that to happen, but he has to say something, something that will establish…human contact. He doesn't get an answer, but suddenly the creature stiffens and looks over its shoulder. The banging and scraping noises stop.

It quickly grows dark as the cloud comes closer, and through the windscreen Peter can see that the black wall in front of him has become diffuse and hazy. Twenty metres ahead of the car the grass seems to be moving in his direction. The creature jumps down from the bonnet and its screams change character, from pain to fear. Through the rear-view mirror Peter sees all four figures running away from the car.

Only when the movement in the grass has reached the car and the haze has become a fog does Peter realise what it is. Rain. A heavy shower of rain is falling from the black cloud, which now covers the sky so that it is as dark as night. A second later the drops begin to spatter on the bodywork of the car.

The screams grow fainter, and Peter runs his fingers through his hair, scratches his head. Rain. At least that explains how the grass can grow, but why are those creatures so afraid of it? Surely it would bring welcome relief, cool them down?

It is pitch black now, and Peter starts the engine so that he can switch on the headlights, but the water pouring down the windscreen still makes it difficult to see anything. He switches on the wipers, and now he can make out something that the flat light from the sky had not revealed. There is a track. A track running from the wall of darkness out across the field, following the route that the creatures took when they ran away.

Steam rises from the windscreen as some kind of sticky substance appears to vaporise. The next sweep of the wiper blades brings more goo; there is a terrible smell coming through the air conditioning, and now the wipers begin to make a screeching noise as they sweep back and forth.

There is something in the rain. What is it?

Peter lowers his window and sticks his hand out in the darkness, palm upwards. Warm raindrops land on his skin and he withdraws his hand, flicks on the interior light.

Ouch! Fuck! Ouch!

His palm feels hot. Then it begins to burn. There is no sign of fire, but it is as painful as if he had held his hand over a naked flame. The drops of rain have penetrated his skin, and he can smell burning flesh. He wipes his hand on the seat, rubbing it against the fabric, but the pain does not diminish.

A few drops catch the bottom of the window frame, splashing Peter's face, and seconds later his cheek feels as if it is on fire. He gasps and closes the window.

The wiper blades are still screeching, and now he realises why. There are no wiper blades. The rubber has disintegrated and been eaten away. It isn't difficult to understand why the creatures ran away.

Peter examines his hand; the acute pain has lessened, and in two places the skin has turned white around a dark red wound that has the faint smell of acetone. It still smarts, but the process seems to have stopped.

What would have happened if I had held my hand out for longer?

It's not hard to guess. He only has to look at the windscreen wipers.

He turns to look out of the back window, but in the darkness he can no longer make out the burnt creatures. Perhaps they weren't attacking him after all? Perhaps they were just seeking sanctuary inside the car?

The rain is hammering down, but it seems as if the grass is unaffected by whatever is falling from the sky. It bends and trembles just as it would in a normal shower, but it is not being eaten away.

Because it belongs here.

Peter doesn't have time to examine that thought more closely, because he has just noticed something about the car bonnet. He screws up his eyes and pulls down the sun visor to shade his eyes from the interior light and to reflect it forwards. He was right.

'Fucking hell!'

The bonnet is shimmering and shining like oil on water. The diamond-hard lacquer has begun to dissolve and is running across the metal in bubbling streams; the glow of the headlights grows fainter as they are covered with liquid lacquer.

'Fuck!'

If the rain has the ability to dissolve lacquer, then it is not unreasonable to assume that it can also eat through metal. For the moment Peter is sitting here inside the car, nice and cosy, but in five minutes or five seconds he could be sitting in a fucking colander with acid trickling all over his body until...

Until I become like one of them.

He's not about to analyse that thought either. He turns the key, and at the same time feels a burning sensation on the back of his neck. The rain has come through the plexiglas sunroof.

As he puts the car in gear and jolts forward

The tyres. Are the tyres okay?

he leans to the side, twisting his body away from the leak. He swings the car around while looking for something he can use to block up the hole. He can't see anything, so he opens the glove compartment and takes out the thick manual.

A couple of drops land on his shoulder, and he screams as they burn through his shirt and his skin. He changes up to second gear and floors the accelerator, following the track that leads away from the darkness, one hand pressing the manual against the sunroof, which buckles alarmingly under the pressure, as if it is much thinner now and on the point of breaking.

He doesn't know where he is going, and right now it doesn't matter. All he can do is keep his eyes on the track leading away from the darkness, and pray to God that the tyres and the headlights will hold out for as long as necessary.

But he has forgotten something. There is no God here.

All he can do is keep his eyes on the track. Keep his eyes on the track.

*

Stefan has never liked being the boss. He likes doing his own thing, but he has never enjoyed being in charge of other people. During the summer months he and Carina sometimes have five employees in the store, including a couple of teenagers. Stefan has no problem organising and allocating duties, but having to tell off the kids if they're spending too much time hanging out in the stockroom is just the pits. Bossing people around. To be honest, he usually leaves that kind of thing to Carina.

However, it seems as if he is going to have to take charge now. Majvor's discovery of the gold items has created confusion and a lack of focus. There is a great deal of vague chat, and the only concrete suggestion comes from Carina, who thinks they ought to dig a latrine so that they won't use up all their water flushing the toilets. Unfortunately this doesn't lead to direct action, because no one seems keen to tackle long-term issues, so Stefan takes the responsibility and puts into words what everyone already knows.

'Okay,' he shouts, clapping his hands. 'We have no idea how long we're going to be here, and...' Emil is standing beside him, so he changes *we might die here* to: '...it could be quite some time. We need to act on that basis.'

Stefan starts doing what he does best: organising the troops. Lennart and Olof will expand their vegetable patch and lend a spade to Emil and Carina, who will dig a latrine. Stefan himself will carry on building his tower so that they can make phone calls.

'And Majvor...'

He had intended to ask her to sit with Isabelle, but when he sees her eyes sparking with anticipation, he says: 'Check on Isabelle, then perhaps you could search around and see if you can find anything else? That's obviously one of your talents!'

In spite of the fact that his little speech was based on the assumption that they are going to have to stay here for a long time, the mood of the group has lifted as they disperse to tackle their assignments.

The four white figures have become a part of the landscape, standing motionless in the middle of the camp, but still Stefan avoids looking at them as he heads towards his caravan. They remind him of a bomb that has been defused; it is still a bomb.

He is about to go inside to fetch a screwdriver so that he can dismantle the wooden decking, but decides to check out the surrounding area first of all. Peter should have been back ages ago. Stefan clambers up onto the roof and hears a bark. The dog is trotting across the field, accompanied by a cat. Donald is a few metres behind them.

The group is only a stone's throw away, and there is no ambiguity about Donald's mood. His face is red, his hands gripping the strap of his shotgun as he staggers along on stiff legs. Donald is furious, and as he gets closer to the camp he slips the gun off his shoulder. Stefan is about to climb down when he spots something beyond Donald.

Black clouds have begun to pile up on the horizon. They grow in seconds, moving rapidly towards the camp. Stefan hurries down the ladder and glances in the opposite direction. Black clouds are gathering there too, racing across the sky towards the camp. Two gigantic arms, ready to embrace them.

*

Peter has driven out of the corrosive rain. The sky above him is clear and blue once again as he approaches the group of distorted creatures from behind. Only then does he realise that he is still pressing the car manual against the sunroof with his right hand, and steering with his left. When he slowly lowers the thick book, he sees that the rain has eaten virtually all the way through it.

He tosses the manual on the passenger seat and slows down as he drives past the running remnants of humanity. They spot him and turn towards the car, hands outstretched. But it is a half-hearted gesture without conviction; it could just as easily be a plea as a threat.

They really are a pitiful sight, like refugees from a nuclear explosion or the survivors of a fire. Even that does not do justice to their appearance. It is as if everything that is not essential to move forwards has been burnt away, and not even the remaining parts are intact.

Thanks to his own sports injuries and his work as a personal trainer, Peter is reasonably familiar with the muscular structure of the human body. He has studied scans showing how tendons, sinews and ligaments are connected, and these creatures look like a display of those images, although they are incomplete and damaged beyond repair. Some of the muscles have been so badly burnt that the bone is visible behind them, and the powerful ligaments in the thighs have been reduced to scraps that should no longer be able to convey strength. It is hard to understand how they can move at all, let alone run.

Are the hands outstretched because the creatures are hungry, or is this a plea for help? Whichever it might be, Peter has no intention of hanging around to find out. The clouds are growing in the rear-view mirror, and the need to get away overshadows everything else. Away from the corrosive, lethal rain.

But where can he go?

The field is endless.

The thought that gave him consolation not so long ago now seems like a mockery. If the field is endless, then all he can do is drive and drive until he runs out of petrol, then sit and wait for the cloud to catch up with him.

But the field is *not* endless. It ends where the darkness takes over. As Peter drives past the running creatures he scratches the back of his neck, wincing as his nails catch a sore. He moves his fingers a fraction and scratches again, examining the thought.

If there is an end, then it means that the field is not endless, but if that is the case, then what shape is this place? There is a slight curve to the horizon, but is this a sphere or merely a…sloping disc?

He concentrates on driving, because he has spotted something. The track which was so clearly visible in the beam of the headlights can also be seen beneath the blue sky, now that he knows it's there. In the absence of an alternative course of action he decides to follow it, while actively avoiding any speculation about the actual composition of the field.

He is leaning forward to switch on the radio when the horizon suddenly changes. Three long, narrow rectangles appear, and as he keeps going they grow taller, until they take the shape of three caravans. The track leads directly into the camp.

*

Majvor enters the caravan to find Isabelle propped up in bed with several pillows behind her back, her bandaged arms folded over her stomach. Molly is placing a laptop in front of her.

'Are you looking after your mummy?' Majvor says. 'That's a good girl. Mummies need looking after too, sometimes.'

'I'm a good girl, I am,' Molly says. 'Aren't I a good girl, Mummy?'

Isabelle nods slowly, but there is nothing to suggest that she knows why she is nodding. Her eyes are as empty and cold as two frozen lakes, and if it hadn't been for the movement of her head, Majvor would have thought she was dead.

'How are you, sweetheart?' Majvor asks, and Isabelle turns her head towards the sound of her voice. A cold shudder runs down Majvor's spine when their eyes meet. There is not the faintest spark of life in the two glass orbs set into the damaged face.

What has happened to her?

When Majvor was trying to stop the bleeding, Isabelle had been dazed and confused, but at least you could see that in her eyes. Now there is nothing, and Majvor doesn't know what to do. It is a relief when she hears Benny barking; it gives her an excuse to go outside and see what's going on.

Stefan jumps down from the ladder at the back of his caravan as Donald marches into the camp, followed by the dog and the cat, shotgun at the ready as if he is out hunting. The idea of taking him out into the field was to give him time to calm down; it looks as if he

281

has spent the period of isolation doing the exact opposite.

'Stop right there, you little bastard,' Donald yells, pointing the gun at Stefan, who does as he is told and holds up his hands.

'Get out here, the lot of you!' Donald thunders; his voice is so loud that Benny and the cat slink away under the farmers' caravan. 'Out here so I can see you!'

As Majvor walks towards Donald he fires a shot into the air, making the metallic walls of the caravans vibrate. She stops. However ridiculous his behaviour might be, there is no getting away from the fact that he is carrying a loaded gun. He shot at her before, and he could do it again.

Lennart and Olof leave their gardening and Carina emerges from her caravan with a spade in her hand. She signals to Emil to stay inside.

'So you thought you could dump me like a fucking scapegoat in the desert, did you?' Donald says, waving the barrel of the gun at the assembled company. When he reaches Harvey and the three incarnations of James Stewart he stops, then smiles scornfully and mutters: 'Oh no. You can't fool me. No way.'

'Donald,' Stefan ventures, pointing to the left and right. 'There are black clouds…'

'That's your problem,' Donald interrupts. 'You might just get wet. Because you're going to bring back my caravan.'

Stefan's comment has broken the concentration of the group, and they all start looking around to check out the clouds, which makes Donald even more furious than he already is.

'Did you hear me!' he bellows. 'You are going to bring back my caravan, and then you are going to fix it, and where's that bastard Peter, by the way?'

'He hasn't come back,' Stefan says, taking a step forward. 'Donald…'

Donald lowers the gun and fires a shot into the ground a metre in front of Stefan, which makes him jump back.

'I'm serious!' Donald yells. 'Get going, right now! Otherwise,

God help me, I'll kill the lot of you, one by one.'

Donald raises the gun to his shoulder and takes aim at Stefan, who hunches his shoulders and holds up his hands. Lennart clears his throat and says: 'Calm down, Donald. Olof and I will go and fetch your caravan.'

The clouds have grown bigger and moved closer in the short period since they first appeared.

'You're all going,' Donald insists, gesturing towards the farmers' Volvo. 'Get out of here. And fix the caravan.'

Over the years Majvor has developed a range of strategies for dealing with Donald's mood swings, but she has no experience of the state he is in now. The final resort usually involves telling him off in a sharp tone of voice, but she doesn't think that would help at the moment, so she troops over to the battered Volvo with the rest of them. The only person who doesn't move is Carina.

'I'm not leaving my son,' she says.

'Oh yes you are,' Donald says. 'Otherwise I'll shoot you.'

Carina's lips tremble as she lowers her arms. 'Go on then. Because I'm not leaving him.'

Majvor can't predict what might happen, but Donald's stressed expression and bloodshot eyes suggest that things could go really badly as he places his finger on the trigger.

'Donald!' she shouts, and manages to divert his attention. She smiles as sweetly as she can, and says: 'I'm useless anyway. Wouldn't it be better for me to stay here and look after you?'

The muscles around Donald's eyes twitch as he lowers the gun. Perhaps he is not ready to shoot an unarmed woman in spite of his insanity; perhaps he needs Majvor's care and attention. Whatever the reason, he lets out a snort and says: 'Okay, yes. But the rest of you need to get going right now!'

Majvor catches Carina's eye and nods reassuringly, a nod that means she will take care of Emil while they are away. Carina hesitates for a couple of seconds then returns the nod before joining the rest of the group.

Donald sits down in the folding chair and lays the shotgun across his knees, mumbling to himself as he follows the preparations for departure through narrowed eyes. Then he notices Majvor, standing alone a couple of metres away.

'Don't just stand there looking stupid,' he says, waving towards the refrigerator. 'Fetch me a beer.'

The Volvo has just started up when everyone becomes aware of the sound of another engine approaching the camp. All activity stops, and before anyone has the chance to react, Donald's Cherokee appears, with Peter at the wheel.

It stops next to the Toyota and Peter leaps out. With no grasp of what is going on, he runs over to the other car, shouting: 'We have to get out of here! Right away!'

The plan is to slam the Toyota into reverse then hook up his own caravan. Donald gets to his feet, the gun in his hands, and Majvor knows him so well that she can tell from his back view that he is smiling. Beaming, in fact.

*

'Don't moving a fucking muscle, Peter. I've got you in my sights. Hands up!'

One of Peter's talents as a player was the ability to make a decision in a fraction of a second. He didn't waste time fiddling around with the ball while he made up his mind. Better to do something unexpected, take a major risk, than to allow the other team to close ranks.

He can tell from Donald's tone that this is serious; he also realises that Donald has the gun. His eyes are still fixed on the tow bar, but he is able to work out roughly where Donald is from his voice. He decides to raise his hands slightly first of all, so that Donald will think he is cooperating, then he will throw himself under the caravan and roll out on the other side. After that he will have to improvise. If he can just explain about the clouds, the situation might change.

Peter lifts his head and begins to raise his hands. Then he stiffens, frozen in mid-movement. There are four people standing in the middle of the camp, staring at him. No, not four people; four versions of the same person. The final version, which is the most unpleasant, is something he has never seen in reality. His jaw drops and he whispers: 'Dad?'

When his father came out of prison, it turned out that the woman he had abused had a big family, who didn't think that prison was the best punishment for knocking women about. They thought someone who did that kind of thing should be bound naked to a tree in the forest before a number of significant wounds were inflicted with a pair of secateurs. In conclusion the perpetrator should be castrated using the same implement, then left to bleed to death. That was their view, which was soon translated into action.

By the time Peter's father was found, predators had started eating away at the soft tissue, and the organ that had been responsible for Peter's conception was never found. There was little doubt about who had carried out the attack, but there was no forensic evidence, and the entire family provided one another with watertight alibis. The court concluded that a person or persons unknown had tortured Peter's father to death.

Peter has already established that God does not exist in this place. He has also briefly considered the natural progression from this thought: that this is the *only* place where God does not exist—hell, in other words. However, he dismissed the idea as ridiculous. Why would four families from the same campsite be condemned simultaneously to eternal torment in hell? It just didn't make sense.

As he looks over at the middle of the camp, it seems a lot less ridiculous. If there is one person in his life who deserved to end up in hell, it is his father. And here he is. Four versions of the same man.

One is the drunken monster who almost killed Peter's mother, one is the vicious brute who smashed up their caravan, a third comes from Peter's early childhood, before the booze took over. But the figure that makes Peter forget his planned manoeuvres is the fourth, the one he has never seen, only imagined, over and over again.

A naked man with the corners of his mouth slashed to form a broad smile, his body marked with eight or ten gaping wounds, and no sex organs. His dead father, bloodless and clean, but still on his feet.

Without lowering his hands Peter closes his eyes, squeezes them tight shut. When he opens them again the father figures are still there, but Donald has moved closer. Majvor is behind him with a can of beer in her hand, while Stefan, Carina and the dairy farmers are getting out of the Volvo. There is no sign of Molly or Isabelle.

Donald stops ten metres away from Peter, puts the gun to his shoulder and takes aim. 'Now you're going to die, you bastard.'

Everything Peter had intended to do or say is gone. He realises that Donald really does mean to shoot him, that the time has come. He must remain calm. Breathe evenly, prepare himself.

Peter closes his eyes once more, takes a deep breath and thinks about the darkness, the smell of shower gel and disinfectant. He thinks *Anette*, he turns all his senses into a phallus and drives into her sweetness. Then Donald fires.

*

It's not that Donald hates Peter. Not really. But because Peter did what he did, Donald has no choice but to shoot him. In the real world he wouldn't act this way—he doesn't want to end up in jail after all—but in this pretend world it is the only thing he can do.

One of Donald's key characteristics is his ability to hold a grudge. He is well aware of this, in fact he often boasts about it: 'I've got a long memory, let me tell you.'

If someone has wronged Donald, there are virtually no lengths to which he will not go to restore the balance, preferably by doing something even worse to the perpetrator.

For example, take the wholesaler who sold a huge consignment of untreated wood to Donald at a good price, because he was supposed to be winding up his company and moving to the Costa del Sol.

Eighty thousand kronor down the pan; the entire consignment was riddled with woodworm after being kept in an unventilated storeroom for years and years. Worthless timber, firewood.

Donald bided his time, made sure he kept an eye on the person in question. When he still hadn't set foot in Sweden after a couple of years, Donald spent a considerable amount of time making the right contacts, then paid certain people to pay the former wholesaler a few visits.

Three local thugs were temporarily employed to wreck his garden, scratch his car, start a fire in his garden shed, and to break into his house a couple of times. Nothing major, but as the incidents were spread out over a period of several months, they had a significant impact on the man's peace of mind.

Eventually Donald sent him a postcard: 'Hope you're very happy in your house, and that things are going well. Best wishes, Donald'. After all, there was no point in doing all that if the guy didn't *know*.

As a result the man called Donald, weeping and promising to pay back the money for the wood, if he could just make it all stop. Donald said he had no idea what he was talking about, but he was happy to accept the money because the consignment really had been rubbish.

He hadn't done it because of the money, but he wouldn't be much of a businessman if he turned down eighty thousand kronor. At least it covered the amount he had spent to break the bastard, but the important thing was the victory itself, the fact that he had sat there shaking in his shoes in the heat of the Costa del Sol, and had realised that you couldn't get away with ripping off Donald Gustafsson.

Such measures are not an option when it comes to Peter. He dragged Donald away like a dog, wrecked his caravan and stole his car. The Bloodman turned white when Donald shot him, the mask disintegrated. What will happen to this fantasy creature called Peter? There's only one way to find out.

Donald closes one eye and aligns the crosshairs with the middle of Peter's forehead. He pulls back the trigger and takes a deep breath to steady his hands.

A yellow flame bursts into life in the back of his head, he hears a hissing sound, and the gun goes off.

*

Come on, Majvor. Come on.

Stefan's thigh muscles are tensed, his body leaning forward as he gets ready to run. He hasn't had time to reflect on whether he actually has the nerve, but perhaps his new role as leader has given him the extra courage he needs.

He was the one that Majvor looked at. As Donald walked towards Peter, Majvor followed him with an unopened can of beer in her hand. When it became clear that Donald really did intend to shoot Peter, Majvor raised the can, pointed to Donald's head, then looked over at Stefan. Stefan, nobody else. He swallowed hard and nodded. And got ready to sprint.

'I've got you in my sights.'

Donald places the butt of the gun to his shoulder and rests his cheek against it. His finger is on the trigger.

Come on, Majvor. Don't miss.

Majvor was probably intending to hit Donald over the head with the can, but suddenly it is urgent, and she has to act fast. She is only two metres away from Donald when she raises her arm above shoulder level and hurls the can with unexpected force. It flies through the air like a red and white stripe and strikes the back of Donald's head.

Stefan has been concentrating so hard on adopting the correct position and on his run that it seems only logical that he hears a starting gun go off as he charges at Donald with the aim of snatching the shotgun.

The can has caught Donald at an angle; it bounces upwards and forwards over the top of his head, then down in front of his face. At the same time the can flips open and there is a hissing sound as a stream of Budweiser spurts over Donald's face and chest in a white, foaming cascade.

The can hits the ground and continues to spurt, all over Donald's feet. If he turns around to see who threw it, he will see Stefan, but fortunately he looks down at the projectile itself first of all, and as he leans forward to get a better look at the hissing, bubbling object at his feet, Stefan reaches his goal.

Once again he surprises himself. His aim was to get hold of the gun, and he had pictured himself whirling past and grabbing it. Instead he stops dead right next to Donald. Without any particular sense of urgency, as if he were relieving a teenager who had been shoplifting of his ill-gotten gains, he takes the gun out of Donald's hands and says: 'Okay!'

Donald's reaction is not dissimilar to that of the beer can. As if a valve has been opened, releasing some internal pressure, Donald's shoulders drop, and with beer dripping from his face he looks at the gun, at Majvor, at Stefan, and says feebly: 'What the...fuck?'

There is nothing to suggest that Peter has been hit; he is standing open-mouthed, gaping at the four white figures.

'Peter!' Stefan shouts, backing away from Donald with the gun raised. 'Peter!'

Stefan doesn't know what Peter sees when he looks at the figures, but judging by his expression it is something terrifying. Stefan points the barrel of the gun at Donald, but realises that it is only the after-glow of the heat of battle that is making him do this. Without the shotgun, Donald is just an angry old man. Stefan lowers the weapon and goes over to Peter, obscuring his view of the figures.

'Peter?'

Peter isn't *completely* out of it. 'My father,' he says. 'He's dead. So how can he...how...'

Stefan slips the strap of the gun over his arm so that he can place both hands on Peter's shoulders. When Peter tries to move his head to the side so that he can look at the figures, Stefan places his hands on Peter's cheeks, holding his head still, and locks eyes with him.

'Peter, listen to me. That's not your father. They're just pretending to be whatever might scare or upset us, so that...blood will be spilt.

289

Do you understand me? They are *not* your father, nor anything else. They're just...nothing.'

Peter abandons the attempt to turn his head, and Stefan removes his hands. Then Peter gives a start as if he has just remembered something.

'Clouds,' he says. 'There are clouds coming.'

'I know, I've seen them.'

'Something falls from the clouds, something corrosive. It eats through metal, through everything. We have to get away from here. Right now.' Peter points in the opposite direction from which he came, then turns his attention back to the tow bar.

'It's no good going that way,' Stefan says. 'There are clouds coming from that direction too.'

Peter presses his hands to his temples. 'Bloody hell, Stefan, it eats through *everything*. And there are...'

He falls silent. Listens. Stefan can hear it too. Screams of pain in various keys are coming from the field, from both directions. And they are getting closer.

*

'Have you calmed down, Donald? Have you calmed down now?'

However crazy everything might be, Majvor cannot deny that she finds a certain amount of satisfaction in the current situation. She has always had to deal with Donald's unpredictable moods alone, picking her way through the minefield of his capricious nature. Now at least she has help.

Lennart and Olof have stayed with Majvor so that they can keep an eye, or rather six eyes, on Donald who seems anything but calm now that the initial shock has passed. He pulls a face and sets off towards Stefan, muttering something about his gun, but Lennart and Olof grab an arm each and hold on to him.

'Stop it, Donald!' Lennart says. 'You can't go around *shooting* people, for heaven's sake!'

Donald twists and turns in their grip, yelling: 'Let go of me, you bastard cowfuckers!'

'You're in a state,' Lennart says. 'We can't have you like this.'

'So what are you going to do? Shoot me? Go on then, shoot me, just like you shoot your bloody cows when you've finished fucking them!'

Olof looks at Majvor, who blushes. Donald can be foul-mouthed, but he doesn't usually go this far. He is her husband, after all, so she feels guilty by association when he says such terrible things to Lennart and Olof, whom she has come to regard as two fine men.

'Shut up, Donald!' she says, and perhaps it is his tasteless comments that make her add: 'Shut your mouth!'

Donald's eyes open wide, and he falls silent in the face of this unusually fierce reprimand. He jerks his body, trying to escape from Lennart and Olof, but without success. Lennart sighs and nods towards the breast pocket of his dungarees.

'Majvor, I've got a roll of tape here.'

Majvor has seen enough films to know what he means. Lennart and Olof twist Donald's arms behind his back so that Majvor can wind the tape around his wrists as she says: 'I really don't want to do this, Donald, but you are behaving like a madman right now. As soon as you calm down, we'll let you go.'

She sighs, breaks off the tape and pats him on the back. 'Goodness me, what a mess.'

Regardless of how Donald has been behaving, this feels wrong. That business with the can of beer was a necessary evil, an emergency measure, but she has wound the tape around his wrists with cold deliberation. You just don't *do* that to your husband. She walks around so that she can look him in the eye, and says: 'Sweetheart, I know all this has been terrible for you, and that you're confused. I just want to prevent you from doing something you might regret. Do you understand?'

Donald nods, and Majvor feels a spark of hope; perhaps he is starting to come to his senses. Then he looks at her and smiles nastily.

291

'Oh, I understand. The farmer wants a wife. It's one of your favourite TV shows. So now you've got a wet pussy, hoping to get a bit of farmer's cock, yum yum...'

He doesn't get any further; Majvor rips off a strip of tape and clamps it over his mouth. *That* doesn't feel wrong. Not at all.

Donald's face is bright red as he continues to utter muffled curses, which are fortunately unintelligible. The colour of Majvor's face isn't far behind as she turns to Lennart and Olof to apologise for her husband.

The two men are turning their heads from side to side as if they are listening, concentrating hard. Now that Donald has been more or less silenced, they can hear something else. The sound of screaming, as if someone somewhere is in great pain, and a whiff of...fried food. Majvor sniffs. Fried food and something else.

Sulphur.

Fire and brimstone. Majvor looks around, and what she sees approaching from the field makes the association even stronger.

Lord have mercy on us sinners.

*

Carina goes into her caravan, ready to console Emil. He must have witnessed the terrible scene with Donald, and how his father risked his life—things they would never allow him to see in a film, for example.

But Emil is not where she expected to find him, glued to the window that overlooks the middle of the camp. Instead he is kneeling on the sofa, looking out of the window on the other side. His fists are clenched, his body tense.

'You don't need to be scared any more, sweetheart,' Carina begins.

'Look, Mummy!'

Carina sits down beside him, strokes his head. Then she looks out of the window.

The first thing she sees are rainclouds covering almost her entire field of vision, and she thinks: *Lovely*. The unchanging blue sky has made her feel uncomfortable, and has contributed to her thoughts about disappearing. The clouds are something different, and they also mean water, life. Then she lowers her gaze.

Her mind tries to find an explanation for what she is seeing, and her first thought is marathon runners. Skinny black men whose thin bodies seem to be made up of nothing but muscle and sinew. A group of marathon runners is approaching from the field, but there is something wrong with their technique. They are struggling, throwing themselves forward in a series of jerky movements, as if the component parts of their skeletons are inadequately linked together. She hears the screams, and as they come closer she can see their bodies more clearly. If this is a race, then it started in the kingdom of the dead.

'Zombies, Mummy!'

Carina has no idea what these ragged creatures are, but she does know one thing: they must not get into the caravan.

'Stay here, sweetheart,' she says, and as she gets to her feet she sees the Lego fortress. The four walls, the three knights.

With thick walls so it can withstand the attack. The door is the weakest point. Is there anything bigger that lives on blood?

Somehow Emil has known all along. What else did he say? Something about whatever it is that lives on blood, but what was it? There isn't time to ask him now. She has to go and find Stefan.

When she reaches the doorway she sees her husband standing in the middle of the camp holding the shotgun high above his head as if he is wading across a river. Before she can say anything he shouts: 'Listen everyone! We need to get inside the caravans! The rain contains some kind of corrosive acid. We need to take cover!'

Carina steps back to let Stefan in. He has the gun in one hand, and with the other he closes and locks the door behind him.

'How are you two?' he asks. 'Are you okay?'

Stefan is essentially a very calm person, and it takes a lot to get him worked up. On one occasion a truck ran into a petrol pump outside the store, and thousands of litres of fuel gushed out across the car park. Just one spark and ICA Ålviken would have been nothing more than a memory. Stefan took charge of evacuating the premises, cordoned off the area and called the emergency services. Everything turned out okay in the end, but it's the only time Carina has seen him really stressed.

Until now; this is much worse. His voice has a metallic tone and his eyes are darting all around the caravan as he brandishes the shotgun. Carina temporarily pushes her own fears to one side so that she can put her arms around his trembling body. 'You're my hero. You're the bravest person I know. I love you.'

The trembling subsides a little, and Stefan takes a deep breath, then exhales in a long sigh. He puts down the gun on the worktop and hugs her back.

'Thank you,' he whispers into her hair.

Emil squeezes in between them so that he can join in with the hug. With his head between their stomachs he says in a broken voice: 'They're here now.'

There is a crash and the caravan shudders as the first runner crosses the line.

*

Peter has given up. As he was driving towards the camp, his plan of action was clear in his mind: hook up the caravan and head away from the clouds. Now it turns out that the clouds are coming from both directions, and his head is empty. All he can do is sit and wait. Let others say their prayers, if they so wish.

Before he goes into the caravan he looks around. Stefan has just slammed the door shut behind him, while the two farmers are manhandling Donald into their caravan, followed by Majvor. The four versions of his father are still standing in the middle of the camp, staring in different directions.

'I hate you,' Peter says to them. 'I know it isn't you, but I hate you anyway. If I had the gun, I'd shoot you. And you. And you.' He looks at the last figure, the kinder version from his childhood. 'And you.'

The clouds are now so close that they are visible above the roof of the caravan. Peter nods to the four fathers. 'I hope you burn.'

He steps inside, checking that Isabelle and Molly are already there. He closes the door behind him, and as he turns the lock he *sees* what he just saw, the horrific vision of Isabelle, sitting up in bed with his laptop open in front of her.

'What the hell have you *done?*'

Isabelle's face is so swollen that she is barely recognisable, and there are patches of dried blood on her cheeks and chin. Both arms are encased in duct tape, and a string of pink saliva is dangling from the corner of her mouth, heading for the laptop's keypad.

'Hi, Daddy!' Molly says. 'We're watching a film!'

The approaching screams from the creatures outside mingle with similar noises from the laptop's speaker. Peter sits down on the bed and turns the computer so that he can see the screen.

A woman is hanging on a metal frame while a man flays her alive, his face expressionless. The woman screams and screams as the man uses a scalpel to remove yet another sliver of skin, exposing red, gleaming flesh. He throws the scrap of skin into a metal bowl, looks into the woman's eyes, which are hysterical with fear, then begins to slice off another piece.

'It's *brilliant!*' Molly says, clapping her hands. 'Come and watch it with us, Daddy!'

Peter has gone through a range of emotions over the past few hours, many sensations have surged through his body, but he has not experienced the entire spectrum until now: he feels ill. Bile rises in his throat as he looks at Isabelle's distorted face, the martyred woman on the screen, and Molly's beaming smile.

Sick, this is…sick.

The sky outside grows dark, and the light from the screen flickers in nauseating shades of blue and green over his wife, his daughter. With his hand covering his mouth Peter gets up from the bed just as one of the creatures reaches the caravan and starts banging its hands against the metal. Peter jumps and takes a step back as the claw-like fingers scrabble at the window.

'Nooooo, please God! Nooooo!'

For a moment he thinks that the creature's inarticulate cries have turned into words in English. Then he understands, reaches across the bed and slams the laptop shut. He grabs it and places it on the highest kitchen shelf.

'Daddy, no!'

'Molly, you're not to watch that kind of thing.'

'But I *love* that kind of thing!'

Peter looks out of the window. There is no longer any sign of the burnt creature, nor can he hear the sound of scrabbling as it tries to find a way in. Fifty metres away a ripple passes through the grass as the curtain of rain comes closer. Forty metres. Thirty.

There is nothing he can do. The nausea subsides; the internal voices urging him to run, to do something, think of something, fall silent. Slowly he sinks down onto the bed. There is just one thing he would like to know before it all ends.

'Molly,' he says, and his daughter looks up at him, her expression sullen. 'What exactly *are* you?'

The sullenness disappears and Molly's face changes as she straightens up; it is as if she has been waiting for this question for a long time. 'Don't you know, Daddy?'

'No, Molly. I don't know.'

Molly looks at her mother's ruined face to check if she is listening, but Isabelle is lost, her gaze turned inward. Molly shuffles closer to Peter and whispers: 'I am a fountain of blood in the form of a girl.'

And then the rain is upon them.

*

Benny doesn't like whatever it is that has crawled under the caravan to join him and Cat. He doesn't like it at all. It smells kind of like when there is a fire, it is neither He nor She, and Benny barks at it, hoping it will go away. Cat must be of the same opinion, because she hisses and makes herself enormous.

Benny wishes he could make himself enormous too, just like one of those Dogs people are scared of, because the thing that smells of fire takes no notice of the noise they are making, but simply edges closer as if it wants to grab hold of Benny.

A few seconds ago they could have run across to another caravan, but this is no longer possible; it is raining, and you only have to sniff the rain to realise that you will be a dead dog if it touches you. They are stuck here with the firecreature.

Benny and Cat shuffle backwards, barking and hissing. The firecreature has a noise too, a horrible noise just like when He or She have hurt themselves really badly, and it makes this noise all the time, as if it is constantly hurting itself.

Benny and Cat have reached the far side of the caravan; there is nowhere else to go. Benny peeps out and sees that the four big Grandchildren are still standing there; the rain is pouring down on them, but they are not dead. Benny is so preoccupied by this sight that he has no time to react when the firecreature seizes his collar.

The barking changes to a howl as Benny is dragged across the grass towards the firecreature's mouth. He can see its teeth. Big white teeth, gleaming in the darkness. Benny's claws scrabble and slip on the grass without finding any purchase, and he whimpers in terror as the teeth part and the mouth opens, ready to bite his throat.

Then he sees an orange stripe out of the corner of his eye. Cat's fur tickles his nose and Cat sinks her sharp little teeth into the firecreature's hand. Cat is now so big that she only just fits beneath the caravan, and her eyes are wild.

The firecreature lashes out at Cat, striking her on the back, but she refuses to let go of its hand. At the same time her claws come out and she scratches the firecreature's eyes.

The noise it is making grows louder and it lets go of Benny, who takes the opportunity to bite its other hand. More noise. Then it withdraws to the other end of the caravan and lies there on its belly. It is still looking hungrily at Benny and Cat, but it daren't come any nearer. Benny and Cat move back to their own side. There is blood in the fur on Cat's back. Benny nudges her in the stomach and she lies down, then Benny begins to lick her wounds.

*

The rain is hammering down on the roof of Lennart and Olof's caravan when they hear barking from under the floor. Barking, hissing, and screaming that seems to come from a person in agony. Majvor covers her ears with her hands; Donald is on the sofa, still struggling to free himself from Lennart's grip. The paraffin lamp they have lit and placed on the table wobbles and almost falls over.

'Will you stop it?' Lennart roars. 'Aren't things bad enough already?'

Olof looks at the floor and says: 'Maud. Maud is down there.'

'Yes,' Lennart agrees. 'I guess she is.'

The barking turns to howling and then a terrified whimpering, Maud's hissing intensifies and Olof pulls a face. 'I can't listen to this.' He gets up and moves towards the door. 'I'm going to…'

'Olof, didn't you hear what Stefan said?'

Olof fiddles with the strap of his dungarees and looks out of the window at the thick drops of rain sliding down the glass against a backdrop of darkness. 'Yes, but it doesn't make sense.'

'And what exactly has made sense in this place so far? At least test it out first.'

The sound of fighting under the caravan stops, and Olof picks up a puzzle magazine with a caricature of the pop singer Måns Zelmerlöw on the cover. He opens the window a fraction, pushes the magazine outside for a few seconds, then pulls it back in.

The cover is smoking as Zelmerlöw's face disintegrates, revealing completed crosswords which also dissolve, until the magazine is perforated by a number of holes. Donald hurls himself from side to side, yelling something from behind the tape. Lennart shoves him away.

'Okay,' he says. 'Enough. You think all this is a dream you're having, right?'

Donald looks at Lennart through narrowed eyes, then he nods.

'Right. And neither I nor anyone else can do or say anything to convince you that this is not the case, because then you just assume it's part of the dream?'

Donald says something, but when he realises that no one can understand him, he nods again.

'Okay. Listen to me. There was some philosopher who said: *I think, therefore I am.*'

'Descartes,' Olof says. 'Came up yesterday. In a crossword.'

'That's it, Descartes. And you *think*—don't you, Donald? Sitting there glaring at me right now, you can *think*, can't you?' Lennart goes on without waiting for a response from Donald. 'Now I'm no philosopher, and I might not be very good at putting things into words, but neither are you, so...'

Majvor has uncovered her ears and is leaning forward with her eyes fixed on Lennart's lips as if she doesn't want to miss a word.

'We're all here,' Lennart says. 'In this place, this...bizarre place. And you're walking around here, Donald. And you're *thinking*. So this is where your head is. Regardless of your opinion, it means that *you're* here too. Just like we are. Thinking. Do you understand what I'm saying?'

Donald's eyes flicker from side to side and it seems as if he is making use of the faculty Lennart has just ascribed to him: he is thinking. Then he nods once more.

'Good. In that case I'm going to remove this tape, Donald, because to be honest this is just ridiculous.'

Gently Lennart pulls off the tape; Donald moans as it tugs at his stubble. He smacks his sticky lips and says: 'The hands too.'

'First of all I need to hear that you understand,' Lennart says.

'I understand. I understand that you're talking a load of crap.'

Lennart closes his eyes and his shoulders slump. He gets to his feet, and Donald, unable to use his hands, clumsily follows suit. Lennart opens a drawer, takes out a serrated knife and cuts through the tape binding Donald's wrists. Then he sits back down and waves towards the door.

'Be my guest, Donald. You saw what happened to the magazine, but if all this is a dream then you're in no danger, because it's impossible to die in dreams, from what I've heard. Go for it.'

There are several rusty patches on the old caravan, places where corrosion has begun to eat away at the metal. So far there are no holes, but one of the worst spots is just above the door. As Donald puts his hand on the latch, the rain comes through and a few drops land on his bald patch. He runs his hand over his head, then his face crumples and he lets out a yell as he scrubs at the affected area with both hands.

'Ow ow ow, fuck, it's burning...ow!'

He runs to the sink and turns on the tap to sluice his head with cold water; meanwhile, Lennart, Olof and Majvor lean closer together.

'What are we going to do?' Majvor asks, glancing up at a patch of rust above the table, where a single drop of rain is just about to fall. It slowly lengthens, frees itself and lands on the laminate tabletop, where it leaves a small, hissing crater. Majvor cannot take her eyes off it.

Fire and brimstone from the sky.

They are not going to get out of this alive; there is no point in pretending any more. As Lennart and Olof get to their feet, Majvor puts her hands together, closes her eyes and begins to pray.

She knows a lot of prayers, both those sanctioned by the church and those she has made up herself. Most are addressed to God the Father, the creator of heaven and earth. But in really difficult times, such as the time when she was pregnant with Albert and thought she might be losing the baby, it is not God who is closest to her.

No, when darkness falls and she feels that there is no hope left, then God is—forgive the blasphemous thought—merely an omnipotent judge, a man among other men, and the only one who can understand her is another woman, another mother: the Virgin Mary.

There is a cracking sound as something in the kitchen is torn free. Majvor concentrates on the boundless inner space where Mary will open her arms to receive her.

'Holy Mary, Mother of God,' Majvor murmurs. 'Help us in our hour of need and forgive us our sins which are as innumerable as the grains of sand on the seashore. Show us the way out of this...hell.'

Majvor listens, but all she hears are the external sounds of wrenching and breaking wood.

'Where are you?' she whispers. 'Mother Mary, where are you?'

Nothing. Absolutely nothing.

Until now everything has somehow been bearable. Majvor has known all along that if her need becomes too great, if she prays from the bottom of her heart, then the answer will come. It always does. But not this time. She has nowhere to turn, and the depth of her isolation does something to her. Something critical.

*

'I need the outdoor cushions too! And the rugs!'

Stefan is standing on the loft ladder, throwing soft furnishings into the alcove between the roof and the ceiling as Carina passes them up from below. Their only hope is that the corrosive rain is a temporary phenomenon, and the alcove gives them the chance to create a layer of insulation above the kitchen table, which should at least buy them a few extra minutes.

Even though Stefan has not really recovered from the incident with Donald, he has already been thrown into a new cycle where lives, their lives, are at risk. He feels like a character from Emil's Nintendo, a Raving Rabbid. His hands seem as if they are not attached to his body, but are living a life of their own where they carry out the necessary actions when someone else operates the controls. Up the ladder, down the ladder, jump forward, duck to avoid being shot, try to survive until the next level.

'The sleeping bags!'

Now the idea has taken hold, he can't get it out of his head. It seems odd that he is talking, issuing orders and appearing to be quite sensible, when all he really has to say is what Raving Rabbid says. Those crazy, wide-open eyes, that gaping mouth, and 'BWAAHHH!'

'Daddy!'

For a moment Stefan isn't sure. Did he really just yell like those lunatic rabbits? If so it's hardly surprising that Emil sounds so frightened.

'Daddy!'

'What?'

'My cuddly toys! You have to save them!'

'Okay, pass me the torch.'

Emil grabs the flashlight and passes it up to his father.

Bwaahhh!

The rain has come through the roof in at least a dozen places and has begun to destroy Emil's bedclothes, mattress, and everything they have thrown in the alcove. An acrid mist hovers in the air in the cramped space, thickening as the drops continue to fall.

'Sweetheart, I just can't do it, it's…'

If Emil had said *Please Daddy*, or *Daddy you have to*, Stefan wouldn't have done it, even though he knows how much Bunte, Hipphopp, Bengtson and the others mean to his son. Wherever the family goes, the five soft toys have to come too, and in a way they are his closest friends. But acid is dripping from everywhere now, and there is no possibility of Stefan reaching the toys around Emil's pillow without it landing on him.

Emil says nothing, probably because he realises that retrieving his toys is out of the question. Instead he takes a deep breath and swallows a sob. He won't even allow himself to cry, and Stefan's heart, which is already at breaking point, cracks a little more.

He shines the beam of the torch into the mist. At the very end of the milk-white cone he can just see the outline of Sabre Cat. Down below he hears Carina's voice: 'Sweetheart, we have to wait until this has stopped. It's…No, Stefan!'

Stefan grabs a bath towel, throws it over his head and back and crawls into the alcove.

What if it doesn't stop...

That was the straw that broke the camel's back. In spite of their efforts to create a barrier between themselves and the rain, every indication suggests that this is a futile exercise. They will end up cowering on the sofa until the rain starts dripping onto them, and Emil won't even have his soft toys to cuddle for consolation when his mummy and daddy's arms have

Bwaahhh!

disintegrated and can no longer protect him; the thought is unbearable. So Stefan begins to crawl as Carina begs him to stop.

The first metre is no problem. A few drops land softly on the towel, but Stefan is unaware of the smell of acid and burnt fabric because he is holding his breath to avoid inhaling any of the mist. But his eyes are stinging, and he sees Sabre Cat through a veil of tears as he reaches out and grabs the animal's shaggy coat.

A drop hits his hand at the same time as the dampness penetrates the towel and the legs of his trousers. It feels as if red-hot nails are being driven through the roof and down into his back, his thighs and the back of his head, and he has to summon every ounce of willpower to stop himself from screaming. He bites his lower lip so hard that it starts bleeding as he grabs the remaining soft toys, and for one insane moment

Bwaahhh! BWAAAAAHHHH!

he can't decide whether to shuffle backwards or turn around, but instead he thinks, *I'll just stay here*, because now he comes to think of it, his body is also insulating material that could give his wife and son another minute or two before the rain finds its way through to them down below, but as is so often the case when the battle is between good intentions and physical pain, it is the pain that

I am on fire

takes the victory because it is no longer red-hot nails but a huge, white-hot iron that is pressing down on Stefan's back, and now it is not possible to suppress the scream.

Stefan lurches sideways in a quarter turn, the cuddly toys clutched in his arms, then pushes off from the wall of the alcove with one foot as if he were in a swimming pool, and manages to thrust his body half a metre closer to the ladder. He mistakenly takes a breath, and a network of sticky, stinging threads spreads through his lungs, making him cough as he wriggles forward using his elbows. Not only can he feel the skin on his back being eaten away, he can also *hear* it sizzling, just like when a pork chop is dropped into the hot fat in a frying pan.

His body is burning, he is coughing so violently that he is almost throwing up, and tears are pouring down his cheeks when he reaches the edge of the alcove without even realising, and tumbles over.

Some sane corner of his mind or the sheer instinct for self-preservation makes him twist his body in mid-air so that he lands on his chest, with the bundle of soft toys partly cushioning his fall.

He still lands quite badly. One shoulder hits the floor hard, and his forehead slams into the linoleum-covered metal, releasing a chaotic starburst inside his skull.

'Darling, you crazy...'

He feels Carina's hands under his arms, dragging him towards the kitchen table. His sole focus during the overwhelming starburst is to hang on to the cuddly toys.

'I'm so sorry, Daddy, I never meant...'

Stefan lets out a yell as Carina heaves him up onto the sofa and his thighs make contact with the coarse fabric. He leans forward so that his back won't touch anything, and the stars begin to fade as he opens his arms and drops the toys on the table. Emil gathers them up, remorse written all over his face.

'Sorry, sorry, sorry...'

Stefan waves a hand to indicate that it's okay. He daren't open his mouth for fear that the only thing that will come out is

Bwaahhh!

something that might frighten Emil even more. Carina strokes Stefan's arm, gazing at him with the kind of love that is usually reserved for lovers on a sinking ship or a plane that is about to crash, a love that might not even be love, but something more fundamental: *I'm here. You're there. I see you.*

And the rain just keeps on falling.

*

Peter is sitting on the bed next to Molly, doing something that he hasn't allowed himself to do properly for a long time: he is thinking. The rain is hammering on the roof, sliding down the window panes; a few drops find their way in through a tiny gap above the sink and burn holes in the dishcloth. How can rain like this exist? Why *shouldn't* rain like this exist?

Peter can't remember the exact figures, but the series of coincidences that must be combined in order for new life to be viable is an astronomical number. It is usually too hot or too cold, or there is no atmosphere, or the atmosphere that does exist is toxic, or covalent hydrocarbon bonds cannot form, or there is no water; there are thousands upon thousands of other factors that make life impossible.

We shouldn't exist.

The existence of humanity borders on unimaginable, so it is not too far-fetched to think that there must be a plan behind it all, a God who has set the machinery in motion and perhaps continues to keep a watchful eye on what is going on. But if this creator, this engineer and caretaker, is removed from the equation, then what is left? Perhaps nothing more than an endless field where humanity and its attributes have no right to exist, and must be erased from the clean surface.

'What are you thinking about, Daddy?'

Peter shines the beam of the torch on Molly, and to his astonishment sees that there are tears pouring down her cheeks. Molly can sound desperate and tearful if she thinks it will serve her purpose, but Peter can't remember when he last saw her actually cry.

I am a fountain of blood...

'I'm thinking about God.'

305

Molly grins and there is nothing in her voice to suggest that she is crying when she replies: 'There's no need for that.'

The tears leave pink streaks on Molly's skin, and Peter's suspicions are confirmed when another drop of liquid falls from the ceiling onto her forehead, then runs down her nose without causing any serious damage, merely a slight irritation.

…in the form of a girl.

The drip reaches Molly's chin, and before it has time to fall, Peter wipes it away with his index finger. For a moment he thinks that the rain has changed, that it has become diluted and less dangerous. Then his finger begins to burn as if he had held it over a lighted match. The nail turns white and grows as a few millimetres of the cuticle are eaten away.

Molly runs a hand over her face, sounding surprised as she says: 'It hurts. It stings.' She looks at her damp hand and shakes her head. The words that come out of Peter's mouth are unexpected; he hasn't had time to think the thought through.

'You belong here, don't you?'

'I don't know. Not *yet*.'

A few drops land on Peter's head, and however much he would like to give up, fall backwards onto the bed and let the rain pour down on him, it is out of the question, because it is so bloody painful.

Humanity…

Hanging by its fingertips above the abyss, drowning in the ice-cold sea, standing on the window ledge of a burning building. Always trying to get a *slightly* better grip, hold its breath for just a *few* more seconds, withstand a *little* more heat before the fall, the end. To squeeze the very last drop out of life.

Peter doesn't know what Molly is, but he is a human being, and he can't help trying to survive for as long as possible. He crawls to the top of the bed, tucks his hands under Isabelle's arms and drags her into the kitchen area. He checks the ceiling for holes, then props her up against the sink.

His back and arms feel as if they are on fire as he strips the bed and removes the thick cushions that serve as a mattress. He opens out the table and places the cushions on top, creating a refuge underneath, a den with a half-metre thick roof of foam rubber. He knows that he is only putting off the inevitable, but he cannot do anything else; he is a human being.

'Come on!' he shouts, turning and sweeping the beam of the torch around the caravan. 'You need to...'

Molly is standing there looking expectantly at him with liquid running down her face. Isabelle is not there, and the sound inside the caravan has changed. The hammering of the rain on the roof mingles with a rustling, splashing noise as the rain falls on the grass; the door is open. Peter shines the torch in that direction and sees the outline of Isabelle's body as she walks through the rain, away from the caravan.

'No, Isabelle!'

He takes a step towards the door, but is stopped by Molly, who grabs hold of his thumb. She shakes her head. The curtain of rain visible through the doorway is so dense that it is difficult to see through it; it is incomprehensible that Isabelle manages to stay on her feet for long enough to disappear beyond the range of the torch.

Molly pulls him towards the den, and Peter allows it to happen. He can no longer feel individual places where the rain has landed on him; his entire skin is a blanket of pain enfolding his body, and his head is boiling so much that he actually sees red as he and Molly crawl into the cramped space.

He drops the torch on the floor, curls up and screams as the blanket of pain shrinks and the burning heat is turned up yet another notch.

No more. No more. I can't bear it.

A cool hand is laid on his forehead, small fingers run through his hair. Through the veil of red Peter can see that Molly has drawn up her knees and is sitting with her chin resting on them as she smiles at him and continues to stroke his head. 'It's just you and me now, Daddy. Isn't this cosy?'

Under different circumstances you could say that Lennart and Olof, Majvor and Donald have been *lucky*. The worktop that Lennart and Olof ripped off turned out to be exactly the right length when they laid it above the kitchen table, resting on the top of the window frames. In addition, the roof of their old caravan is significantly thicker than modern versions. It was several minutes before they could hear drops splashing on the worktop above their heads as they sat there hunched around the table, with the yellow glow of the paraffin lamp playing over their faces.

Majvor has been unreachable for some time; her eyes are closed, her lips are moving. Donald's aggression has temporarily abated, but his face is set in a scornful grin, as if he finds the situation ridiculous and beneath his dignity. However, he has taken advantage of the extra protection available.

The whole thing seems so bizarre that Olof had to stick out his hand to catch a drop a little while ago. It wasn't a very good idea, because now the palm of his hand is sporting an angry red crater, which is sending stabbing pains all the way up his arm.

This is really happening.

Olof has a tendency to daydream, and since he and Lennart threw in their lot together, he has sometimes dreamt of their old age, when the hard work on the farms is over at long last.

They will sit in their rocking chairs on Olof's porch, or perhaps they will lie in hammocks—why not—gazing out across the fields where Ante and Gunilla have taken over, having provided them with a grandson and a granddaughter.

Lennart and Olof will chat about the past, satisfied with what they have been able to pass on to their children. Sometimes Ante or Gunilla will come to ask for their advice, and sometimes the little ones will come along, wanting help with some project.

They will move quietly through the days, content to be together now that life's toil and struggle are over. There will always be a beautiful twilight, with the sun setting the cornfields ablaze, and they will take each other's hands and sigh as they share a sweet melancholy.

A drop of rain penetrates the worktop and lands on the laminate surface of the table in front of them. The acrid, chemical smell of acid and burnt plastic reaches Olof's nostrils, and he thinks that the daydream he has just enjoyed once more is going to be his last.

If only I could...

Lennart's hand finds his, and there is no reason to pretend any more; it is too late for that kind of thing. Olof turns and hugs Lennart. There is a rasping sound as stubbly cheek meets stubbly cheek, and Olof whispers in Lennart's ear: 'I love you.'

Lennart caresses the back of Olof's head and the nape of his neck, and he whispers in return: 'I love you too, Olof.'

They sit with their arms around each other for a little while in silence, then they hear a snort and Donald's voice: 'Fuck me. The things you see when you haven't got your gun.'

Lennart and Olof move apart. Donald is sitting up straight on the opposite side of the table, righteous indignation in every fibre of his body. His scornful smile has changed into a grimace of disgust, while his wife is still curled around her own internal world.

'I'll spare you the sight,' Lennart says, turning off the paraffin lamp.

In the darkness Olof feels Lennart's hands moving across his face. Although they have never done it before he understands what is happening, and leans closer until his lips find Lennart's. It feels strange when they kiss at long last, but at the same time it feels right.

*

Certain people reach a point or several points in their life where they feel that *this is where I have been aiming for*. Defining moments that might involve a blessing or a curse, torment or joy, but the key thing is that they are a consequence, the sum of previous actions, desires and choices distilled into one place, one time. Isabelle's point is the moment when she steps out of the caravan into the rain.

Here. Now. Me.

The smell of swimming baths or a laundry room fills her nostrils. Chlorine and bleach, falling from the sky and rising from the ground. Her hair is drenched in seconds, and the rain runs down her face and body, over the tape that covers her arms as she walks away from the caravan.

Two steps. Three. Then comes the pain, and it is beyond all reason. Every nerve in her body with the capacity to transmit suffering begins to vibrate, every muscle relaxes or tenses in a series of uncontrollable, jerky movements. Faeces and urine pour out of her, but the receptors that should be able to detect what is flowing down her thighs have already been burnt away, and *shame* has no place here. This is where she is meant to be.

Isabelle's worst fear has always been to be burnt on a bonfire. Of all the horrific images she has seen on film, it is a simple scene from a mediocre production that made the greatest impression on her. *Silent Hill.* The woman who is tied to a frame and slowly tipped towards the fire until her skin begins to boil and her facial features disintegrate.

Four steps, five. This is worse.

At least fire heats the blood quickly, until the heart collapses and death takes over. The rain covering Isabelle's body is slowly gnawing through the skin, the sinews and the muscles, tearing at the nerves and causing a pain more intense than she would have thought possible.

Six steps, seven.

The silver tape on her arms has dissolved into a sloppy mess of plastic and fine threads, slipping down towards her hands where the skin over the knuckles has been eaten away, exposing white, rounded bone. The hair on her head comes away in stinking clumps that slide down her face and would have tickled her lips, if she had any lips. Chunks of skin cover her eyes, and her already blurred vision deteriorates still further as she takes with her eyes closed as the colours behind her eyelids go from black to red to orange and soon they too will dissolve and then the rain will reach her eyeballs and then everything will go black and there will be nothing but pain, pain until it is finally over.

Isabelle has no control over her body, and the pain is so immense that she can no longer feel it; her nerves have given up the struggle. In a final attempt at deliberate action, she concentrates all her energy on her now yellow eyelids, and opens them to a beautiful summer's day.

The first thing she sees when she manages to focus is an overweight man in a Hawaiian shirt, on his way to the kiosk to hand in his mini-golf club. An equally overweight woman is waddling along beside him, rolling two golf balls around and around in her hand. Meanwhile a stick-thin little girl is bouncing up and down on the trampoline, and the smell of fried food is in the air.

Fried food.

That's it. Not burnt, but deep-fried. Slowly boiled in oil until the skin falls off and the eyes turn white. Isabelle looks at her arms, where her lightly tanned skin is covered in pale, downy hairs. She touches her face. She can feel her lips and her jawbone now that her cheeks are no longer swollen. She runs her tongue around the inside of her mouth, presses the tip against her front teeth, licks her top lip; she can taste salt. She opens her mouth and says: 'Fuck.'

She is back where their caravan used to be, along with the other three. The caravans are gone, and no one else has come to take their place. When she looks down she sees that her sandal-clad feet are covered in ash, because she is standing in the communal barbecue area, a circle of stones in the middle of the camp.

You would think the other campers might be interested in the sight of a model standing in a pile of ash, taking deep breaths as she tries to work out what has happened to her. But although there are plenty of people around, no one is looking in her direction. It's as if she is invisible.

The idea is no stranger than anything else that has happened to her today. Isabelle looks over at the child on the trampoline ten metres away, and brings her hands together in a loud clap. The braids whirling around the girl's ears break their trajectory and whip across the top of her head as she immediately turns in Isabelle's direction. Their eyes meet for a fraction of a second, then the girl looks away and concentrates on her bouncing.

Not invisible.

People *can* see her, but consciously or unconsciously they don't *want* to see her. As if she were something that shouldn't be here, a smelly junkie—best to ignore her. Otherwise why is no one looking at her? People *always* look at Isabelle.

She rakes her nails over her forearms. They're *itchy*. When she looks more closely she sees two long, narrow cruciform scabs, running from her wrists to the crook of her arms. She scratches a little more and fragments of scab come away and get stuck under her bitten nails as one of the wounds begins to bleed.

Slowly she spins around in a complete circle. There is a track running towards the kiosk, another in the opposite direction, into a grove of trees. The track leading down to the sea passes through the spot where Isabelle is standing and continues further up into the campsite, at right angles to the first. She is standing at the crossroads and her wounds are itching.

*

Carina, Stefan and Emil are sitting very close together, hunched around the kitchen table. The rain hasn't yet penetrated the alcove with its layers of insulation, but the far end of the caravan is in a bad way. The roof has been perforated in countless places, and the rain is dripping or rather pouring down on their belongings.

Stefan has stopped shining the torch over there because it doesn't make him feel any better to watch the coffee machine melting or to see the rug his mother wove disintegrating from the inside as it absorbs the liquid. He sits with his arms around Emil and Carina's shoulders. Emil is curled up in a ball, his cuddly toys pressed close to his tummy. Carina's cheek is resting on Stefan's shoulder, the top of her head nestled into his neck.

Sometimes, just before he falls asleep, Stefan is haunted by terrible images. When he was young they were primarily of the white figure and what would have happened if he had obeyed the call. Since Emil was born the focus has shifted to his family, and what could happen to them.

His brain tortures itself as he lies awake for hours, unable to shake off scenes of concentration camps, being separated from his wife and son on the platform at some dirty, wintry train station, or being dragged through mud by people who wish them harm. He forces himself to watch, while at the same time he is ashamed of the fact that he is putting Emil and Carina through such horrors, even though they're not aware of it.

His only consolation as he lies there, his throat constricting, is that perhaps there is a purpose behind it all. Perhaps this is happening so that he will be prepared if the day ever comes—God forbid—when something similar actually does befall his family. However, in spite of all the variations on fire, water, and evil individuals with which he has castigated himself over the years, the current situation has never featured in his personal chamber of horrors. Nothing has prepared him for this.

'I love you,' he says into the darkness, and hears a clatter as the knives crash down onto the draining board; their plastic rack has been eaten away. 'You're the best thing that's ever happened to me.'

Carina nestles closer and Emil says: 'Daddy, I'm scared.'

There is a moment in certain films that makes Stefan absolutely furious. A terrified child in an apparently hopeless situation expresses his or her fear, and someone says: 'It's gonna be okay. I promise.' How the fuck can you promise something like that? Stefan certainly can't. He tightens his grip around Emil's shoulders, pulls him closer and says: 'We're here, sweetheart. We're all in this together.'

The movement nudges the torch, and its beam illuminates Emil's fortress, which is still on the table.

'Emil?' Carina says.

'Mmm?'

'How did you know? How did you know those creatures were going to come?'

Emil doesn't say anything at first, and the only sound is the patter of the raindrops and a protracted hiss as yet another object dissolves

soon it will be us

and Stefan thinks he can feel a slight change to the burning pain in his back; he imagines that the rain has penetrated the alcove and that the fatalistic calm he has fought to achieve is about to be destroyed

we're going to die, we really are going to die, all three of us are going to die, slowly and in agony, we won't exist any more

He wants to run, to fight, he wants to sacrifice his life, he just wants to *do* something, anything at all.

'Molly told me.'

'Molly told you they would come?'

'Mmm.'

'Did she say the rain would come too?'

'No. She said…' Emil's voice changes, shrinks from scared to pathetic as he breaks off, then says: 'We took the hoses.'

The first drop falls from the alcove and lands on a loose piece of Lego, which collapses in on itself as the plastic softens. Stefan clenches his fists and swallows hard.

The gas cylinder.

What will happen when the rain reaches the fuel? It doesn't matter. The metal cylinder is thick, and before the rain manages to eat through it all three of them will be dead, melted away like the piece of Lego, which is now a shapeless clump of plastic.

Emil must have realised this too, and wanted to unburden himself before it was too late. He is hanging his head in shame, and there is absolutely no need for him to feel like this *now*. Stefan strokes his hair and says: 'It doesn't matter, sweetheart. It doesn't matter at all. Was it Molly's idea?'

A faint hint of light passes across Emil's face and he nods. 'She said it was a good thing to do, but I knew it wasn't.'

Stefan looks at Emil. Blinks. Looks again. The hint of light was nothing to do with a brightening of his mood. Emil still sounds just as pitiful as he makes his confession. But the interior of the caravan *has got lighter.*

'Stefan...' Carina whispers.

He sees. He hears. The rain is no longer hammering on the roof of the caravan, and as if a roller blind is slowly being raised, the room begins to fill with daylight.

*

It may be an old wives' tale, but they say you can pinch yourself to find out whether you're dreaming or not. But has anyone ever been in the middle of a dream, pinched their arm and woken up? As a testing strategy it's probably about as effective as checking for radiation with a barometer. However, it has had some impact on Donald.

He hasn't been pinching himself, but as the rain punches holes in the kitchen worktop above him and more and more scalding droplets land on his head and body, he has begun to reassess his previous conviction. He is in so much pain that he is ready to crawl out of his skin, and the experience is so *physical*, right down to the bone, that it is impossible to believe the body being subjected to this torture is only a dream.

However terrible it is to admit it, and however meaningless it might be as he stands at the edge of his grave, he is actually *here*. This is happening to him. He is sitting at a table next to his disloyal wife with two gay dairy farmers, and he is about to be killed by acid raining down from the sky. You could almost die laughing.

He can just make out the shape of Lennart and Olof as they sit there slurping each other's faces; it's the most disgusting thing Donald has ever seen. He doesn't really have anything against dykes and queers, but he does think they should keep it to themselves! Normal people shouldn't be forced to look at what they do.

But here he is, with Lennart and Olof *snogging* right in front of him. If he needed any further proof that this is not a dream, there it is. He would never dream something so repulsive; such images do not exist inside his mind. Unfortunately, however, they do exist in reality. And they are getting clearer and clearer.

Donald is about to yell at them, tell them to pack it in for fuck's sake, when he realises that his night vision has not in fact improved; the light is returning. The darkness outside the window is fading, changing from black to grey to pale grey. It has stopped raining.

Lennart and Olof move apart, and Majvor opens her eyes, looking as if she has just woken up. Donald clenches and unclenches his hands, which look as if he has stuck them in an open fire, because he used them to protect his head. The skin is blistered and broken, and some of the nails have been partly eaten away, exposing the angry red flesh beneath.

'Fucking hell,' he says. 'Fuck fuck fuck fuck fuck.'

'Donald!' Majvor snaps. Her face is disfigured by long sores running from her temples and down her cheeks. A few clumps of her permed hair have come away, and are lying on the table in a pool of liquid.

Donald looks at the pool, at Majvor's hair. The acid that has corroded the metal roof of the caravan ought to consume the hair in no time, but nothing happens. Donald cautiously touches the liquid with his index finger, but it has obviously lost its potency; all he can feel is a faint warmth.

'Good God,' Donald says, gripping Majvor's shoulders and bringing his face close to hers as he emphasises every syllable: 'Good. God. Jesus. Mary.'

A lingering, harmless drop falls from the makeshift ceiling onto his bald head. He pulls a face and emerges from the shelter. The roof looks like a colander, and through the holes he can see a pale blue sky.

Donald turns to face the table, where Lennart, Olof and Majvor are huddled like three injured crows.

He has been a good husband to Majvor; he has always put her safety and wellbeing first. In spite of the fact that he worked his fingers to the bone to provide for his family, he was never an absent father. He has also helped out around the house whenever he had the time. Majvor is a lucky woman.

Now that he has cast aside the dream theory, he finds her disloyalty utterly atrocious. It is the real Majvor, the woman he has spent almost fifty years taking care of, who has rewarded him in this way. She has stood in his way, injured him, and finally *bound his wrists*! He looks at her, with tufts of hair sticking up all over the place. She is *nothing* to him from now on.

'Donald,' Majvor says. 'Stop that.' She frowns. 'Are you okay?'

'I'm fine,' Donald says, rubbing a particularly sore patch on his forearm. 'I'm going to go and fetch our caravan. Are you coming?'

Majvor glances at Lennart and Olof, which infuriates Donald. It's as if she wants to see what they think, check if it's okay. What do you think, my dear arse-bandits? Should I go with my husband? Donald swallows his anger and says calmly: 'I no longer believe I'm dreaming. Come and fetch the caravan with me, Majvor.'

Puffing and sighing in the way that makes Donald grind his teeth, Majvor extricates herself from beneath the shelter. If he can just get her in the car, she will soon see that he has plans for her, oh yes indeed. But until then he will just take things slowly. Very slowly.

Donald has just turned to open the door when he hears something scrabbling at the metal. Then the sound of banging. A brownish-black hand is fumbling at the kitchen window, while another is hammering on the window above the sofa. The door handle jiggles up and down as someone or something tries to get in.

*

The rain has stopped. The light has returned. Peter is sitting with his knees drawn up to his chin beneath the mattress through which no moisture has penetrated. He is virtually unharmed. Molly has brought out a small mirror and is contemplating her face.

Isabelle is dead, she must be. And if she's not dead, Peter doesn't want to see the state she is in. He just wants to sit here and wait. Wait for this to end. For the hand that picked them up and placed them here to decide that it is time to put them back. He has no intention of praying for anything; there is no one to pray to. He is just going to wait. Look at Molly.

You belong here, don't you?

I don't know. Not yet.

There are pink lines where the rain trickled down Molly's face, as if she has raked her nails down her cheeks. She contemplates herself doubtfully, touching the lines with her fingers and shaking her head.

'I don't understand,' she murmurs.

Peter has spent all day racing from one task to another, on and on, as he always does. Now that he has given up, surrendered his will, it is possible to think simple thoughts, do simple things. Molly said something. Now he is going to say something.

'What is it you don't understand?' That is what he says.

'It's not supposed to be like this,' Molly says, tossing the mirror back in the drawer.

Peter considers whether he has anything further to ask, a comment to make, but nothing occurs to him. Instead he says: 'Isabelle must be dead. Mummy is dead.'

'Perhaps,' Molly says absently. 'Or perhaps not. Perhaps both.'

It is obvious that the question does not interest her. This could be regarded as peculiar, not to mention horrific, but Peter is incapable of summoning up such emotions at the moment. He just looks at Molly, as she flings her arms wide and says, with a despair he believes to be genuine: 'I don't know what to do!'

'No,' Peter says. 'That's just the way it is sometimes.'

There is a knock on the door, and it takes Peter a few seconds to work out how he is supposed to react to such a thing. Someone knocks on the door, you go and answer it. Before he has time to convert this knowledge into action, there is a knock on the window. And the wall. Then the sound of scratching. Scratching and tapping. Molly looks out of the window and her eyes widen. She crawls into the shelter, presses herself close to Peter and clutches his arm.

'Daddy,' she says. 'I'm scared. I really am scared now.'

*

A pallet of herring. Herringpallet. Palletherring.

When the burnt creatures start tapping on the caravan and trying to get inside, Stefan can't even manage to be afraid. He has already been so frightened, so convinced that he and his family are about to die, that he can't do it any more. As he gets up to fetch the gun, he thinks about the herring order that he hasn't managed to cancel. In a way it is a relevant thought.

The same thing happened in the summer of 2010, although on that occasion it involved potatoes. An extra zero had crept into the order, and instead of a thousand kilos of new potatoes, they ended up with ten thousand kilos. It was their mistake, and they just had to try to get rid of them.

They ran an advertising campaign with big colourful posters, customers got free potatoes when they bought other things, and in the end they dropped the price to fifty öre a kilo. They still didn't manage to shift all the potatoes, which is where the relevance comes in. Saturation. Everything has a saturation point, when the pain receptors switch off, fear becomes ordinary, and no one wants potatoes, even if they're free. Enough is enough.

That's how Stefan feels right now. The bodies he can see through the window are horrible, but he merely registers this as he would register a seagull flying across the sky. He picks up the gun and discovers that the butt and other parts look as if they have been attacked by woodworm, crumbling away when he touches them.

The metal is largely intact, apart from certain areas which are corroded and discoloured. He pumps the slide backwards and forwards a couple of times; he thinks the gun should still work.

He hears the dog barking, and looks over at Carina, who is still sitting on the sofa with her eyebrows raised. For a moment he thinks her eyes are wide with fear, but then he sees that her lips are twitching as if she is trying not to laugh. She feels the same as he does.

'It's too much, isn't it?' he says.

'Mmm,' Carina says with a nod.

'It'll be the same with the herring.'

'The herring?'

'Yes, there'll be too much. Too much herring.'

Emil looks anxiously from Stefan to Carina.

'Stop it!' he says, pointing at the window with a trembling finger. 'Stop talking like that! They're dangerous!'

'Sorry, sweetheart,' Stefan says, running a hand over his face; tears have sprung to his eyes without his even noticing. 'It's just that...we're *alive*!'

'And what if they get in? Do you think we'll be alive then? Mummy! Stop laughing!'

*

Children are dependent on their parents. Not only for food, a roof over their heads and love, but also as a touchstone when it comes to interpreting the world, both intellectually and emotionally. As Emil looks crossly from his mother to his father, and they carry on laughing, it just happens somehow; eventually he starts laughing too.

He really ought to carry on being terrified, because the zombies are trying to get in, but with Mummy and Daddy laughing like that it all seems a bit silly and kind of pretend. Pretend zombies pretending to try to get in! And after all, that's how it is. Almost.

Once when Emil was at his friend Sebbe's house, Sebbe's older brother was watching a zombie film, and the two younger boys sneaked a look. The zombies were super horrible—rotten and fast and strong, and the people didn't stand a chance.

The zombies outside the caravan aren't like that at all. Admittedly they look horrible, but they're just scratching and tapping, like a cat that wants to come in even though it's not allowed. It's actually quite funny, but Emil's chest still hurts when he laughs, because their screams are so awful. It's like laughing at someone who's broken their leg. Emil stops laughing and shuffles over to the window on his knees.

The zombies are moving away from the caravan, and Emil is so pleased that he can't help smiling, in spite of the dreadful screams. He looks up and his eyes narrow. He saw what the rain did to his father's back, and to the things in the kitchen. So how come the four white figures, who now only *almost* look like stormtroopers, are still standing in exactly the same spot as when the rain started? Surely they should have melted away completely?

The rain has left the window pane pitted and buckled, and Emil moves his head until he finds a point where he can see more clearly. He is thinking about stormtroopers; what do they actually look like underneath their armour? Will we ever find out?

He finds a spot, no bigger than a five-kronor piece, where the window is the same as it was before the rain. He can't close just one eye, so he covers his left eye with his hand and peers out, as if he is looking through a peep hole.

The zombies are heading towards the stormtroopers, and Emil feels as if he is watching a film, a bit like when he and Sebbe peeped through the gap in the doorway. *Zombies versus Stormtroopers!*

But it doesn't look as if there is going to be a fight. The stormtroopers simply lean forward, as if they are bowing to the zombies. Emil laughs out loud, because everything is just too weird and silly even to be a film, and if it weren't for the fact that Mummy and Daddy can see *more or less* the same things as him, he could easily believe that he's made it all up.

What are they doing?

Emil presses his eye so close to the glass that the picture becomes

321

blurred. He blinks a couple of times, then looks again. Four zombies have climbed onto the backs of the four stormtroopers, and suddenly it's not fun any more because the zombies aren't zombies, they're vampires. All four have sunk their teeth into the necks of the stormtroopers carrying them, and it is obvious from the movement of their bodies, from the jerking and shuddering, that they are drinking.

Emil looks past the horrible sight and sees Molly, staring out of the window of her caravan. She knew it was going to turn out like this. That creatures wanting blood would come. So why does she look so scared?

3. Beyond

Gradually everyone emerges to watch the drama in the middle of the camp. They stand outside their caravans, arms hanging by their sides, observing what is going on at the crossroads. Some see the same thing, others see something completely different. There is a feeling that *something should be done*, but no one does anything.

One by one the burnt creatures climb up onto the backs of the white figures and drink their blood. The white figures allow this to happen. They allow it to happen as they stare at the people, and the people feel that *something should be done*, but no one does anything.

It is not unlike a ritual, but there is no need to go that far. It is an agreement. Something that has to happen, and is therefore in order. Perhaps that is why no one does anything. They are standing outside an event in which they have no part. Not any longer. Not yet.

The lustre of the white figures' skin grows dull and disappears, the stormtroopers' armour begins to look worn, their bodies stooping. Jimmy Stewart ages rapidly, the travelling salesmen appear to have spent decades on the road, and when the last of the burnt creatures clambers down, the tigers seem to be dying. The screaming has abated as the creatures leave the white figures and head back across the field, following the same tracks that brought them into the camp.

The white figures in their various manifestations remain where they are for a minute or so, until they have the strength to straighten their bent bodies. They gaze at the people for one last time with their dull, black eyes, then they begin to stagger along the tracks leading out into the field.

The people stand there with their arms hanging by their sides, watching them go. It is over. For this time.

*

'What was that?'

Olof watches the burnt creatures as they head off into the distance, while Lennart focuses on the four travelling salesmen, who look as if they will soon be at the end of their travels, dragging themselves along their eternal road.

'I don't know,' Lennart says. 'It almost felt as if it was…meant to be. Like when a mink kills a chicken with a single bite.'

'Well, yes, but then chickens don't just stand there waiting to be bitten.'

'That's often exactly what they do.'

They don't look at one another during this exchange. That kiss is still burning on their lips. If it hadn't been for the rain, death falling from the sky, it would never have happened. Never in a million years. Now the rain has passed, and things are very awkward.

Just over three years after Ingela and Agnetha had shot through, Lennart and Olof got drunk one night. Neither of them was much of a drinker, but the children were with their mothers, it was Saturday, there was plenty of schnapps, and they were having such a good time playing old albums on Olof's record player. They both had a glass or two more than usual.

When it was time for Lennart to go home, Olof said he was welcome to stay so that he didn't end up in a ditch. By this time Lennart was so far gone that he simply fell into the bed Olof used to share with Ingela; he didn't even bother getting undressed.

Olof stood there for a little while contemplating his sleeping friend and hanging on to the bed head for support, because the floor was moving up and down like the deck of a ship caught in a violent storm. He would go and lie down on Ante's bed as soon as he had sorted out his balance. But Ante's room was ten metres away, and there was space in the bed right there in front of him. Without further thought he took three steps and crashed down on the bed next to Lennart and immediately fell asleep. When he woke up it was gone nine o'clock.

Both Lennart and Olof's bodies were used to waking up at five to see to the cows. Olof in particular had found it difficult to sleep since Ingela disappeared; he would often wake two or three times during the night, and sometimes he couldn't get back to sleep.

Therefore, his first thought when he woke up and saw the clock was: *Oh my God! The cows!* His second thought was: *I've slept really well.* Then a sour, fluffy wave came surging through his skull, bringing with it his third thought: *I'm never going to touch another drop.*

He would get up in a minute, get on with the day, but first of all he gave himself a little time to think about how he was feeling. In spite of the hangover there was a kind of peace in his body, the peace that comes from being fully rested. He turned over and looked at Lennart's broad back. The movement woke Lennart, who peered at him in confusion.

'What are you doing here?'

'It just turned out that way,' Olof said.

'What time is it?'

'Nine o'clock.'

'You're kidding me!'

'Nope.'

Lennart made a move to get up, then fell back on the pillows, staring up at the ceiling.

'I might have had a bit too much to drink last night,' he said.

'Yep.'

'We need to see to the cows.'

'I know. Did you sleep well?'

Lennart rubbed his eyes, blinked a couple of times, then shook his head in an attempt to clear his mind. 'Like a baby,' he said. 'I never sleep that well these days.'

'Same here. Strange.'

'Very strange.'

They looked at one another. Smiled shyly. Shook their heads. Then they got up and tackled the day. That evening they had just a couple of drinks and discussed the matter. In spite of their respective hangovers, both of them had experienced an unusually high level of energy during the day. With cautious hints, half-questions and a great deal of circumlocution, they finally agreed that they might possibly sleep better if they shared a bed.

It would be a couple of days before Ante and Gunilla returned, so Lennart and Olof decided to try it once more, with less alcohol involved this time. The same thing happened again, in spite of the fact that they both slept fully dressed. A whole night's wonderful sleep.

After another day filled with energy, they met up in the evening for a serious talk.

'I mean, this isn't a long-term solution,' Lennart began.

'No, I expect you're right.'

'What will the kids think?'

'What do you mean?'

'You know what I mean. Two men sleeping together. It's just not possible.'

'No,' Olof said, thinking how reassuring it felt to hear another person's breathing when you were just about to fall asleep, to know that there was no risk of being overwhelmed by the sense of being all alone in the world. 'Then again, why not?'

'You know that just as well as I do.'

'No, I don't. But then perhaps I don't know much at all.'

Lennart's eyes narrowed as he looked at Olof, who was sitting opposite him at the kitchen table, hands neatly resting one on top of the other.

'Can I ask you something?' Lennart said.

'Ask away.'

Lennart shuffled, rubbed his chin. 'The thing is, I'm not...I mean I'm not the kind of person who judges others, each to their own, but....have you got any...*tendencies* in that direction?'

Olof began to say, 'I don't know what you...' but Lennart slammed his hand down on the table and interrupted him.

'For fuck's sake, Olof! Don't make this any more difficult than it already is! You know exactly what I'm talking about.'

Olof sighed. 'Right, yes. No, I don't have any *tendencies*. As far as I'm aware, never have had.'

'Okay. Okay. Good. Just so we know where we stand. Because

I haven't either. None at all. As I said, it's not that I have anything against those who are that way inclined, but...'

'But?'

Lennart glared at Olof. 'To be honest, I think you're being really difficult. To deal with. As far as this is concerned.'

'Sleep on your own then,' Olof snapped. 'Lie there tossing and turning, or sit up and wait for the dawn. Like I do.'

There was a long silence, broken only by the ticking of the grand-father clock in the living room, the rasp of fingernails on stubble, and a faint rustling as they both shifted uncomfortably in their seats. Eventually Lennart spoke: 'But what about the kids?'

'They'll understand. They will.'

When Ante and Gunilla got back and were told about the new arrangement, they had quite a lot of questions. However, these questions mainly concerned what was going to happen to their rooms and where they were all going to live. Lennart's house was bigger, and there was a guest room that was hardly ever used, so that was to be Ante's new room. He had no complaints, because it was much nicer than his old one.

If the children had any questions about the nature of Lennart and Olof's relationship, they kept them to themselves. Everyone thought that living together was much more fun, and more practical. Ante and Gunilla already got on very well, and after the move they became best friends.

Lennart and Olof continued to sleep well at night. As time went by they even ventured to get undressed down to their vests and long johns at bedtime. A year or so after they had moved in together, their hands happened to brush against one another, and somehow they got into the habit of lying there holding hands for a while before they went to sleep.

That was as far as the physical aspect of their relationship had gone, until acid raining down from the sky made them take an enormous step into the unknown.

*

Side by side, but not too close, they amble over to their little planta-tion and discover that, as they suspected, everything that had been flourishing so unnaturally has been annihilated by the rain. There is not a leaf to be seen, not a stem or a stalk; all that is left is a patch of black earth.

'This grass...' Olof says, rubbing the sole of his shoe over the bright green surface.

'Yes,' Lennart says. 'Let's not talk about it.'

'You think we shouldn't talk about things we don't understand?'

Lennart sighs and gives Olof an apologetic look. 'Was there some-thing you wanted to say about the grass?'

'Not really; I was just thinking that it must be specially adapted to grow here. To survive these conditions.'

'What do you mean?'

'I don't mean anything. Just that whatever exists here must be specially adapted to survive. Everything else disappears.'

They walk over to the space where Donald and Majvor's awning used to be. The sun lounger has been reduced to a corroded skeleton, the little refrigerator has lost its white coating, and all that remains of the treated decking is a greenish, rotten sludge. Lennart pokes it with his foot.

'This isn't going to be much use when it comes to building a tower,' he says.

'No. But then I never did think that particular plan was going to work—did you?'

'Not really. But it would have been good to be able to phone home at some point.'

'It would,' Olof agrees.

The tone of their conversation is getting back to normal; both of them can hear and feel it. They glance at one another, tentatively venturing a smile.

'Lennart...'

'No. Not now. We'll talk about it later. I need to...'

'Digest it?'

'Yes. Exactly. Something like that.'

They look around the camp. Since the white figures' enchanted circle broke up, everyone has gone back to their usual tasks, insofar as any task is normal in this place. Carina is checking her water tank, Peter is throwing out possessions that have been destroyed, while Donald and Majvor are getting ready to set off.

Judging by surface appearances, everyone is acting as if a temporary crisis has passed, and it is now time to tackle the situation afresh. But that is only superficial. Their faces, the way they move their bodies, the sound of their voices—everything has changed following their collective near-death experience. An undercurrent has seeped in, as dark as the sludge at Lennart and Olof's feet.

They have stopped believing that they can survive. For the time being they are getting on with what needs to be done because there is nothing else to do, but they all know that it will take only one or perhaps two showers of rain to reduce them to any items made of precious metals that they might be wearing, just like Erik and the others. It might not be for a day or two, perhaps even a week, but sooner or later it will happen.

*

Isabelle's itchy arms are so irritating that it is almost a relief when a familiar sensation begins to make itself felt, fighting for the space available to deliver discomfort: hunger. She steps out of the barbecue area and walks towards the kiosk, ash whirling around her feet. A few mosquitoes pick up the scent of her sweaty forehead and start whining around her ears.

Fuck. Fuck.

She was supposed to melt, be burnt out of the picture, go clean and pure to her death. Instead, this. The stench of urine and faeces from the toilet block makes a lump of vomit rise into her throat as she reaches the kiosk. The boy inside is perhaps eighteen years old, and suffering from a bad case of acne. His flat face is red and pitted with scars; he looks shy and unsure of himself. Isabelle straightens her back, sticks out her chest and asks: 'Have you got any chocolate?'

The boy glances up at her, then he looks away, shakes his head. Isabelle checks that her nipples are sufficiently erect to show through her thin top. His eyes should be out on stalks, but instead he is refusing to look at her. He actually turns around and starts fiddling with something on the shelves.

There is a box of chocolate bars on the counter. Isabelle grabs a couple and backs away as she rips the wrapping off one of them, bites off a huge chunk and begins to chew. She can hear chomping and crunching, but the only thing she can taste is ash. She takes another bite, munches harder, runs her tongue around the inside of her mouth, but the taste of ash merely grows stronger. She begins to sweat, and her hands are shaking.

She looks around. Three indolent middle-aged men are sitting at a camping table messing around with fishing lines, weights and floats. There are three bamboo rods propped against a tree beside them. Isabelle's arms burn and sting as she goes over to them and says: 'Hi, guys.'

The men nod and murmur in response, but they don't even look up. They carry on attaching hooks, clipping on weights, threading floats.

You're the most beautiful woman I've ever met.

How many men have said that to her? Five? Seven? Ten? And now these three are sitting here; they ought to fall at her feet and worship her, but instead they only have eyes for their fishing equipment. Isabelle pulls off her top and steps out of her pants, drops the items of clothing on the table. She stands naked before the men, spreads her arms wide and yells: 'See anything you like? Well, do you? *Look* at me, for fuck's sake!'

One of the men moves her top, which has landed on his jar of worms, then returns to his task. Isabelle's body is seething with hunger, a rushing sound fills her head, and the itching in her arms is unbearable.

The two tracks lead away from the table at an angle. She chooses the one on the right, which leads into the trees. She uses what remains of her nails to scrape at her wounds until they start to bleed, then she breaks into a run.

Blood is dripping from her arms as she enters the forest. The track is narrow; twigs and branches scratch her bare skin, and at last something begins to feel real, at last she can actually feel something, and she extends her bleeding arms so that everything that is sharp can stab and tear at her, and eventually the pain is so great that it washes away everything else.

There are five of them moving across the grass, whimpering and groaning. Isabelle slows down to match their pace. Her flesh is screaming, and the muscles that have not been burnt away are throbbing with a pain as deep as the earth itself; her entire body is a ganglion of pain, but it is a pure pain from which there is no hope of redemption, a pain that simply *exists*.

The thing that used to be Isabelle opens its ruined mouth, widens its throat and allows its voice to blend with the others in the lament that never stops, the lament about life, about pain, about hunger and movement. She follows the track that leads out across the field, together with her tribe.

*

Donald has demonstrated many different moods over the past few hours, above all a range of variations on anger and fury, but Majvor has not yet seen the emotion that is etched on his face when he looks at his car. Donald looks *distressed*.

He takes great pride in looking after his car. Washing, polishing, waxing. Donald is rarely as amenable as on a Sunday afternoon, when he comes indoors after spending a couple of hours on the drive with Turtle Wax and a chamois leather, leaving the car shining like the still surface of a lagoon in the setting sun. He might forget to shave, he might wander around for several days with unattractive hairs protruding from his chin, but he polishes that car until you could eat your dinner off the bonnet.

No miracle cloth in the world is going to be able to restore his car now. Most of the lacquer has disappeared, leaving only odd patches. The plastic housing over the indicators has melted away, leaving a yellowish gunge all over the hub caps.

But that's not the worst of it. The metal bodywork has survived, but the sunroof has not. The plexiglas has dissolved, giving the rain free access to the interior. It has splattered all over the instrument panel, destroying buttons and display screens; it has shredded the leather covering on the steering wheel, and it has burnt big holes in the front seats. For a second Majvor thinks that Donald is going to burst into tears as he looks at the car.

But he opens the door, gets into the driver's seat with some difficulty, then reaches for the key in the ignition. Majvor crosses her fingers behind his back. *Don't start, don't start.* It seems unlikely that the car will spring into action, given the way it looks.

Unfortunately it seems that the vital components must have escaped serious damage, because the engine immediately roars into life, and Donald beckons Majvor impatiently. She opens the passenger door and gets in, shifting her weight around on the craters in the seat until she finds an acceptable position, then she closes the door.

The gearstick has partly dissolved, and the gearbox screeches as Donald puts the car in first. But it begins to move forward, against all expectation. Donald follows a black skid mark on the grass, and when it disappears he continues along the same line.

'Donald,' Majvor says. 'Is this a good idea? How are you doing?'

'I'm fine. I just want somewhere to live.'

He definitely sounds saner than at any time since he returned to the camp—and before that, to tell the truth. Could it be that the experience of the rain has really made him see the situation more clearly?

'What do you think about all this?' Majvor says. 'What can we do?'

Will Lockhart, the Man from Laramie, appears ahead of them on the field; he is staggering along and appears to be in an even worse state than he was in the film after he had been dragged through the camp fire and had his hand shot up. Donald's eyes narrow as he spots Will, and he puts his foot down. Majvor doesn't know what he's thinking, but to be on the safe side she says: 'You mustn't run over him. We have no idea what might happen.'

Donald grunts, but turns the wheel so that the car is no longer on a collision course with the figure. As they drive past, Majvor glances out of the side window.

Will Lockhart looks as if he has been wandering through the desert for days without finding a watering hole. His eyes have sunk deep into his skull, his skin is lined and yellowing. He has lost so much weight that his gun belt is almost sliding off his hips. Overall, it seems that his only possible goal must be his own funeral. It is so upsetting that Majvor's eyes fill with tears. Her dream, her hero, reduced to a wreck.

What is this place doing to us? What can we do with this place?

'We're doomed,' Donald says. 'We just have to accept it.'

'Doomed? What do you mean, doomed? Why should we be doomed?'

Donald gives a wry smile. 'Isn't this your area of expertise? Guilt and sin and damnation? I think *you* should be able to explain why we've ended up here. Go on. What does the Bible say about this place? Eh?'

'Stop it, Donald.'

'Seriously, I'm interested. I mean, you usually come out with quotations from the Bible at the drop of a hat. Surely there must be something that fits the current situation?'

Of course Majvor has considered this. She has thought about Moses, wandering in the desert for forty years, and about the trials of Job. Gehenna. The truth is that there is far too much that fits, which makes any interpretation impossible. However, that isn't the real problem.

'It wouldn't be appropriate,' she replies.

Donald lets out a bark of laughter. 'What do you mean, *it wouldn't be appropriate*? At long last we're in a place where all that crap might finally come in useful! Back home you start banging on about Jesus if I so much as think about fiddling a bill, but now, now it could really be…You're so funny, Majvor.'

'It has nothing to do with this place,' she insists. 'It wouldn't be appropriate.'

Even if she wanted to, she couldn't explain it to Donald, but she has realised that this place lies beyond normal concepts, both earthly and celestial. The usual rules do not apply here, and prayers will not help.

This realisation left her shocked at first, then empty. After a little while she began to get used to the idea, and surprisingly enough it happened quite quickly. There isn't such a huge difference; this is merely the other side of the same coin. Her everyday world is populated by ethereal characters from the Bible, the air is filled with invisible angels, and no occurrence or action escapes the watchful eye of the Lord.

The total *absence* of all this brings its own fulfilment, in the same way that total darkness is to a certain extent the same as a blinding light. It is hard to grasp and even harder to explain. And besides, she has no desire to try.

Donald continues his harangue and Majvor continues to keep quiet. After a few minutes they can see their caravan on the horizon. Donald slaps his thigh and says: 'There she is, Majvor! You'll soon be able to start baking buns again!'

There is nothing pleasant about his tone of voice. Quite the reverse.

*

The mattress that was closest to the roof has been totally destroyed. When Peter tries to lift it down it disintegrates completely; he carries the pieces outside and dumps them behind the caravan. The second mattress is damaged, but he turns it over and concludes that it can be used.

By him and Molly. When it's time for bed.

He stops what he is doing and looks at Molly, who has crawled up onto the kitchen worktop and is sitting watching him. He can only cope with contemplating the future in short segments. The last thing that came into his mind was: *Turn over the mattress. Check the other side.* Now he has done that, and for the moment the future is over. He sits down on the mattress.

Which can be used by him and Molly. When it's time for bed.

Even such a simple thought seems unfathomable—the idea that a distant future when they might both go to bed should even exist. Bed. Molly.

'Molly? Why didn't the rain harm you?'

Molly touches her face, where the pink marks are still visible. 'It did. It hurt.'

'You know what I mean.'

Molly chews her lower lip and her eyes dart around the caravan; she glances through the door then meets Peter's gaze for a second before eventually fixing on the perforated ceiling. Peter can't remember ever seeing her so unsure of herself.

'I don't know what I am.'

'Sorry?'

'I don't know what I am.'

'Have you forgotten? You're a fountain of blood in the form of a girl, aren't you?'

Molly shakes her head. 'Maybe not. I don't know. It went wrong.'

'I don't understand. What were you supposed to be?'

There is a long pause before she answers. 'Something else. It happened when I was little. Like those white creatures.'

'What white creatures?'

'The ones that were here. They were in the tunnel too. I became like them.'

'What tunnel? Molly, I have no idea what you're talking about. I haven't seen any white creatures.'

For the first time since they started talking, Molly looks at him directly, her eyes full of sorrow. 'I know what you see,' she says. 'But you don't know what I see.' The contact is broken as she looks out through the open door and nods towards the field. 'Mummy is one of them now.'

A slimy worm of fear has begun to crawl through Peter's guts, and he's not sure if he wants to continue this conversation. He rubs his belly as if to massage away the fear, and pretends it's just a touch of stomach ache.

'What do you mean, one of them?'

'They eat creatures like me. I didn't know they existed. It was horrible.'

Peter stands up, his hand still resting on his belly, which is grumbling and gurgling as if an angry little animal is trying to get out. He goes over to Molly and touches her foot.

'Sweetheart. Darling Molly.' Her lips twitch and she snorts as if he has made a bad joke. 'I really don't understand what you're talking about. You say that you know what I see. What do you mean by that?'

Molly glances at Peter's hand, which is resting on her foot. He moves it away and looks down at the top of her head, the spot where he once gently stroked her fontanelle, the thin layer of skin covering the brain that is now a mystery to him. It seems like a lifetime ago. The memory brings with it a wave of tenderness, then Molly lifts her head and looks up at him.

The animal in his belly unsheathes its claws and attacks. Molly's face has changed. Behind it and through it, like a double exposure, he can see his father's face. Her clear blue eyes are looking into his, but inside these eyes there is another pair, brown bordering on black, narrowing in uncontrollable rage. Molly opens her little mouth, which is simultaneously another mouth, and says: 'Not even Jesus wants your fucking cunt.'

Peter is bent double by a sudden cramp in his belly. He clenches

338

his buttocks, steps to the side and yanks open the toilet door. He just manages to pull down his pants before whatever has been building up in his stomach comes gushing out. The cramped space is filled with the stench of diarrhoea, and he covers his mouth with his hand to stop himself from throwing up, on top of everything else.

Not even Jesus wants your fucking cunt.

The words have been etched on his mind in burning letters ever since the night his father almost killed his mother. He has never told Molly about it, of course; he hasn't even told Isabelle. He has never told anyone.

He breathes rapidly through his nose, inhaling the terrible smell once more, which causes a fresh wave of nausea.

Not even Jesus.

There is a knock on the door, and the sickness is overlaid with fear. His father is standing out there right now. The hammer is in his hand, and this time there is no crucifix to hold him back. And if there was a crucifix it wouldn't help because *the field is endless.*

Peter clutches his belly; the pain has eased now. He remembers a soft little body, a comforting bundle of warmth against his skin, he remembers Diego, taken from him by God, he remembers all the sorrow, all the fucking sorrow life has thrown at him, and of course he's going to end up like this, nauseous and stinking in a disgusting toilet. There is another knock on the door, and he hears Molly's voice.

'Daddy?'

Peter swallows. Exhales. Molly's voice sounds just the way it always does. No connotations of a violent father's voice. Just a little girl who says: 'It's not my fault, Daddy. Mummy left me in the tunnel. Why did she do that? Daddy?'

Peter finds that he can breathe through his mouth without the risk of being sick. He takes a deep breath, then wipes his bottom. He gets to his feet, stands up and looks at the brown slop that has splattered all over the toilet bowl.

Water. Save water.

What's the fucking point? He flushes. Nothing happens. The rain hadn't penetrated the water tank, and yet nothing happens. There's no water. Yet another thing to add to everything else. He closes the lid and opens the door.

Molly is standing outside; she wrinkles her nose as the smell hits her. Peter closes the door.

'What tunnel?' he asks.

'Where we used to live. When I was little.'

'The Brunkeberg tunnel?'

'I don't know what it's called.'

'Isabelle left you in the Brunkeberg tunnel?'

'Yes. For a long time. It was dark. I don't understand.'

Peter can only shake his head. 'Me neither.'

Molly looks around the caravan, clamps her lips together resolutely, then nods to herself. 'We need to get rid of Mummy's things.'

Peter sees no reason to protest as Molly opens closets and drawers, gathers up Isabelle's clothes and dumps them on the draining board. He flops down on the mattress and watches as she grabs tattered fashion magazines and Isabelle's ruined laptop and throws them in the sink. There is a suppressed rage in everything she does, as if she were a landlady cleaning up after the departure of a particularly filthy tenant. When she has collected up everything she can find, she comes over to Peter.

'Better now?' he asks.

Molly shakes her head and points to the drawer on Isabelle's side of what used to be their bed.

Peter opens the drawer, which had been protected by the mattresses and is undamaged by the rain. Molly tips the contents onto the bed. Mostly films with titles such as *Macabre*, *Guinea Pig*, *A Serbian Film*. More fashion magazines. Make-up, sweet wrappers, a brochure from a luxury hotel in Dubai. And a box.

Molly picks it up and turns it over. 'What's this?'

'I've no idea. I've never seen it before.'

The box is about the same size as a Rubik's cube, and is made of black wood, inlaid with complex patterns in gold or imitation gold.

Peter can't decide whether it's a piece of tat or an antique, but the precision locking mechanism would suggest the latter. Molly runs her finger over the thin bolt securing two hasps, which in turn keep the lid closed, and her eyes are shining as she whispers: 'It's Mummy's secret.'

In spite of the fact that Peter has no emotional reserves which would enable him to engage fully with the issue, he does feel a pang of simple human curiosity—*What will happen if I press the button? What's in the box?*—as Molly slides back the bolt and flips back the hasps.

She opens the lid and Peter doesn't know what she sees when she looks inside, but normal, childish tears pour down her cheeks as she contemplates Isabelle's secret. When Peter leans forward, Molly slams the lid shut, dashes the tears from her eyes and glares at him.

She makes a noise that is almost a bark and hurls the box at Peter, then runs out of the caravan. Peter is about to get up and go after her, but realises that he has neither the strength nor the inclination. Instead he lies back on the mattress and opens the box.

It is empty.

He settles down and closes his eyes.

*

'Stefan, we need to rinse your back.'

'Yes, but the water...'

'We've got water.'

'Not an unlimited amount.'

'Come over here.'

Stefan begins to undo the buttons, and although the least touch on his back is painful, at least it is a relief to find that the fabric isn't stuck to the skin as he cautiously removes his shirt.

'Daddy, no!'

Emil covers his eyes with his hands and shakes his head. So it must look *really* bad. Stefan sits down on the kitchen stool and lets out a groan as pain sears through his buttocks and thighs. He gets up again.

'Take everything off,' Carina says. 'We need to wash your whole body.'

She turns on the tap, fills a jug. When Stefan starts to undo his belt, it's all too much for Emil. He grabs Sabre Cat and heads for the door.

'Don't go wandering off,' Carina stays. 'Stay close by.'

'Mmm. Thank you for saving my animals, Daddy.'

Emil jumps down the step and Carina gasps when she looks at Stefan's back.

'How bad is it?' he asks.

'I don't know anything about this kind of thing, but…it must be incredibly painful. I hope this will help a bit.'

The finer sensory nerves in his back must have been damaged, because Stefan experiences nothing more than a slight change in temperature; he isn't even sure Carina has started pouring until the water splashes around his feet. When she asks how it feels, he tells her it feels good.

'I think we need to do a *lot* of rinsing,' Carina says, filling another jug. 'The tank holds two hundred litres, doesn't it?'

'What did you see?'

'Sorry?'

'When you looked at those four figures. You said it was a long story—I want to hear it.'

Carina carries the jug over to Stefan and slowly pours the contents over his back, bottom and thighs. 'It was another life. Nothing to do with what we have now.'

Stefan waits until she has finished. As she heads back to the sink, he grabs her arm and turns her to face him.

'Carina, if there's one thing I think I've learned about this place, it's that not knowing each other is dangerous. Not knowing what the other person is thinking, what burdens they might be carrying.'

Carina extricates herself and leans over to refill the jug, but Stefan can see that his words have made an impression, which encourages him to go on.

'I know virtually nothing about what happened to you between that evening at the dance and the night you came back. That's eight years, Carina. Eight years of your life that I know nothing about. Now Emil isn't here, I can say what we're both thinking: we might never get out of this. And I think the risk is greater if we don't know each other. Isn't it time?'

Carina has been listening so intently that the jug is overflowing. The lines of her body suddenly soften.

'Do you remember?' she says. 'That night at the dance?'

'Of course I do. Why would I forget the night my dreams came true?'

It was called a disco. It used to be called a barn dance, but nowadays it was a disco, held in the pavilion next to the old steamboat jetty. First of all there was a local folk group, the Salty Sailors, playing evergreens and classics from the archipelago, then a disco.

Carina and her friends uttered the word with studied irony—'Shall we go to the *disco* tonight?'—but they went because there was nowhere else to go.

Carina's mother had died six months earlier and her father had sunk into a deep depression, which among many other things meant he had forgotten to give notice on the holiday cottage, and by the time summer came it was too late. Since he was going to have to pay anyway, they decided they might as well go.

It was a mistake. Memories of childhood and love and bright summer days lurked in every corner of the house and garden. Carina and her father crept around among those memories like two ghosts, incapable of doing anything to create a life that was about here and now. Before long Carina was only sleeping at home, and often she didn't even do that.

Back in town she had started hanging out with a different crowd, but out in the sticks her old summer mates would have to do. She was the most popular member of the gang, the one everyone wanted as

343

their special friend. The fact that she wanted to go to the *disco* made it cool.

They pre-loaded with a witches' brew of as much booze as they could lay their hands on, listening to Dr Alban and laughing their heads off. At about ten-thirty they headed down to the disco, where the bass beat of 'Living on a Prayer' floated out across the inlet, woppa-wo-wa, woppa-wo-wa. A few over-thirties were dad-dancing, and perched on a fence with a can of Fanta in his hand was Stefan. Kamilla with a K pointed to him: 'Check out the guy from the store! I bet he's *actually* got Fanta in there!'

She could well have been right. Stefan was wearing a pair of dark blue jeans that looked brand-new, and a red checked shirt buttoned almost to the top. His large black-rimmed glasses reflected the glow of the coloured lights, flashing out of time with the music.

'See anyone you fancy?' asked Camilla with a C, and Carina shrugged.

'I see someone who's been hit with the ugly stick!' Jenny said, waving her hand in Stefan's direction.

It was just an idea. Suddenly Carina heard herself saying: 'What do I get if I snog him?'

The girls slurred 'a thousand' and 'ten thousand', but when they realised that Carina was serious, they settled on fifty kronor each. A hundred and fifty. Carina insisted on two hundred, and after a brief period of negotiation the deal was done.

Carina and her father had got into serious financial difficulties after her mother's death. Carina received only half of her student grant, and two hundred kronor was a lot of money to her—something the others didn't know, of course. They came from well-off families, and assumed she was haggling just for fun.

Carina sashayed across the dance floor and stood in front of Stefan. 'So,' she said. 'What you got?'

Stefan held out the can, and she took a swig. To her surprise there was a noticeable kick of rum. She handed the can back and asked: 'Got anything neat?' Stefan nodded. 'Fancy sharing?' Carina said.

Stefan shrugged. This was going better than Carina had expected. As she followed Stefan off the dance floor, her friends made meaningful gestures, egging her on.

Stefan's hiding place was an upturned rotting skiff that had been in the same spot for as long as Carina could remember. He pulled out a half-full bottle of Bacardi, and Carina whistled. 'Wow. Were you going to drink it all yourself?'

'No. I've had it for quite some time.'

Carina laughed. 'Hang on, have I got this right? You've got a bottle of Bacardi, and you just...have a little drop now and again?'

'On special occasions.'

'That's kind of crazy. I mean, that's like what *adults* do!'

'And?'

Stefan passed her the bottle, then reached under the boat for another can of Fanta. Carina took a swig of the neat rum. When Stefan straightened up, she took another swig before giving him back the bottle. She loved the burning sensation in her throat, and warm fumes filled her brain. Stefan waved the can: 'Aren't you going to...?'

'No, I'm fine, thanks.'

Carina looked over at the dance floor where people were staggering around to 'Moonlight Shadow'.

'You dancing?' Stefan asked, his eyes fixed on the ground.

'What?'

'You dancing?'

'No, I'm just standing here.'

'I mean...'

'I know what you mean. Come here.'

She grabbed the front of Stefan's shirt, pulled him close and fastened her lips on his. When she thrust her tongue into his mouth, it was a couple of seconds before he responded. She closed her eyes, and actually enjoyed the sensation for a moment. His lips were soft, his tongue warm as it whisked over hers. Then her nose bumped against his glasses. She pushed him away, said, 'Okay. Thanks for the drink,' then walked away.

She went the long way round, trying to avoid her friends, but they came rushing to meet her. When Kamilla with a K held up her hand for a high five, Carina felt a sudden urge to slap her face instead.

Stefan kept giving her long looks for the rest of the evening, but she ignored him. A couple of times she crept back to the skiff and helped herself to the Bacardi until the bottle was almost empty. She didn't know if Stefan realised what she was doing, nor did she care.

At some point the dance ended without her even noticing. By that time she was sitting on a rock at the water's edge with her head between her knees. The music had stopped and the lights had gone out; the moonlight over the sea was the only source of illumination as she got to her feet, fell over and sliced her elbow open on a sharp stone.

'Fucking hell,' she muttered, fumbling for something to get hold of. She found a hand.

'Come on, let me help you.' It was Stefan's voice. He pulled her to her feet and looped her arm around his neck. She allowed herself to be led; they were going in the same direction after all. They had been walking in silence for a while and her head had cleared when Stefan suddenly said: 'You shouldn't drink so much.'

'You shouldn't wear such ugly glasses,' she replied, and that was the end of that. They followed the dirt track leading to both their houses, and Carina saw that the kitchen light was on in the cottage; her father was still up. She stopped, and with her arm still around Stefan's neck she asked: 'Do you know how to fuck?'

His shoulders tensed. 'What do you mean?'

'I mean do you know how to fuck? Have you done it before?'

'I have.'

Carina let out a long, drunken sigh. 'I can't handle having to teach you, you know.'

'No, I've done it before. Once.'

'Okay. Shall we do it then?'

'What, now?'

Carina withdrew her arm and rubbed both hands over her face.

'No, let's go back to yours. Not for coffee or anything, just to fuck. And I'll stay over. Okay?'

Stefan had a small place of his own next to the main house. His walls were adorned with photos of birds, and a picture of some guy made of fruit. Carina wondered whether he had been lying when he said he'd fucked before.

Without further ado she stripped off and placed Stefan's hand on her pussy. She squeezed his crotch and was relieved to find that he was both hard enough and big enough. She lay down on her back on his bed, spread her legs and said: 'Come on then. I'm on the pill.'

It wasn't good. It wasn't even okay. Stefan was far too cautious. If he had at least made up for it with a thorough exploration of her body, it might have been all right, but he couldn't even bring himself to do that. There was just a gentle thrusting which went on for a couple of minutes, during which time Carina lay and looked at the picture of the fruit man, wondering if it was a photograph or a painting. Then Stefan let out a whimper, and it was all over.

He curled up beside her, stroked her hair and said: 'I lied. That was my first time.'

'No shit, Sherlock.'

'I wasn't very good, was I?'

'I've had better. But it's okay.'

'Do you want to smoke?'

For a moment Carina thought he meant did she want to *smoke*. That he had some gear. Then she understood; he was asking if she wanted to smoke one of her own ordinary cigarettes now they'd had sex. He'd probably seen it in some film. There wasn't the faintest whiff of smoke in Stefan's cottage, and she realised he was making a major concession. To make up for what had just happened.

'Sure,' she said. 'Pass me my jeans, will you?'

She dug out a crumpled packet of Marlboro Light and her lighter as Stefan picked up an empty Fanta can from the floor. He was obviously a Fanta guy. While she smoked and dropped her ash into the can, Stefan caressed her breasts, her stomach. He shook his head.

'You have no idea how long I've dreamt about this,' he said. 'Ever since I started having that kind of—'

'I know,' Carina interrupted him.

'And then it turns out like this.'

He frowned and a shadow passed across his eyes. He was on the verge of tears. Carina patted his cheek. 'Hey, it's cool. It's fine. Really.' *If he starts crying, I'm out of here.*

Stefan pulled himself together and gently stroked her pubic hair. Carina felt a tingle, and pressed herself against his hand. He didn't seem to notice. With his eyes fixed on a picture of eight birds that all looked exactly the same, he said: 'I know this is a one-off. Is there anything I can do to change that?'

Carina looked at him. Now that he had taken off his glasses, he could have been any one of a thousand ordinary, boring guys. Even though the movement of his hand felt good, she felt no attraction whatsoever. She shook her head slowly.

He carried on stroking her. 'In that case I just want you to know that…I think you're the best girl in the world. Every summer I wait for you to arrive, just so that I can see you. And if there was anything I could do…'

Carina stubbed out her cigarette and put the can on the floor. She pressed herself harder against him. 'You can carry on doing that. I'm not leaving just yet.'

A little while later they did it again; this time it was okay, and Carina looked at Stefan rather than the fruit man. Afterwards they lay there chatting for a while, and Stefan took a drag of Carina's cigarette, which made him cough.

In the morning she left via the window and cut across the neighbour's garden so that nobody would see her on the road as she walked home. The following week she and her father went home, and it would be eight years before she saw Stefan again.

She blew the two hundred kronor on cigarettes.

*

'So why did you do it?' Stefan asks. 'The first time you kissed me—why did you do it?'

Carina doesn't know if sluicing his back is having any effect at all; it looks like a pizza that has just started cooking. White strips of skin and dark red muscle tissue, and several blisters the size of a five-kronor piece. It's difficult to grasp that human skin can look like this, that the person whose skin it is can speak rather than scream, and that the person in question is Stefan. Her Stefan. Her poor Stefan.

'You were kind of cute,' she says, pouring water over his neck and shoulders. 'A bit lost, somehow.'

'Is that true?'

Carina is glad Stefan can't look her in the eye as she nods and says: 'Absolutely.'

Stefan might well be right when he says it is dangerous if they don't know each other in this place, but wherever they are it's also dangerous to hurt each other, and Stefan has already been hurt enough. The exposed muscles have a life of their own, twitching like tiny fish when the water runs over them. However, Stefan refuses to give up.

'I just think it's so weird,' he says. 'I mean, I know what I looked like, what you looked like, who you were—'

'Stefan,' Carina breaks in as she empties the jug. For a moment she considers telling the truth, but reducing the amount of money. Twenty kronor. Telling him it wasn't about the money. The truth is that back then she would have kissed the Salty Sailors' bass player, and he looked like a pig that was tired of life.

But that lie would be worse, more elaborate, so when Stefan says, 'Yes?', she pushes up the sleeve of her T-shirt and points to the tattoo on her shoulder. 'Do you know what this is?'

'Two eternity symbols.'

'No, it isn't.'

Carina goes over to the sink and refills the jug. Anything but that kiss. Stefan asks more questions, but she doesn't start talking until she is standing behind him once more. She tells him about the tattoo and how she got it. About the people she used to hang out with, about her life up to the point when, in a final attempt to save herself, she went out to Ålviken and knocked on Stefan's door.

Her story takes twenty jugs of water. When she has finished, there is silence, and in that silence they hear a car start up. Carina doesn't know if it is because she is afraid of how Stefan will react, but suddenly her whole body feels cold, as if someone has stabbed her in the heart with an icicle. She has been so taken up with her account that she has forgotten.

'Emil,' she says. 'Where's Emil?'

*

'Come on.'

'I'm not allowed to hang out with you.'

'Why not?'

'I don't know, but I'm not allowed.'

Emil clutches Sabre Cat to his stomach like a shield when Molly comes over. Her eyes are red, as if she has been crying, and there are pink lines on her face. Ever since Emil met her for the first time she has been kind of *double* in a way that he can't understand. Just as Transformers can be two different things. She is a girl, and something that isn't a girl.

Now, with puffy eyes and marks on her face, she is almost nothing more than a girl, particularly when she pouts as she looks at Sabre Cat and says: 'Nice cat.'

'It's not a cat. It's a lynx.'

'What's it called?'

Emil can't remember where he got the name Sabre Cat from, and since he's just said it's a lynx, it seems like a silly name. He feels as if he's letting Sabre Cat down, but because he's just been thinking about Transformers, he says: 'Megatron. It's called Megatron.'

'Like in *Transformers*?'

'Mmm.'

350

'Cool. I've got a lion called Simba.'

'Like in *The Lion King*.'

'Yes. He's at home, though. I've got the DVD as well.'

'Me too.'

Without thinking about it, Emil has tucked Sabre Cat under his arm and moved closer to Molly. 'Do you know Star Wars?' he asks, and Molly shrugs. 'A bit.'

He really wants to show someone, and even if Molly might not understand how *amazing* it is, perhaps she might understand to some extent if she knows a bit about Star Wars. Emil takes the two Darth Maul figures out of his breast pocket, but leaves the lightsabers where they are so that he won't lose them. 'Check these out.'

'Oh!' Molly says. 'Can I have a look?'

Emil hands over the figures and is pleased to see that Molly seems seriously impressed as she examines them. Although it is disappointing when she asks: 'Who are they?'

'You said you knew Star Wars.'

'Only a bit. I'm guessing he's evil?'

'And then some! That's Darth Maul.'

Emil tells her about Obi-Wan and Qui-Gon Jinn, and Molly listens, wide-eyed. In a way it's better than if she had known everything already. When he has finished, Molly says: 'We can play Star Wars!'

'With Darth Maul?'

'Yes! Come on!'

Emil has almost completely forgotten that he's not allowed to hang out with Molly, and as he doesn't know *why*, it doesn't really matter, as Daddy would say. The image of his father's back flickers across his mind as he and Molly walk towards her caravan, but it disappears when Molly says, 'The emperor strikes again!' and crawls underneath the caravan.

Emil sighs and says, 'The *empire* strikes *back*,' then he crawls in beside her and lies down on his tummy.

Molly places the two figures on the grass outside the caravan, making them say things that are nothing to do with Star Wars, so Emil has to take over. She laughs when he makes his voice as deep as possible and intones: 'Fear is my ally.'

'Hang on a minute, I'll just go and get something,' Molly says.

She wriggles out and runs off. Emil stays where he is; he rolls over on his back and looks up at the sky while kicking at the underside of the caravan. He's glad that Molly is being nice now; this place is boring and horrible at the same time, and it's good to have someone to hang out with, even if it is a girl.

Emil picks up the two Darth Maul figures and makes them walk up the side of the caravan as he whispers: 'Fear is my ally.'

Then he hears a car start up.

*

Molly knows what to do, she has seen Daddy do it loads of times. The key is on the passenger seat, and it's the kind of key that doesn't have to be inserted in a lock. You have to push down the brake pedal, though.

Molly stretches full length so that she can reach the pedal and press the start button at the same time. The engine roars into life. She takes her foot off the brake and slowly begins to accelerate.

*

Peter is dreaming of a football pitch as big as the whole world, an immense green surface with people moving around in regular patterns. There are no goals, there is no ball, no apparent purpose to the game. Is it even a game? The only thing to suggest that there is something to win or lose is the tense concentration on the people's faces as they run, jog or amble across the pitch. As if it were a matter of life and death.

As is always the way with dreams, logic has no part to play, and Peter is watching the whole scene from high above, while at the same time he is down on the pitch. He knows that he must run and he knows why, but it is impossible to put it into words. When he tries, he finds himself enveloped in darkness that smells of shower gel and disinfectant.

Another body is there with him. This body is the goal and the ball and the point of the game, and yet curiously enough it is *outside* the pitch, even though the pitch encompasses the whole world. Peter holds out his arms in the darkness. Something bumps into him, and he opens his eyes.

The caravan jolts and Peter just has time to realise that it is moving, has time to think for a second that Donald is driving off with him and for an image of Goofy from the usual Christmas Eve TV show to flash through his mind

So who's driving?
Why, I'm driving, ho ho ho!

Then the caravan tilts slightly as one wheel rolls over something. Peter hears a high-pitched scream which is cut short after a fraction of a second, to be replaced by a cracking sound, just like when a dead tree falls and the dry branches splinter on the ground. Then the wheel comes down with a bump, the caravan rights itself and all is silent. The caravan travels a few metres further on before it stops.

*

Emil doesn't know that the caravan is hitched up to the car, so when he hears an engine start up, he simply wonders who is about to drive off. He considers getting out the lightsabers and letting the Darth Maul figures have a fight. Then the wheel immediately to the left of his chest begins to turn.

He just manages to bring down his arms to try to push himself out when his shirt is trapped between the wheel and the ground. He screams as the wheel grips the skin below the crook of his arm and twists it like a vice. His nipple is dragged to the left as the full weight of the caravan lands on his thin chest.

He throws his head back, looking at the world upside down as all the air is forced out of him. His ears pop, and he doesn't hear his ribs breaking, he is just aware of fiery blue thrusts of pain stabbing through his body and warm liquid surging up into his throat and he knows it's blood and

I'm too little to die

a bird that he is able to identify as a flycatcher in the fading light darts across the sky before his eyes. He turns his head to the right and sees it land on the fence surrounding the campsite, where it waggles its bottom up and down a couple of times before it is sucked down into the darkness.

*

Something that had been forgotten in the general confusion was the digging of the latrine, so Lennart and Olof have taken on the job. They have dug down and hacked at the earth, which smells of blood. It is good working together. Good because the conversation is restricted to the task in hand.

'How deep do you think we should go?'

'Half a metre ought to be enough for the time being.'

'We could do with some turf or something. To use as a cover.'

'Yes. That would be useful.'

'Then again, if we have any more rain...'

'If that happens I think it will put paid to most of our problems, so to speak.'

When they have finished digging the trench, they straighten up with aching backs and admire their work. It isn't really big enough for ten people, but at least they've made a start, and perhaps those with younger muscles can carry on later, if it proves necessary.

'What about you?' Olof asks, nodding towards the hole. 'Do you need to go?'

'Well, not right now,' Lennart replies. 'But we ought to put up some kind of screen.'

'Yes. But that's quite funny. Under the circumstances.'

Lennart gives Olof a look. 'You could say that depends on your sense of humour.'

'You don't find it funny?'

'Maybe a bit.'

They have dug the latrine twenty metres behind their own caravan, and as they walk back to the camp they see Molly slide into the black Toyota. Nothing strange about that. They carry on walking. It does seem a little strange when the engine starts up, and by the time they reach their door, they see that both the Toyota and the caravan have begun to move.

'Is Molly...' Olof begins. 'Bloody hell!'

Both of them see what happens. Emil's arms appear, his head jerks back as the wheel of the caravan is dragged across his chest. They hear the sound of breaking ice and splintering branches as his bones crack. Emil's eyes roll back so that only the whites are visible as a fountain of blood is forced out of his mouth in a single gout, spurting all over the grass. His arms drop and the caravan stops.

Lennart and Olof race over to Emil and drop to their knees beside him. Peter appears in the doorway.

'What's going—' He catches sight of Emil's head protruding from beneath the caravan, his forehead and cheeks covered in blood. Peter's face is distorted in a tortured grimace and he whispers one word, 'Molly...', which is drowned out by the sound of Carina howling.

*

Four pairs of hands lift Emil and carry him to his own caravan, trying keep him perfectly flat in case his back is damaged. Is this the right thing to do?

The front of his shirt looks horribly sunken, because his ribcage has been compressed. His breathing is faint and gurgling, as if there is fluid on his lungs. It ought to be drained, isn't that the procedure? But no one knows how to do it.

Emil's eyes are closed, and his fingers are twitching. Occasionally a drop of blood trickles from his mouth. His life is as fragile as a bubble. It could burst at any moment, the shimmering rainbow colours disappearing in an instant.

He is lying on the sofa, with Carina on the floor beside him. She gently presses the palm of his hand to her forehead, as if she is trying to transfer her own life force to Emil. She is no longer screaming. Stefan is sitting by his son's head, gently running his fingers through the boy's hair.

Peter, Lennart and Olof watch helplessly. From time to time they look at one another as if they are about to say something, but nothing comes out. Someone should be issuing clear instructions, explaining what can be done to improve Emil's condition, to save his life. But no one knows. No one has a clue. The only thing they can do is wait and hope.

Emil's broken ribcage heaves, straining the fabric of his shirt. Everyone holds their breath. Then he coughs, just once. More blood spurts out of his mouth. Carina sobs, pressing his hand harder against her forehead. Was that…? No, Emil is still with them, his breathing shallow but even.

Stefan's hands are shaking so much he can hardly get a grip when he leans over Emil to unbutton his shirt, exposing skin in shades of blue and yellow. However, no broken bones are poking through, there is no external bleeding. Although perhaps that would have been better than the internal bleeding? To let it flow? No one knows.

They all notice it at the same time, or more or less at the same time. The red cross imprinted on the skin over Emil's heart. As if he has been marked, branded.

Stefan cautiously slides two fingers into Emil's breast pocket and takes something out: two thin lengths of neon-coloured plastic. Their outline must have been pressed into Emil's chest by the weight of the caravan.

'The lightsabers,' Stefan whispers. 'The lightsabers.'

*

'The lightsabers.'

Peter can't stand it any longer. His own body was part of the weight that crushed Emil. He heard the sound of the boy's ribs breaking, felt it like a faint clicking and scraping that went right through the metal, through the mattress and into his back as he lay there sleeping like a pig instead of keeping an eye on Molly.

His body is a hole, a coal-black vacuum where nothing can live. He has helped to carry Emil, he has stood with the others watching the boy fight for his life, but essentially he has ceased to exist.

He was the kind of person who brought happiness. Helped people to regain control of their lives and their bodies. A source of inspiration and a role model. He will never be able to do that, be that person again, and therefore he is nothing. It's over.

Without saying anything to the others—what could he say?—he turns and heads for the door. As he is about to step down, he stops dead.

Molly.

Under normal circumstances he would have thought about his daughter, about how she might have been affected by what had happened. But for one thing these are not normal circumstances, and for another he has stopped thinking of Molly as his daughter. His paternal feelings are not enhanced by what he sees from the doorway.

Molly has stripped naked and is lying face down on the grass where Emil vomited blood after he had been run over.

Mummy left me in the tunnel. I became like them.

Slowly he steps down from the caravan. If it hadn't been for Molly's long blond hair, he wouldn't have recognised her. The pale pink skin has faded and turned white. Her body is jerking as if the heart of the earth is punching her in the stomach, jolting right through her. As Peter moves closer she lifts her head and her hair stays on the

357

grass like a discarded wig. The person who gets up on all fours is his father.

Peter is not afraid. To be afraid, you must have something to lose. Peter has nothing to lose. Everything has been taken from him, and all he has now is a task which he must complete. He unhooks the caravan from the tow bar and hears his father's voice behind him. Or from the side or in front of him. He hears it.

'Peter,' says the voice in that drunken, slurring tone that Peter hates. 'Come and talk to your daddy, there's a good boy.'

'Go to hell,' Peter says. 'I know it's not you, but go to hell anyway.'

He gets into his car; it has no sunroof, so the interior is undamaged. The key is still lying on the passenger seat. He presses the start button and the engine springs into life. He looks up at the horizon.

I'm coming.

The hole that is his body will be transported to where it belongs, the task will be completed. He puts the car in gear and sets off to meet the darkness. This time he will not turn back.

*

'Pik-pik-pik, pik-pik-pik!'

Pied flycatcher.

Emil can identify twenty-two birdsongs, including the pied flycatcher. The bird is singing just above his head, and he opens his eyes.

The last thing he saw before everything went dark was a flycatcher landing on the fence surrounding the campsite. Now he has somehow moved; he is lying next to the fence and the bird is directly above him.

'Hello,' Emil says, and the bird tilts its head on one side, contemplating him with its beady eyes for a second before it flies away.

Emil sits up and rubs his eyes. He really is on the campsite, near the spot where their caravan stood before everything got weird. A few metres away is the communal barbecue area where they cooked sausages one evening; he can also see the kiosk, and the trampoline, which no one is using at the moment.

358

Emil wonders whether to go over and have a bounce for a little while, but when he stands up and takes a couple of steps, he feels a burning pain in his chest. It's like being stung by a wasp, and he cries out and rips open his shirt to let the insect out.

There is no wasp. Emil looks at the spot where it hurt, just over his heart. He sees two intersecting lines, a cross drawn on his skin, burning and smarting as if it has been etched there by a wasp's sting.

Or a laser.

This makes him think of the Darth Maul figures; he was holding them just before…before what? He can't remember. He was playing with the Darth Maul figures, and then he was here. He is no longer holding them, and when he checks his breast pocket he discovers that the lightsabers are gone too, and he is on the verge of tears.

Daddy will be really cross. No, worse than that. He'll be really sad.

The mark on his chest burns like fire as Emil searches all around, but there is no sign of either the figures or the lightsabers. Occasionally the pain subsides, and unconsciously at first, then deliberately, Emil begins to take a step in different directions, like someone searching for the hidden object in a game of Hot or Cold, trying to work out where it's

Warm, cool, warm, boiling hot

and he works out that it is least painful, in fact it hardly hurts at all, when he is standing on the track. The track that cuts through the camp, and is intersected by another track by the barbecue. He stands still, and after a while the pain comes back. He moves forward a couple of steps, and it subsides.

He has to walk right through the barbecue area to avoid deviating, then he carries on along the narrow track that leads further into the camp. He has to put his feet one directly in front of the other, almost taking baby steps so that he stays within the boundaries, and it's like a game.

Walk the line.

Although he's not looking for birds this time, but something else. Something that the track is leading him to.

Walk the line, he thinks again, the words of the song running through his head.

It might be fun if he weren't so terribly tired. It's as if he has a temperature, a really high temperature, and his legs feel like jelly. He can't go on. Where are Mummy and Daddy?

He can barely keep his eyes open as he looks around. He knows what's supposed to happen. If a child is poorly, grown-ups are supposed to come and help. He is a child, but all the grown-ups are looking in different directions. As if they don't want to see him.

In spite of the fact that the pain in his chest is getting worse, he has to stop and rest. He stops. Sits down. Lies down. Just for a minute. Then he'll carry on. He closes his eyes, fumbles around in the grass and finds his mother's hand.

*

Carina feels the pressure of Emil's hand in hers; she gasps and looks at his face. His eyes are screwed tight shut as he concentrates hard. As she gazes at him his expression softens, the muscles relax and he opens his eyes.

'Emil?' Carina says, forcing back the tears. 'How are you feeling, sweetheart?'

Emil says something she can't make out, and she leans closer. 'What did you say, my darling boy, my precious...'

'Walk the line,' Emil whispers. 'I walk the line. Mummy...'

Stefan's hands are joined as if in prayer, and he presses them to his chest as he looks at Emil.

'What is it, sweetheart?' Carina is so close now that her lips are touching Emil's cheek. 'What do you want me to do?'

'Mummy. Must go.'

Emil's eyes close, and Carina's tears run down his face as she kisses his cheeks, his forehead, and whispers: 'No, no, no, no, you can't go, sweetheart, don't go.'

Emil's eyes remain closed, but the thing Carina fears most in all the world does not happen. He carries on breathing, carries on living, even if he is inaccessible. Carina flops down onto the floor, stroking his hand.

'What did he say?' Stefan asks; it is difficult to hear the words because he is now pressing his joined hands to his mouth.

'Must go,' Carina replies. 'Mummy. Must go.'

Carina's fingers stop moving. *Mummy. Must go. Mummy must go.* She hears a discreet cough behind her, then Lennart's voice.

'Perhaps we should leave you in peace. But if there's anything we can do, anything at all—'

Carina interrupts him. 'He wants me to go.'

'I'm sorry?'

'That's what he said. *Mummy. Must go.*'

Carina pulls herself to her feet and is already on her way to the door by the time Stefan says: 'Hang on, where do you think you're going?'

'I don't know, but that's what he said. That I must go. So I'm going.'

If there's one thing Carina thinks she has understood about this place, it's that they don't understand anything at all. They are like newborn babies thrown into an incomprehensible reality where everything is new. Chaotic. But just as a child, deep within its genetic make-up, has at its disposal a machine built to bring order out of chaos, little by little, Carina has gradually begun to discern patterns. As soon as she tries to make sense of them or to think rationally, they slip beyond her grasp, but they are there. The machine recognises them.

Why else would she have become so obsessed with the crosses on their caravans, and felt such dread when she discovered the crossroads? And now the mark over Emil's heart. It's all connected. She doesn't understand it, any more than a baby understands the link between the nipple and the warm, delicious taste in its mouth, but the connection is there, and all she can do is act on that basis. She is not going to die, Emil is not going to die. There are tracks. Mummy must go along one of these tracks. But which one?

In spite of the fear kicking deep inside her belly, she laughs out loud when she steps down from the caravan; it is the laugh that is forced out of someone riding the ghost train, when something scary but oh-so-obvious leaps out of the darkness.

Of course.

The tiger is waiting for her. It is lying next to the spot where Emil had his accident, its head resting on its front paws. When it sees her, it gets to its feet and yawns, exposing a row of sharp, white teeth. It is the beautiful tiger, the terrible tiger. The tiger from the Brunkeberg tunnel.

The tiger turns around, glances over its shoulder and begins to walk out into the field. Carina is about to follow when she feels a hand on her shoulder.

'Carina,' Lennart says. 'What are you doing?'

'I don't know. But I have to go. Tell Stefan...' A series of alternatives that might make her conviction sound reasonable flash through her mind. None of them work, so she simply says: 'Whatever you like.'

The tiger is now about twenty metres away, and it is following one of the tracks. Perhaps it is important to stay close to it, so she hurries along until she is five metres behind the swishing tail, then she slows down and continues at a steady pace.

For so many years she has felt this tiger creeping up behind her, following her every step, lurking in the shadows, ready to pounce. Perhaps she has misinterpreted the whole thing. Perhaps it was just waiting. Waiting for *her* to follow *it*.

*

Donald has parked a short distance from their caravan and got out of the car. When Majvor fails to follow suit, he walks around to her side, opens the door with a chivalrous flourish, and says: 'Madame!'

Majvor doesn't know what Donald is planning, but she feels obliged to clamber out of the uncomfortable seat, using the doorframe for support. She accompanies him on an inspection tour of the caravan: most of the contents appear to have fallen on the floor, and the remains of her unbaked cinnamon buns are smeared all over the parts of the sofa that haven't been eaten away.

'Dear oh dear oh dear,' Donald says, wringing his hands. 'Dear oh dear oh dear.'

He opens the cupboard under the sink and takes out a couple of plastic bags, which he fills with undamaged food. He fills a third bag with bottles of booze from the drinks cupboard. Majvor has found a corner of the sofa that is more or less intact and is not covered in sticky dough, and she sits down, folds her hands neatly on top of one another, and watches his activities.

'Donald,' she says eventually, 'what are you doing?'

'What am I doing?'

'Yes.'

Donald has reached the tool drawer, and he places the hammer, the small axe, the drill and several screwdrivers in a basket, then adds rags, rust remover and glue. He puts the basket on the draining board and sits down opposite Majvor.

'Surely it's perfectly obvious,' he says. 'I'm gathering up things that might come in useful.'

'What then?'

'Then I intend to get out of here.'

'How?'

'I'll drive until I get to the end. It must end somewhere.'

'But don't you think we ought to...'

'Mmm-mm.' Donald wags his index finger at Majvor. 'Wrong. There's no *we*. You're staying here.'

Majvor looks around the devastated and now plundered caravan. 'Here?'

Donald leans closer and lowers his voice, as if he is about to share a confidence with her. 'Majvor, would you say you've been loyal to me?' Majvor is about to protest, but Donald silences her with a gesture. 'I'm talking now. You can't gag me this time, you know.'

Donald summarises everything that has gone on during the course of the day, and from his point of view Majvor really does come across as the most perfidious of wives. Donald does not, however, include details of his own ridiculous behaviour. This is hardly the time to correct him, because he is gradually working himself up into another frenzy of rage. He snorts and shakes his head as if he cannot believe the words coming out of his mouth as he concludes: '...then you taped me up like some fucking parcel.'

There is a brief pause in the onslaught, and Majvor dares to speak: 'You're wrong, Donald.'

Donald nods thoughtfully. 'That's possible, Majvor. That is possible. But it really doesn't matter. Do you know why?'

Majvor doesn't really want to hear what is coming next, but nor does she know how to avoid it, so she says nothing.

'Because, Majvor, I am sick to death of you anyway. I am tired of your saggy body and I am tired of your stupid face. I am tired of your cinnamon buns and the food you cook, and I am tired of bloody Jesus. Everything you say makes me tired, and everything I am not allowed to do makes me tired. I have been trying to work out how I can get rid of you so that I can spend a few years without you dragging me down with your rolls of fat and your pathetic personality. And now the chance has come, and I intend to take it.'

A hard lump has formed in Majvor's throat during Donald's monologue. Their life together over the past few years hasn't exactly been hearts and flowers, but she thought they had a mutual understanding, an acknowledgement that they would stick together and make the best of it. The revulsion in Donald's voice suggests that she was completely wrong.

The way he is looking at her, like a disgusting insect he has just squashed and can't wait to wipe off his fingers, means that she can't help letting out a sob as she gets up from the sofa. Donald gets up too, ignoring her as he goes over to the bedroom area and starts rummaging around for his reading glasses.

Tears blur Majvor's vision as she walks towards the door, then stops and looks back at Donald who is now kneeling on the bed with his back to her. To think that she once wrapped her arms around that back, digging in her nails in a moment of pleasure.

She pulls herself together and opens a cupboard, takes out the spare car keys. Then she steps outside; behind her Donald is still muttering because he can't find what he's looking for.

Halfway to the car, she stops. Will Lockhart is leaning on the boot to stop himself from falling over. The cowboy shirt and jacket hang loose on his sloping shoulders, the gun belt is dragging him down, and his body seems ready to give up as he breathes heavily, his hands fumbling at the metal. The eyes that gaze into Majvor's do not belong to the Man from Laramie, just a very old James Stewart.

Jimmy. Oh, Jimmy.

Because not even the wretched state he is in can extinguish the openness, the kindness deep down inside. Her Jimmy. She moves a little closer, and he holds out his hand.

'Majvor,' he whispers. 'Help me.'

She takes his hand, brings it to her lips and kisses the wrinkled skin, marked with liver spots.

'Of course, Jimmy,' she says. 'Whatever it takes.'

Majvor is not a good driver; she has been told this over and over again. She got her licence when she was thirty, mainly so that she could drive the children around, and she had to take her test five times before the examiner reluctantly signed her off. She hadn't actually done anything *wrong*, but…she just wasn't a very good driver.

Since the children have grown up Majvor has had no need to drive, and since the incident with the carport four years ago, which resulted in twenty thousand kronor's worth of damage to the bodywork, she has put her licence on the shelf, quite literally. The shelf above the extractor fan in the kitchen.

As she settles down behind the wheel, she realises that she has never driven this car. She doesn't know where the ignition is, and when she eventually finds it she fumbles with the key for some time before managing to insert it. She isn't sure what to do, because she doesn't really know where she's up to. Everything Donald said, the way he looked at her, has changed the world, made it messy and confusing.

She starts the engine and studies the gearstick, trying to understand how it works. First, second, reverse.

A kindly word at the right time helps the world go round.

Whatever happened to that wall hanging? It could be anywhere. Many self-evident truths have been lost in this place. She will just have to find new ones.

Donald must have heard the sound of the engine; he emerges from the caravan with a plastic bag in each hand. It seems his intention was to transfer anything of value to the car, then leave Majvor here. That's not very kind, is it?

A kindly word...

Majvor glances in the rear-view mirror. Jimmy Stewart is standing behind the car, staring at the horizon with eyes that have grown cloudy with age and weariness. What is more real: what we dream of, or what is right there before us?

First or reverse?

A kindly word... She will let kindness decide. Donald is standing in front of the car, looking straight at her. She smiles at him to give him a push in the right direction, but perhaps he interprets her smile as scornful, or else he just doesn't care what she does, because he yells: 'Get out of the car, you miserable fucking—'

That's it. Not a hint of kindness. Majvor puts the car in first gear and accelerates. The wheels skid on the grass before they find their grip and hurl nine hundred kilos of metal straight at Donald, who only has time to drop the bags before the grille hits him in the stomach. He is pushed backwards three metres with his upper body draped over the bonnet, then the whole thing crashes into the caravan. Majvor is thrown forward, the world explodes in a burst of white, and she loses consciousness for a few seconds.

When she comes round, she is jammed between the seat and the airbag, which is blocking her view. Her ears are buzzing as she opens the door and manages to get one leg out; she wriggles free and grabs the edge of the roof to haul herself out. She rests her chin on the top of the door and looks at the front of the car.

Oh dear. How very unfortunate.

Donald is still bent over the bonnet, arms outstretched towards the windscreen. He is facing Majvor, but his eyes are blank. His mouth is twitching as if he is trying to say something. Perhaps he wants to ask a question? Or make a confession?

Majvor feels a presence behind her back, and turns her head. Jimmy Stewart is gazing at her, his eyes loving and pleading for her help. Then he looks at Donald.

'I know,' Majvor says. 'But it's difficult.'

Jimmy Stewart nods and gently caresses her cheek. Majvor closes her eyes, picturing what she must do. The only consolation is that there is a kind of logical consistency to it all; Donald has often said the same. Majvor leaves Jimmy Stewart and goes into the caravan. The tools Donald gathered together are still exactly where he left them. She picks up the axe, weighing it in her hand.

Fortunately Donald has not come to life by the time she emerges; that might have made things too difficult. She walks over to the car and weighs up his left arm, measuring the angle with the axe.

'You said it yourself, Donald. Lots of times. That you wished it could have been you. So that…well. I guess this is how it's meant to be, somehow.'

Without waiting for a response, she brings down the axe. Blood pours from a deep gash just above Donald's wrist, and his hand starts flapping on the bonnet like a flounder on the shore, which makes it hard to aim. Majvor grabs hold of Donald's arm just below the elbow, carefully picks her spot, then brings down the axe once more.

When the hand has been chopped off and the flounder has stopped flapping, Majvor twists Donald's stump so that the blood runs down the side of the bonnet and onto the ground.

'Come along,' she says. 'Let's go, Jimmy.'

*

367

'Hey hey…'

Stefan is half-humming, half-singing, but the sound emerging from between his lips isn't even a whisper, just a series of uneven breaths with neither notes nor words. He is standing on the stairs looking towards the kitchen, where Emil is balancing on Carina's feet as she walks around. The soft morning light on the wooden floor, the gleam of the toaster, the aroma of coffee and newly baked bread in that eternal moment.

'Hey hey…'

Everything is falling apart.

The aroma of coffee metamorphoses into the metallic smell coming from Emil's mouth as he lies there on the sofa with his head resting on Stefan's knee, breathing in short, shallow gasps. His chest rasps and wheezes, and every breath could be his last, but Stefan can't allow himself to think that, because Emil is so *fragile* that even the thought that he could break might make it happen.

And yet Stefan cannot stop those four words whirling around and around in his head, like orbiting satellites falling towards a black hole.

Everything is falling apart everything is falling apart everything is falling apart

His damaged back is hunched as he strokes Emil's damaged body, which is flickering like a flame that cannot get enough oxygen. There is no room to think about Carina's story, but there it is again: damage. A damaged life where

everything is falling apart

as if normality, happiness, love were only temporary. Brief moments or short periods where chance weaves the threads together to form a whole, and it is possible to walk down the stairs humming 'Hey Hey Monica' in spite of the fact that the damage is always waiting to tear apart everything you have taken for granted, and you find out that what you have always thought were eternity symbols actually meant *Heil Hitler*.

Emil's legs are twitching. Left, right, left, as if he is walking along an invisible road. Stefan softly touches the cross imprinted over his heart.

My precious boy. Don't leave me. Don't leave...

Once again the picture fills his mind. Emil balancing on Carina's feet in the kitchen. His laughter when they move one step forward, then another, as he learns to walk. This is how you learn to walk.

Stefan stops on the stairs, his hand resting on the newel post as he takes in the moment. The dust motes dancing in the sunlight, a strand of Carina's hair that has fallen over her face, Emil's downy head that Carina will kiss in a moment. There is an unevenness beneath Stefan's fingers, a scratch in the newel post in the form of two crossed lines, and Stefan gasps as he realises that somehow he is actually *there*.

It is as if he were watching an old family film, but he is there too, and the perspective shifts imperceptibly so that he is part of the film; he can see himself sitting on the sofa watching himself. Both versions are equally true.

Stefan runs his fingers over the two lines and the newel post is covered in Emil's skin and Emil's skin is made of wood.

'Offee!'

Emil shouts from the kitchen as he continues to move around on Carina's feet, and a shudder runs through Stefan as he brushes against an understanding of the basic relativity of time and space, but it is whisked away as his fingers leave the two lines, and all that remains is:

Don't leave me. But walk. Walk, little man.

Stefan is back in the caravan. He blinks. The road home is endless, but at the same time it is only a heartbeat away.

*

Emil is back on his feet, taking baby steps along the track. He passes caravans where grown-ups are barbecuing, playing darts, or simply lying around in the sun. Older children are preoccupied with tablets or smart phones. No one looks in Emil's direction as he walks by. The only person who notices him is a little girl of about three. She is wearing a bright red swimsuit and is not entirely steady on her feet as she toddles towards him with her finger in her mouth and says: 'Hlm.'

Emil stops. 'You're not supposed to suck your thumb.'

With a plop the girl extracts her saliva-covered finger and holds it up in the air. 'Not thumb.'

'No. But you shouldn't suck your finger either.'

The girl examines her finger, then asks: 'What you doing?'

'I'm walking,' Emil replies.

'Why?'

Emil has been standing still for only about ten seconds, but the pain is already beginning to build. 'Because I have to.'

'Why?'

There is a boy at Emil's day care who does exactly the same thing. He keeps on asking *why, why* until someone says, 'Just because,' but still Emil wishes he had an answer to the girl's question. For his own sake.

'Because there's a track,' he says.

The girl looks at Emil, then to the right and the left. She wrinkles her nose and says: 'Isn't.'

'Yes there is.'

'*Isn't.*'

A woman in a brightly coloured dress who is presumably the girl's mother comes rushing over and grabs the child's hand. She doesn't look at Emil, but merely says, 'Come along, Elsa,' and drags the girl towards one of the caravans.

The heat in Emil's skin is now a burning pain, and he places one hand over his heart and closes his eyes. For a moment he has the feeling that the fingers stroking his chest are not his own. They feel more like a grown-up's fingers, like Daddy's fingers.

The feeling passes and he opens his eyes. It doesn't matter what Elsa said; the track is perfectly clear. It leads right through the middle of the campsite and out into an open field. Perhaps it ends in the distance, where Emil can see something glinting as it is caught by the rays of the setting sun. That's where he is going.

The pain fades as he begins to put one foot in front of the other again. It's nice to remember the sensation of Daddy's fingers touching his skin, and as he walks it seems to Emil that there is something different about his feet too. It is as if he is balancing on someone else's feet, a greater power that is helping him to make progress.

Walk, little man.

He walks.

*

Master and Mistress have gone off in the car without Benny. It doesn't matter, because Master and Mistress are no longer important. Cat is important. As long as Benny and Cat are together, everything is as it should be. But Benny is hungry. He hasn't had any food for a very long time, and his tummy is rumbling.

Benny and Cat walk around side by side, checking everything out. The firecreatures have gone away, and there is no longer anything that is actually dangerous. But there's not much else either. A lot of things have disappeared, and what is left doesn't smell too good.

Benny lets out a little whimper, which makes Cat prick up her ears and look at him. Benny whimpers again, his hungry whimper. Cat seems to understand. She does something with her tail and her head which Benny interprets as *follow me*. He has started to understand Cat a little better.

Cat trots over to her caravan and jumps inside. Benny hesitates, but Cat makes a noise that seems to mean he is allowed, so he follows her. Cat's masters are there, and they aren't cross with Benny for coming into their home. They pat both Benny and Cat, and say something that includes the word 'Food', among other things.

They get out two bowls and open a tin that looks more or less the same as the tins of Benny's food, except that this one has a cat on it. It is cat food. Benny sniffs. No, it doesn't smell the way it's supposed to. He sneezes and Cat's masters laugh.

Cat looks up from her bowl and Benny shakes his head. His

tummy rumbles again. Oh well. He takes a mouthful; it doesn't taste particularly good, but it's edible. He really is very hungry; he gobbles up everything in the bowl, and when the masters give him some more, he gobbles that too.

When they have finished eating, Benny and Cat creep under the table. Benny curls up and Cat lies down beside him, with her back against Benny's tummy. After a while Cat begins to hum and vibrate. It is a soothing noise, and Benny wishes he could do the same.

The masters pat Benny and their voices are kind. Cat has nice masters. Benny wishes they were his masters too. Perhaps they are? Perhaps Master and Mistress won't come back?

That would be good. Really good.

*

'Come back!'

Donald's despairing howl becomes more and more distant, grows fainter and fainter.

When he came round, he started off with a flood of curses so toxic that Majvor was amazed he even knew words like that. So many references to sexual organs, prostitution and figures from both heaven and hell—in the end she had covered her ears while James Stewart finished doing what he had to do.

It wasn't until Majvor and James Stewart started to walk away that the imprecations gave way to pleading. Donald invoked all the years they had spent together, all the good times they had had, everything he had done for her. She almost allowed herself to be persuaded, but then the Man from Laramie took her hand and said: 'Let's go, honey.'

It was good that he said it in English. It made everything more real, so Majvor took his hand and went with him as Donald's begging came down to one simple plea—*Come back*—which is now growing ever more feeble as he loses blood.

Majvor would never have thought she was capable of what she has done, and she would never have done it if she hadn't come to realise that God does not exist here. This place is silent and empty. Therefore, she had to make a choice: stay in this silent, empty reality, or for once follow what her fantasies and her body are telling her to do.

Will Lockhart's spurs jingle as he walks beside her, his warm hand holding hers, and she is aware of the manly smells of desert dust, sun and leather. Maybe a touch of horse as well. She glances sideways at him, and when his blue eyes meet hers, she makes up her mind.

Not Will Lockhart. She will stop thinking of him as Will Lockhart, a vengeful and not particularly nice man. He is James Stewart. James Stewart and no one else.

'James?'

His hand squeezes hers. 'Call me Jimmy. Everyone does.'

'Yes, I know. Jimmy?'

'Mmm, Majvor?'

'Where are we going?'

'Does it matter?

Majvor looks towards the horizon. They are heading away from the direction in which the camp lies, away from the rest of the group. She is alone with Jimmy Stewart in a place where no one else exists. Somewhere deep down she knows that this is not real, that she is making this happen.

But does it matter? If Donald believed the whole thing was a dream and therefore dismissed it, Majvor has decided to embrace the idea instead. Her dreams have come true, so she would be pretty stupid if she didn't choose to regard them as reality.

She stops. The jingle of the spurs falls silent as Jimmy stops too. They look at one another. Majvor decides to see how realistic this fantasy is. She takes a step towards him, lifts up her face to be kissed, and he kisses her. She just has time to think it's a good job the dream *isn't* realistic, because Jimmy Stewart would never...

Then she feels his hands on her body, and she stops thinking, gives herself up to the moment. They undress one another and she lies down on her back on the coarse grass. He kneels between her legs, and when she looks down at his stiff cock she catches sight of her sagging breasts spilling to the sides, the pallid rolls of fat. Tears spring to her eyes.

This can't happen.

Has she ever even dreamt of this? No, this is not part of her fantasy. She might have thought it was—it felt that way when his hands were caressing her, undressing her—but when he parts her legs and she feels his manhood rubbing at her dry labia, seeking a way in, she knows that it was never about this. In fact it is about something completely different.

She is about to lift her head and tell him when Jimmy, with the help of a little saliva, penetrates her anyway.

Oh!

Eventually it will no doubt become clear what it's all about, but meanwhile.....it's been a long time, and it's nice to feel that hard, slippery warmth pushing deep inside her. When he begins to thrust, she wraps her arms around his back, opens her eyes wide, looks into his face. Jimmy Stewart. Blue eyes, blue sky.

A few seconds pass. Something shuts down in her head. She *hasn't* dreamt about this; to tell the truth she's never been all that keen on the sexual side of things. Perhaps she is naive, but her image of romantic love is more like the stories she reads in her magazines. 'He takes her in his arms, kisses her tenderly, then dot dot dot', or 'their hungry bodies found nourishment at last' or something along those lines. A paraphrase.

What she and Jimmy Stewart are doing is definitely not a paraphrase. It is thrusting and sweat and her pale, wobbly flesh and it is *ugly*. She tries to shove Jimmy away, but that makes him push harder, and she feels like crying.

At last he stops and leaves her lying on the ground, spread out like a flayed rat. And ugly, ugly, ugly. As she crawls around naked, gathering up her clothes, she feels like the ugliest woman in the world. She has given up everything for this.

By the time she is dressed and on her feet, Jimmy Stewart is several hundred metres away. Only now does Majvor notice the band of darkness resting on the horizon. She turns around and sees her caravan far, far away. She *cannot go there.*

She winces as her hand brushes against her aching pudenda. 'Oh, why is everything so terrible?'

So what is it you want, Majvor?

It's not Jimmy Stewart's voice. Her innocent fantasy has lost its value now that it is no longer innocent. She could almost weep when she realises she doesn't even have that any more.

What do you want?

Nor is it the voice of God, which has never been this clear. No, it is just Majvor, talking to herself in this empty place where there seems to be nothing left for her.

What?

Perhaps she knows something, perhaps she doesn't. In any case there is only one thing to do. Majvor smoothes down her sweatpants, fastens her sandals and sets off after Jimmy Stewart, heading towards the band of darkness.

*

Peter has driven fast this time; he knows where he is going, and even if he had no idea of direction, the pull in his blood would guide him.

However, when the wall of darkness becomes visible on the horizon, a feeling begins to sprout within him, getting stronger as the wall grows higher and the pull increases. He is empty. He is finished. Everything has been taken away from him, and anything he might have had has been left behind. There is a strange serenity in this knowledge. He allows himself to rest in this serenity, and discovers that he understands Isabelle.

To disappear. To escape.

To relinquish one's will is hard, and requires a particular kind of strength. Under normal circumstances it is virtually impossible, but normal circumstances do not apply here. Help is available here. A weight lifts from Peter's shoulders as he gives himself up to the pull of the wall, which now fills the entire windscreen. He feels...at peace.

With only a hundred or so metres to go before he reaches the wall, Peter switches on the radio. After a couple of seconds of silence Jan Sparring starts to sing another Peter Himmelstrand composition. It's the one about life being good to him; Sparring sings about how much it has given him, everything he ever wanted.

Peter pulls up but doesn't switch off the engine. He leaves the radio on and gets out of the car. He tips his head back and gazes at the wall, which reaches right up to the sky.

He hears Sparring singing still, about how his troubles have been small, quickly passing by, never more than 'shadows in the sun'.

Peter takes a few steps forward and the grass in front of him begins to blur. At first he thinks it's because he is almost inside the darkness, then he realises that his eyes are filled with tears. He knows the song, knows what message it is trying to convey. He keeps on going as Sparring reaches the chorus. Somebody up there must like him, he sings—somebody who gives him all he has.

Peter lets out a sob and wipes his eyes; the tears are pouring down his cheeks now, dripping onto his shirt. He covers the remaining distance and is immediately embraced by the darkness.

Just as the glow of a lamp can linger on the retina after it has been switched off, so Jan Sparring's voice continues to echo in Peter's ears, even though it was cut off as soon as he stepped into the darkness.

It is silent here. Pitch black. The only sound is his own breathing. He clicks his fingers, claps his hands. The noise spreads in all directions without bouncing off anything. This place is empty.

He spins around in a circle, then does another half-turn so that he is facing in the direction from which he came. He thinks. He isn't sure. He can see nothing. He walks forward a couple of steps without coming out into the light. Goes back. Tries a different direction. Nothing but darkness. With no concept of left and right, backwards and forwards, it is difficult to be sure, but after a minute or so he thinks he has investigated every direction without finding his way out. It could easily be five minutes. The concept of time is also fluid, meaningless. He is lost. He is in the darkness.

He sits down on the grass which is still grass, but when he runs his hand over the surface it is metal. Or plastic, flesh or stone. It could be any material at all, depending on what he chooses to believe it is.

I am in the darkness. Not a darkness which is the absence of light, but the darkness.

He folds his arms across his chest and rocks back and forth. He is frightened. What is he frightened of? The darkness. Why is he frightened of the darkness? Because of everything it can hide. But this is not that kind of darkness.

Peter relaxes, manages to take a deeper breath. Then another. He blinks. It makes no difference. Another deep breath. He runs his hand over the tiled floor on which he is sitting. He has come here, he chose to come here, to complete his journey. Free falling. Yes. It is a darkness that resembles free falling.

He stands up and slides his foot across the smooth floor. Then he begins to walk. He no longer believes that the direction has any relevance. After a dozen or so steps the quality of the sound around him changes, as if it is bouncing off walls close by. He is in a tunnel. At the mouth of the tunnel far away in the distance he can see cars driving along…Sveavägen?

The Brunkeberg tunnel.

He carries on with his hands stretched out in front of him, because he is expecting to bump into a wall, but there is no wall, and when he looks over towards Sveavägen he sees only darkness. He keeps on walking.

Once or twice he catches a glimpse of another place, a way out, but as soon as he tries to focus on it or to move towards it, it is no longer there, perhaps because his efforts are half-hearted. He doesn't really want to get out. What he is looking for is *here*.

Sometimes he thinks he is aware of movement in the darkness, other bodies, but there is nothing to see. Perhaps he is going around in a circle, but he doesn't think so, because he has started to follow the only trail he can sense: the smell of disinfectant and shower gel, which grows stronger and stronger, until he can just make out a single point of light.

He stops, rubs his eyes. When he opens them again the light is still there, a lone firefly in the darkness. Perhaps it is very small and very close, or very large and far away. When he starts walking again the light quickly gets bigger, forming a rectangle the size of half a sheet of A4 paper, and after just a few steps he is close enough to read the words written on it.

'Will the last person to leave please turn out the lights!'

The white paper has an internal glow of its own, enabling Peter to see the worn tiled floor beneath his feet. He falls to his knees and breathes in deeply through his nose, inhaling the smell of the showers, lingering steam and human perspiration. After a second he hears her voice:

'Come on then.'

She is sitting below the sheet of paper. Sitting or lying. It is impossible to tell, because her body is so immense. She is naked and her white skin flows out across the tiled floor in rolls of fat, oily with sweat, slipping and sliding over one another like whales in a pod. It is difficult to form an impression of her face, because it lies buried in layer upon layer of fat, billowing as she nods invitingly to Peter.

Somehow it is Anette, but in the guise of the Fat Lady, something way beyond what Anette could be. Something that belongs to the darkness and to Peter's real desire, which he would never have been able to put into words in the light.

He shuffles over to her and crawls onto her lap. She wraps her enormous arms around him and he sinks into her flesh. He wants to make love to her, and he will—all in good time. There is plenty of time, an infinite amount of time.

*

The campsite is far behind them. When Carina turns around, the caravans and cars look like toys. For a moment she thinks that something terrible will happen as a punishment for turning around, but what could be worse than everything that has already befallen them? She carries on following the tiger, walking two metres ahead of her with its tail swinging from side to side.

The tiger is my punishment.

She didn't understand what Emil meant when he said she had to go, she didn't know where or why, but the only available guidance when she wanted to do what he said was to follow the tiger. So she followed the tiger.

To fly. Into the sun. To disappear from the picture.

All day she has been haunted by images relating to her obliteration. Perhaps it is time to complete the eradication of herself that she attempted in her teenage years, the process that Stefan prevented. Maybe those years with Stefan were merely a pause, and she was on her way here all along.

These are Carina's thoughts as she follows the tiger out into the field. That must be the case. There is no one and nothing here but herself and the creature that is the symbol of all the bad stuff she has done. They are walking along together, and it must involve a sacrifice, what else could it be? She is to be sacrificed so that Emil may live.

She puts one foot in front of the other, her eyes firmly fixed on the tiger's powerful thigh muscles, rippling beneath the skin, on the tail swishing across the grass like a pendulum measuring out time. They keep on walking, and nothing else happens.

'What do you want?' Carina asks, and the tiger pricks up its ears. 'What do you want from me? What do I have to do?'

The tiger keeps on walking, following the track that leads off into the distance as far as the eye can see. The image of Emil's broken body comes into Carina's mind, and she cannot bear it any longer. He might have taken his last breath while his mother is engaged in this seemingly pointless excursion. She spreads her arms wide and yells: 'What do I have to do, what do I have to do, what do I have to do?'

The tiger takes no notice of her, and the swishing of the tail does not falter, not even for a fraction of a second. Tick-tock, time is passing. Carina darts forward and grabs hold of the tail, tugs it hard and drops to her knees. The tiger stops, turns around and growls.

Their faces are level now. The row of sharp white teeth is exposed as the tiger draws back its lips and growls again. Carina holds her breath. Instinct tells her to *run! run! run!* as the killing machine that is the tiger's head comes closer, and she tenses every muscle in her body to stop herself from giving in to the impulse.

The tiger looks at her. She looks at the tiger.

'What?' Carina shouts. 'What!'

The tiger tilts its head on one side as if it is trying to understand what she is saying. Then it sits down and starts meticulously washing its coat.

*

The sun is going down and Emil has goose bumps on his arms as he leaves the campsite and follows the track out into a field which is now in shadow. In the middle of the field is a caravan hitched up to a car. Emil has seen cars and caravans like that before, but never together.

The car is a little round one, the same model as Herbie. Daddy says it's called a Beetle. The caravan is also small and round, and you could fit two of them inside Emil's caravan. They turn up on campsites occasionally, and Emil usually stops to have a look at them. They make him laugh, and he thinks it's funny that this model is called the Egg.

That is where the track is leading. To the Beetle and the Egg. They are both silver-coloured, and there is a man sitting outside doing something with his hands. As Emil approaches the man looks up and nods to him. This is the first adult who has paid any attention to him, and Emil edges closer. When he is a couple of metres from the man, he stops and says: 'Hi.'

'Hi yourself,' says the man, who is wearing jeans and a sweatshirt.

He is slightly older than Daddy and he has less hair; he looks neither nice nor nasty. He's just an ordinary man. He shows Emil what he is working on, and Emil sees that it is a piece of knitting. Not an ordinary man after all. Men don't usually knit.

'It's getting too dark to do this,' the man says, putting down the knitting. He looks at Emil. 'And what are you doing here?'

'I don't know. I was supposed to come here, I think.'

'I see,' the man says with a sigh. 'I was actually thinking of packing up and moving on, but...'

The chair creaks and squeaks as the man gets up and goes over to the door of the caravan. Emil sees a glass under the chair, with the dregs of some kind of dark liquid in the bottom and the handle of a paintbrush sticking up above the rim.

The man is about to open the door when Emil asks: 'Was it you who painted the crosses? On the caravans?'

The man shrugs. 'Of course. That's what I do.'

Even though it makes him feel like a little kid, Emil can think of only one question: 'Why?'

'How should I know? The flaws are there. I paint the crosses, I drive around with the caravan. That's what I do. Are you going in?'

He opens the door and at first Emil thinks there is a black curtain hanging just inside. He moves forward, and when he is only a metre or so from the opening he sees that it is not a curtain. Whatever is inside the door isn't *flat*, somehow.

The man leans against the frame. His eyes narrow; he is listening. Then his features soften and he smiles, nods to himself and actually rubs his hands together.

'Well, what do you know,' he says. 'It seems as if I need to go in there as well.'

The man eagerly beckons Emil, but Emil hesitates. Even if he thought really hard, he wouldn't have been able to come up with a situation that was a more perfect match for everything his mother had warned him against. Unless of course the man said he had sweets or a fluffy bunny rabbit inside the caravan. Something to tempt him. The man isn't doing that; on the contrary, he seems totally uninterested in Emil, and is completely focused on whatever it was that he heard. When Emil doesn't move, the man says, 'Please yourself,' and turns to go inside.

'Hang on, I'm coming.'

Emil doesn't think the man is dangerous, and even if he doesn't seem all that *nice*, Emil is glad of some company as he enters whatever is behind the door. His chest is starting to hurt again, so he takes the last few steps up to the caravan.

No, it's not a curtain. Behind the door is a darkness so compact that it ought to seep out like runny chocolate mousse. But it stays where it is, and nothing happens to it when the man walks in. However, the man is immediately swallowed up. Emil hurries after him, up the step and into the blackness.

He can't see a thing; it is darker than when he closes his eyes. When he turns around he can see the doorway and the campsite a few hundred metres away, the lilac glow of twilight which doesn't reach one single centimetre over the threshold.

Then he hears the man's voice. When Emil went in he was afraid of bumping into the man, who must be just in front of him. But the voice comes from far away, and Emil can't even work out the direction as it says: 'Could you close the door so that—'

Emil doesn't hear the rest of the sentence; it is drowned out by the noise of the door slamming shut, and now there is nothing but the darkness. His heart is pounding and he wishes he had Sabre Cat with him. But he is alone. Completely alone. He calls out, 'Hello?' but no one answers.

The pounding fills his ears, and even if it isn't a very nice sound, it is still a sound, something that means he is alive, he is here. Emil touches his face, sticks his finger up his nose, and it feels just the way it always does when he picks his nose, although of course he's not supposed to do that.

A lilac rectangle begins to appear before his eyes and Emil realises it's the door. As his eyes grow accustomed to the gloom he can see the outline, but when darkness falls outside it will vanish.

He takes a deep breath and turns away. Then he starts walking. He senses that he will not bump into a wall, and it turns out he's right.

*

Stefan picks up Emil's soft toys one by one, examining them carefully. Apart from the odd burn mark, they are all undamaged. He doesn't know how many hours, days, weeks Emil has spent constructing imaginary worlds where these five animals have been his brothers in arms, his fellow travellers, his companions.

Sometimes Stefan joins in the game, and over the years their characters have crystallised. Bengtson the bear is a little slow on the uptake, but he is totally reliable. Sabre Cat is the one who comes up with crazy plans. Sköldis the tortoise always thinks too highly of himself, and claims that he has been around for a thousand years. Hipphopp the rabbit is modelled on Little Hop from the Bamse the Bear cartoons, and he is always scared. Bunte, who doesn't appear to be a specific animal, often tries to start a quarrel.

Stefan carefully arranges the five animals around Emil in a protective circle, keeping vigil, and whispers: 'Help him. Please help him.'

The plastic eyes stare blankly into space, and as Stefan looks from one to the other he is struck by a realisation so painful that it stabs at his heart.

The animals are going to die.

He can't bring himself to face the terrible possibility that Emil might die from his injuries, but the adjacent thought attacks him and the knife is twisted around and around.

Without Emil the animals are nothing. Without Emil, these most loyal friends and most courageous adventurers are no more than five worthless objects made of fabric, stuffing and plastic. What would Stefan do if...He wouldn't be able to throw them away. Put them in a box. Put the box in the shed. Try to forget about the box. Find the box after ten years. See Emil's best friends ruined by damp and mildew. Dead.

'Please...' Stefan whispers to the animals, to Emil, to the universe. 'Please don't die...'

Emil suddenly coughs and raises one hand. He gropes in the air and opens his eyes.

'Daddy?' he says in a voice thick with blood and phlegm. 'Where are you?'

Stefan takes Emil's hand and leans over him. 'I'm here, sweetheart. Daddy's here.'

He tries to catch Emil's gaze, but there is nothing to catch. His son's eyes are as empty as those of his animals, and his restless pupils are so dilated that they almost fill the iris. His other hand is now groping at the air as if he is feeling his way in a dark room, and he says: 'Mummy?'

'Mummy isn't here, sweetheart.'

Emil takes a few laborious breaths; it sounds as if his tongue is sticky as he asks with difficulty: 'Where is...she?'

'She left. She...'

He breaks off as Emil's head twitches from side to side. 'Fetch... Mummy. Hurry. Go...'

There is a rattling sound from Emil's throat and he starts to cough; droplets of blood fly out of his mouth and land on the back of Stefan's hand, which is still clutching Emil's. There is a part of Stefan that can't take any more. One version of Stefan goes crazy and starts screaming and lashing out inside the prison of his brain, while another version carries on holding Emil's hand, pretending that he can cope.

The coughing fit subsides and Stefan asks: 'Where? Where do you want me to go?'

Emil takes the deepest breath he can manage with his broken ribcage. 'The darkness. You. Me. Mummy. Hurry. Soon...dark.'

'What do you mean, sweetheart? The darkness, soon dark, I don't understand, what...'

But Emil has closed his eyes, and his hand is limp. Stefan gently lays it down next to Emil's chest, which continues to rise and fall with each shallow breath.

Hurry. The darkness.

There might be a darker line on the horizon—isn't that what Peter said? Stefan had intended to ask him about that, but the opportunity never arose. He has thought about that darkness, wondered whether this world does have some kind of borderline after all, some kind of end.

Hurry.

It is doing nothing that has created the mad version of Stefan that is roaring inside his head. Anything is better than sitting here shaking with his hands clasped, terrified that the crazy Stefan will break out and take over.

The skin on his back pulls and tears as Stefan crouches down and slides his arms under the sofa cushion on which Emil is lying. Sores that were starting to heal break open, and he has to clench his teeth to stop himself from screaming as he straightens up, carrying Emil and the cushion.

He sidles out through the door and manages to get Emil on the back seat of the car. Sköldis and Hipphopp have fallen off en route; Stefan runs and picks them up, then places them next to Emil. He stands there irresolute, holding the seatbelt as he considers different ways of making his son secure.

Hurry.

The madman is waving his arms around in his prison, shouting: 'What does it matter, for fuck's sake! Put on a helmet when you're drowning, don't forget your lifejacket when the house is on fire, just go you fucking idiot!'

Stefan lets go of the belt, kisses Emil on the forehead, slams the door and gets behind the wheel. He turns to look at Emil, but his eyes are still closed, so instead Stefan addresses the animals, using the phrase he has heard Emil utter so many times: 'Are you with me?'

Bengtson, who is usually Chewbacca and the co-pilot, nods in agreement.

'Good. In that case, let's go.'

Donald is slumped over the bonnet, his cheek resting on the still-warm metal. He has stopped calling out; he has neither the strength nor the desire left. He doesn't actually want Majvor to come back, partly because he doesn't want to see her ugly face, and partly because he would prefer not to know what state he is in.

The intense pain from shattered bones in the pelvic area has turned into a constant burning that is slowly easing as the blood continues to flow from the stump of his arm.

The loss of blood has made him dizzy and apathetic, and the way things are right now, this is a desirable state of affairs. If the car was moved away, allowing the weight of his body to come down on his midriff, the pain would explode again, to no purpose. He is finished. There is no redemption. Perhaps his condition is making him tractable, but through the mist in his mind he is still surprised at the readiness with which he accepts that fact.

You're going to die, Donald.

Okay. If you say so.

He has always thought, or rather hoped, that Death will be a figure that comes to him in extremis. Nothing to do with solace or comfort; he just wanted Death to appear in some concrete form so that he could punch it right on the nose. Go down with all guns blazing, as it were.

Now the time has come, he doesn't feel that way. He just wants to dissolve, to fade away and disappear in the red mist that is filling more and more of his brain and obscuring his vision.

He mumbles, 'Buchanan, Lincoln, Johnson, Grant,' as he returns in his mind to Graceland. It is a different Graceland from the one he visited. The other tourists are gone, Majvor is gone, and he is free to stroll through the empty rooms as he pleases.

'Hayes, Garfield, Arthur...'

He stops in the TV room. The yellow fitted carpet, the huge sofa, the three televisions set into the wall. This time he doesn't have to stay behind the barriers, he can wander into the room, and he drifts towards the glass table and the white figure who is sitting there.

'Cleveland, Harrison, Cleve...Cleve...land...'

Almost there.

The white figure is a monkey. A monkey made of porcelain, with one arm looped around its knees. Its eyes are round and black. Donald is drawn towards those eyes. The red mist turns dark red as the black sphere that is the monkey's eye comes closer.

Donald reclaims his awareness for one last look at the world before he goes to the monkey. His vision is blurred and he is incapable of focusing on the figure walking towards him across the field.

For a moment he thinks it really is the monkey, and he tries to clench his remaining hand into a fist so that he can deliver that final blow in spite of everything, but discovers that he cannot even bend his fingers towards his palm.

The figure stops beside him.

'Hi there,' it says. 'I have a suggestion.'

*

Neither Lennart nor Olof is completely sure of the year, but it could have been the spring of '98. Olof maintains it was the year Olof Johansson stepped down as party leader, while Lennart tends to think it was around the time that Holmberg's dog was killed by the wolf, which was '99. Or it might have been '97.

Some of the neighbours used to gather towards the end of April for a logging weekend. They had been collecting logs all winter and piling them up on Lennart's land. They would spend the weekend turning the pile into firewood, which was then divided up between all those involved.

At their disposal they had a combined saw and splitter hooked up to a tractor. After the logs had been split, the wood was carried along on a conveyor belt from which it fell onto a growing heap. Everyone could help themselves, take the wood home and stack it safely so that it would be lovely and dry for the following winter.

It was both pleasanter and more efficient to work together. It was the custom to switch between tasks, so that everyone had the chance to bring the logs, chop them, split them and carry them away. The women and children also joined in if they felt like it.

That particular spring, people kept dropping out, one after the other, for various reasons: an illness here, an injury there, visiting relatives, an unexpected calving. As a result, Lennart and Olof ended up standing there at midday all on their own. It wasn't really a problem, the machinery could be handled by two people, but obviously it would take longer.

Lennart and Olof set to work. After half an hour they had found a good rhythm, and the woodpile was growing so fast that you would have thought three people were doing the job. If not four.

The blade of the saw whined and sliced through log after log, then each section was split into four pieces which travelled along the conveyor belt. Lennart and Olof worked as if they were in a trance, caught inside a bubble where nothing else existed apart from the two of them, the machinery and the growing pile of wood.

At two-thirty they took a fifteen-minute break; they simply sat in silence contemplating the fruit of their labours, smiling and nodding to one another. Then they set to work again. By the time they called it a day at five o'clock, they had managed to get through half the logs all on their own.

Olof switched off the tractor which was driving the machinery. The hydraulic compressor fell silent, and the whine of the saw died away. The low sun made the new buds on the birch trees glow, and the air was filled with the fresh smell of sawdust as Lennart and Olof settled down side by side on a log that had rolled away from the rest. No doubt Ingela and Agnetha would have dinner ready back home, but the two men wanted to enjoy the satisfaction of a job well done for a little longer.

'Would you look at that,' Olof said, nodding towards the mound of split wood.

'Not bad,' Lennart said. 'Not bad at all.'

They sat quietly, appreciating the pleasant aches and pains in their bodies and the peace of the late afternoon. Something passed between them during those few moments. In spite of the fact that they spent a great deal of time together, both in their work and with their families, it was only then that a simple truth crystallised for the two of them. They were each other's best friends.

Either of them could have expressed what came next, but since Lennart was the more talkative of the two, he spoke first.

'I've been thinking about something,' he said.

'Oh yes?'

'What I mean is, I just thought about it now.'

'Go on?'

Lennart brushed the sawdust from the folds in his dungarees and looked around as if to check that no one was listening, then said: 'What I thought was…couldn't we…you and me…couldn't we kind of promise one another that…'

Lennart was struggling to find the right words, and Olof helped him out: 'That we'll look after one another? If things go wrong?'

Lennart nodded. 'Yes. Something like that. Not that I have any reason to think things will go wrong, I'm not trying to set up some kind of insurance, but…'

'I understand,' Olof said. 'Sounds good to me. If things go wrong for you, then I'll help you, and if things go wrong for me, then you'll help me. Good.'

Lennart stared at the ground, wondering if there was anything to add, but decided that Olof's summary covered all the bases. When he looked up again he was met by Olof's outstretched hand.

'Let's shake on it.'

They shook hands, and patted each other on the shoulder. And so the matter was decided.

As it turned out, neither of them benefited from the agreement alone. When things did go wrong, it affected both of them at the same time. Ingela and Agnetha went to the Canaries and never really came back. Lennart and Olof took care of each other, and gradually their relationship developed into something else.

389

*

Olof and Lennart stand side by side next to their caravan, watching Stefan's Volvo disappear into the distance. There are only the two of them left now. Everyone else has left the camp, except for Benny and Maud of course.

'Do you remember that time with the logs?' Olof says. 'Everyone dropped out, and there were just the two of us left?'

'Yes,' Lennart says. 'Ninety-eight.'

'Or ninety-nine.'

'Something like that, my friend.'

Lennart turns and holds out his arms. The two men embrace, then stand for a long time with their cheeks resting on each other's shoulders until Lennart whispers: 'What are we going to do?' They move apart, arms hanging by their sides.

'It will soon be over, won't it?' Olof says, carefully examining his hands.

'Yes, I think so. One way or another.'

'In which case we ought to...'

'What?'

'Try to...to work things out, somehow.'

'You mean...?'

'Yes. While there's still time.'

They stand there looking at the ground, at their feet, out across the field, fiddling with the straps of their dungarees.

'I mean, it's nothing to be ashamed of,' Lennart says.

'No. Those days are gone.'

Lennart scratches the back of his neck and looks shyly at Olof, contemplating his body as if he is trying to decide to what extent it is suitable for the intended purpose.

'Of course I don't know if it's possible,' he says. 'I don't know if I can do it.'

'Me neither,' Olof says. 'But we can try. At the eleventh hour, so to speak.'

Lennart smiles at the unusual expression, then he shrugs and says: 'You're right. We can always try.'

*

By the time Majvor catches up with James Stewart, the darkness on the horizon has grown so tall and wide that it forms a wall which seems to be moving towards her under its own steam. The gun belt slaps against Jimmy's hip as he strides along; he doesn't turn around when Majvor calls out: 'Jimmy, where are we going?'

He mutters something in response, and Majvor has to make a real effort to keep pace with him. She looks over at his dogged profile; the Jimmy she knew and loved has gone, leaving behind only the bitter Will Lockhart.

'What did you say, Jimmy?'

'Stop calling me that. And quit following me.'

'What else can I do? I have nothing, I've left…'

'That's not my problem. You know who I am. What I am.'

Yes, Majvor thinks, *in spite of everything you're just another one of those guys who ruin a poor woman and then…*

At the same time she knows this isn't true; that's what happens in the stories in her magazines. Jimmy has sprung from her own mind. He is her creation, her responsibility. You don't get that kind of thing in a women's magazine.

'What are you actually doing here? You and…the others?'

'We're walking,' Jimmy replies. 'First we walk in one direction. Then we walk in the other direction.'

The darkness continues to grow ahead of her; Majvor stumbles along, still trying to keep up with the man she has conjured up from her dreams. Sweat is trickling from her armpits, and her body is giving off a sour smell.

'Jimmy,' she says, tugging at his sleeve. 'Please, Jimmy…'

She runs her hand over his chest, she caresses his cheek from his chin up to the brim of his hat, and she desperately wants him to take

391

her in his arms and hold her, nothing more, just like in the sweetest story. Just so that she can pretend for a little while that everything is as it should be.

'For fuck's sake, Majvor,' he says, pushing her away. She stands in front of him, blocking his way. When he takes a step to the side, she does the same. Eventually he stops and stares at her. She tries to smile.

'Majvor,' he says, his hand moving towards his hip. For a second she has the foolish idea that he is going to produce a wedding ring and go down on one knee. Then she sees the revolver in his hand, the barrel pointing at her belly. 'I'm going to count to three. One...'

What happens if I die? Can I die here?

She stares at the piece of metal in Jimmy Stewart's hand. Is it real? Can it shoot? If it can shoot then surely it must contain dummy bullets, they wouldn't give an actor real ammunition...

They? Who are they?

'Two.'

She daren't risk finding out, she doesn't want to risk a red-hot bullet drilling into her belly. Before Jimmy reaches 'Three', she holds up her hands and backs away from him, then turns around. The darkness is only a few steps away from her now. She takes those steps.

*

Blood. Blood soon. Soon it will start to bleed.

The thing that used to be Molly is sitting motionless, contemplating the thing that is still Carina. The name Carina no longer has any meaning. The thing kneeling in front of Molly is merely a container filled with blood. Soon that blood will come out.

The thing that used to be Molly has always existed. It has been waiting. In mountains or in seas. Sometimes it has entered into a human being. Waited for the blood to come so that it can live again. 'Live' is an unknown concept. Continue to walk. Continue the movement.

There are many of them. If one ceases to exist, the darkness creates another so that the movement can continue. 'Blood' is an unknown concept. Blood is life. And life is the movement.

When the thing that used to be Molly looks at Carina, it sees the opportunity for continued movement. Its task is to demonstrate. So that the blood can come. Soon it will come. First the liquid from the eyes, the scream from the mouth. Then the blood. Now. Carina is using her teeth. Biting her arms.

Then there is an interruption. Noise and movement. The movement becomes a car and out of the car steps a person. The person takes Carina before the blood has had time to come. They drive off.

The thing that used to be Molly gets up and continues to walk, continues the movement. There will be others. There are always others.

*

Majvor is so unhappy and disappointed that it is a relief to enter into the darkness. It enfolds her like the embrace she has longed for.

Out of the darkness we call unto you.

Majvor tips back her head, but there is nothing but darkness. She wouldn't call out or pray even if she thought there was someone who could hear her. It is too late.

What do you want, Majvor? What do you want from the darkness?

Buried deep within her there is a burning point, a feeling. When she glimpses just such a point in the darkness, she walks towards it. The glow fades, moves, grows brighter, then fades once more.

The third time the glow burns brighter she thinks it is illuminating a face; she can see the contours of a face shimmering, fiery red. Then it vanishes as the glow fades yet again, moving to the side. Majvor edges forward as the glow intensifies, moves higher; the face reappears. Suddenly she realises what she is looking at. A cigarette. Someone is sitting here smoking a cigarette. With each drag the glow lights up an emaciated face. Majvor stops a metre away as the face is once again plunged into darkness.

'Hello?' she says, as if she were talking to someone far away.

The voice that responds is hoarse and croaky; she thinks she recognises it as it says: 'Hi there.'

The cigarette flares again, revealing sunken cheeks in a long, narrow face, grey hair in a pudding bowl cut. It is the unflattering hairstyle that gives it away.

'Peter Himmelstrand,' she says. 'It is you, isn't it?'

'Too right,' he says after a brief coughing fit. 'And who are you?'

'My name is Majvor. Majvor Gustafsson.'

'Majvor, Majvor…no, I've never written a song with a Majvor in it. But it's never too late.' Peter Himmelstrand laughs, and the laughter turns into another bout of coughing before he adds: 'Not here, anyway.'

The cigarette is down to the filter and Peter Himmelstrand uses it to light another, takes a deep drag. Majvor's expectations of what she might find in the darkness were unclear, but one thing she does know: she *wasn't* expecting Peter Himmelstrand.

'What are you doing here?' she asks.

'I'm responsible for the songs. That's kind of my thing.'

'But how did you get here?'

'Fuck knows. I was offered the gig and the alternative was crap, so I went for it. What about you?'

'Me?'

'Yes—what are you doing here?'

If only she knew. There are so many questions Majvor would like to ask Peter Himmelstrand, mostly to do with the nature of this place, but there is plenty she would like to know about Peter himself. As a dedicated listener to the Swedish pop charts, Majvor knows lots of his songs by heart, and she thought it was really sad when she heard that smoking had killed him back in 1999. But here he is, puffing away as if nothing has happened.

What really went on between him and Mona Wessman? How much of that song about the priest is taken from their life together? How do you come up with a lyric like *hambostinta i kort-kort*? And her favourite, the one that Björn and Agnetha from Abba sang, what was that called again?

But that's not the question right now. The question is what she is doing here, and *What do you want, Majvor?*

'I don't know,' she replies. 'I have no idea. I thought…'

'Yes?' There is a hint of impatience in Peter Himmelstrand's voice. 'What did you think? Let's hear it. I'm pretty busy here, you know.'

Majvor doesn't understand how sitting in the dark smoking constitutes being pretty busy, but he is the first *celebrity* she has ever met, and it is not her place to doubt him. Besides, she has a feeling that this is real, in a different way from James Stewart.

'I thought there would be something here. Something for me, something that…I don't know, and please don't take this the wrong way, but surely it can't be *you*?'

'Nope,' Peter Himmelstrand says, taking an even deeper drag that highlights the crater-like shadows on his cheeks. 'Seems unlikely. But hang on a minute, if you just chill, then…'

In the faint glow Majvor can see him fumbling around on the ground, until his fingers find what he is searching for. He picks it up and holds it out to Majvor. 'Could it be this? Is this your thing?'

The object that is placed in Majvor's hands is a revolver, and as her fingers close around the grooved butt, she knows he is right. This is why she came here. This is what she was supposed to find. She spins the cylinder around and hears a series of clicks.

Peter Himmelstrand is in the middle of another coughing fit; he points at the revolver. When he has recovered, he says: 'Two shots have been fired, so there are only four bullets left. Make sure…well, you know.'

'No,' Majvor says. 'What?'

Peter Himmelstrand sighs. 'Well, I'm no expert, but if you're thinking of using it, make sure there isn't an empty chamber in front of the hammer. Got it?'

Yes, Majvor has got it. The gun is heavy, and in spite of the fact that she has never fired a pistol or a revolver, it feels completely natural. You could say it fits her like a glove, as if it has been waiting for her fingers and hers alone.

'Where has it come from?' she asks.

'Haven't a clue. It was here when I arrived.'

Majvor raises the revolver, aims it into the darkness. *Two shots have been fired.*

As Peter Himmelstrand sucks on his cigarette once more, Majvor takes the opportunity to read the inscription on the barrel. *Smith & Wesson .357 Magnum.*

Just as few Americans can hear the date *9/11* without thinking about the Twin Towers, so there are few Swedes who can hear *.357 Magnum* without seeing the image of Hans Holmér, chief of the Swedish National Security Service, with two revolvers dangling from his forefingers. Not the actual gun, but the *type* of gun that killed Olof Palme. The actual gun has never been found.

A shudder runs down Majvor's spine, and as if he can read her mind—perhaps he *can* read her mind—Peter Himmelstrand says: 'No idea. Maybe, maybe not. But it's yours now. Do you know what you want?'

The words stick in Majvor's throat, so she merely nods.

'Excellent. Off you go, then. Life is short.'

He starts to laugh, and once again the laughter turns into a bout of coughing, much worse this time. Majvor turns and walks away. When the coughing subsides, she stops and says: 'By the way, I love "This Is How Love Begins" by Björn and Agnetha. Fantastic song. Thank you.'

'Yeah, yeah,' Peter Himmelstrand's voice says from the darkness. 'Didn't help much, did it? Good luck.'

Majvor takes a few steps and finds herself back in the light. She clicks open the cylinder, ejects the two spent cartridges and puts them in her pocket, flicks the cylinder shut and spins it so that there is a bullet in front of the hammer. It is as if she has never done anything else.

*

Carina is slumped in the passenger seat, her hands resting limply in her lap. When Stefan strokes her head, she doesn't react. He glances at her left wrist, which is covered in angry red bite marks, and asks: 'What were you thinking?'

There is no response, and Stefan looks towards the horizon, where a dark cloud is growing bigger and bigger, as if a gigantic black disc is being inexorably pushed up out of the green grass.

Hurry.

He doesn't know if he is doing the right thing, if this was what Emil meant, but he can see no alternative. He turns to the back seat, where Emil is lying quietly, surrounded by his cuddly toys. His ribcage is moving and his feet are twitching.

'Get rid of me,' Carina says. 'Get rid of me and everything will be fine.'

'What are you talking about?'

Carina's voice is a monotone as she goes on: 'It's what I've been thinking. All day. That I have to go. All the bad stuff I've done. I'm the one who's marked us. I'm the one who has to pay.'

'Carina, we don't know that.'

'It was a bet.'

'What was?'

'When I kissed you. My friends scraped together two hundred kronor. Which I would get if I kissed you.'

The darkness is growing fast, and already covers such a large part of the sky that the light inside the car is beginning to fail. Stefan thinks back to that evening by the jetty. How it began, how it ended. He clears his throat and says: 'In that case I'd better write and say thank you.'

'Who to?'

'Your stuck-up friends. Who would have thought something good would come from them? I'll send them a postcard.'

'But Stefan, you don't understand...'

'I understand perfectly. I also understand that if they hadn't scraped together that money, I would never have stood on the stairs

397

watching you and Emil in the kitchen.'

'What? When?'

It is like dusk now, and Stefan can see that the darkness has a clearly defined edge approximately twenty metres in front of the car. He pulls up, turns to Carina, takes her head between his hands and says: 'God *did* make the little green apples. We're sticking to that, okay? I love you.'

Together they lift Emil out of the car, still lying on the sofa cushion, and carry him towards the darkness.

'Stefan,' Carina says. 'Why are we doing this?'

Stefan really wishes he had a good answer. Something else about little green apples, about faith, hope, love, or the road we have to travel. But when he looks down at his son's broken, struggling body, there are no such answers. They must go into the darkness because they are already in darkness. Because there is nothing else left.

*

Jimmy Stewart is standing on the field with his chin raised as if he is checking out the lie of the land. Or sniffing the air. As Majvor walks towards him he turns and sets off in the same direction from which they came.

'Hey you!' Majvor shouts. 'Stop right there!'

She has a real weakness for cowboy films. She has seen all of Jimmy's, of course, but also everything featuring John Wayne and Clint Eastwood. She knows this scene.

The two men meeting in the middle of nowhere. Eyes locked, getting the measure of one another. Who will draw first? Majvor daren't risk that kind of confrontation. For a start she doesn't have a holster, and even if the figure in front of her isn't Will Lockhart, she knows that Jimmy Stewart was also a competent marksman in real life.

In real life?

Honestly, a person could die laughing. Majvor doesn't even wait for Jimmy to turn around; she simply raises the revolver, pulls back the hammer, aims at his back and fires.

BANG!

She was expecting the recoil, and made sure she was holding the gun firmly. It was nowhere near enough. The impact that travels from her wrist and all the way up her arm makes the barrel jerk upwards. It feels as if someone has punched her hard, and she staggers.

Her ears are buzzing as she straightens up and rubs her shoulder. Jimmy is facing her now, taking his time as he draws his gun and aims at Majvor, his arm outstretched. This is no duel. It is more like an execution.

Fate gives her one last chance as she throws herself to the ground a fraction of a second before the gun goes off.

If she had thought that none of this was real and therefore she couldn't be shot here, that idea is swept away by the sound of the bullet whining past just above her ear. The next one will find its mark, and as Majvor lands painfully on her belly, she knows that essentially she is already dead. Shot by Jimmy Stewart.

However, she is determined to play this lethal game to its conclusion. She grips the revolver with two hands, supporting herself on her elbows, and aims at Jimmy, who is slowly lowering the barrel of his gun in her direction. A smile plays across his lips as he pulls back the hammer.

Majvor doesn't have time for such niceties; she simply pulls the trigger as hard as she can. The hammer is pushed backwards and slams down on the bullet.

BANG!

As soon as she fires, she knows that her aim is true. Jimmy Stewart's eyes widen and he clutches his chest.

She doesn't know what she was expecting. Did she think he would drop to his knees, fall backwards, whisper a few last words? That's not what happens. Jimmy's face begins to dissolve. His clothes become as transparent as gossamer, and the revolver which was so lethal just seconds ago fuses with his hand and disintegrates.

In no time the Man from Laramie has disappeared, and in his place a smooth, white, only vaguely humanoid creature is standing looking at her. It is still wearing a hat, which means the hat must be similar to the gun in Majvor's hand. Something that actually exists.

As Majvor gets to her feet and walks towards the white creature, revolver at the ready, the last vestiges of shape and colour disappear, and there is nothing left of Jimmy Stewart.

'The hat,' she says, pointing the gun at the creature's head. This time she allows herself time to pull back the hammer. 'The hat, if you don't mind.'

If her bullet really did penetrate the heart, there is no longer any sign of a wound. The skin is just as white and smooth as over the rest of the body. Presumably the white creature cannot be killed, but perhaps it still has the capacity to feel pain, because it grabs the hat by the brim and throws it on the ground in front of Majvor.

They look one another in the eye, whereupon the creature turns and sets off along its eternal track. Majvor bends down and picks up the hat.

What do you want, Majvor?

The feeling she had turns to certainty as she puts on the hat, and finds that it fits perfectly. It's just a shame the gun belt disappeared like that. It would have felt good, buckling it around her hips.

How stupid. How wrong can you be.

For more than half her life, Majvor has sighed over James Stewart, indulged herself in half-baked fantasies about what it would be like to be with him, just once.

Typical woman, she thinks.

Because her longing wasn't actually about being *with* James Stewart, it was about *being* James Stewart.

Now she has won that right. Won it fair and square, with the smell of gunpowder and her skill with a gun. Majvor tips back her hat and allows the hand holding the revolver to dangle by her side as she heads out into the wilderness.

Emil doesn't know how long he has been walking when the darkness thickens and begins to solidify. It is becoming harder to breathe. When Emil waves his arms he can feel the darkness touching his hands, like millions of tiny strands of gossamer or candy floss, getting more and more dense. He is gasping for air and he can feel something being *pressed down*, just like in *Star Wars* when they are in the trash compactor and the walls are closing in so that they will all be crushed to death.

The darkness is tightening around him, and an image comes into his mind. He gets the idea that he is about to be *squeezed out*. That there is another Emil in here, and there isn't room for both of them. One of them will have to be squeezed out.

Emil doesn't want to be squeezed out, it's bound to hurt, just like being *run over by a caravan*. He remembers now. Molly, Darth Maul, his shirt getting trapped, the wheel rolling over his chest.

The pressure is coming from all directions. Emil can't even get enough air to scream. He falls to the ground and wraps his arms around his body as the vice tightens still further. He can't hear a thing, and he rocks back and forth, until suddenly he is not hugging himself, but his cuddly toys. He is no longer rocking himself, he is being rocked. Back and forth. Whatever he is lying on is rocking. A cushion.

'Mummy?' he says. 'Daddy?'

At long last they are with him in the darkness, patting him, stroking him, kissing him. He can't see them, but he can hear their voices; he recognises their hands and their smell. *Dark soon.* Emil gets up from the cushion and says: 'We have to go. Before it gets dark.'

Mummy and Daddy's hands, which have mostly been caressing his face, are now moving over his body. There are tears in Daddy's voice as he says: 'Sweetheart, you're...you're whole again.'

'You were injured,' Mummy says. 'You were very badly injured, you were...' Then she starts crying too.

'That was the other one,' Emil says. He knows what he means, but it's hard to explain, and there isn't time. 'Stop crying,' he says instead, tucking his cuddly toys inside his shirt. 'We have to find the door.'

Emil has no idea which direction to take. There are no directions here. But they set off. Mummy is holding one of his hands and Daddy the other. It's nice. The darkness is terrible and they are as lost as it is possible to be, but it is better to be in the darkness with Mummy and Daddy than to be alone in the light. Emil tells them about the campsite, about the Beetle and the Egg. About the door that was closed, and the faint light around the opening. He knows it sounds really weird, but Mummy and Daddy believe him.

They walk and walk, and even though Mummy and Daddy are with him now, a lump forms in Emil's throat. He doesn't know how much time has passed, but he is afraid it is far too long. What was it the man said? *I was thinking of packing up and moving on.* Emil has no idea what that means, but he fears the worst and the lump grows.

'There,' Daddy says. 'What's that?'

It is impossible to see in which direction he is looking. They stop. 'Where?' Emil asks.

Daddy places his fingers on Emil's temples and gently turns his head to the left. Emil screws up his eyes. He can just make out something red, a faint glow like the dying embers of an open fire.

Emil grabs Daddy's hand again and drags him and Mummy towards the glow; as they get closer it takes on the form of a rectangle, flickering at the edges as if it is about to sink into the darkness. When they are standing right in front of it, Emil lets go of Mummy and Daddy's hands and gropes until he finds the handle. He pushes it down and the door opens.

The campsite is burnished by the last moments of twilight, a dark red band across the top of the pine trees. Emil pulls Mummy and Daddy out of the little caravan. They stagger a short distance, then stop and blink in the light, which grows dimmer as their eyes become accustomed to it.

Mummy and Daddy can't even speak. As they look around they

402

are making noises that mean nothing; they don't seem to hear the caravan door closing behind them. Only Emil turns back.

It isn't the same man this time, the one who was knitting. It's the man with the big caravan, the one who was horrible to his dog. He looks nastily at Emil and says: 'You were lucky there.'

Now Mummy and Daddy turn around too. 'Donald?' Daddy says.

Donald shrugs and folds up the camping chair. In spite of all the strange things that have happened, Emil still can't help being surprised when Donald walks over to the car, opens the *bonnet*, and puts the chair inside, where the engine ought to be. Then he remembers: it's a Beetle. The engine is at the back.

Donald is just about to get into the car, but Daddy takes a few unsteady steps towards him.

'Hang on,' he says. 'Wait, what…was it *you* that…?'

'Nope,' Donald says. 'But I'm in the driving seat now. Until further notice.'

Daddy's mouth is hanging open like a fish on dry land. Emil understands; he has so many questions that it's like searching for water when there isn't any water. The only words Daddy can manage as Donald settles down behind the wheel are: 'But why?'

Donald shakes his head. 'Good luck with working that one out.' Then he closes the door and starts the engine; they can hear it humming away in the boot, which probably isn't called the boot in this instance. The car moves away, towing the caravan along behind.

Mummy, Daddy and Emil watch the silver-coloured vehicles drive through the campsite and out onto the road, where they gradually disappear into the shadow of the pine trees.

'Daddy?' Emil says, taking out his cuddly toys one by one. 'Where are my lightsabers?'

*

The thing that used to be Isabelle is walking.

There has always been a hunger, an emptiness, and no one has been able to satisfy it. The hunger is still there. It is strong and it hurts, but it is *simple*. There is a track to follow. If you just follow the track, then the hunger will be sated, sooner or later. Across the field she walks, together with those who are like her. The song of hunger rises from their throats.

The thing that used to be Isabelle is no longer capable of thinking as humans do, but if she could, she would be thinking something along the lines of: *I am happy.*

*

Lennart and Olof are lying naked in bed, looking at one another. Benny and Maud are sitting on the floor, looking at Lennart and Olof. It is a moment of stillness. Four pairs of eyes, drinking in one another. Then Lennart sits up, scratches the back of his neck and says: 'Well, it was worth a try.'

It didn't work. They had unfolded the bed, then undressed clumsily and with a certain amount of embarrassment. They had got into bed and lay there caressing one another, they kissed a little, but nothing happened.

Olof had put forward the hypothesis that perhaps it wasn't working because the dog and the cat were sitting there staring at them, but they both knew that wasn't the real problem.

They could agree on the fact that neither of them saw anything disgusting or shameful *in principle* in making love the way two men can. It was just that they couldn't do it, couldn't find the spark, so instead they lay there for a long time, naked before one another, reaching the level of intimacy that was possible for them right now, and that was good in its own way.

Lennart pulls on his pants and socks, clambers into his dungarees without bothering about a vest. He nods to Olof and strokes his foot before leaving the caravan, accompanied by Benny and Maud.

It's moving in.

A band of darkness has begun to rise in all directions, all the way along the line of the horizon, and as Lennart watches it grows a few more millimetres, like a sack that is slowly being pulled upwards. The world is shrinking, closing down.

Lennart goes back inside and fetches the gadgets. Olof is getting dressed.

'It seems to be getting dark,' Lennart says. 'Pretty quickly.'

'I'm coming.'

They stand side by side, watching the approaching darkness as it closes in around them. Benny lets out a short, sharp bark. Olof pats him on the head and says, 'Not much we can do about it, is there?'

'No, I don't think so. Anyway, I'm ready for that lesson now.'

'Lesson?'

Lennart crouches down on the grass where he has placed the iPod and speakers. He scrolls through the playlist; he doesn't know which song he is going to choose, but he finds exactly the right one and puts it on repeat. That means it will go on playing for as long as it is possible to play, which is only right.

Olof bursts out laughing when he hears which song Lennart has chosen: it is Abba, 'Dance (While the Music Still Goes On)'. He opens his arms and Lennart moves into his embrace. It's not much of a lesson; they just move slowly in each other's arms, closing their eyes as what is going to happen happens, and the song begins over and over again.

They dance, while the music still goes on.

They dance.

I switch off the light.